MW00625962

HARBOR *of* REFUGE

A novel by
Joseph A. Tringali

CALKINS HARBOR
PUBLISHING

North Palm Beach, Florida

Harbor of Refuge

Calkins Harbor Publishing
441 Marlin Road
North Palm Beach, FL 33408

View our website at *http://www.calkinsharbor.com*. For sales inquiries, contact *sales@ calkinsharbor.com*

ISBN: 978-_-_____-_-_

This book is dedicated to
the woman who was the model for
"Marilyn Dupré"

*"What the heart has once owned and had,
it shall never lose."*

—Henry Ward Beecher

*"Harbors" are places of refuge
in which protection and shelter are sought
within the inclosures of land . . .*

—THE CUZCO, VOL. 225
FEDERAL REPORTER, PAGE 169
(WESTERN DISTRICT OF WASHINGTON, 1915)

*"Harbor" in its most strict
and proper sense means a safe station . . .
a place of refuge, shelter, rest.*

—THE AURANIA AND THE REPUBLIC,
VOL. 29, FEDERAL REPORTER, PAGE 98.
(SOUTHERN DISTRICT OF NEW YORK, 1886)

Chapter 1

Marilyn Dupré stopped her small car at the end of the shell-rock road and sighed. Ahead of her, past the unpaved parking lot, sprawled Cap'n Kelly's Marina, a rambling, worn-out, shabby monument to man's indifference. If she had been in a romantic mood, she might have seen the place as "cute" or "quaint" or even "nostalgic." She wasn't in that kind of mood and, as the Florida sun beat down on the dusty, pockmarked lot, the weathered concrete block building and the rickety docks beyond, the only word that came to her mind was "dingy."

Why Theo Grant had assigned her to this God-forsaken place was anybody's guess. But Marilyn wasn't being paid to guess. She was marking time in early 1985, waiting to take the Florida Bar examination in July. She would have preferred to spend the time working for a law firm, but she had learned the hard way that clerking jobs in Florida were no easier to come by than they had been back in Louisiana. The job with Walker & Grant, Certified Public Accountants, was the next best thing. Next best thing? Who was she kidding? It was the only thing. With tax season in full swing, the firm needed help. After completing more years of school than she cared to remember, Marilyn wasn't about to go back to waitressing. Although Walker & Grant wasn't paying her much she had to admit that—as the old saying went—the firm wasn't charging her for the experience, either.

The marina in front of her occupied a small cove off a larger bay known as Calkins Harbor. The bay, along with the adjoining town, took up the central portion of Bonita Key, an island off Florida's southwest coast. Calkins Harbor was a town where time appeared to have stopped somewhere in the 1950's. The newest building in town was a 7-Eleven store. Other than that one lonely symbol of "convenience," Marilyn guessed the Calkins Harbor town council—if there was such a body—hadn't issued a building permit in a long time. It was a far cry from the mainland city of Bonita where Fred Walker and Theo Grant had their offices and where, with uncharacteristic good luck, Marilyn had managed to find an apartment she could afford. If the town of Calkins Harbor was a far cry from the city of Bonita, it was an even farther cry from the wealth and glamour that existed on the north end of the island.

More than mere distance separated Calkins Harbor from the northernmost tip of Bonita Key. The "north enders" as the denizens of the town derisively called the people who shared their island, were an upscale group of professionals whose lives revolved around the exclusive

Bonita Key Yacht Club. The clubhouse at the north end of the island was built even before a bridge linked the Key to the mainland, and the club-owned Bonita City Station still provided launch service to its members. Old timers complained that the launch was as close as some of the newer members ever got to a real boat.

Anyone who was anyone in Bonita belonged to the B.K.Y.C. Marilyn recalled the day barely a month ago when Theo Grant excitedly announced he had heard from "certain people" that his application was finally being considered by the membership committee. When she pointed out that he hadn't been accepted yet, Theo told her it had taken him a year just to get the application. She guessed that by the time he actually became a member, she would be on her way back home to New Orleans.

The only thing Cap'n Kelly's had in common with the Yacht Club was the island they shared. The marina was laid out in the shape of a square that nature had tried to squeeze into a triangle. A dilapidated, two-story building was located along its base; short, narrow wooden piers extended from the sea wall behind the building, and boats were tied up in slips between them. The other two sea walls extended at right angles from the first one, but about halfway to the cove entrance they suddenly angled in toward each other, until only a narrow inlet separated them. More boats were berthed in single files along each wall.

The boats in the water were a motley collection of old, new and home-built vessels. Around the yard, a number of other boats sat dry-docked in various states of disre-pair. Some of them were being worked on as Marilyn watched, while others seemed to be slowly succumbing to the elements.

As she sat there taking in the scene, Marilyn wondered what the "Calkins Boys" would be like. She had met Mrs. Calkins, the widow of Captain Kelly Calkins, only once when the woman came to Fred Walker's office for a pri-vate conference. Mrs. Calkins—no one but Mr. Walker ever called her by her first name—was five feet of gray-haired iron determination covered with a soft patina of Southern gentility. She was the product of a bygone era, with knowing eyes that appeared to have seen much and a quiet smile that said she remembered all she had seen. She was the kind of woman who could draw people out and, without really willing to, Marilyn found herself engaged in an intimate conversation in response to the older woman's gentle questions. When she thought about the incident now, sitting in her hatchback at the edge of the unpaved parking lot, Marilyn realized that some of those questions were surprisingly personal, but they hadn't seemed to be that way at the time. Marilyn had quite enjoyed the wom-an's company. "Well," she said to herself, "I guess it's time to meet the rest of the family." She put the car in gear and bounced forward over shell-rock sending up a wake of dust to mark her passage.

The main building was about twice as wide as it was deep. Four overhead doors covered perhaps two-thirds of one side of the first floor and gave the place the appearance of a large, two-story garage. The doors were open and the contents of the building spilled out onto a concrete pad that projected into the arid lot. Marilyn got out of her car, clutched her new leather portfolio and smoothed her gray business suit with the pink blouse she had bought for the occasion because it went so well with her dark brown hair and eyes. Although the building must have been open for business, no one had bothered to turn on the lights, and she had an uneasy feeling she was trespassing as she entered the deserted structure.

She picked her way through an assortment of small boats and equipment, hoping that someone would appear out of the gloom and help her find her clients. No one did. Nor did anyone respond to her "Hello's" that echoed off the concrete walls. Directly ahead of her a wooden, windowless door bore a hand-lettered sign announcing the fact that it led to an office; to its right, a second, identical door was unmarked. A counter to the left of the office door sectioned off an area filled with shelves. Once upon a time it might have been a parts department, but the yellowed cardboard boxes and the dust on the cans clearly showed that no one had bought parts there in years. Along the far left wall, a stairway led to a second floor; whatever was up there would have to remain a mystery for the time being. Marilyn took a deep breath and opened the office door.

A blast of cool air hit her. "Thank God the place is air conditioned," she thought, half expecting it not to be.

Two portly men sat at desks facing one another. One was reading a newspaper that was meticulously laid over the top of an empty desk; the other man was half turned away, either dozing or looking out the window. The room was a combination of all her worst nightmares; the air was thick with the smell of stale cigars and an odor she would later learn was diesel fuel. Along one side of the room, a frayed couch was far too dirty to even consider sitting on, and the wooden chairs were piled high with papers that, like the boxes outside, had yellowed with age. The two desks that dominated the center of the room must have been reclaimed from the same trash heap that supplied everything else in the room. Someone with an oversupply of gray bilge paint had repainted them long ago. Now burn marks scarred the ancient linoleum tops, and tired oak peeked wearily though places where the paint had worn off.

Mr. Newspaper looked up when Marilyn entered the room.

"Hello," she began tentatively, "my name is Marilyn Dupré. Theo Grant sent me."

"Oh, yeah. Hi," Mr. Newspaper responded without getting up. "I'm Doug Calkins. This is my older brother, Kelly Junior."

The other man turned when he heard is name. "Your office is in there," he said, without taking the stump of a soggy cigar from between his teeth. He jerked his head in the general direction of the closed door to his back.

Mr. Newspaper got up and took her hand. "Don't pay

any attention to my brother. I'm the friendly one around here. Come on, I'll show you where we set you up."

This is it, Marilyn thought. Bar exam or no bar exam, I'm not going to spend my time in some dingy office with cigar smoke and furniture left over from the Depression.

Before she could think of anything to say, Doug Calkins let her through the adjoining door and she unexpectedly found herself in a freshly painted room, standing on a clean carpet and looking at new office furniture. The room itself was about half the size of the other office and appeared quite comfortable. An air conditioner like the one in the brothers' room poked though the wall and gave the place its own temperature control. Best of all, there were two additional doors: the one she had seen leading to the floor of the main building and another that went directly outside. If she was going to be required to spend her days here, at least she could get in and out without fighting her way past smelly cigars.

"This is . . . this is very nice," she stammered, not knowing what she was expected to say.

"Mom wanted you to be comfortable. We don't get many women . . . ladies . . . in the office, so she told me to clean the place up and get new furniture. She insisted on brand new," he replied.

"Your mother . . . Mrs. Calkins?" Marilyn asked, wondering how the older woman had found out about her assignment and why someone Marilyn barely knew was so interested in her comfort.

"Yeah. I guess Theo Grant must have told her you were coming. Anyway, it wasn't any trouble. Arlo painted the room. I wouldn't have put in the carpeting except that he made such a mess out of the floor."

"Arlo?"

"Arlo Woodbrace. He's sort of our handyman. He ain't much of a painter though. Got more paint on himself than he did on the room. Anyway, the carpet was on sale, and it smells good."

"Mr. Calkins . . ."

"Call me 'Doug.' Everybody else does."

"All right, Doug," Marilyn began again. "What, exactly, am I supposed to do here?"

"Heck, I don't know," he replied. "Take care of the books, I guess. You're working for Theo Grant. I was told to set up the room. The rest is up to you and him. You can read the newspaper all day for all I care. That's what I do most of the time."

"Doug!" Junior boomed from the other room. "Somebody's here to pay!"

"Duty calls. Got to take their money. It's a tough job but somebody's got to do it." He chuckled at his own lame joke and bolted back through the connecting door.

Marilyn wondered why the older brother couldn't take the payment, whatever it was. Surely he knew how to write out a receipt—provided they used receipts! Her mind suddenly flashed back to undergraduate days filled with talk of cash journals and double-entry ledgers. She wondered if these people had been pocketing the daily cash. Theo Grant was far too careful to allow his name to be associated with such a thing. He may have decided to assign her here to monitor the situation.

On the other hand, it wasn't likely that someone as far down the firm's pecking order as she was would be given such an assignment. The Calkins family was one of Walker & Grant's biggest clients, going back to the days when Fred Walker worked alone, long before Theo Grant came to Bonita. Theo had simply told Marilyn to "take care of things and keep them happy." There didn't seem to be much use in asking Doug what that meant, and she had already made up her mind never to ask Junior anything. So the only thing to do was to settle in and start taking care of things. Tomorrow morning she could stop by the office before coming across the bridge and get more specific instructions from Theo.

With little else to do, the large window behind her desk suddenly commanded her attention. Like the window in the office next door, it looked out over the entire marina. Across the cove, to the right of the inlet, a woman in a very small bikini lounged under a beach umbrella between two fuel pumps. Closer to the building, two men worked on a large dry-docked boat that was balanced on its keel and seemed to be held up rather precariously by assorted rubble. The younger of the two men kept glancing toward the fuel dock; he probably wasn't interested in the price of fuel.

To her left, in the corner of the marina, a commercial fishing boat quietly rotted away. Larger than any of the other boats, it was obviously out of place. The accountant in Marilyn wondered who paid to keep it there. Far ahead of it, past the point where the wall angled in toward the marina entrance, another boat caught her attention. It was built along the same lines as the fishing boat, but it was clearly a pleasure craft that gleamed white in the Florida sun. The yacht was larger than most of the other pleasure boats and seemed as out of place as the rusted hulk it resembled.

Behind the yacht, in the line of nondescript boats along the left hand wall, one other boat intrigued her. It wasn't the boat itself—a rather modest houseboat—but the setting that was so unusual. Someone had built a white picket fence on the sea wall alongside. At the bottom of the fence, window boxes spilled over with bright flowers, and matching boxes were carefully placed around the boat itself, giving the whole place the appearance of a floating summer cottage. As Marilyn watched, a man in a floral shirt and straw hat emerged from one of the doors. He filled a watering can from a hose and began carefully watering the flowers. The scene made Marilyn think of her mother, tending her potted plants long ago on their wrought-iron balcony in the French Quarter of New Orleans. Whatever that boat was, it appeared to be the man's home: a real home; the kind of home that Marilyn had not had since she was a little girl. The man appeared content. And Marilyn envied him.

Chapter 2

At that moment, Jack Townsend pushed himself away from the word processor on his salon table and surveyed the same scene from his trawler yacht on the other side of the marina. As usual, Arlo Woodbrace and Les Leslie were hard at work on Les' boat. Les had been working on that boat for the entire two years Jack had been living aboard, and he appeared to be no closer to completion now than the day Jack first found refuge at Cap'n Kelly's.

Everyone acknowledged that Les was one of the best shipwrights around. His problem lay in completion. He could never stay with any one thing long enough to actually finish it. The only reason he managed to complete the contract jobs the Calkins brothers forced him to accept was the fact that they constantly rode herd on him. Their incessant nagging, combined with the implied threat of throwing him and his boat out of the marina, forced him to do the unthinkable: actually finish those jobs. On Les' own project there was no such mandate, and he went from one plan to another, continually revising the design in his own mind, forever making it better and ignoring the fact that all forward progress on the project had ceased long ago.

Les and Arlo were pounding wooden plugs into the hull, caulking and covering the bronze screws Les had used recently when he re-fastened the longleaf yellow pine planks. As they worked with their backs to the cove, Jack noticed the furtive glances Arlo sneaked in the direction of Erlene, the Gas Girl. About a month ago, Arlo had been pounding plugs and watching Erlene, just as he was doing at the moment. Only that time when she bent over, Arlo took an extra-long look and knocked himself out cold with his own mallet. Jack had been trying for weeks to work that episode into a book he was writing, but no matter what he did with it, it just came out too unbelievable.

In a way his life had become unbelievable. He had always wanted to live aboard a boat; now he was doing it, but it had not happened the way it was supposed to. He had managed to get away from it all, but he had done it alone and for all the wrong reasons. Now he was the victim of his own isolation as much as he was the author of it.

Jack had written a few magazine articles when he first came to the marina. How he was writing a book that would probably never be published. He started it at the end of his first year of living aboard, and, much like Les' boat, all forward progress had come to a halt. At first it seemed like a good idea, using his experiences as the basis for a novel. But the manuscript had become nothing more than a way of filling up his days, and sometimes his nights. The thought came over him that he was wasting his life, and he accepted it; since his life no longer had a purpose, wasting it didn't seem like such a bad idea.

Out of his aft starboard cabin window, Jack watched Eddie Miles in his sunbonnet watering the flowers he had planted in the boxes Jim Lacey built for him. Jack made it a point to mind his own business, but it was no secret that Eddie hated anything to do with the water. In spite of that, he and Jim lived aboard, and Eddie was doing his darnedest to turn the houseboat into a cottage. He even hung miniature lights on the picket fence Jim built for them along the wall. It was curious: Eddie always seemed happy in spite of his aversion to all things nautical. Maybe he had discovered the secret of what life was really about after all.

Jack hadn't been happy in a long time—just about two years, to be exact. He wasn't particularly melancholy any longer; he had simply given up on the idea of finding happiness, whatever it was, and he no longer sought out its company. He had replaced his fruitless search for happiness with objectivity. He told himself that he had become an observer of the human condition. In a few years, he might graduate into a full-time curmudgeon, but for now he kept his opinions to himself and he appreciated it when others did the same.

At first Jack had relished his self-imposed exile, but recently he had come to admit that he felt, if not lonely, at least left out of things. He decided to be nicer to Arlo Woodbrace the next time Arlo came around.

ഇ യ

It was almost a week before Jack saw him. Arlo came by in his guise of marina handyman, walking down the pot-holed, dusty shell rock road, picking up trash in a hopeless attempt to make the place look neater. Jack went out on deck when he got closer.

"Afternoon, Arlo."

"Huh?"

"I said, 'Good afternoon, Arlo,'" Jack repeated.

"Ya' mean me?" The man's dark bronze skin was an amalgam of African and Caribbean cultures and his voice carried a trace of the Islands.

"Unless there's another Arlo around," Jack said with a grin he could not suppress.

"Oh, yeah. Afternoon, Mister . . . ah, Mister," Arlo stumbled.

"Townsend. Jack Townsend."

"Yeah, I knew that, Mr. Townsend. See, I just didn't know what ya' liked to be called."

"Call me 'Jack'."

"Well, yeah. Okay, Jack. My name's Arlo."

"Yes, I know," Jack said with a bigger smile. "Would you like a beer?"

"A beer?" Yeah, sure, I guess."

"Why don't you come aboard and I'll get you one."

"Come aboard? Yeah, sure, if ya' don't mind and everythin'."

Arlo followed Jack into the salon of the trawler yacht. It was even nicer than it looked outside. There was wood everywhere from the mahogany walls to the teak parquet floor. Built-in shelves, each with its own pinrail, held a number of books. It was obvious Jack Townsend liked to read. The salon table was covered with word processing equipment, papers and more books.

Jack went down to the galley and started poking through the full-sized refrigerator.

"Uh, if it's all the same to you, Mr. Townsend, I'd just as soon have a Pepsi," Arlo said. It looked like he was not going to accept Jack's offer of familiarity.

"Pepsi? No kidding? That's my favorite, too. I hate beer. And call me 'Jack'," Jack reminded him.

"Me, too," Arlo said as Jack handed him the soft drink.

"I used to keep beer around for visitors but I don't get many of those these days," Jack continued. Without really thinking about it, he maneuvered Arlo into a seat on the end of the settee, then moved one of the chairs to the port side of the salon and sat across from him. It placed Jack between his guest and the door, and it meant Arlo would have to get past him to get off the boat. It was a habit Jack had picked up from too many visits to too many jails, where you always made the other guy sit farthest from the exit.

There was an uneasy silence as they sipped their soft drinks.

"This is quite a boat," Arlo said as he looked around. "It's comfortable."

"How big is she?" Arlo asked. It was the inevitable question, Jack thought, and one that confirmed Arlo, whatever his shortcomings might be on land, had a heart that belonged in the world of boats.

"A little over forty-two feet," Jack told him.

"A forty-two foot trawler. Wow. This must 've set ya' back a bundle."

He said it the way a child would say it: completely honest and without a hint of guile. Only a person as open as Arlo Woodbrace could say a thing like that to a virtual stranger, Jack thought.

"What's this stuff?" Arlo said, pointing to the salon table.

"I'm writing a book . . . or at least trying to," Jack said. "Sort of 'The Life and Times of Jack Townsend'."

"Writing a book. Wow." Jack noticed that Arlo said "wow" a lot. "Who's in it?" he asked, taking another sip of his Pepsi.

"A lot of people I know," Jack replied.

"What kind a' people?" Apparently a lack of curiosity was not one of Arlo's faults.

"All kinds: murderers, drug dealers, you know, the finest members of society," Jack said sarcastically.

"You know drug dealers?" Arlo's brown eyes widened into saucers.

"Big dealers," Jack replied coolly. "Bad ones, too. I know a guy who took three guys out to one of the Keys and executed them because a deal went bad."

"Executed? Ya' mean like killed?" Arlo's mouth suddenly got dry. He took a long swig from the Pepsi bottle.

"Killed like shot in the head. He and another guy who owned a van tied them up hand and foot, drove them out to the middle of nowhere one dark night and left them in a swamp. And then, after the other guy went back to the van, the first guy shot each of them in the head, one at a time."

"Wow," Arlo took another long pull from the Pepsi bottle. "What happened ta' him?"

"As a matter of fact he's on Death Row right now, waiting to be executed himself," Jack said quietly.

"Executed? Wow," Arlo repeated. "How'd they catch him?"

"The other guy, the one who drove the van, squealed to the cops and turned State's evidence at trial. The State wanted the killer so badly that they made a deal and eventually let the driver go. The best part was he knew where the three guys hid the missing drugs and, after everything cooled down, he went and got them. He made himself quite a nice profit."

"Nice guy," Arlo said, attempting to imitate Jack's cool sarcasm of a moment earlier.

"Hey, it happens all the time in that business," Jack replied bluntly. "You do it to them before they do it to you."

Arlo shifted around uncomfortably on the settee. He looked like most people look when they confronted by the reality of crime: he apparently wanted to know about it, but not this much and not this close. It seemed the nightly news and an occasional movie was quite enough for him.

"Well, look, it's been real nice talkin' to you, Mister . . . Jack. But I really got to get goin'. Ya' know, lots a' stuff ta' do and everythin'."

"Sure, I understand," Jack said with a smile as he extended his hand. "Stop by anytime, Arlo. I'll let you know how the book is coming along."

"Yeah. Sure. Okay," Arlo replied. "I mean if it's okay with you and everythin'."

"Any time, Arlo." Jack repeated as he escorted his guest to the door.

Jack returned to the table and looked at the unfinished manuscript in front of him. He flipped through the pages and wondered if he had the guts to go on with it. The execution/murder had not been the worst thing he had touched in this life. There was more—much, much more. The stories in his head and the guilt they inspired were what caused him to start writing a book in the first place.

He truly had started writing a book. Part of the manuscript was right there, right in front of him. But now, well over a year after he had begun writing, he couldn't finish it. It was too depressing, too rotten, too meaningless. It was the depressing, rotten, meaningless story of a depressing, rotten, meaningless existence. He needed a whole new subject. He needed to start over—his book as well as his life.

"I guess I've been alone too long," Jack said out loud to the empty room as he thumbed through his unfinished work. "Arlo's beginning to look like good company."

Chapter 3

"I'm tellin' ya', y'r crazy, Arlo," Les Leslie said as he chipped away at one of the toerails on the foredeck and exposed another ancient screw. Their discussion had gone on all morning and they were no closer to a conclusion than when they started. They were on the foredeck now, getting ready to remove the old brightwork and hardware. Les had decided he didn't like the canvas-over-plywood deck. He was going to remove it and replace it with individually laid teak planks. True to his form, he had dropped work on the hull in favor of stripping everything off the deck.

"And *I'm* tellin' ya', the guy's a drug dealer," Arlo insisted. "Well, he's a retired drug dealer, anyways."

"A retired drug dealer," Les repeated for the hundredth time, in a voice that spoke of too many years at sea, sharing quarters with the crews of too many nations. His blue eyes squinted about his gray bushy beard. "An' I suppose he just up an' told ya' that ... right?"

"Yeah, he told me," Arlo insisted. "Like I told ya'." Arlo saw the look in Les' eyes and added, "Well, he didn't 'tell me' tell me. He sort a' told me."

"What in Hades do ya' mean, he didn't tell ya', tell ya', he sort a' told ya"? Ya' sure ya' didn't do somethin' permanent when ya' beaned y'rself with that mallet?"

"Look," Arlo said defensively, "the guy couldn't come right out and tell me he was a drug dealer . . ."

"Ya' got that right," Les interjected.

" . . . so he sort a' told me . . . in a story. Ya' know, like he *knew* a guy who did this, and he *knew* a guy who did that. That sort a' thing."

"And just what did the guy he knew do?" Les demanded.

"Like I told ya', he squealed on another guy who *killed* three other guys. An' then, after the guy that killed the guys got sent to the electric chair, the guy went back an' dug up the drugs and sold 'em. That's how he got the money to buy that boat." Arlo's voice rose as he pointed to the white trawler and presented Les with his inescapable conclusion.

"Arlo," Les said patiently, "first of all, ya' got too many guys and not enough names. Second, anybody does somethin' like that ain't gonna tell nobody . . ."

"But . . ." Arlo tried to insist.

" . . . ain't gonna tell nobody, not even in a story. An' third, anybody does somethin' like that an' gets away with it ain't gonna end up livin' here at Cap'n Kelly's."

"But don't ya' see?" Arlo insisted. "This is the perfect place ta' hide out. Who'd ever think a' looking fer anybody here?"

"Why hide out here? Why hide out anywheres? If all a' the guys 're dead or in prison, why not take the money an' spend it? Go someplace nice?" Les demanded.

"Ah don't know. Maybe he likes it here," Arlo suggested.

"Now I know y'r crazy," Les retorted.

"Well, crazy or not, I still say he's a drug dealer," the younger man insisted before he turned away to dig out another screw.

℘ ℘

From her office window, Marilyn Dupré watched the two men with increasing interest. She couldn't hear them, but she didn't need sound to know they were engaged in a heated discussion. As their words became more animated their work became less so, until they dropped their tools and knelt facing each other, their hands mirroring their debate. It ended with Les placing his hands on his hips, and Arlo turning away to continue doing whatever it was he had been doing before the conversation began.

Marilyn had been on the job for a week now, a week during which the Calkins brothers studiously avoided her and Theo Grant gave her no direction. Left on her own, she had begun to organize the books and records. Today, she would begin the process of putting those records together with names and faces. A knock at the door signaled the arrival of her first appointment.

"Hello?" The woman gingerly opened the door. "I'm Erlene Rodgers," she said. "Ah take care a' the gas dock."

"Yes, I know," Marilyn replied. "Won't you come in?"

Erlene was wearing her bikini halter-top and had slipped into shorts and tennis shoes for her visit to the office. Even though everyone around the marina referred to her as "the Gas Girl," Marilyn could see that Erlene had not been a girl for quite a while. She appeared to be about thirty-five, but Marilyn had to admit she still had a dynamite body. Her tawny skin and lilting accent could have originated only in the Bahamas.

"Is everythin' all right? I mean, I'm not in any kind of trouble am I?" she asked nervously.

"What do you mean, 'trouble'?" Marilyn replied quizzically. "I don't understand."

"Doug said you wanted ta' see me. I guess you're in charge now, right?" Erlene asked by way of confirmation.

"Miss Rodgers . . ." Marilyn began.

"Erlene," the Gas Girl said.

"Pardon me?"

"Most people call me 'Erlene'," she continued.

"Okay, Erlene," Marilyn said. "My name is Marilyn Dupré. I work for the firm of Walker and Grant, and I'm not in charge of anything."

"Then I'm not in trouble?" Erlene said with obvious relief.

"No, you're not in trouble. I told Doug Calkins that I wanted to speak with all of the employees so that I could check on their withholding arrangements. Who told you I was in charge?"

"Doug Calkins," Erlene said quickly. "He said you was

in charge, and that anythin' I wanted I should just go ahead and ast you."

"That's just Doug's way of escaping responsibility," Marilyn complained, almost to herself. She had seen a lot of that in the past week. Doug Calkins was a nice enough person but he seemed incapable of independent thought. He could carry out orders with the best of them, leaving all of the decisions to his older brother. Now it appeared he decided to fall back on Marilyn as well.

"Doug does that a lot," Erlene observed. The response was so perceptive that Marilyn was taken aback for a moment. Maybe there was more at the gas dock than an empty head and a dynamite body.

"What do you mean?" she asked. The answer might tell her as much about Erlene as it did about her employer.

"What you said about excapin' responsibility," Erlene said straightforwardly. "Doug does that all the time. He never says nothin' is his idea. He blames everythin' on Junior. He makes deals with people an' says it's that way 'cause that's the way Junior wants it. Sometimes I wonder, though."

"Wonder about what?" Marilyn asked.

"Sometimes I wonder if Junior wants it that way, or if Doug just says he does so's he'll have someone to blame it on. 'Course it don't matter," she observed brightly, "'cause the deal comes out the same on their end either way."

Well, well, Marilyn thought, I guess there's something more than just a stuffed bikini on the gas dock after all.

"And what kind of deal do they have with you, Erlene?" she asked.

"Forty percent."

"What do you mean?"

"I get forty percent of the profit from the gas dock. After they pay the power and taxes and stuff."

"Let me get this straight," Marilyn said. "You give them sixty percent of the profit . . ."

"Heck, no. That ain't the way it works at all," Erlene said defensively. "I give 'em everything."

"You give them all of the money from the gas dock?"

"That's right. Ev'ry dime. Ev'ry day."

"Then how do you get paid?" Marilyn asked.

"At the end of the week, they tell me how much I brought in, and they take out my share of the power bill and the taxes and stuff . . . Junior's got a way of figurin' it . . . an' they give me forty percent a' what's left."

"And you trust them?" Marilyn demanded. She might be working for the Calkins family accountants, but she knew a raw deal when she saw one.

"Heck, no!" Erlene said more defensively than before. "I ain't stupid, ya' know. Ah keep track of every gallon I sell. Junior's never shorted me neither," she added, thrusting her head up proudly.

"But how do you know he's not overcharging you for the expenses?"

"Oh, we sat down one day an' Junior figured it all out with pencil and paper. Showed me in black and white."

I'll bet he did, Marilyn thought. Erlene might be perceptive but she did not appear to be a match for Junior Calkins when it came to a pencil and paper.

"Anyway, it's legal, ain't it?" Erlene asked. "I got my two kids to take care a' an' I don't want no trouble."

The mention of children brought a whole new dimension to Marilyn's mental image of Erlene the Gas Girl. "You have children?" she asked incredulously.

Erlene nodded. "My girl's seventeen ... the same age I was when I became her Mommy. 'Course she's smarter'n I was. She's startin' at Bonita College in the fall. An' my little guy, he's seven. His Daddy walked out on us when he was born, so he's grown up with two Mommies, me an' Faith."

"Is that your daughter's name, 'Faith'?"

Erlene nodded again. "It seemed like a good name at the time. I knew I had made one mistake but I wasn't gonna make another one by just ... you know ... gettin' a operation 'r somethin'. Ah had faith that if I did right by my baby, everythin' would work out. It did, too." Erlene said with a warm smile that seemed to come easily.

"What did?" Marilyn was thinking about how low a man like Junior would have to sink to take advantage of the Gas Girl.

"Everythin'. I took care of her and she was there f'r me when I needed help bringin' up Tommy. Now I got me my own bidness. It's legal, ain't it? Lettin' me run my gas dock like that?" Her face clouded momentarily while she sought

Marilyn's approval. "Kind a' makes me my own boss," she added proudly.

"Of course it's legal," Marilyn said, slipping quickly into her role of counselor. "Naturally, you have to pay your self-employment tax, and file your quarterly returns just like any other small business . . ."

"Oh, Junior told me not to worry about that. He said I was covered by the marina."

"I see. Well . . ."

"It's legal, ain't it?" Erlene's face clouded again.

Marilyn looked across the desk and saw a single mother: a woman with little education who was making her own way in the world. What she was doing was most assuredly not legal. But how could Marilyn begin to explain the myriad forms and filings that would be required to make it so? It was a safe bet the Calkins brothers were not paying all of the required taxes, which meant that if Erlene picked them up she would have even less net profit. The woman desperately wanted approval and Marilyn, the soon-to-be-lawyer, was faced with her fist ethical dilemma. Seminar discussions in "Law in Modern Society" hadn't covered anything like this. She wondered for a moment what Sister Jean-Marie, back at her old high school, would say about ends justifying means. Finally, she took a deep breath and, before she really knew what she was saying, she blurted out, "Don't worry about it, Erlene. If there's a problem, I'm sure I'll be able to straighten it out."

A knock at the door cut off further conversation and

Marilyn, relieved to be off the spot for the moment, gratefully told the visitor to come in. It was the younger of the two men she had been watching at work on the dry-docked boat. It was his first visit to the office.

"'Mornin'," he said. "Is everythin' all right?"

"Yes," Marilyn answered, "everything is fine."

"I mean th' color an' everythin'. Do ya' like it?" he asked.

"Oh, yes, the color's fine," she said.

"'Mornin', Erlene," he said to the Gas Girl." "I'm goin' to get a Pepsi. Would ya' like one? You too, Miss?"

"Sure," Erlene responded.

"Thank you, that would be very nice," Marilyn added.

The man closed the door leaving a greasy handprint on the frame. Erlene turned to Marilyn and said, "That's Arlo Woodbrace. He's sort a' the handyman around here. Lives on that sailboat between here and the gas dock. Works nights at the Solid Waste Authority. I sure wisht I knew what he does with his money."

Chapter 4

J ack Townsend stared at the empty screen of his word
processor and waited for inspiration, but the only
ideas that would come into his head that morning
had nothing to do with writing. Arlo had not come back
after that first visit, and Jack was alone as usual. Something
had changed in the ordered regularity of life at Cap'n Kelly's: a new person had been added to the office. The person
in question happened to be a woman—a very attractive,
petite, brunette woman with intense, smoldering eyes. If
Jack had been interested in getting involved with a woman
ever again, she would be just his type. Of course he wasn't
interested. He was only thinking about her, he told himself,
because, in a place where very little ever changed, she was
bound to be noticed. Besides, she was new and the polite
thing to do would be to invite her to dinner or something.
Not that he was interested in her. Because he wasn't.

Her name was Marilyn Dupré. He had learned that
from Doug Calkins, along with the fact that she was at the
marina on assignment from Walker & Grant, the family

accountants. Jack ran into her—literally ran into her—in the parking lot one morning on his daily walk to the post office. She was going into the old side door of the building when he came around the corner and almost knocked her down.

"No one ever uses that door," he blurted out at the time, offering an excuse for his own clumsiness.

"Well, I'm using it!" she shot back, her dark eyes flashing at him.

She was heart-endingly beautiful, and he had stood there like a fool, unable to say anything else, so he mumbled and apology and got the hell out of there.

Jack had not been able to get her out his mind since that encounter, and the thought of her working nearby somehow made his isolation more intense. She appeared to be young, far too young for him to think about seriously. Still, there was something in her eyes that would not leave him. He began walking past that side of the building every day, hoping to run into her again, thinking of what he might say this time, what excuse he might use, to strike up a conversation. The encounter never came. In desperation he even thought of calling Fred Walker, the senior partner of Walker & Grant, and asking him about the firm's new employee. But, on second thought, he realized that he would feel pretty foolish asking Fred about a young woman. Besides, Fred was semi-retired and he no longer had much to do with the operation of the office. Jack hardly knew his new partner, Theo Grant, and he certainly wouldn't ask a virtual stranger for information about a woman. Anyway, he told himself, the woman appeared to be, well . . . young.

Jack cursed himself and stared at the blank screen on the table in front of him. He hadn't planned on feeling so old, and so lonely, and so foolish at this stage of his life.

ഇ ര

At the other end of Cap'n Kelly's Marina, Marilyn concentrated on trying to make herself useful in spite of a complete lack of direction from anyone. Theo Grant's only response to her repeated inquiries was to "take care of things and keep them happy," and the Calkins brothers barely spoke to her. She decided to learn everything she could about the operation of the marina and compile that information into a written report that Walker & Grant could use in making future recommendations to the Calkins family. None of the partners said they wanted recommendations, but then, they never said they didn't want them, either.

Several days after speaking with Erlene, Marilyn approached Les Leslie near his boat. Les appeared to be around sixty, perhaps twenty years older than Arlo, his constant companion—a companion who wasn't around at the moment. Les was working a wood plane over a large piece of wood that was becoming something he called a "toerail." Whatever a "toerail" was, he planned to install it over the teak deck—whenever that project was finished. She stood there in the hot sun, admiring how the mahogany shavings curled in the plane. Thin ribbons of wood clung to Les' hair and beard, and they littered the ground around him.

"My name is Marilyn Dupré," she began by way of introduction.

"Yes, Miss, I know. Erlene told us," Les said, without looking at her. "She said you're gettin' things in order around here. Sure hope nothin's goin' ta' change."

"What do you mean?"

"Liveaboards, Miss. Lots a' marinas don't want 'em anymore. They're tryin' ta' get rid of 'em all over Florida. Hope it don't happen here."

"Do you think it might?"

"You bein' here don't make it look good," Les replied, still not looking up from his work.

"Mister Leslie, I promise you, I'm only a . . . well, I'm sort of an accountant. And I'm only here because . . . well, I don't know why I'm here, actually. I'm just trying to get the books in order. I'm sure that nothing is going to change."

As she spoke those words, Marilyn had an uneasy feeling that Les might be right. The Calkins family might have just wanted her around for window dressing; their own "professional" on the "staff" might make the place look more legitimate to a prospective buyer. She hoped she was wrong. Although she hardly knew these people, she would not want to hurt them.

"I'm only here doing my job," she continued, gently touching his shoulder. "And I would appreciate it if you would talk to me for a minute."

"It don't cost nothin' ta' be polite, my Pa used ta' say," Les responded, putting down the plane. "An' if changes are goin' ta' come, I guess they'll get here soon enough whether I talk ta' ya' 'r not. What would ya' like ta' know?"

"Do you live here?" Marilyn began.

"Well, now that's a good question," Les said, scratching his beard and doing nothing to hide the fact that he was avoiding the answer. "Let's just say that I stay aboard . . . sometimes."

"Then you live aboard?"

"I didn't say that. I said, I stay aboard . . . sometimes."

"Then you live somewhere else?

"What difference does it make?" Les asked.

"Well, sometimes you do contract jobs for the marina, don't you?" Marilyn asked.

"Yeah, that's right," he admitted.

"Okay," she said, "I need your mailing address for your tax records."

"Oh," he said, obviously relieved, "that's no problem. I pay my taxes, all right. An' I get all my mail right here."

"Then you live here?" she asked.

"No, I stay here. Sometimes. When I work late, I stay here, aboard *Elena*. And I get my mail here. And when *Elena* is finished, I'll live aboard . . . legally live aboard, if ya' get my meanin'. But right now, I only stay here . . . sometimes. Understand?" Les gave her a broad wink and Marilyn found herself liking Les Leslie in spite of herself. He saw that she was looking around, so he quickly pulled out a large red handkerchief and brushed off a place for her to sit. Then he made himself comfortable on a concrete block across from her.

"Mister Leslie," she said, trying to remain objective in the face of Les' homey charm, "I don't care if you live up there in your dry-docked boat or not. What I really need to know is how you get paid for the jobs you do."

"The boys pay me with checks, all nice an' legal," Les replied.

"But you're working on other people's boats," she protested.

"That's right," he explained. "Them people hire Cap'n Kelly's ta' fix up their boats, and Cap'n Kelly's hires the work out ta' me."

"But if those people know you're doing their work, why don't they just come to you directly?"

"Because I don't do no work f'r nobody except Cap'n Kelly's. That way, the boys don't look too close if they see me spendin' a night 'r two aboard *Elena*."

So that was it, Marilyn thought. That was why he was being so evasive. The boys weren't above their own form of blackmail. The next question was none of her business but she just had to ask it.

"Mister Leslie," she said, trying to sound as innocent as she could," how much do the boys mark up your work?"

Les scratched his beard again. "Well, Miss, I don't know f'r sure, but I've heard a hundred percent."

"A hundred percent! You mean they pay you and then

get double your price to the customer for doing nothing?"

"That's what I've heard, Miss. 'Course, you'd know more about that 'n I would."

"I'm afraid I don't know very much, Mister Leslie," Marilyn replied as she stood up to leave. "But I'm learning."

"Anytime, Miss," Les said, extending a callused hand. "Just don't make no changes."

"There won't be any changes, Mr. Leslie," she replied. "At least not if I have anything to say about it."

Marilyn started back to the office, then suddenly stopped and went back. Les had already returned to work.

"Mr. Leslie, I hate to bother you again . . ."

"No bother, Miss," Les said, not looking up from his toerail.

"Who is that man who walks by my office every day?"

Les looked up. "What man is that, Miss?"

"Tall, light hair, blue eyes and glasses. He looks like he might be around forty," she reported. "He never drives a car and he walks past my office every day."

"Never drives a car? Sounds like that could be Mr. Townsend, Miss," Les said.

"Does he live here? Really live aboard a boat, I mean?"

"Yes, Miss, he sure does." Les pointed to the boat that had caught her eye the very first day. "He lives on that forty-two foot Grand Banks: the white trawler . . . the one without a name over there."

"You mean the one that looks kind of like a fishing boat?"

"That's no fishing boat, Miss. That're 's one of the finest yachts afloat. Why, a boat like that'll shrug off seas that'd make others run f'r home. 's shame he never takes her out."

"Never goes out? That's odd. What does he do? For a living, I mean?"

"No one seems ta' know, Miss. Just stays aboard an' minds his own business, mostly."

"Thank you, Mr. Leslie," she said. "I guess that's something else I'll have to find out for myself."

"Oh, I wouldn't do that Miss. Nobody bothers Mr. Townsend much. Not even Junior."

Marilyn was about to head over to the trawler in spite of the warning, but she was interrupted by Doug Calkins who called from the office door. "Telephone!" he shouted. "Theo Grant wants to talk to you!"

Thank God, she thought. I'm about to be paroled. She ran back to her office and picked up the phone expectantly.

"Marilyn," a familiar voice said, "Theo Grant here. How goes it?"

"Fine, Mr. Grant," she lied gracefully. "I'm learning quite a bit about the operation of the business."

"That's good. Great. Wonderful," he replied and then added, "Marilyn, Mrs. Calkins called. She needs your help balancing her checkbook. Could you stop by her house and see what the trouble is?"

"Stop by her house?" Marilyn wasn't sure she heard him right.

"She's an important client, Marilyn. Megabucks. Buck-aroos. Buckaroonies. She lives over there in Calkins Harbor. I'm busy here and you're already out there, over the bridge."

"Of course, Mr. Grant, Marilyn signed. "No need to explain. I'll go see her this afternoon."

"Thanks, kid," Grant said. "I'll buy you lunch at the Yacht Club someday if those people on the membership committee ever get off their duffs. Keep in touch. Call me if you need anything."

Marilyn hung up thinking the only thing she needed was to have her head examined for having taken this silly job. Still, it got her out of Louisiana and out of a relationship that was going nowhere. And if she hadn't made it back home yet, at least she had plenty of free time to study for the Florida bar exam.

It was afternoon before Arlo showed up at Les' boat.

"The new gal was around ta'day," Les said as he started to plane another block of wood.

"What'd she want?" Arlo asked.

"It don't look good. She was astin' a million questions."

"What kind a' questions?"

"Everythin'. If ya' ast me, they're gettin' ready ta' sell this place an' we're all gonna be out on our ears."

"Gosh, I hope not," Arlo said.

"'Hopin' don't get the job done,' my Pa used ta' say," Les responded. "She was askin' about y'r friend Townsend, too."

"What'd you tell her?"

"I told her what I knew," Les said, looking Arlo straight in the eye. "I told her he lives on that trawler, an' he minds his own business. Which is what you should be doin'."

"You mean you didn't tell her he's a drug dealer?" Arlo demanded.

"No, I didn't tell her any such thing. An' ya' better just f'rget that silly notion a' y'rs, Arlo."

"It's not a silly notion, Les! The guy told me so himself."

"Here we go again," Les said. "Look, he didn't tell ya' nothin'. An' ya' better stop repeatin' it all over the marina."

"I ain't told nobody," Arlo lied.

"Well, just make sure ya' don't, 'cause I'm sure it ain't true."

"I'm going to get a Pepsi," Arlo said, changing the subject. "Want one?"

"Okay, sure," Les replied, digging into his pocket. "Here, I'll treat."

Arlo's route took him right past the outside door that went into Marilyn's office. As he approached the building he looked back and saw that Les was busy with his latest block of wood. He knocked and quickly slipped inside. Marilyn was standing behind her desk, putting some papers into a briefcase.

"I'm sorry, Arlo. I'm just about to leave," she apologized.

"That's okay, Ms. Dupré," he replied. "It's just that, well, it's . . ."

"What's the matter, Arlo?"

"It's just that I hear you was astin' about Mr. Townsend, and I thought . . ."

"Yes?"

"Well, I kind a' thought ya' should know . . ."

"Know what?"

"He's a big drug dealer."

Arlo's revelation was a whopper, even for Arlo, and Marilyn felt her knees get weak. "What did you say," she asked, sitting down and hoping she had misunderstood him.

"He's a big drug dealer," Arlo repeated. "Well, he's a retired big drug dealer, anyways. He told me so himself. 'Course, he didn't tell me straight out 'r anything. I had ta' kind a' worm it outta' him."

"Arlo," Marilyn said, recovering her composure, "I have an appointment with Mrs. Calkins in fifteen minutes. I don't want to be late. We'll just have to talk about this some other time."

"Sure, no problem," he replied. "Like I say, I just thought ya' should know."

Chapter 5

Marilyn's mind raced as she drove away from the marina. The thought of a major drug lord living nearby made her skin crawl. But, still, she just couldn't believe Jack Townsend was such a man. She had watched him walking past her office every day; he looked harmless enough, even pleasant. She had almost invited him in a couple of times. On the other hand, she had to admit that Arlo was much more familiar than she was with Cap'n Kelly's and the comings and goings of its residents. If anyone knew everybody's business, Arlo did. She also had to admit Townsend had all the characteristics of a man on the run. He certainly kept to himself. All the same, if wanting to be left alone were illegal, half the population of Florida would be in jail. And yet, Arlo said that Townsend had admitted he was a drug dealer. But what did Arlo know? Maybe he had gotten things mixed up. Marilyn was willing to bet it would not have been the first time. Or maybe Townsend *had* smuggled drugs at one time. She could imagine him as a pilot, perhaps, flying in a load of cocaine, just once, so he could make enough money to buy the boat of his dreams and then disappear. It wasn't the right thing to do, of course, but he might have reformed. Sister Jean-Marie used to talk about divine mercy and the spark of goodness in every human soul. Jack Townsend might have truly regretted his one act of youthful indiscretion. He couldn't return home; that was why he was in hiding. She could understand that. It could have happened that way. The man who walked past her office every day, and once even appeared to hesitate as though he might come inside, that man was no "drug dealer." Maybe he was a smuggler, but only once, and then only a very long time ago. By the time Marilyn finally settled the matter with herself she was at the Calkins home.

The two-story house on Magnolia Avenue was surprisingly modest for people who were supposed to have what Theo Grant called "buckaroonies." The sloping roof covered a wide front porch that had been designed for sitting in the evening air. A bay-window dormer capped by a cupola sprouted from the roof and announced the presence of at least one second-floor bedroom. The view from that room must have commanded the front yard as well as the bay just across the street.

If the house was modest, the grounds were unusually large. Two Magnolia trees dominated the front yard. Marilyn wondered which had come first, the trees or the street that took its name from their blossoms. Farther back, on either side of the house, she could make out the last of the citrus fruit still clinging to the branches of other trees, and here and there coconut palms swayed in the afternoon breeze. The grounds were immaculate, and as Marilyn walked up the brick path, she concluded that Mrs. Calkins had a very good caretaker. The lady of the house was waiting at the front door.

"Good afternoon, Marilyn. It's so nice of you to drop by."

"It's good to see you again, Mrs. Calkins," Marilyn said.

"Won't you come in? I have tea ready."

The older woman led Marilyn into a house of white stucco walls accented by dark wood trim. The whole of it appeared to be filled with antiques, and a young blond woman was playing a baby grand piano in the living room. The music stopped when they entered.

"Marilyn, this is my granddaughter, Jennifer. Jennifer, this is Marilyn Dupré."

"Hi, Marilyn. My grandmother's told me so much about you," Jennifer said, extending her hand from the piano bench. Then, turning to her grandmother she added, "Grandma, the piano sounds just fine."

"Well, if you say so, Dear," Mrs. Calkins replied. "Anyway, I love to hear you play. Now why don't you ladies chat a bit and I'll get us our tea."

Mrs. Calkins disappeared through a dining room into what must have been a kitchen at the back of the house, and Jennifer left the piano bench to sit on a love seat opposite Marilyn.

"Grandma loves her afternoon tea. She says it's what separates civilized people from the unwashed."

"Your grandmother is quite a lady," Marilyn agreed.

"She thinks you're special, too," Jennifer said.

"Really?" Marilyn asked. "I can't imagine why. She barely knows me."

"You're a professional woman, that's why. And you have a career. Those things count with Grandma. I'm just finishing my last year at Bonita College, and she's already working on me to find something to do. Of course, she would never come right out and say that, so she's been using you as an example."

"'That Marilyn Dupré,'" Jennifer said, mimicking her grandmother's voice, "'Do you know, Jennifer, why, she's almost a lawyer. It just goes to show you what a woman can do with herself these days.'"

Marilyn smiled. "What are you majoring in?"

"Fine art. I've always been interested in it, and in the past couple of years I've gotten into interior design as well. But I'm afraid that's not enough for Grandma. She's worried that I won't be able to earn a living."

"So what are your plans after graduation?"

Jennifer looked toward the kitchen. "I could make that lady the happiest person in the world if I suddenly announced in the middle of our tea party that I had decided to move to Palm Beach and work for some exclusive gallery on Worth Avenue."

"Then why don't you?"

"Because I don't know if that's really what I want anymore. Besides, it would mean that I would have to leave her. She doesn't have much of a relationship with my father, and Uncle Doug . . . well, you've met him. He's kind of useless. I don't have any brothers or sisters, and . . . well, I'm afraid of what might happen to Grandma if I go."

"Does she know that's how you feel?" Marilyn asked, although she already suspected the answer.

"God, no!" Jennifer confirmed. "She'd have an absolute fit if she thought she was holding me back. Besides, I'm really *not* sure if that's what I want to do. Right now we've sort of compromised. I told her I wasn't sure of what I wanted, and we agreed that I would stay at Bonita College after I graduate and get a Master's degree."

"In what?" Marilyn asked.

"In anything," Jennifer replied. "Anyway, I have the whole summer to come up with the answer to that question. Meanwhile I'll just live here with Grandma, drink tea and play the piano."

Marilyn felt an immediate fondness for the younger woman, and intuitively felt it was returned. It was a special chemistry, an immediate bond that sometimes blossoms between two people. It was hard for Marilyn to believe that Jennifer was the daughter of Kelly Junior, a man who was hated and avoided by everyone at the marina. Jennifer was the antithesis of her father; she was as warm, genuine and outgoing as he was cold, introverted and devious.

"You must love your grandmother very much," Marilyn observed.

"She's all I have, really," Jennifer responded. "My parents

split up when I was six. I don't remember much about it, except they were always fighting about something. My father was always walking out and coming back. Then one day he walked out and didn't come back. After a while, my mother left me here at this house with my favorite doll and a suitcase full of clothes. Grandma and Grandpa became my parents."

"But your father did come back," Marilyn said. "I mean, he's here right now . . . at the marina."

"Dad came back when I was ten," Jennifer continued. "I guess he wanted to take me away, but Grandma and Grandpa wouldn't hear of it. They were all set to go to court or something when they all just made up. Grandpa gave Dad a job at the boatyard and I stayed here."

Jennifer paused. Marilyn sensed her sudden embarrassment, as if she had said too much to a woman who, after all, was a complete stranger. Marilyn broke the silence with a revelation of her own. "At least they all wanted you," she said. "After my mother died, all I had was Sister Jean-Marie at a convent school."

Their exchange of secrets ended when Mrs. Calkins called from the dining room and told the "ladies" their tea was ready. Marilyn and Jennifer took their places at a table set with linen, fine china and sterling silver. The biscuits and cakes made it look more like a meal than an afternoon snack.

"Indeed it is," Mrs. Calkins said. She explained that in England, where the custom of afternoon tea originated,

the evening meal was a light "supper" that was served quite
late. An "afternoon tea" filled the gap between the midday
"dinner" and the late evening meal.

"Have you always done this?" Marilyn inquired.

"Goodness, no," Mrs. Calkins said with a smile as she
stirred her tea. "When my late husband and I came to
this part of Florida we were lucky to have three meals a
day, and never mind their order or what you called them.
But he's been gone these five years, and afternoon tea is .
.. well," she said softly, "it's something to take up an old
woman's time."

"What was it like when you came here?" Marilyn asked,
hoping to cheer up her hostess.

"It was hard at first, very hard," Mrs. Calkins replied.
"We came down from Biloxi, down the Florida coast in an
old shrimp boat. That boat was our first home, Casey and
me, and of course the two boys. Air conditioning? Bosh!
We were happy to have an electric fan!"

"Grandma, why do you call Grandpa 'Casey'? I've never
understood that," Jennifer said.

"Jennifer! I'm surprised at you! Kelly Calkins' initials were 'K.C.' All of the old timers from Biloxi called
Grandpa 'Casey,' and I did, too." She thought for a moment
and added, "But they're all gone now. And Grandpa only
gave that privilege to a very few people around here." She
smiled a moment and added, "Nowadays you'll only hear
it from those who knew us back then."

Mrs. Calkins took a sip of her tea and continued her

story. "Most folks think we founded this town, but that's not so. The bay was here, of course, and so was a small town called 'Kelly's Landing.' Casey said that was a good omen, and he dropped the hook in a cove off the bay, and we lived aboard for the first few months."

"Casey was a smart one. By and by, he made a deal for us to live in a small house, and then he got up a fishing crew by guaranteeing them shares. He would have had to sell our boat if they hadn't caught anything on that first trip. Things were hard, but we saved our money and eventually they got better. Every time we had a few extra dollars, Casey would buy a piece of land. People thought he was crazy, but he just said, 'It's the only thing they're not making more of,' and he bought it."

"Where did you get the idea for a marina?" Marilyn asked.

"That was Casey's idea too," Mrs. Calkins explained. "More shrimpers were beginning to come down the west coast, and Casey figured they'd need supplies and one thing or another. Land was cheap, so he bought the little cove where we'd first dropped our hook. The inlet was too shallow to get through except at high tide, so Casey went out and got a load of old steel bedsprings and dragged them back and forth to deepen the channel. By and by the boatyard grew. Strangers just naturally called it 'Kelly's Boatyard,' and many referred to Casey as "Captain" because of his Coast Guard service. So we named the place "Captain Kelly's." The 'marina' part came later when the pleasure boaters moved in."

"Then how did 'Kelly's Landing' become Calkins Harbor?" Marilyn asked.

"Well," Mrs. Calkins said, taking another sip of tea and putting her cup back on the china saucer, "that's a story in itself. The bay itself didn't have a name when we got here. During World War II, Casey put in quite of bit of time with the Coast Guard. After the War, he was something of a local hero and a friend of his in the Government put the name 'Calkins Harbor' on the charts of this area. By and by the folks around here voted to rename the town after the harbor . . . and they named it after us in the process."

"'Everything happens for the best,' right, Grandma?" Jennifer said as if she had heard this part of the story a million times and already knew the ending.

"Yes, Love," Mrs. Calkins responded. "Everything does happen for the best, after all."

"How about you, Marilyn?" Mrs. Calkins asked, turning to her. "Are things working out for you?"

"Yes, thank you," Marilyn answered. "It was especially nice of you to have that office painted for me. I just wish I knew . . ." She didn't know how to say what she was thinking.

"Yes, Dear?"

"Well," she went on, "I only wish that I could . . . that I knew what it is that everyone expects me to be doing there."

"Everything will work out, Dear. You'll see," Mrs. Calkins said confidently. "Tell me, have you met any of the residents?"

"Arlo Woodbrace is very nice," Marilyn began. "He tries to be so helpful to everyone. And I have a lot of respect for Erlene Rodgers, the woman who runs the gas dock. Did you know she's working there to support two children? In fact, her daughter starts college this fall."

"I'm so happy to hear that," Mrs. Calkins said. "And how about Mr. Townsend, have you met him?"

The mention of Jack Townsend caught Marilyn off guard. She had no idea that Mrs. Calkins actually knew these people by name. What could she say? That she had heard Townsend was involved in narcotics trafficking? Did Mrs. Calkins know about it already? Did she even know such things existed, especially right here in Calkins Harbor? Marilyn decided to take the safer course and plead ignorance.

"You mean the man who lives on the fishing boat?" she asked innocently.

"A trawler yacht is hardly a fishing boat, Love," Mrs. Calkins said. "But yes, that's him."

"I only bumped into him once," Marilyn said honestly. "Really bumped into him, I mean. I guess he wasn't used to the idea of anyone using the side door of the building and we collided there my second day on the job."

"Wonderful relationships have been built on stranger meetings," Mrs. Calkins laughed.

"Oh, I don't think . . ." Marilyn began. "I mean, I couldn't see myself . . . I don't think that's possible," she concluded, obviously flustered.

"And why not?" Mrs. Calkins demanded lightly.

"Well, to be honest," Marilyn began, looking for a way to say what was on her mind, "Mrs. Calkins, do you know whether Jack Townsend is involved in any . . . illegal activities?"

"Good Lord, I should hope not!"

"Yes, but do you know? I mean are you sure? Marilyn insisted.

"My Dear, in this life we can't be sure of anything, but I am quite certain that Mr. Townsend would never be involved in anything that was not completely respectable."

"But how can you know that?"

"Marilyn, Mr. Townsend was very highly regarded by my late husband," Mrs. Calkins said firmly. "Casey Calkins would not have had anything to do with anyone who was less than honest."

"But you said Captain Kelly died five years ago."

"Yes, that's right."

"Well, maybe Mr. Townsend became involved in something recently."

The older woman cut her off sharply. "No. I am absolutely certain that Mr. Townsend did not become involved in anything illegal. I would stake my reputation on it."

Mrs. Calkins appeared to be getting a little testy on the subject, and it did not appear to be a good idea to challenge her again, but Marilyn could not resist asking her one more question.

"Mrs. Calkins," she began, "do you know what Mr. Townsend did for a living before he . . . retired?"

A smile returned to the older woman's lips. "Well, Love," she said, stirring her tea, "perhaps it would be better if you asked him that question."

The rest of the afternoon went well. Marilyn avoided any further discussion of the marina and its residents. It was plain that Mrs. Calkins knew more about the place and the people who lived there than she let on, and Marilyn wanted to avoid any more disagreements with her. It was almost five o'clock when she remembered what it was she had been sent to do.

"Mrs. Calkins," she began, "I'm sorry, but Theo Grant told me you needed some help balancing your checkbook."

"Yes, Dear, that's right. Thank you for reminding me," Mrs. Calkins replied. "But it's much too late now. Perhaps you could come back another day?"

"Tomorrow?"

"No," she said, "I'm afraid I'll be busy tomorrow, and the rest of the week as well." She thought for a moment and then said, "I have a wonderful idea! Today is Wednesday. Why don't you come back a week from today, and we'll have another tea? I'll have the checkbook ready for you and you can look at it then."

"Well, if you don't think it needs any immediate attention . . ." Marilyn said.

"My Dear, in this life the only things that need immediate attention are health and happiness. Now you run along. I'll see you next week."

Chapter 6

Marilyn got to the marina early the next morning, determined to unravel the mystery of Jack Townsend. Drug dealer, smuggler or hermit, she would solve the riddle once and for all that day. As she pulled up to the building she noticed Junior and Doug Calkins loading fishing tackle into a station wagon.

"Well, take care of things, Marilyn," Doug said. "We'll see you in a few weeks."

"What . . .what do you mean?" Marilyn stammered.

"Our annual fishing trip. I told you about it, didn't I?" Doug replied a little too offhandedly.

"No," she frowned, "I'm afraid you didn't tell me anything about a fishing trip."

Marilyn knew she was right, of course, and that this was just another way of Doug avoiding responsibility. If he didn't tell her about it, she couldn't object to being left to babysit the place until it was too late.

"Well, it doesn't matter," Doug continued. "Junior and I go fishing for two or three weeks every summer. We're trying our luck early this year. Just sit in the office and make yourself comfortable until we get back."

"But ... what if something comes up?" she demanded.

"It won't. We usually just lock the door and leave the place to run itself. The slip fees have all been collected and Arlo's around for emergencies."

"Can you at least tell me where you're going?"

"Don't know. North," Doug replied. "Either to the Carolinas or Kentucky. Maybe west to Arkansas. Wherever they're biting."

Junior banged his hand on the roof of the car. "C'mon Doug," he said through his cigar, "let's hit the road." The station wagon shook as he heaved his bulk into the passenger seat.

"Got to hit the road, Marilyn," Doug said as he got behind the wheel. "See you in a couple of weeks."

The engine roared to life and they bounced across the parking lot, leaving Marilyn standing in a cloud of shell-rock dust. No sooner had they reached the road than the telephone rang. Marilyn had a good mind to let the fool thing ring itself out, but she was the kind of person who had to do a good job in spite of herself. She ran inside, picked it up and said, "Good Morning, Cap'n Kelly's" in her best Sainte Anne's Convent School voice. The caller wanted information on slip fees, and Marilyn began a very long and busy morning.

After she got the telephone under control, Erlene came in to report that the fuel distributor had failed to make his regular "drop" and the marina's storage tanks were nearly empty. By the time Marilyn found the number and arranged for delivery and payment, all thoughts of Jack Townsend had been swept from her mind, replaced by thoughts of the slow, painful murder of Kelly Calkins Jr. and his little brother, Douglas.

℘ ☙

The morning was less hectic but no less serious at the Calkins home. This was the day Mrs. Calkins had selected for her follow-up visit to the doctor. She usually went alone, but this time she asked Jennifer to take her.

"Is anything wrong, Grandma?" Jennifer asked as they got into her grandmother's roomy yellow Cadillac.

"Wrong? Of course not, Love," Mrs. Calkins replied with a gentle smile. "I've just been a little tired of late, and I thought it would be nice to have someone else drive for a change."

Jennifer knew her grandmother too well to be completely satisfied with that answer, but she also knew it was useless to press the woman on a subject she did not wish to discuss. On the way to the office, Mrs. Calkins began to talk about how much the town had grown since she first came here. "It's so nice to have someone else drive so that I can sightsee," she said. "Lord, how some of these sights bring back memories."

They crossed the bridge into Bonita, and Mrs. Calkins asked Jennifer to drive by her college. As they passed the campus she said, almost wistfully, "Perhaps you should pursue a degree in the law, Dear."

Jennifer was startled by her grandmother's statement. "Oh, Grandma, what makes you think I'd want to be a lawyer, anyway?"

"It's a good profession, Jennifer," Mrs. Calkins responded. "And you and Marilyn Dupré would make such a lovely team."

"Marilyn?" Jennifer asked. "Grandma, she'll be on to bigger and better things than the boatyard after she passes the bar examination."

"Perhaps, Dear," Mrs. Calkins said. "But I think not. At least I hope not."

Dr. Greenman's office was on the first floor of the Bonita Gardens Medical Center. His nurse asked them to have a seat in the waiting room while he finished up with another patient. It was a few minutes before they were called, and Jennifer stood up to accompany her grandmother inside.

"Jennifer, dear," Mrs. Calkins protested, "there are some things a lady does not discuss, even with her dearest grand-daughter. Be a Love and wait here. I'll be out in a moment."

The "moment" was much too long for Jennifer. Twenty minutes became thirty. As the hands of her watch crawled to the forty-minute mark, she knocked on the reception-ist's window.

"Is anything wrong? I mean, is everything all right in there?" Her concern showed on her face and the reception-ist tried to reassure her.

"Yes, Miss, I'm sure everything is fine. Doctor just likes to take his time with patients."

"Yes, but . . . it's been an awfully long time," Jennifer reminded her.

"Well, sometimes he takes longer than others, but I'm sure everything is fine."

Jennifer decided to wait another five minutes. If her grandmother wasn't out by then, by golly, she would burst in there and demand to know what was going on. Once she made the commitment to herself she was afraid she might be forced to keep it, and she wondered if she would have the nerve. At forty-five minutes she stood up to ask the receptionist if she could go inside. At that moment the door opened and Mrs. Calkins appeared.

"Grandma!" she said in a voice mixed with worry and relief, "What took so long? I was worried sick!"

"There, there, Dear," her grandmother said, "There's nothing wrong, nothing at all. Dr. Greenman just likes to talk."

"But you were in there so long," Jennifer protested.

"Yes, well, we both did our share of talking, I'm afraid. Now where shall we have lunch? I haven't been to the Yacht Club in ages," Mrs. Calkins said as they walked out of the waiting room.

Jennifer knew that her grandfather had been a member of the Club and remembered going there with him a few times. They hadn't been back since he died, and she always assumed their membership had expired with him.

"Are we still members?" she asked.

"Of course, Love," Mrs. Calkins replied. "Your grandfather was a member, and I am still Mrs. Calkins, after all. It's a courtesy the Club extends to the widows of deceased members.

Jennifer always hated the word "widow" and was particularly upset when her grandmother used it to describe herself. Yet that was what she was, the widow of Captain Kelly Calkins and, like it or not, the word fit.

"We must do something about getting you your own membership one of these days," her grandmother continued. "I believe I still know one or two members who could put in a good word."

As they drove back across the bridge to their island, Mrs. Calkins smiled to herself at the thought of the widow of Captain Kelly needing anyone to put in a good word for her anywhere on Bonita Key. Soon—perhaps sooner than she wished—Jennifer would learn the truth, and she prayed that her granddaughter would be able to handle it when she did.

Sam DePasquale, the Club manager, recognized the yellow Cadillac and came outside to open the door in person.

"Mrs. Calkins," Sam said, "it's so nice to see you again. Surely this can't be Jennifer?"

"It can be and it is, flatterer," Mrs. Calkins replied, playfully slapping his cheek. "Now be a dear and have one of the boys park the car so that we can have lunch."

Sam did not even bother to try to explain the Club did

not provide valet service until evening. He asked one of the bartenders to park the vehicle and personally escorted Mrs. Calkins and her granddaughter to the second-floor Members' Dining Room where he seated them at a table overlooking the yacht basin. After they ordered the "BKYC Special," Mrs. Calkins reminisced about how she had to inveigle her late husband into joining the Club years ago.

"Didn't Grandpa want to be a member?" Jennifer said with astonishment. "No one ever turns down a membership in this Club, do they?"

"Grandpa was probably the only man in the history of the Club who had the Membership Committee come to him and beg him to join," her grandmother replied. "He almost did turn them down, too, but I convinced him that it would be good for business. Grandpa was much too practical to join a club like this for any other reason. Of course, he would never put in the time required to become Commodore. I always regretted that, and I suspect he did, too, in his later years. But by then other, younger men were in line, and he had lost his chance."

The story was one that Jennifer had never heard. "Tell me more," she said, fascinated.

"There's not much more to tell," her grandmother continued. "We attended a few of the social functions, but, you know, we never owned a boat other than that old shrimper." She chuckled at the thought and added, "And that's not the kind of boat one takes on a BKYC cruise."

"The boat's still at the boatyard, isn't it?" Jennifer asked.

"Yes," Mrs. Calkins replied. "the *Margaret* is still there. He named her after me, of course. It's a tradition with those men, you know . . . naming their boats after their sweethearts. Perhaps we should visit her after lunch. There's another matter to which I must attend anyway."

Early afternoon found them at the marina, another place they had not visited since Captain Kelly died. "Just go around to the left of the building and out along the seawall, Dear," Mrs. Calkins instructed. "There's a shell-rock road there, and I'll tell you when to stop."

The order came when they were alongside Jack Townsend's white trawler. The arrival of an unexpected, early-afternoon visitor, especially one in a large yellow Cadillac, was an event to be noticed at the marina, and Townsend came out on deck to greet them.

"Permission to come aboard, Captain?" Mrs. Calkins asked as she got out of the car.

"Of course, my dear lady," he replied. "And that goes for the lovely young lady at your side as well."

"Flattery will get you everywhere, sir," Mrs. Calkins said as she turned her head so that he could kiss her cheek. He extended his arms and wrapped Jennifer in a hug. "Jennifer," he said, "it's so nice to see you. Please come inside."

Jennifer was surprised at how Townsend acted toward her and her grandmother. Her grandmother, too, acted like she was in the presence of an old friend although Jennifer could not quite place him.

The boat was blessedly air-conditioned, and the main

cabin was ample. It appeared that Mr. Townsend was a writer. The salon table was covered with word-process-ing equipment and papers and books, which he quickly brushed out of the way.

"And now, my dear lady," he said, pulling two chairs up to the table and taking a seat on the settee opposite them. "how may I be of service?"

"A cup of tea would be very nice," Mrs. Calkins suggested.

"Certainly," Townsend said. "Jennifer? Tea? A soft drink?"

"No, thank you," she replied. "We just finished lunch."

Jack went to the galley and put a small pot of water in the microwave. "I see you're writing a book, Dear," Mrs. Calkins said. "I should hope that it's not your memoirs."

"As a matter of fact it is . . . or it will be, if I ever finish it," he replied, returning to the table for a moment.

"You're too young for that, Jack," Mrs. Calkins said, with even more familiarity. "You haven't lived your life yet."

"I've lived about as much of it as I care to," he responded with a touch of bitterness in his voice.

"You left your path and had a setback, Dear," she said. "Now it's time for you to get back on it and move on."

"I don't think I can," he said.

"Yes you can, Dear. And you will, too," Mrs. Calkins assured him. "Trust me."

"I haven't seen any forward progress," he protested.

"Well, Dear, perhaps you haven't been looking," she said.

Townsend did not reply, and in a few moments the chime of the microwave oven gave him a reason to escape from a conversation that appeared to make him uncomfortable. "I'll get our tea," he said lamely as he went to the galley.

Jennifer had watched the dialogue between her grandmother and Townsend with growing amazement. Her grandmother seemed to know a lot about the man, and it was obvious she took a great deal of interest in him. More than that, she allowed him a degree of familiarity that she did not permit in other people, especially people who were more than twenty years her junior.

Jack brought out mugs and a pot of hot tea and apologized for the lack of fine china.

"Lord, you of all people should know that when we first came here Casey and I would have been happy to have mugs with handles, never mind fine china," Mrs. Calkins replied.

Jennifer saw Townsend smile at the mention of her grandfather's pet name. "Yes," he said, "I heard that from Casey himself. But that was a long time ago."

"Those were glorious years," Mrs. Calkins laughed dreamily. "We were as poor as church mice. We didn't know how happy we were. It was only later, at the end, when we realized that true happiness is found in the struggle for the goal rather than the attainment of it."

The room was silent as Mrs. Calkins stirred her tea. "I recall," she said after a moment, "there was a time when you took on a struggle on behalf of your friends."

"But I was younger then, dear lady," he replied, "and I believed in their cause. I've gone out of the cause business since that time."

"And yet," she prodded, still stirring her tea, "I wonder if you might be willing to take on one more cause?"

Jack smiled, completely charmed by her way of putting things. No wonder she could get Casey to do anything she wanted, he thought.

"If the cause were just, and one in which I truly believed, I supposed I could be persuaded," he replied.

Mrs. Calkins acknowledged her granddaughter for the first time since they boarded Townsend's vessel. "Jennifer," she said, "be a Dear and go . . . visit Marilyn for a while. Mr. Townsend and I have something to discuss."

There was something in her grandmother's voice, something in the words, "be a Dear and go . . ." that struck a hidden chord deep inside Jennifer Calkins, as if the next words should have been, ". . . go play outside." A wave of *déjà vu* swept over her. She had been a part of this scene once before, but she could not say where or when. It took a moment for her to gather her thoughts, and when she finally spoke it was as if she was inside a dream from long ago. "Okay, Grandma," she heard herself say, "Call me when you want me to come in."

Chapter 7

The presence of the long yellow Cadillac parked next to the trawler was not lost on Marilyn Dupré as she watched from her office window. She had seen the car drive up and watched as Jennifer and her grandmother went aboard Townsend's boat. No matter what she did, Marilyn could not put the pieces together in any logical fashion. Now Jennifer came alone, walking back toward the office, and Marilyn stepped outside to greet her.

"This place brings back memories," Jennifer said, looking around. "You know, I haven't been here in years."

"You mean you never come to visit?" Marilyn asked.

Once in a while Grandpa would bring me when I was a child, but I haven't been here at all since he died," she replied.

"So what's the occasion today?" Marilyn said.

Jennifer's expression grew more serious. "Marilyn, I wish I knew. Grandma wanted to come here, and she told me to drive directly to that boat over there."

"Jack Townsend's boat," Marilyn confirmed.

"That's right," Jennifer continued. "And when we got there, he acted almost like a part of the family." She paused for a moment, as if trying to remember something. "And I have the strangest feeling that I know him from somewhere, but I just don't know where."

"Mr. Townsend seems to have a strange effect on a lot people," Marilyn agreed.

"Yes, but, " Jennifer added, "he seems to know me . . . really know me, I mean. And honestly, I just can't place him."

"Jennifer," Marilyn said, "I'm going to ask you a question, but promise me you won't be angry with me after I do."

"I'm too confused to be angry right now, Marilyn"

"Promise?

"Okay, okay, I promise," the younger woman responded. "Cross my heart and hope to die. How's that?"

"Do you think," Marilyn began, groping for the words, "I mean, if Jack Townsend is . . . or was . . . a drug dealer . . . is it possible he and your grandfather ran a very quiet smuggling operation years ago?"

"Oh, that's . . ." Jennifer caught herself in mid-sentence, turned and looked at the yacht and yellow Cadillac for a long moment before beginning again. "I wish I knew, Marilyn, I wish I knew."

Marilyn put her arms around the younger woman as they stood together looking at the boat and the car and wondering what the widow of Captain Kelly Calkins could possibly have in common with Jack Townsend. Finally, Marilyn broke the silence.

"Come on, Jen," she said quietly as she escorted the younger woman inside. "Let me show you around my world."

"This was my grandfather's office," Jennifer said, overcome with nostalgia. "They certainly cleaned it up. What happened to his big roll-top desk?"

"Darned if I know," Marilyn replied. "This is the way I found the place when I arrived."

"Well, looks comfortable enough," Jennifer said, "But what do you do?"

"I'm afraid I don't know that, either," Marilyn sighed. "Of course, right now it looks like I'll be in charge for the next couple of weeks."

"In charge?" Jennifer asked before she quickly added, "Wait, don't tell me. It's the annual fishing trip, right? Isn't this a little early?

"How did you know about that?" Marilyn asked.

"They've been going fishing together since my father came back," Jennifer explained. "Usually later in the summer, though. This is only May. Anyway, Grandpa and I would come over to run the place while they were gone. Come to think of it, that's when he would bring me here. Gosh, I used to have a wonderful time, pretending I was Grandpa's secretary," Jennifer added with a sigh.

"Well, Jen, if you want to re-live your childhood, you're welcome to spend your time with me for the next two weeks."

"Do you really mean that?" Jennifer said excitedly. "I could come here when I'm not in class. It would be a lot of fun, wouldn't it? We might even solve . . ." she lowered her voice to sound like the coming attraction for a movie ". . . The Mystery of Jack Townsend."

"Seriously," Marilyn said when they both stopped laughing, "I'm going to find out about Mr. Townsend. I just need to figure out how to run into him."

"That shouldn't be hard, considering you've already done it," Jennifer observed.

"What do you mean?"

"At Grandma's house," Jennifer continued. "You said that you bumped into him outside the door. Why don't you just do it again?"

"That was an accident," Marilyn protested.

"So what?" Jennifer shrugged. "It seems to be just a matter of timing."

so ca

Back on the trawler, Jack listened to Mrs. Calkins' proposal. "It does raise some problems," he said, "particularly with me living here."

"Are they problems that can't be solved?" she asked.

"My dear lady," he replied, "anything can be solved given enough time."

"I'm afraid time might be a precious commodity, Jack," Mrs. Calkins said. "I should like to have this resolved by next week."

"That's a tall order, but thanks to a severe case of writer's block, I have very little to occupy my time right now," he replied, nodding toward the equipment on the table.

"I'd prefer not to come here, in case they've returned," Mrs. Calkins continued.

"I agree. I'll come to your place," Jack said. "How about next Wednesday?"

"No, I afraid I have another engagement that day," Mrs. Calkins replied as she got up to leave. "Better make it Thursday, a week from today."

"Thursday it is," he agreed. "I'll have an answer for you by then."

As they reached the door, Jack bent down to bestow the expected kiss on the old lady's cheek, but she suddenly wrapped her arms around him and whispered, "You've always been very special to me, Jack. I'll get you back on your path. You'll see."

Jack offered to drive her back to the office, but Mrs. Calkins wouldn't hear of it. "I'm fine," she protested. "And I'm a better driver than most. I'll pick up Jennifer on the way out." She executed a three-point turn on the narrow road next to the sea wall and bounced her way back to the office. Jack returned to the confines of the salon, and cleared away the remainder of his book material. She had made a most unusual request, and it would take some doing to accomplish it.

℘ ℭ

"Did you have a nice visit?" Jennifer asked her grandmother from the passenger seat of the Cadillac.

"Yes, Dear, it was very nice," Mrs. Calkins replied.

"I don't suppose you'd care to discuss it?" Jennifer asked.

"You know, Dear, something doesn't seem quite right about the brakes," Mrs. Calkins said. "Perhaps we should ask Mr. Leslie to check them."

ℴ ℭ

As Marilyn drove home that evening, she kept thinking about Jennifer's words, "It's just a matter of timing," Jennifer had said. "Just a matter of timing."

"Jack Townsend," Marilyn said quietly to the empty car, "whether you're ready for it or not, tomorrow morning you and I are going to have a meeting."

ℴ ℭ

Jack woke up the next morning with a lot on his mind. He knew what Margaret Calkins wanted to do, and yes, he believed she was right. All the same, it meant the end of a peaceful way of life. No doubt many people's lives would be changed by what she intended, his as much as anyone's. It was a distracted Jack Townsend who started out on his daily walk to the post office that morning. He wasn't thinking about Marilyn Dupré who was waiting in her office. He didn't see her watching him as he approached the building; didn't know she was counting the seconds as he rounded the corner. And he didn't see her open the door.

He walked right into her. The papers in Marilyn's hand went flying across the parking lot as she fell.

"I'm terribly sorry," Jack apologized as he knelt down to help her. "Are you all right?"

"Yes, yes, I'm fine," Marilyn answered, her dark eyes flashing at him as she brushed herself off on the ground.

"I guess I'm supposed to say, 'We have to stop meeting like this'," he joked.

"Maybe it would be better if we just set up a schedule," she shot back angrily.

"Here, let me help you up," he offered.

Marilyn took his hand and winced in pain when she got to her feet.

"What's wrong?" Jack asked with a look of concern on his face.

"My foot!" she cried. "I think it's broken!"

"It can't be broken . . ." he protested.

"Well why don't you try walking on it?" she cried. "No, don't bother. You already did that!"

"Let me get you inside," he said, genuinely concerned.

"Don't touch me! You've done enough damage!"

He suddenly picked her up, carried her into her office and set her in a chair.

"You . . . can't just pick up women and carry them around like . . . sacks of potatoes!" she sputtered.

"What did you want me to do?" he demanded, raising his voice in return. "Call an ambulance? Anyway, let me check your foot." With that he knelt down, took off her shoe and gently began to massage her foot.

"Ow!" she protested. "Should you be doing that? You're not a doctor, are you?"

"No, I'm not a doctor," he replied. "But I know enough about broken bones to know that if something was broken you wouldn't be letting me touch it like this. It's probably just a bruise."

"Ow! Be careful!" she said as he continued to rub her foot.

"Does that feel any better?" he asked.

"Yes," she admitted, moving her bare foot in his hand. "More on the side."

"You know, I've been meaning to stop in and introduce myself. My name is Jack Townsend," he said, extending his hand.

"Yes, I know," Marilyn said, not taking it. "Please don't stop what you're doing."

"Well, I'm going to have to stop sometime," he said, looking into her eyes.

"Really?" she smiled. "Why?"

He smiled back. "Why don't we discuss that over dinner tonight? There's a little place on the edge of town called the Beach House. It's very informal."

"You don't even know my name," she reminded him.

"It's Marilyn Dupré," he answered.

"How did you know that?"

"Let's just say I have my sources."

At that moment Jennifer walked in. Jack was kneeling on the floor with Marilyn's bare foot in his hands, and

Marilyn appeared to be enjoying every minute of it.

"Oh, excuse me," Jennifer blushed. "I didn't mean to interrupt."

Jack stood up, obviously flustered.

"Jennifer, this is Jack Townsend," Marilyn said from her chair. "Jack, this is Jennifer Calkins."

"Yes, I know," Jack muttered self-consciously. "Good morning, Jennifer."

"What time shall I expect you?" Marilyn continued, not missing a beat.

"Pardon?" he asked.

"You're taking me to dinner," she reminded him. "What time shall I expect you?"

"Oh, I don't have a car," he explained. "You'll have to drive. Why don't I just meet you here after work?"

"I'd like to go home and freshen up first," she said. There was an awkward pause. "Suppose I just meet you at your boat at six o'clock?" she finally suggested.

"Sounds fine to me," he replied as he headed for the door. "I'll see you then. Goodbye, Jennifer."

"What was that all about?" Jennifer asked as the door slammed shut.

"I guess I have a date tonight," Marilyn replied.

"Marilyn! Are you crazy?" Jennifer protested. "What if he really is a drug dealer?"

"So what? I'm not going to be buying drugs from him."

"But what if he tries to kill you or something?" Jennifer continued.

"Why would he want to do that?"

"He might, if he knows we're on to him."

"Jennifer, he's not going to kill me in a restaurant. And we're not 'on to' anything. I'm just going out to dinner with him," Marilyn said as she stood up, slipped her foot back into her shoe and walked to her desk.

"What's the matter with your foot?" Jennifer inquired.

"My foot?"

"Your foot. Mr. Townsend was rubbing it when I walked in," Jennifer reminded her.

"Oh, my foot," Marilyn smiled. "My foot never felt better in its life."

Chapter 8

The Beach House was not the kind of place where people took dinner guests to impress them. It occupied what had once been a single story frame cottage across from the beach on Bay Street. It was a neighborhood kind of place, where tiny Christmas lights that permanently twinkled in the windows provided "atmosphere." Three picnic tables stood in various positions on the front lawn and acted as an *al fresco* dining room for take-out orders or anyone foolish enough to sit out there and expect table service. Two frazzled waitresses who were hardly distinguishable from the patrons as they hurried around in tee shirts and shorts did their best to ignore those people.

Other than the Christmas lights, the décor consisted mostly of nets, driftwood, shells and assorted flotsam that had washed up the beach across the street at one time or another. Here and there, a model of a sailing ship perched on a small shelf, and the whole of the interior was set off by neon lights in each window that proclaimed the names of different brands of beer. Jack found a small table in the corner ell that probably had been a back bedroom in the building's past.

"Well," Marilyn said as they squirmed their way into the corner, "this is . . . quaint."

"No," he responded, "it's a dive. But the food is good. And besides, dives are great places to study humanity."

"What do you mean?" Marilyn asked.

"Look at those two," Jack said, indicating a very overweight couple across the room. "The guy's got a napkin tucked in his shirt so he doesn't drip barbeque sauce on his gut. And look at Ma attack that cole slaw. Places like this are better than television. I could make up a whole story about those two right now."

"Like what?" Marilyn laughed.

"Well, let's see," Jack began, adopting a thick Southern drawl, "They been out fashin' all day. Didn't cotch nuthin', so he says ta' her, he says, 'Tell ya' whot, let's get us some ribs down ta' th' Beach House.' 'Sounds good ta' me,' she says. 'War'n't in no mood f'r fish anaways.'"

"Jack, stop," Marilyn whispered, smiling. "They'll hear you."

"Wait 'till I get to the part about him dribblin' sauce on his plum-clean shirt."

"Behave yourself," Marilyn chided. "One of the waitresses is coming over."

"That's okay," he whispered in reply. "I've been thrown out of better places than this."

The girl explained that the kitchen was "pretty backed up," and warned that it might be a while before they got their dinners. "That's fine," Jack told her. "Bring us a carafe of your best wine. We need time to talk."

"I don't know if that was such a good idea," Marilyn said as the girl walked away.

"What was?"

"Telling her to take her time. I used to be a waitress. You might have put us in for a very long wait."

"I don't have anywhere to go," Jack said, looking intently into her eyes. "And I can't think of anyone I'd rather be with."

Marilyn looked away for a moment as she felt herself blushing. She was relieved when the waitress returned quickly with a wine carafe and two glasses. Jack filled them and offered a toast to a pleasant evening, touching her glass with his own. They sipped in silence for a minute. Finally, Jack put his glass down and said, "So, tell me about yourself, Miss Dupré."

"Well," Marilyn began, "I'm almost a lawyer. I have an undergraduate degree in accounting, and I've got an L.L.M. . . . that's a master's degree . . . in tax law. I'm registered to take the Florida bar examination in July, and then I guess I'll go out on my own. I think someday I'd like to have my own firm—not too big. I'm working at the marina right now taking care of the books and other things for Walker and Grant. I guess there's not much more to tell."

"Only that you're single," he offered. "Your career is the most important thing in your life. And you're the first one in your family to have gone to college."

"How did you know that?" she demanded.

"Let's see," he continued. "You're from Louisiana . . . New Orleans, probably. Your family isn't wealthy by any means, but they own their own business . . . or at least did at one time. You put yourself through college . . . Louisiana State University, perhaps? Oh . . . yes . . . and you graduated in the top half, but not the top ten percent, of your law school class." He paused and added, "At L.S.U."

Marilyn's dark eyes flashed angrily. "Have you been spying on me? Because if you have, I don't like it."

"Calm down," Jack said with a disarming smile. "It's just a couple of old lawyer's tricks."

"What do you mean?" she asked, still not sure if she should believe him.

"Whenever you're picking a jury," he explained, "you always start with an open-ended question. Something like, 'Tell me about yourself, Miss Dupré.' Usually the person will begin with the most important thing in his or her life—sort of the way they define themselves. In your case, you started out by telling me about your career. Therefore, it's a good bet that it's the most important thing in your life right now."

"How about the rest of it?" she asked, still unsure of him.

"Simple observation and inference," he replied. "You're not wearing a wedding ring, and you're out having dinner with me. Either you're not married or you have a very under-standing husband. You're much too attractive for any man to be that understanding, so the inference is that you're single."

"Thank you . . . I think," she said, calmer now. "But how about all that stuff about my family? You must have known something!"

"Only what you told me," he said.

"But I didn't tell you anything like that!" she protested.

"Sure you did. You just didn't know you did. It's called 'assuming facts not in evidence,'" he explained. "You pres-ent the witness with a conclusion and watch her reaction. She makes an admission because she thinks you have information you really don't have."

"But how . . . ?"

"I made certain assumptions based on what I knew . . . or inferred . . . and presented them to you as though they were established facts. The expression on your face told me I was right, so I made other assumptions and kept going until you stopped me."

"I don't know whether to believe you or not," she said.

"Look," he explained, you're extremely proud of your education, even to the point of mentioning your degrees. By the way, I know what an L.L.M. is . . . and it's quite an achievement. You have a right to be proud of it."

"Thank you again," she said quietly.

"Is it so hard to guess you're the first one in your family to have gone to college?" he continued. "Your name is French, and you ordered oysters and blackened redfish for dinner. Where else could you be from other than Louisiana? The 'New Orleans' was just a lucky guess, but since you didn't deny it, it's probably true. The rest of this gets to be a little bit more tricky."

Marilyn leaned back in her chair and relaxed. She sipped her wine and said, "Okay, let's have it."

"Well, you mentioned being a waitress. That had to mean you worked your way through school . . . at least partially. It's an honest job but, let's face it, it's not professional. That means, to me at least, that your family didn't have any connections that could help you back home. They're probably not professional people. You have an idea of working for yourself; your parents probably did the same thing."

"Okay, okay," she interrupted, "but how about L.S.U. and my class standing? You couldn't have guessed those!"

Jack was laughing now. He could hardly believe he had scored such a direct hit after being out of practice for so long. "No, honestly," he chuckled, raising his right hand. "I swear. The only law schools I could think of in New Orleans were Louisiana State University and Tulane. L.S.U. sounds like it would be cheaper, which would be a big consideration if you were paying your own way. As far as your grades, well, you're obviously a pretty sharp lady. It didn't take any lawyer's tricks to figure out that you graduated high in your class . . . but not high enough to be snapped up by a big firm back home.

"All right, all right, I believe you," she said. "Where did you learn to do that, anyway?"

"In the courtroom," Jack replied. "I was one of the best."

"Ho, ho, ho. No ego problems here," she scolded.

"It isn't an ego problem; it's true. I was very good at what I did."

"So you're a lawyer?"

"I used to be."

Marilyn looked at him intently. "So . . . if you were so good, why did you give it up and get involved in drugs?

"What do you mean?"

"That's what got you disbarred, isn't it?"

"Disbarred? What are you talking about?" he protested. "I've never been involved with drugs *or* disbarred."

"But Arlo said . . ."

"Whatever Arlo said, he's wrong," Jack said testily. "Be careful about assuming facts not in evidence, Miss Dupré. It doesn't always work."

"I'm sorry," she said, averting her eyes from his. "Now I'm embarrassed."

He reached across the table and took her hand. "Please don't be. Besides, it's kind of my fault. I made the mistake of telling Arlo some old war stories, and I guess he jumped to the wrong conclusion."

She looked at him again with eyes that captivated him. "So why did you give it up?" she asked gently.

"I got tired," he said. "Tired of being around people I didn't like . . . tired of listening to people I didn't believe . . . tired of laughing at jokes that weren't funny. Most of all, I got tired of compromising with myself: telling myself that

I was only doing my job, that I was upholding the integrity of the system. What I was really doing was selling my talent to a bunch of scumbags. It was prostitution, pure and simple, regardless of what anyone called it."

He stopped for a moment and looked at her intently. "Do you believe in Karma, Marilyn?"

"I . . . I'm afraid I don't understand," she said.

"Karma," he repeated. "It's an old Hindu belief."

"You mean like reincarnation? I'm Catholic; I'm afraid I can't accept that."

"Reincarnation might be part of it, but it doesn't have to be. The Law of Karma says that we pay a price for what we do. We all pay. I paid."

Jack downed the rest of his wine and fell silent. Whatever it was that troubled him, was too intense, too personal for him to say more. Jack Townsend was a very troubled man, but whether the trouble was real or imagined, whether it was deserved or not, Marilyn could not tell. The arrival of their dinners thankfully broke the silence.

Jack was right about another thing: whatever its shortcomings in formality, the Beach House provided excellent food. Her Oysters Rockefeller and blackened redfish were perfectly prepared, and Jack was a marvelous dinner companion. He kept up a running commentary about the patrons of the place, entertaining Marilyn with stories told in various accents, and once or twice she suspected he even slipped in a few "war stories" in the guise of fiction.

"You're really good at this stuff," she said, laughing at his latest character. "You should have been an actor."

"I wanted to be," he said, "but my family wouldn't hear of it. You see, I had a tradition to uphold. Anyway, Perry Mason was big on television when I was a kid, and court-room drama seemed to be the next best thing."

The mention of the program seemed to bring Jack down a little. "The only difference between Perry and real life," he added bitterly, "is that Perry always represented innocent people."

"Jack," Marilyn said, taking his had gently in hers, "ever since I was a little girl, I've had . . . I don't know . . . feelings . . . intuition, I guess. Whatever happened to you, whatever you did, it wasn't anything wrong. I know that. I can feel it."

He held her hand tightly, looked across the table and said softly,

"Sally Dupré, Sally Dupré,
With eyes that are neither black nor gray,
Why do you haunt me, night and day?"

The lines of the poem startled her for a moment. They recalled something out of her own past, something that not even Jack Townsend could have guessed—all the bit-tersweet memories of her teenage years at the convent school. They were memories she had buried deep and tried to forget. Now a few lines from a long-ago poem ripped open her heart and she remembered all too well the lone-liness of those days.

She tried to make a joke to deflect the pain. "Whah, Cap'n Townsen'," she said in her best movie-star Southern drawl, "Ah nevah thaought Ah'd meet a Yankee who could recaite po'try."

"It's from an American epic poem by Stephen Vincent Benét," he said, smiling at her, "and I'll bet fifty bucks no one in this place ever read it."

A thousand thoughts were still running through her head. "Hand over the money," she said at last. "When I was in high school I was sure that some of it had been written about me. Let's see . . . how did it go?" Marilyn looked off in the distance and recited the words she knew far too well:

"And she looked like her father, the dancing master.
The scapegrace, elegant, 'French' Dupré,
Come to the South on a luckless day,
With bright paste buckles sewn on his pumps,
A habit of holding the Ace of Trumps,
And a manner of kissing a lady's hand,
Which the county could not understand."

There was a long silence before she spoke again. "That was Papa, all right," she finally added. "Living on borrowed dreams and costume jewelry. He and Mama owned a small café in New Orleans . . . you were right about that, too. But Mama died when I was twelve, and Papa couldn't wait to ship me off to a convent school in Baton Rouge. Then he just fell apart. He stopped opening the café, and the bank foreclosed. He lost our house . . . everything. Whenever I went home for a visit, he had a different job . . . chef, maitre d', headwaiter . . . and a different 'housekeeper.' So I stayed

at Sainte Anne's and later worked my way through L.S.U."
She looked at him with a coy smile and added, "Which
is also in Baton Rouge, by the way, so you did not earn a
perfect score."

Jack smiled his acknowledgement but didn't speak,
unwilling to interrupt her story.

She sighed and continued, "After that I . . . just kept
waitressing for a while. And then one of the Sisters
arranged for me to get a scholarship to law school." She
sighed and added, "And after I graduated, I didn't have
anything better to do, so I stayed there for an extra year
and got an L.L.M."

"Your father must have loved you," Jack said quietly.
"Places like convent schools don't come cheaply."

"That was the problem, wasn't it?" she demanded, suddenly angered by the memory. "I didn't have to go there.
I could have stayed home where I belonged. Do you have
any idea what it's like to be the only one in the whole
school who can't afford to be where you are?"

"No, I'm sorry, I don't," Jack replied, suddenly painfully
aware of his own pampered upbringing.

"When everyone else was going skiing in Colorado,
I was answering the telephone in the school office," she
continued. "Do you have any idea of the things I missed,
always because we couldn't afford it?" She turned away
again, embarrassed by her outburst. "I just didn't belong
there," she added lamely.

"I'm sorry," Jack said gently.

She shook her head, it seemed more for her own benefit than his. "That's okay. It wasn't your fault," she reminded him.

"What happened to your father?" Jack asked quietly.

She looked at him again. The pain had not left her eyes and it affected Jack deeply to think of her like that. "Papa's still living in New Orleans; still living in the same dreary apartment, still behind on the rent. He never lacks for female companionship, but I don't think he ever really loved another woman after Mama died."

Her words hit him like a punch in the gut and brought him back to reality. He took a deep breath and stood up. "I have to leave," he said quietly.

"What do you mean? What happened?" Marilyn asked. "Did I say something wrong?"

"Not at all," Jack replied. "You just reminded me of something." He took her hand for a moment as if he wanted to say something, but then he appeared to think better of it. He shook his head and walked away. Marilyn caught up with him as he was thrusting money into the hand of a startled waitress.

"Jack, please. Wait. I have to drive you home.

"It's not far," he said. "I'll walk. I need to walk right now."

She followed him out the door and onto the porch steps where she grabbed him. "Please tell me! Is it something I said? What did I do?

He shook his head again, this time with a look of unbearable regret. "You didn't do anything except be young and beautiful and remind me that I'm old enough to be your father," he replied.

"You are not!"

"I'm not?" he said. "How old are you, anyway?"

"What difference does it make?" she demanded. "Who cares?"

"I care."

"All right," she said, "I'm . . . almost twenty-nine."

"Well, I'm *almost* forty-one," he said, mimicking her attempt to sound a year older.

"Come on," she said, "that doesn't mean anything."

Jack raised her hand to his lips. "I'll see you around the marina," he said. Then he kissed her hand and walked off into the night.

Chapter 9

The telephone rang early the next morning at the Calkins home. Jennifer, barely awake, picked up the extension in her bedroom.

"Hello?" she asked groggily.

"Jennifer?" It was Marilyn's voice and she sounded troubled. "I know it's early," she said, "but may I come over? I really need to talk to someone."

"Marilyn? What happened? What did you find out?"

The previous day's game suddenly seemed very childish and Marilyn was embarrassed by her role in it. "It's not what we thought," she began. "It's . . . it's much too complicated to discuss over the phone. May I come over?"

"Yes, yes, of course," Jennifer said. "I'll be waiting for you!"

Jennifer was wide-awake and out of bed in an instant. 'Complicated'? What did Marilyn mean by 'complicated'? Was Townsend somehow linked to a larger drug cartel? Was this a matter for the F.B.I.? Or Interpol? How did one go about calling Interpol? Did it even exist, or was that just in the movies? She banged around the kitchen paying little attention to what she was doing, with a head full of questions and no answers.

The noise brought Mrs. Calkins down from the second-floor master bedroom. She was dressed in a morning "house-coat" not expecting to receive company.

"Jennifer, what's the matter?" she asked. "What's going on?"

"Grandma," Jennifer replied, unsuccessfully trying to steady her voice, "Something happened to Marilyn last night."

"Oh, Lord, no! What happened?"

"I don't know yet. She's on her way over here to tell me."

"She's all right then?" Mrs. Calkins said with a small measure of relief. "She's not injured or anything, is she?"

"No, but she had a date with Jack Townsend last night, and she needs to talk to me right away. Something terrible must have happened. He's probably a major drug dealer."

Mrs. Calkins collapsed into a chair with a sigh of relief. "Jennifer Scott Calkins!" she chided, "You mean to tell me you scared the daylights out of me because Marilyn Dupré had a date with Jack Townsend last night and needs to talk 'girl talk'?"

"Marilyn is my friend, Grandma," Jennifer retorted. "We've become really close . . . almost like sisters. And something important must have happened or she wouldn't have called me this early." As she spoke, Jennifer scurried around the kitchen, putting out cups, saucers, plates and silverware in a distracted effort to keep busy.

"Jennifer, sit down," her grandmother said firmly. "I care for Marilyn, too. But I know a good deal more about Jack Townsend than either of you. Whatever happened, I'm sure it's not what you think. Now, I'm going to start a pot of tea. When you're settled down, you can put scones in the oven, and take the egg poacher out of the cabinet. We'll have a proper breakfast when she arrives."

The minutes ticked past as the two women busied themselves in the kitchen. At long last the doorbell rang.

"Goodness, I must look a fright," Mrs. Calkins said. "And the kitchen is no place to receive guests. Well, what must be will be."

"Marilyn isn't a guest, Grandma," Jennifer said as she hurried to the front door.

Marilyn appeared to be healthy enough when Jennifer saw her. Still, the young blonde could not help throwing her arms around her and asking if she was all right. Marilyn was as shocked by the greeting as she was by Jack's abrupt departure the previous evening.

"I'm all right, Jennifer," she said testily. "I'm fine."

"He didn't attack you?"

"No."

"He didn't threaten your life?"

"No, he was a perfect gentleman."

"Then why are you here?" Jennifer asked, mildly disappointed.

"I'm here because . . . may I come inside?" Marilyn asked.

"Of course, I'm sorry," Jennifer replied. "Grandma is waiting in the kitchen with breakfast for us."

Marilyn followed her young friend into the recesses of the house. She sensed that entry into the kitchen was a rite of passage of sorts. Mrs. Calkins was not the kind of woman who allowed strangers into her inner sanctum. The kitchen was the "family room" in the truest sense of the phrase. Only family entered the Calkins kitchen, and only Grandma Calkins decided who would be accorded the privilege of being a member of the Calkins family.

The room they entered seemed somewhat gray although, on closer inspection the walls appeared to be painted a pale blue. The linoleum floor was gray, as were the matching countertops. To the right, a built-in china closet was centered between two windows that looked out to the side yard. The same linoleum-topped counter divided the piece halfway up, and above that, glass-fronted cabinets extended to the high ceiling. Against the back wall, an old-fashioned commercial refrigerator with thick wooded doors and glass windows dominated the far right corner of the room. To its left, a porcelain sink held station beneath a window that provided a view of the back yard. Closer to them, a new electric range stood along the left-hand wall. It was the newest appliance in the room. Obviously, no expense had been spared when it was purchased. The motto of the Calkins family seemed to be, 'Buy the best, and don't get rid of it until it's worn out.' Mrs. Calkins was sitting in one of the four chairs surrounding solid carved oak table in the center of the room. Two matching chairs, one under each of the windows on either side of the china closet, completed the set.

"Come in, come in, my Dear," Mrs. Calkins said. "Now you sit right down here at the table and tell us all about it."

Mrs. Calkins poured the tea while Jennifer buttered the scones from the oven, brought eggs from the poacher and sliced the remains of a pecan pie she found in the refrigerator. Marilyn related every detail of the previous evening, beginning with the peculiar little restaurant and ending with the moment Jack left her on the front steps. When she finished, Mrs. Calkins shook her head slowly and sighed, "Poetry! Oh, my! I declare. If only I were thirty years younger. You hooked him good, Marilyn. Now you'll just have to be patient and wait 'till the fight goes out of him so you can reel him in."

"Grandma!" Jennifer exclaimed. "Marilyn doesn't want to 'reel in' any old, broken-down, has-been lawyer. Do you Marilyn?"

"Well, I . . ." Marilyn began before she was interrupted by Mrs. Calkins.

"Jack Townsend isn't old or broken down, Dear. And as for his being a has-been, well, he's just gotten off his path, that's all. He only needs someone to help him find his way back."

"Well, he's still 'way too old for Marilyn," Jennifer protested. "Isn't he, Marilyn?"

"Well, I don't . . ." Marilyn began again.

"Too old?" Mrs. Calkins shot back. "What's too old? Your grandfather and I had more than a decade between us. That didn't matter because we loved each other." Then, turning to Marilyn she asked, "Do you love him, Marilyn?"

"I just don't . . ."

"Grandma, how could she possibly love him? She hardly knows him. They've only been out to dinner once . . ."

"She knows," Mrs. Calkins insisted. "She knows right now, if you'll just be quiet for a moment and let her listen to her heart."

"Is that what you want, Marilyn?" Jennifer asked.

"I don't know," Marilyn sighed. "I'm really confused. And anyway, what would it matter? Even if I did, he doesn't love me. I just wish I had never met him."

"There, there, Dear. Have some more tea," Mrs. Calkins said, refilling Marilyn's cup and smiling softly. "Everything happens for the best."

♠ ♣

On the white trawler, Jack was no less confused but more alone with his thoughts. He knew he had botched things the previous evening, but he had not been able to control himself. Marilyn's mention of her unhappy child-hood and the untimely death of her mother touched him in a way he could not explain. He wanted so badly to pro-tect her from the hurt she felt in those years. Then, when she said her father never really loved another woman after her mother died, John DeWitt Townsend, the cold, calcu-lating trial lawyer, the man who could not be rattled in a courtroom, felt a desperate need to head for the door. And Marilyn Dupré, the woman who at first probably thought he was merely a clumsy oaf, now undoubtedly though he was a lunatic as well.

Jack couldn't get her out of his mind, and at the same time he couldn't stop feeling guilty about that. Surely enough time had passed, he thought. He couldn't live like this forever. No one would expect that of him. It would be inhuman. But she was only twenty-nine . . . twenty-eight, rather. Alex would have been nearly twenty if Jack and Linda hadn't waited.

He went out on deck and surveyed the marina in the early morning quiet. The sun was still low in the sky and the place was dead calm in the gray morning air. Across the cove, the boats cast their reflections on the flat water while an egret paced the shore searching for breakfast. At the gas dock a pelican stirred, stretching its wings from its perch atop one of the pilings.

"I could live here forever," Jack whispered, knowing as he spoke that such a thing was impossible. Cap'n Kelly's was only a harbor of refuge. Someday he would have to pick up the pieces of his shattered life, leave this splendid isolation and continue the voyage that was meant for him. "I'll just stay away from her," he muttered. Hell, she was only there temporarily taking care of something for Walker and Grant. How much longer could it take? A week? Maybe two? He would just avoid that end of the marina for a couple of weeks and forget the whole thing happened.

※ ⚬⃝

Jack need not have worried. Jennifer decided that Marilyn needed some time off, and declared they would spend Saturday engaged in recreational shopping. The next day, Marilyn would join her and Grandma at the Magnolia Avenue house for Sunday afternoon dinner, and Monday, with no exams scheduled at Bonita College, Jennifer would open the office with her.

"I couldn't ask you to do that," Marilyn protested. "You have a life of your own."

"Oh, Silly, it'll be fun." Jennifer replied. "I'll be your secretary just like I used to be for Grandpa. Besides, I can study there as well as I can here. We'll have a great time."

They spent the weekend shopping on the mainland, and, as Jennifer predicted, they had a wonderful time. Marilyn, the petite, buxom brunette, and Jennifer, the tall, willowy blonde, followed each other in and out of various dressing rooms, trying on clothes and expressing opinions about their outfits. "I have an idea," Jennifer said as they piled into Marilyn's small hatchback with their packages. "Let's go to a movie tonight. Some new people in Calkins Harbor are trying to get the Rivoli started up again by showing old films. Tonight they're showing Bogart in 'Casablanca'."

"You know, I've never seen it," Marilyn replied.

"Never seen 'Casablanca'? Neither have I, but I've certainly heard a lot about it," Jennifer said. "That settles it. Tonight we're going to the movies."

"I don't know, Jen," Marilyn protested. "I'd hate to drive all the way back home that late."

"That's even better!" Jennifer clapped. "We'll stop by your place now, pick up a few of your things and have a pajama party after the movie!"

"I don't want to put your grandmother to any trouble," Marilyn said.

"My grandmother? In case you've forgotten, this morning she practically made you a member of the family. I'll probably be the one who gets in trouble if I let you drive back here alone. Come on, what do you say?"

"I say it sounds like a great idea," Marilyn grinned.

They arrived back home in time to set the table for dinner. Mrs. Calkins was overjoyed at the idea of Marilyn spending the weekend with them but declined their invitation to accompany them to Oldies Night at the Rivoli.

"I'm happy to hear that someone has sense enough to show a good picture there, but I think I'll stay home. You girls enjoy yourselves," she said.

"But you like Humphrey Bogart, Grandma," Jennifer reminded her.

"Yes, Dear, I do," Mrs. Calkins replied. "But I've been tired of late and I need my beauty rest. You two run along and have a good time."

They did have a good time. In fact, they had a great time. The next morning found them in the kitchen making breakfast and humming "As Time Goes By" when Mrs. Calkins came down.

"What have we here?" she asked rhetorically. "It seems Mr. Bogart has some new fans."

"Grandma," Jennifer gushed, "that was a terrific picture. Bogart was wonderful . . . 'Here's looking at you kid,'" she said, imitating the actor with a glass of orange juice in her hand.

"Louie," Mrs. Calkins responded with her best Bogart imitation, "this could be the start of a beautiful friendship."

"Grandma," Jennifer said with surprise, "when did you see that movie?"

"When both it and the Rivoli were much younger," Mrs. Calkins said. "But then, I was much younger too. Lord, your grandfather and I loved that picture."

She turned her attention to Marilyn who was busy stirring a batter of some kind. "And what is my newest granddaughter doing?" she asked.

"This is my father's recipe for crepes. I thought I would fill them with the applesauce I found in the refrigerator and top them with whipped cream," Marilyn replied.

"My, my," Mrs. Calkins said as she inspected her handiwork. "You must spend more nights here. Jennifer will have to learn some of your secrets before some lucky fellow spirits you away."

"Don't worry about me, Grandma," Jennifer said as she set out the china. "I won't be ready for cooking lessons for a long time yet."

"It's best to be prepared, Dear," Mrs. Calkins replied as she took her place at the table. "Well, it seems that I shall be a lady of leisure this morning, and you two shall do all the work."

"And we shall be delighted to do it," Marilyn added.

The three ladies enjoyed a long, leisurely breakfast. Mrs. Calkins was especially delighted with Marilyn's culinary skill and couldn't help remarking about it.

"You mean your father taught you how to cook?" she repeated as they finished.

"That's right," Marilyn confirmed. "Papa was a master in the kitchen. Mama and I were his favorite audience until she died." Marilyn paused for a moment, and then added, "Poor Mama. All she ever wanted was to move across the river to Algiers Point where she could live in a little shotgun house and plant her flowers in a real garden. She wanted so little, and she never even got that."

"In this life we get what we need, Dear. Not what we want—what we need," Mrs. Calkins said.

"Need for what?" Marilyn asked.

"Why, to grow, of course," came the reply. "To learn and to grow."

"Then why did she die so young? It seems so unfair."

"Everything happens for the best, Dear," Mrs. Calkins replied. "Whether we know it or not, there is a plan of each of us. And even though we might not like it or agree with it, everything does happen for the best."

"But why . . .?"

"Mrs. Calkins took her hand, looked directly into her eyes and said gently, "Marilyn, each of us is put on this earth for a purpose. We're here to learn a lesson."

"'Learn a lesson by performing a task.' That's what Sister Jean-Marie used to say," Marilyn offered.

"That's right, Dear. That's a lovely way of putting it." Mrs. Calkins continued. "Perhaps your lesson was to learn how to be self-reliant, how to trust yourself. Or perhaps it was to learn the importance of love. You learned those things after your mother died, didn't you?"

"So God took away my mother when I was twelve years old to . . . to teach me to be self-reliant? I'm sorry," Marilyn said, "that's pretty harsh. I can't accept that."

"But you did become an independent woman," Mrs. Calkins reminded her, "and you learned that people cannot live without love. Now what do a few years matter compared with important lessons like that? If we are truly eternal beings . . . and there's no doubt that we are . . . we shall someday stand apart and watch this old earth as it enters a new Ice Age. We'll see glaciers form and move down over what was once North America. We'll watch as the seas recede and leave dry land between our little island and the mainland. You'll have plenty of time to be with your mother then. What are a few years compared to all of eternity?"

"But what lesson did my mother have to learn?" Marilyn demanded. "She was so young."

"I don't know, Dear," Mrs. Calkins replied, "but she sounds like a good person. I'm certain she learned whatever it was she had to learn before she moved on."

"You make it sound so normal, so natural," Marilyn protested.

"It is natural, Love." Mrs. Calkins insisted. "We all move on, sooner or later. That's not important. What's important is what we do with our time while we're here. You have Jennifer and me now, but one day I'll move on, and then you and Jennifer will have each other and your own families. Then someday, far in the future, your turns will come, and those who are here then will have each other and the lessons you leave them. It's life, Dear. It's what living is all about."

Chapter 10

Marilyn and Jennifer drove to the marina together and opened the office early Monday morning. The first item of business was to summon Arlo Woodbrace to the office and put a certain rumor to rest.

"Did ya' want ta' see me, Miss Dupré?" he said, poking his head into the room and leaving a greasy handprint on the door.

"Mr. Woodbrace," Marilyn said, attempting to keep her French Creole temper in check, "kindly come in and close the door behind you."

"Is anythin' wrong, Miss?" Arlo asked, putting on his best innocent expression.

"Did you or did you not tell me that Jack Townsend is a big drug dealer?" Marilyn demanded.

"Yeah, well, no, I mean . . . I guess I did, yeah," Arlo answered as a knot began to form in his stomach.

"And did you or did you not say that he had told you so himself" she continued, her dark eyes flashing.

The knot in Arlo's stomach grew larger. "Well, he didn't exactly tell me," Arlo replied, looking for a crack in the floor big enough to crawl into. "He sort a' told me."

"And would you mind telling Miss Calkins and myself how he 'sort of' told you?"

"Well," Arlo began, shoving his hands far down into the depths of his pockets, "he told me a story . . . about these guys he said he knew who were dealing drugs and murdered these other guys over a deal that went bad."

"Mr. Woodbrace," Marilyn interrupted him, her voice escalating now, "did it ever occur to you that a lot of perfectly normal people might know drug dealers and murderers? People like lawyers, for example?!"

Arlo looked up and his eyes widened. "Ya' mean Mister . . . Jack is a lawyer?"

"That is exactly what I mean!" Marilyn shouted with her hands on her hips. She pointed to the door and added, "Now you can just go out there and tell the truth to everybody you told that foolish story to!"

"Sure, sure, I'll . . . I'll do that right away," Arlo fumbled. "I guess I better get started, huh?" he added, looking for an excuse to scram out of the office.

"I guess you had better!" Marilyn shouted, her eyes still blazing.

Arlo left as quickly as he could, slamming the door behind him. Jennifer got some paper towels out of the desk drawer and began wiping his handprints off the door. "You really care for him, don't you?" she asked.

"Who?" Marilyn replied.

"You know who," Jennifer said.

"I just want to set the record straight, that's all," Marilyn insisted.

"Sure," Jennifer agreed. "The same as you'd do for any perfect stranger who meant absolutely nothing to you."

⚮

"So now he's a lawyer," Les said. "That's a pretty big leap, ain't it? From a drug dealer ta' a lawyer in what, a coupl'a weeks?"

"This time I know I'm right, Les," Arlo insisted. "I got this straight from Miss Dupré."

"Miss Dupré?" Les said. "Don't tell me ya' got her playin' y'r guessin' game. Why don't you folks just mind y'r own business like he minds his? If he wants ta' tell ya' who he is and what he does, he'll tell ya'."

"Well, I'm goin' over and talk ta' him," Arlo said. "At least I don't have to worry about gettin' my head blowed off anymore."

"Wouldn't be too sure 'a that," Les called out after him as Arlo walked away. "Wouldn't blame him if he did!"

⚮

This time it was Jennifer's turn to watch from the office window.

"Isn't that Mr. Leslie?" she asked Marilyn.

"Yes, do you know him?" Marilyn responded.

"He's our caretaker. What's he doing here?"

"Your caretaker?" Marilyn said. "Honestly, Jennifer, sometimes I think this whole place is nothing more than an extension of your family."

"Yes, but what's he doing here?" Jennifer repeated.

"I'm not sure," Marilyn answered, "but I think he lives here."

"Where?"

"On the boat he's working on."

"But the boat isn't in the water," Jennifer protested.

"Yes, I know," Marilyn said with just a hint of sarcasm.

"You mean Mr. Leslie lives on a dry-docked boat?" Jennifer asked again as though she could not believe what she heard.

"Well, I've never seen him get here, and I've never seen him leave," Marilyn explained. "And he told me he 'stays aboard' when he works late. I think he works late pretty often . . . like every night."

"Mr. Leslie lives on a dry-docked boat," Jennifer said, almost to herself, still looking out the window.

"Why not, Jennifer?" Marilyn asked. "The idea fits this crazy place, doesn't it?"

℘ ☙

Jack Townsend stood on the deck of his trawler and watched Arlo approach on the dusty shell-rock road.

"'Morin' Mister Jack," Arlo said, compromising between the 'Mr. Townsend' he felt a lawyer deserved and the more informal 'Jack' by which Jack had introduced himself the last time around.

"Good morning, Arlo," Jack responded.

"Nice day."

"Yes, it sure is," Jack agreed.

"It's a little hot, though," Arlo offered.

"Yes, it is hot."

"Might rain later," Arlo observed.

"Yes, it might."

It was apparent that something was on Arlo's mind, but it looked like he had exhausted his entire stock of polite conversation. Jack stood in silence and watched him bake in the sun and shuffle his feet in the shell-rock. After what seemed to be an unbearably long time, Jack asked, "Would you like a Pepsi, Arlo?"

"A Pepsi?" Arlo looked up and his eyes brightened. Jack had forgiven him. "Yeah, sure. I mean, if it ain't too much trouble 'r nothin'."

"It's no trouble," Jack replied. "Why don't you come aboard?"

"Come aboard? Yeah. Wow. That'd be great," Arlo said as he followed Jack into the salon.

"Pull up a chair, Arlo," Jack said. "I'll get us a couple of Pepsi's."

"Wow, thanks," Arlo replied. "So, I guess y're a lawyer, huh?"

"Word gets around quickly," Jack said from the galley. "Did Miss Dupré tell you?"

"Yeah, she told me," Arlo confirmed. "But I knew before. I kind a' figured it out f'r myself."

"Oh?" Jack said, handing him his drink.

"Sure," Arlo said as he opened the bottle. "When ya' told me all that stuff about knowin' drug dealers an' murderers an' stuff. What else could ya' be?"

"You might have concluded that I was a drug dealer . . . or even a murderer," Jack teased.

"Yeah, well, no," Arlo replied. "Ah mean, I guess I could 'a thought that, but, see, that wouldn't be very smart. I mean, you don't look like a drug dealer 'r nothin'."

"In twelve years of private practice, I found that it's best not to judge people by appearances. Big Jim Janik was one of the biggest crooks I ever met, and he always wore a three-piece suit."

"Is that how long ya' did it, fifteen years?" Arlo asked.

"Yes, about that."

"So why did ya' give it up?" he inquired.

"Because I got tired of meeting crooks," Jack said quickly.

"Did you know a lot of 'em?"

"Arlo," Jack said with a trace of weariness in his voice, "I knew all kinds. I knew guys who stole with guns and guys who stole with pens. Believe me, the guys who steal with guns are more honest. At least they don't pretend to be upstanding members of society."

Arlo was craning his neck, looking out the window behind Jack as he spoke. Jack turned around to see Erlene across the cove, bending over to fill the tank in a small runabout.

"Have you ever told Erlene you're interested in her?" Jack asked suddenly.

"How did . . . I mean, what makes ya' think I'm interested in her?" Arlo asked in reply.

"She's a good looking woman . . ." Jack began.

"Yeah, she sure is," Arlo agreed, craning his neck even farther.

"And you're a . . . personable kind of guy," Jack continued. "Why don't you ask her out?"

"Me?" Arlo exclaimed.

"Yes, you," Jack said. "All she can do is say 'No.'"

"Yeah, an' she prob'ly will," Arlo said glumly.

"But she might say 'Yes'," Jack added.

"An' then what would I do?"

"I don't know; take her to the Beach House or something," Jack suggested. "Whatever you do, it's better than looking at her across the cove. You know, Arlo, sooner or later somebody else will ask her, and you'll lose your chance."

"What kind a' chancet would a guy like me have, anyway?" Arlo asked as he got up and moved to the helm station for a better view.

"I know what kind of chance you have if you don't ask her: none," Jack told him.

"I guess y're right," Arlo observed.

"Of course I'm right, Jack replied. "Besides, she's probably just waiting for you to ask her."

"Ya' think so?"

"I'm sure of it," Jack said. "Hell, I've seen the way she looks at you."

"At me?" Arlo said in astonishment.

"She's always watching you whenever you're not looking," Jack fibbed. Actually, he had noticed Erlene looking in Arlo's direction once or twice, but he had no idea if that meant she ever gave him a second thought.

"Ya' mean she looks at me?" Arlo began breathing so hard it seemed he was about to have an asthma attack.

"All the time," Jack exaggerated.

"Maybe she's waitin' for me to ast her out or somethin'," Arlo suggested, panting hard.

"No doubt about it."

"Maybe I should go over an' talk ta' her. Just ta' be neighborly," Arlo said as he headed for the door.

"Sounds like a great idea," Jack agreed.

"Hey, thanks for the advice, Mr. Jack," Arlo called from the shore.

"Anytime, Arlo. That's my job," Jack responded from the deck. He turned back to the salon and muttered, "I wish everything else were that easy."

୧୦ ଓଃ

By early afternoon Jennifer was bored with studying, and Marilyn was no fun, sitting at her desk, copying numbers into a ledger and waiting for the telephone to ring.

"I wonder what's upstairs?" Jennifer asked idly.

"You mean you don't know?" Marilyn replied.

"Not really," she said.

"You mean in all the time you spent here with your grandfather, you never went up to the second floor?"

"Grandpa took me up there once or twice," Jennifer said. "But all I remember is that there was a bunch of junk up there."

"Then you *do* know," Marilyn said.

"No, not really," Jennifer protested. "I was a lot younger. All this stuff looked like junk to me back then."

"I've got news for you, Jen," Marilyn said dryly. "It is junk."

"Don't you think we should at least look?" Jennifer insisted.

"Well," Marilyn said, pushing herself away from the desk, "we're probably going to find more junk. But what do we have to lose?"

They went out the door that led to the main floor of the building and picked their way through the assorted small boats and equipment. "What was this area for, anyway?" Marilyn asked as they headed for the stairs along the far wall.

"I guess the idea was for this to be a sales area, you know, like a showroom or something," Jennifer said. "If my father and uncle had any ambition, this whole place would be full of runabouts, sailboards and jet skis."

"Why isn't it?" Marilyn asked.

"They don't want a marina," Jennifer replied. "They just want to hold on to this place until Grandma dies so they can sell the land to a condo developer."

"Is anybody interested?"

"Are you kidding?" Jennifer said. "There isn't a week goes by that Grandma doesn't get a letter or brochure from some real estate agent wanting to 'help her' sell her property . . . either this place or the house or both."

"What does she do?"

"Throws them away. One of the men came to the house once. She told him if he didn't get off her porch, she'd take a broom to him," Jennifer reported with a laugh.

"Well, here we are," Marilyn said as they got to the bottom of the dusty stairs along the far wall of the building.

"You go first," Jennifer said, pushing her forward.

"Me?" Marilyn protested. "This is your idea. Besides, you've been up there before."

"You're the 'big sister'," Jennifer said. "You go."

"Oh, all right," Marilyn replied. "I'm sure there aren't any haunts up there or we would have heard them by now."

The stairway was open at the top, but the only illumination up there was whatever daylight managed to fight its way through the filthy windows facing the cove. Marilyn wasn't afraid of ghosts or goblins, but she didn't care for spiders, and the webs got thicker as she moved up the grimy, open stairs with Jennifer at her heels.

"Jen, I swear to God, if I get a spider in my hair . . ." she warned.

"Keep going. Don't be such a baby," Jennifer replied.

At the top of the stairs they entered a world of dust

and decay. At first, Marilyn thought the large factory windows had been painted over from the outside, but on closer inspection they appeared to be encrusted with years of salt and dirt. Behind them, back toward the side of the building that faced the parking lot, a portion of the collapsed ceiling hung in mid-air, the result of a long ago repaired roof leak. In a far corner, an elevator shaft with its freight elevator long since removed, provided easy, direct, and permanent access to somewhere down below. Wherever it ended, the opening had been walled off, and the shaft was swallowed in darkness. The room itself was as large as the entire building, and it was cluttered with the debris of fifty or more years. Boxes were piled everywhere. Ropes, old tires and nets littered the floor. The heat, even in mid-May, was overpowering.

"Look! It's my grandfather's old roll-top desk. How did it get up here?"

"Like everything else got up here I guess," Marilyn responded. "Somebody didn't want it, but they weren't about to throw it away."

"Look at this place," Jennifer said in amazement. "Can you imagine what we could do with it?"

"What do you mean, 'What we could do with it'?" Marilyn said. "Who are 'we' and what could we 'do'?"

"Look at the view," Jennifer said, peering through a spot in one of the cleaner windows. "This is as good as the Yacht Club. Maybe better."

"Jennifer, what are you talking about?" Marilyn asked.

"About this room," she replied. "Can you imagine what it would be like if we had a restaurant up here?"

"A restaurant?" Marilyn demanded. "Jennifer, do you have any idea how much things like that cost?"

"Can't you imagine it though, Marilyn?" she went on. "A real family place with a view of the cove and the harbor beyond. It would be beautiful, wouldn't it? Tourists would go crazy for something like this."

"Come on, Jennifer," Marilyn said. "Let's go downstairs. I think the heat is getting to you."

Chapter 11

By the time Arlo worked his way back around the marina to the other side of the cove entrance, the runabout was gone and Erlene was back under her beach umbrella.

"'Mornin', Erlene," he said for lack of a better opening.

"'Mornin' Arlo," she replied.

"Nice day," he said.

"If ya' like it hot," she answered. "An' I hear it might rain later."

Arlo was dumbfounded. In one fell swoop, Erlene had wiped out his entire opening conversation. For the life of him he couldn't think of anything else to say.

"It's still a nice day," was the best he could do.

Erlene began to spread sun block over her body. The fabric of her bikini top barely covered the roundness of her breasts that peeked out invitingly at the sides. She poured a dollop of oil into her hand and began to spread it on the insides of her thighs.

"Somethin' botherin' ya', Arlo?" she asked.

"Botherin' me? Yeah, well, I mean, no. Why should anythin' be botherin' me? I mean, it's just a nice day, an' all. That's all."

"Yeah, Arlo," Erlene agreed with a sigh. "It is a nice day."

"Yeah, well, I got ta' go," Arlo said quickly. "You know, important stuff ta' do and everythin'. See ya', Erlene."

"See ya', Arlo."

ഇ ര

Wednesday found Marilyn and Jennifer leaving the office early for their afternoon tea with Grandma Calkins. As she drove the now-familiar route to the Magnolia Avenue house, Marilyn had to remind herself that her first visit had only been a week ago. So much had happened in her life since then that it seemed like a lifetime. She could not explain why she felt so at home here. She had begun to feel that she could sit back and accept things as they came to her instead of forcing events into what she thought should be the plan of her life.

Mrs. Calkins was at the front door. "And how are my girls today?" she inquired as they walked up the brick path.

"We're fine, Grandma," Jennifer said. "And guess what? I have the most wonderful idea."

Mrs. Calkins accepted their kisses at the door and ushered them into the living room. "Now, then," she said to Jennifer, reveling in her granddaughter's excitement, "tell me about your wonderful idea."

"Marilyn doesn't know I've been working on this," Jennifer said and Marilyn cringed inwardly. "I've kept it a secret. But I have this wonderful idea for a restaurant at the boatyard."

"A restaurant?" Mrs. Calkins enthused, egging Jennifer on. "My, that is an interesting idea."

"The whole second floor of the building is vacant. Well, it's filled with trash, really," Jennifer continued, responding to her grandmother's approval. "And it has a terrific view, as good as the Yacht Club. We could remodel the building so that people could get up there from the outside. See . . . I made a few preliminary sketches," she enthused, opening a large tablet she had been carrying.

"These are wonderful, Jennifer," her grandmother agreed. "They're very artistic."

"There's even a place for an elevator," Jennifer continued, getting more excited. "And I even have a name for the place . . . 'Sisters' . . . 'Sisters at Cap'n Kelly's'. Don't you just love it? Of course, we'd have to work out the details . . ." her voice trailed off.

"What do you have to say about this, Marilyn?" Mrs. Calkins asked.

The whole thing was preposterous, of course. It was completely impractical. Jennifer hadn't even thought about construction costs and licensing requirements. An entire commercial kitchen would have to be built. Then there was the cost of outfitting the place, and after that the problems that come with any business that has employees. There were withholding taxes, and worker's compensation, disability insurance . . .

"Marilyn?" Mrs. Calkins voice interrupted her thoughts.

"Oh, excuse me," she said. "I was just thinking."

"What do you think of Jennifer's idea, Dear?"

"Well," Marilyn began, trying to deflate the younger woman's balloon as gently as she could, "it has a lot of imagination. Of course, there are certain . . . costs that would have to be considered. And we would have to have a solid management plan before we started." Marilyn stopped, frozen by her own words. She couldn't believe that she just heard herself say "we." Jennifer's enthusiasm was infectious.

"That's what I like to hear!" Mrs. Calkins exclaimed happily. "My two girls, one the dreamer and the other the realist. You two will make a fine team. This calls for tea!"

As Mrs. Calkins left for the dining room, Jennifer reached across, squeezed Marilyn's hand and whispered, "I'm so glad you agree with me."

"I *don't* agree with you," Marilyn hissed. "There are a lot of things about running a business that you don't know and . . . you . . . you can't even imagine."

Jennifer squeezed her hand harder. "That's okay. We'll work them out together . . . Sis."

೫ ೧೫

"The woman wants me, Les," Arlo said as he helped him lift milled teak boards to *Elena's* deck.

"You sure she's ain't a drug dealer?" Les teased.

"C'mon, I'm serious," Arlo said. "She was rubbin' that oil all over her . . . herself and astin' me if anything was botherin' me."

"Well, was it?" Les asked. "C'mon, hand be another board."

"Was what?"

"Was anythin' botherin' ya'?"

"Well, ya' know, I mean, she was rubbin' that stuff all over herself, an' I . . . yeah, it was botherin' me, I guess."

"Well why didn't ya' do somethin' about it?" Les asked. "Hand me another board, will ya'?"

"What was I supposed ta' do? I mean, well, I couldn't even think of anythin' to say," Arlo pleaded desperately.

Les climbed down from *Elena's* deck. "Arlo, when *you* can't think of anythin' ta' say, ya' got it bad. Now I don't know if the lady wants ya' like ya' say, but I *do* know that you want her. Seems ta' me y'r just gonna have ta' tell 'er that."

"Tell her that!" Are you crazy?" Arlo protested. "I can't say a thing like that ta' Erlene."

"Ya' don't just go up an' tell 'er ya' want 'er. Ya' talk to 'er. Ya' invite 'er out for a sunset sail."

"An' how am I supposed to do that?" Arlo protested.

"Ya' live on a sailboat, don't ya'?" Les said. "Ya' must know how ta' sail the fool thing."

"Well, yeah," Arlo said, looking down at his shoes.

"So ya' goes up to 'er. 'Erlene,' ya' say, 'I'm gonna be takin' my boat out f'r a sunset sail this evenin'. I was kind a' hopin' ya'd like to come along.'"

"Ya' think it'll work?" Arlo asked.

Les put his hand on the younger man's shoulder as they stood in the shade of *Elena's* hull. "Listen, Arlo," he said seriously, "ya' only get one chancet in life. If ya' don't take it, ya'll regret it 'till y'r dyin' day. Now get out a' here an' ast the lady if she'd like ta' go sailin'."

ℵ ℭ

Jack Townsend knew what the answer should be before he opened the books he had piled on the salon table. What Margaret Calkins wanted was out of his line. He was a trial lawyer; wills and trusts were another world. This was the kind of thing he would have farmed out if any ordinary client had asked him a few years ago. But Margaret was no ordinary client. Even if he did not like her or respect her, he would owe this one to the memory of Casey Calkins. Besides, he did like her, and he respected her a great deal, perhaps even more than she suspected. He knew their story. Casey had confided the details to him in his office one day, and like any good lawyer, Jack had filed the memory away, never to be divulged.

But there was more than just Casey's memory involved here. Margaret Calkins was tough, and Jack admired that in anyone, even though it could be exasperating. Margaret was the kind of woman who knew what life expected of her, and she was not afraid to meet it head-on. When the Grim Reaper comes for her, Jack thought, he'd better come with reinforcements.

It wasn't just Casey's memory, or Margaret's strength of will at stake. There was another reason to help her. What she wanted to do was so deliciously right, so filled with poetic justice, that Jack longed to have his hand in it, even though he knew that to do so might doom the whole thing to failure before it began. What was this? he thought. The beginning of another ego trip? "Not this time, pal," he said to the empty salon. It was better take a back seat and let someone else serve the client's interest.

He could imagine Junior's face now. Margaret would keep her word to Casey, all right, but she planned to do it in a way his sons could not imagine. They wouldn't be hurt, not really. They had lived on Casey's grit and determination and money long enough. Now, at age fifty-plus they would both have to grow up. Maybe it was the best thing for both of them, but with Jack living at the marina, he could take no part in her plan.

Still, he thought, it would be a kick to have the last line read, "This instrument prepared by John DeWitt Townsend, Esq., Attorney at Law, Florida Bar #134924, P.O. Box 636, Calkins Harbor, Florida." Yes, it would be kick all right. But he would have to save that kick for another time.

෨ ෬

The dining room table at the house on Magnolia Avenue was set with the usual assortment of silver and china. Today, the center of attention was the Key Lime pie and chocolate éclairs, both of which had been delivered from a bakery in Bonita.

"I suppose I could have baked the pie, at least," Mrs. Calkins said, almost by way of apology. "But I've been a little tired of late, and, besides, it's so much more decadent to have someone else do it for us."

"Decadent truly is the word for these éclairs," Marilyn added. "Chocolate has a way of bringing out the worst in me."

"Well, if we must succumb to temptation," Mrs. Calkins laughed, "let it be to chocolate!"

Jennifer stood up and placed both hands on the table. "I would like to make a motion," she said.

Mrs. Calkins intoned solemnly, "The Chair recognizes Jennifer Calkins."

"I move we declare Wednesday to be 'Decadence Day,' and that we celebrate it by having tea and chocolate every Wednesday afternoon."

"Too predictable! Too boring!" Marilyn protested in true English parliamentary fashion.

"All right then," Jennifer continued, "I amend my motion to 'tea and goodies,' provided that one of the goodies always contains chocolate."

"Hear, hear!" Marilyn agreed.

Mrs. Calkins called for a vote, and then, with the imperious bang of a shiny silver teaspoon declared that the motion had been passed by acclamation.

"Now, Marilyn," she said when they all settled down, "we must have your report on your progress in reeling in your catch."

"Well, I . . . really haven't made any progress," Marilyn began. "I'm not sure that I . . . want to make any progress.

I just don't know where my life is going right now."

"Life isn't that complicated, Dear," Mrs. Calkins assured her as she poured another cup of tea. "If you're on the right path, the doors will open in front of you. If you're not, well, you'll have the devil's own time trying to open them. And if you somehow do manage to pry them open, you'll wish you hadn't."

"Listen to Grandma, Marilyn," Jennifer said, licking chocolate icing off her finger. "I know it sounds crazy, but it's true."

"I don't have any reason to doubt her," Marilyn responded. "It's just that I'm not sure I understand what she's talking about."

"Marilyn," Mrs. Calkins said, putting down the teapot, "each of us was put on this earth for a purpose. You believe that, don't you?"

"You said that before," Marilyn replied, "about how each of us is expected to learn something."

"Exactly," Mrs. Calkins said. "Your teacher told you how we learn a thing by completing a task. Well, when you're on the path that is meant for you, the doors will open in front of you . . . in fact, before you even reach them. You just have to have faith that they will."

"But how am I supposed to know . . ." Marilyn began.

"Your path will show you the way. You can't get off it without a great deal of difficulty. If you do, you'll pay a terrible price. You must have faith and follow your heart, that's all. Here and there you'll have a few obstacles, of course; there are obstacles in everyone's life. But those are only tests. They're put there to help you, to make you grow stronger and they allow you to prove to yourself that you can overcome them. You just remain on your path, and the doors will open in front of you."

Marilyn thought for a moment about how her life drifted after she graduated from college. It was as if, in spite of her education, things would just not come together no matter how hard she tried. The law school scholarship that Sister Jean-Marie worked so hard to get for her should have solved everything, but then Marilyn moved in with a boyfriend and things only got worse. She found herself sneaking around and living a lie, and constantly fighting with him because of it. The whole thing had become too much for her. She had to escape. She registered for the Florida Bar exam while she was still at L.S.U. Law, and she came to Bonita only because she had seen it in a magazine. Then suddenly, after she arrived in her tiny, old hatchback car, things began to fall into place.

The Bonita apartment had been almost handed to her. Marilyn had barely finished bemoaning her lack of accommodations to the church secretary after Mass one Sunday, when the woman offered to sublet her own apartment for a year while she went up North to care for her mother. Although the *Bonita Journal* didn't list any jobs for law clerks, Walker & Grant had hired her that first week on the strength of her accounting background. Now here she was, practically a member of a family she didn't even know a year ago, and feeling more at home than she had ever felt anywhere since her mother died. Her life had indeed taken some strange and wonderful turns recently. Maybe Grandma Calkins was right; maybe she should just relax, have faith and enjoy the ride.

Chapter 12

A taxicab delivered Jack Townsend to the Magnolia Avenue house the next morning. As he walked up the brick path to the front door, he thought of the day many years earlier when he first met the Calkins family. Fresh out of the prosecutor's office and eager to make a name for himself in private practice, he took the cases that other lawyers shunned. Captain Kelly Calkins came to him with a most unusual child custody case.

By that time, his five years in the State Attorney's Office had taught Jack the practicality of cutting a deal when that needed to be done. He thought about those days wistfully. Now on the Calkins front porch and wondered what might have happened if he had stayed in Calkins Harbor instead of succumbing to his rush for success. He rang the bell and waited.

"Come in, Counselor," Mrs. Calkins said as she opened the door. She returned his embrace and led him to the living room. "Now, what news do you have for me?" she inquired after he sat down.

"It's not good, I'm afraid," Jack began.

"I knew it wouldn't be," she responded. "You lawyers! You're all so afraid of your own shadows."

"Much as I would love to do it," he continued, "if I represented you in this matter, it could be considered a conflict of interest."

"Couldn't you fight that?"

"Yes, but a conflict of interest would endanger your plan as much as it would me," he said. "In this case, I'm afraid, discretion is the better part of valor."

"I see," Mrs. Calkins said. "Well, what do you suggest?"

"Get another attorney. I called Monty Holcombe over at the Bank of Bonita. He can put someone on it right away if you'd like. I can go over there with you and wait in the car, but you'll have to talk to them alone."

"Very well," she said. "What must be, will be. Can they see me today?"

"I told Monty that would be a possibility," Jack replied. "He said to come over at your convenience. He'll have someone available."

"No time like the present," Mrs. Calkins said, getting up a little slowly, Jack thought. "I would appreciate it if you would drive. I haven't been myself lately."

"Of course," he replied.

The drive to Bonita was nostalgic for both of them. Almost without thinking Jack began talking about his first job as a prosecuting attorney. "Those were the good old days," he said. "I always knew my side was right. When it wasn't, I had enough authority to do something about it. I can honestly say I never went after a guy I didn't know was guilty."

"No regrets?" Mrs. Calkins asked.

"None. There's nothing to regret. I never did anything I didn't believe in back in those days."

"Perhaps you should think about doing that again," she suggested.

"I don't think so," he replied with a patronizing smile. "Even if I wanted to, I'm not on very good terms with State Attorney Deke Stoner. I don't think he would hire me; and even if he would, I'm sure I wouldn't work for him."

"There's a rumor that Deke will be running for Attorney General next year."

"I've heard that."

"If he were elected, someone might persuade the Governor to appoint you to the State Attorney's job . . . on an interim basis, of course."

"Not a chance."

"Politics is in your blood, Jack. Wasn't your grandfather the Governor of New York?"

"Great-grandfather. My grandfather was *only* a federal judge." He smiled across the front seat at her and added, "And I came down here to get away from all that."

"Well, it was just a suggestion," she said as they pulled into the bank parking lot.

He got out and opened the door for her. "Now, you go inside and talk to Monty and his associate, and I'll wait out here. When you're finished, I might even treat you to lunch at the Yacht Club."

Jack waited impatiently for over an hour. As he did the old feelings of guilt began to creep over him. He sat in the car and tried to be inconspicuous, afraid that he would run into an old colleague. He couldn't handle that, not today. Maybe he could face them again someday, but not just yet. Better to be safe and secure on his boat at Cap'n Kelly's. And yet, why was he hiding? He hadn't done anything wrong. The thing just happened; he was as much a victim as anyone. Still, the prospect seeing someone who knew him terrified him in a way he could not explain. The more he thought of it, the more uncomfortable he became, until he deeply regretted his offhand offer to take Margaret to the Club for lunch.

He was sitting in the car, drumming his fingers on the steering wheel when she reappeared. "Let's go," she said, "I'm famished."

"What do you say we make it the Beach House instead?" he asked hopefully.

"The Beach House? I should like to remind you, Sir, that you promised me lunch at the Yacht Club, and I intend to hold you to that promise."

"I don't know . . ."

"Jack," she said softly, touching his arm, "I don't know how many more lunches I'll be having with you. I'd like to have one at the Club . . . for old time's sake."

It was the second time in a week that Sam DePasquale witnessed the yellow Cadillac pull up to the front door, and he hurried outside to meet it. "Mrs. Calkins, he said, "and Commodore Townsend! This is a real surprise!"

"Does the Club still make the best Old Fashioned in southwest Florida, Sam?" Jack asked.

"The best in the whole State of Florida, Commodore," the manager responded.

"Then why don't you escort Mrs. Calkins to a table for two while I park this yellow canal boat," Jack said with a wink.

"Right away, Commodore," Sam responded.

"You be careful with my baby, Jack," Mrs. Calkins scolded. "Yellow canal boat indeed!"

By the time Jack got to the second floor, Mrs. Calkins was already seated and the small past commodore's flag was in place on the table. An Old Fashioned that he had not actually ordered was waiting for him beside it.

"I told Sam you might not want it," Mrs. Calkins explained. "But he insisted it was on the house. He said it was the way you like it—muddled. I hope that wasn't a comment on your current state of mind as well."

"He has a fantastic memory, doesn't he?" Jack said, ignoring what she said. "It seems so strange coming back here after all this time." He looked around the room and added, "I'm glad it's late enough so that all of the regulars are gone. Boy, there are a lot of new people here."

"I was rather hoping you'd meet some of your friends, Jack." Mrs. Calkins said, stirring the tea that had just been placed in front of her.

"I don't know," he replied. "I'm not ready for that yet."

"Yes you are, Dear," she told him. "You just don't know you are."

Lunch was pleasant enough. Margaret told him about her discussion with the trust officer—"young Mr. Meacham" she called him. Apparently she had spent much of the conference probing into his personal life, and had gathered quite a bit of information. As she talked about "young Mr. Meacham's" heroics on the college football field, Jack loosened up and admitted it felt good to be back where he had spent so much time over the years. In a way it was like coming home, and it felt a lot better than he thought it would. By the time dessert arrived, he was absolutely mellow. Whether it was the drink or the atmosphere of the Club, he admitted to himself that he missed the place terribly. Maybe he would come back more often.

"So, I understand you had something of a date last Friday night," Mrs. Calkins said, bringing him back to reality.

"How did you know that?"

"A little bird told me."

No one spoke for a long time. Mrs. Calkins stirred her fresh cup of tea quietly. Finally, Jack broke the silence.

"It just wouldn't work out . . ." he began.

"What wouldn't work out, Dear?" she asked innocently.

"Marilyn and me."

"And why not?" she demanded softly.

"Do you realize she's only eight or nine years older than Alex might have been if I hadn't . . ." he did not finish the sentence.

"You didn't do anything, Jack," she said sharply. "As for Alex, you're talking about what might have been. What matters now is what is."

"She's twelve years younger than I am!" he protested.

"How can you even think such a thing, knowing about Casey and me?" she demanded. He looked at her quizzically across the table. "Yes," she continued, "I knew he told you the whole story. Casey never kept any secrets from me, but you were too much of a gentleman to let on." She reached across the table and took his hand. "Jack," she said softly, "Kathy and Alex will always be a part of your life, just as Casey is a part of mine. But you can't live in the past. You have to let go and move on. That's the only way you'll be able to fulfill your purpose and learn your lesson in this life."

"It seems so . . ." He broke off, unable to find the words for what he was feeling.

"Disloyal?" she offered.

"Yes, all right," he agreed. "Disloyal."

"Disloyal to whom?"

"To them, of course."

"Why?"

"Just . . . because."

"Bosh. Old Judge MacIntyre wouldn't let you get away with that answer and neither will I. Why is it disloyal?"

The man who had always had a way with words couldn't respond, still unable to explain the turmoil of his feelings. Mrs. Calkins let him sit in silence for a minute. "Jack," she finally said softly, "Kathy and Alex did what they were meant to do. They're complete now; but you still have work to do. To do it you must get back on your path. If it's right for you, the doors will open. You know that."

"I guess a very large door is just waiting for me to step through, isn't it?"

"Yes, Dear, it is. But you must be the one to do the stepping."

He looked away, unable to answer her. As they prepared to leave, a poster caught Mrs. Calkins' eye. "The Club's Summer Fling appears to be early this year," she said. "Is June first the night of the full moon?"

"It must be, or at least close to it," he observed.

"It's always such a lovely party," she reminisced. "An afternoon picnic followed by a dance under the stars at night. Jack Townsend, if I were thirty . . . if I were a few years younger, I know who you'd be taking this year." She took him by the arm and held him back. "It's a wonderful way to get to know a person," she said with a knowing look.

There was nothing more to say, and they drove back to the house on Magnolia Avenue, both deeply in thought. Jack parked the car in the garage and escorted Mrs. Calkins to the door. As he was about to leave she suddenly hugged him as though she might not have the opportunity again for a very long time. "You're being given a second chance,

John Townsend," she whispered. "Rare indeed is the soul which recognizes that privilege. Now don't louse it up."

It was a long walk back to the marina, but it was just what Jack needed to clear his mind. Margaret was right, of course. He had to get on with his life. Whether by fate or her manipulation or both, things were moving in a very clear direction.

He had learned that life treated him best when he didn't fight against it. He once heard that bottle-nosed dolphin were so attuned to their environment that they used almost no energy when they swam. They had mastered the art of using what their world gave them rather than attempting to subdue it. It might be that people were meant to be like that. It might be that, like the dolphin, human beings were happiest and went farthest when they worked with what life had given them instead of attempting to bend it to fit their immediate desires.

He once had made the mistake of being dissatisfied with what he had been given. He had allowed himself to be seduced by dreams of money and power, by a childish need to prove something that did not need to be proven. Now he was back where he began, older and a lot wiser. The price had been awful, and, until today, he thought he could never forgive himself. It seemed that Margaret had given him a new perspective. If Kathy and Alex had accomplished their missions in life, then perhaps it was up to him to accomplish his. Refusing to pick up the pieces and move on might be the ultimate disloyalty to them. Perhaps . . .

He could not deny that a door was opening for him, although he suspected that one Margaret Calkins might be giving it a helpful nudge. If she was, okay, what of it? She, too, had a place in the order of things. It might be that her nudge was a part of the universe's plan for him.

It took another mile for him to collect his thoughts. By the time he turned off the paved road onto the shell-rock one that led to the marina, he felt prepared to step through the cosmic door marked "Marilyn Dupré." He hoped that door would not be slammed in his face.

Jennifer, dressed in a tee shirt and jeans, was prowling around the old showroom with a pencil and clipboard, taking measurements and making a sketch. Jack hoped that whatever she was doing would continue to occupy her for the next few minutes. What he had in mind was going to be difficult enough; he would prefer to do it without an audience.

"Hello, Mr. Townsend," Jennifer said as he stepped through one of the open overhead doors.

"Hello, Jennifer," he replied. "I'd like to speak with Marilyn . . . Miss Dupré for a minute, if you don't mind."

"Sure. She's in the office," Jennifer responded, pointing the eraser end of her pencil to the door. Jack hesitated for a moment, and Jennifer added, "I'll be out here for a long time. I have quite a bit of work to do."

She certainly had her grandmother's tact, Jack thought, as he walked inside the office. Marilyn looked up and glared at him from behind her desk.

"Well, *Mister* Townsend," she said, without getting up, "to what do I owe this honor?"

Ouch, he thought, this was going to be worse than he planned. "Look," he said lamely, "I want to apologize for the other night . . . leaving you at the Beach House like that."

"The 'other night' was almost a week ago," she reminded him.

"Yes, I know. I really meant to see you before today and say . . . I'm sorry about . . . the way the evening ended."

Marilyn stood up and her expression softened a little. "You really are an enigma, aren't you?" she said.

"I was hoping to make it up to you this weekend," he continued. "My Club is having a picnic Saturday. I'd like you to be my guest."

"A picnic? Am I going to be left in the middle of a field somewhere?" she teased.

"I promise I'll be on my best behavior." He held up three fingers and added, "Scout's honor."

"You're not a Boy Scout," she chided.

"No, but I was a Knickerbocker Gray, and my mother said that was even better. Besides, I always wanted to be a Scout, and that should count for something."

"I haven't been on a big picnic in a long time," she laughed. "I'm not even sure what to wear."

"Well, it's an all-day thing, so you'll have to bring a change of clothes. The picnic is in the afternoon, and then there's a dance out on the deck at night," he explained.

"Wait a minute," she said. "What kind of picnic is this anyway?"

"I told you, it's the Club picnic. The Summer Fling. They do it every year."

"You mean the Yacht Club?" she asked incredulously.

"Yes, the Yacht Club. It's the only club on island."

"You belong to the Bonita Key Yacht Club?" she repeated, still not believing she got it right.

"Yes," he assured her, "the Bonita Key Yacht Club. It's a really nice place, and I'm sure you'll like the people."

"Isn't it . . . a rather exclusive place?" she asked.

His face broke into a broad smile. "That's okay, we're rather exclusive people, aren't we? Besides, things aren't always what they appear to be."

Marilyn was still in shock. "Shall I pick you up here?" she finally asked.

"Better yet," he smiled, "meet me here Saturday morning and we'll go by boat. It's more fun that way." He turned and headed for the door. "I'll see you about ten o'clock Saturday. "Don't forget to bring a change of clothes; casual in the afternoon, dressy at night," he reminded her.

"Dressy at night," she repeated. Jack closed the door and Marilyn sat down, alone in the office. Boy, she thought, wait 'till Theo Grant hears about this!

Chapter 13

Nature outdid herself Saturday morning. The clear blue Florida sky was dotted with just enough puffy white clouds to give it depth and substance. Jack was up early, and a light breeze wafted through the marina and fluttered with the flags as he "dressed ship." It had been a long time since he'd bothered with things like flags, he thought, as he hoisted the various burgees and ensigns that provided a knowledgeable observer with a résumé of his accomplishments.

Les Leslie and Arlo Woodbrace drank coffee and watched from the shade of *Elena* on the other side of the cove.

"Would ya' look at that," Les said. "I didn't know the guy'd been around that much."

"Maybe he don't know what them flags mean," Arlo observed, not really believing that idea himself. "Maybe he just found 'em somewheres and he thinks they're purdy."

"A guy with a forty-two foot Grand Banks?" Les snorted. "Not likely." He scratched his beard as he squinted at the blue flag with the white anchor and three stars that flapped at the masthead of the white trawler and added, "No, I s'pect he knows what he's doin' all right."

Jack started the engines and allowed them to idle while he checked the latest chart and went over the boat from stem to stern one more time. It would not do to get into trouble on such a short run. If this was going to be his grand re-entrance, he did not want to do it while earning a dreaded "skunk flag."

Marilyn arrived promptly at ten o'clock. She looked fantastic in a peach blouse that complemented her dark hair and white tennis shorts that showed off her very attractive legs.

"You look great," Jack said as he helped her aboard with her overnight bag. "What's in the suitcase?"

"My things, of course," she said. "You told me to bring a change of clothes. It's dressy at night, remember?"

"You need a suitcase for a dress?"

"Jack, a dress means different . . . underthings . . . and shoes, and jewelry, and a purse, and makeup and hair stuff . . . Oh, never mind. The boat looks great," she said, changing the subject. And look at all the flags! I'll bet every one of them means something."

"My dear," he said, placing his hand over his heart with mock solemnity, "on a boat, everything means something."

"Okay," she said, "I'm ready for my first lesson. Tell me what they mean."

"The burgee at the bow is the . . ." he began.

"Wait . . . wait," she interrupted, "I'm new at this. Can we do it in English?"

"The triangular one at the front, blue with a white star, is the flag of the Bonita Key Yacht Club. Up at the masthead . . . at the top up there . . . that blue flag with the anchor and three stars means that I used to be a "somebody" at that Club. On the starboard spreader . . . that's the boat's right side, over there . . . that rectangular flag with the blue and white vertical stripes is the 'ensign' . . . that means 'flag' . . . of United States Power Squadrons. Below it, the swallow-tailed flag with the three panels . . . blue, white and red . . . means I used to be a "somebody" there, too."

"Aren't you anybody now?" she teased.

He hung his head and shook it in mock self-pity. "No, now I'm just a has-been everywhere. Now if there are no further questions, you can stow your gear in the guest quarters, then come out on deck and we'll cast off."

"Pardon?"

"Put your 'things' in the front bedroom, come outside and we'll untie the boat so we can leave."

"Right, Captain. That's what I'm supposed to call you, isn't it?"

"Not exactly, but that'll do," he said with a smile. "And you're supposed to say, 'Aye-aye,' not 'right.' Oh, come on, on second thought since you're a landlubber, I better show you around."

Jack put his arm around her and led her into the magic world of a live-aboard yacht. "This is the main salon," he said. "Technically, it's a 'saloon,' but unfortunately that word got hijacked by the westerns. You might call it a living room, but please don't."

"And what a cute little kitchen," she added, peering into a small area three steps down from the front end of the main salon.

He took her by her shoulders and faced her. "That is the 'galley,'" he said, "and forward of it . . . that means toward the front of the boat . . . are the guest quarters: a stateroom with its own head . . . that's a bathroom." He turned her around and added, "The owner's stateroom and another head is aft . . . that's toward the back, which is also sometimes referred to as 'astern.'"

"I'm sure you don't call this a 'steering wheel,'" she said, running her hand over the polished mahogany wheel and spokes.

"No, that's a helm, he replied, "and to be honest, I've never used it. I've always used the flying bridge topside. Come on, let's get started. If you behave I'll let you steer part of the way."

Marilyn deposited her suitcase in the forward stateroom and hurried to join Jack out on deck. Les and Arlo were alongside on the shore.

"Give ya' a hand castin' off, Commodore?" Les called out.

"Thanks, Les," Jack replied, "that would be great."

"I'll get the stern line," Arlo offered.

Within minutes the trawler was free of her bonds and

Jack took Marilyn up to the bridge above the main salon. With a turn of the wheel and a deft touch of the throttles, he moved the boat away from shore and headed for the cove entrance.

"This is wonderful!" Marilyn exclaimed as the glided into the harbor proper. "See how everything looks so different from here." She was like a kid on an amusement park ride, Jack thought.

"Don't tell me you've never been on a boat before," he said.

"Just the Algiers Point Ferry, but that was nothing like this," she replied.

"Well as soon as we reach open water you're going to take the helm," he warned her.

What should have been a short trip to the Yacht Club took a lot longer. Jack went around the south end of the island and turned the boat northwest into the Gulf of Mexico. "This is wonderful! This is great," Marilyn kept repeating as the sun reflected off the water and the wind caught her hair.

"You should try it at night in a gale," Jack shouted. "Come on, take the wheel."

"Do you really think I should?" she asked in the kind of voice that begged him to encourage her.

"We're about three miles out," he said. "There's nothing to hit out here. Turn us around and head up back toward Bonita Key and I'll give you a quick lesson in navigation."

By the time they got back to the island Marilyn was becoming an old hand. "Want to take her into the Club basin?"

"No, thank you," she replied. "I leave the tricky parts to the experts."

"Nothing to it," he said as he took the wheel. "Just keep it real slow so you can stop if you're not sure of the next move. These things don't have brakes, you know."

Jack guided the trawler into one of the slips at the Club with an ease that surprised her. "You've done this before, I'll bet," she said.

"Once or twice," he replied.

"Come on Jack, step on it!" a man shouted from the dock. "If you take much longer they'll be out of beer!"

"I hate beer!" Jack called back.

"Yes, but I don't," the man replied. "And I volunteered to handle your lines."

"Marilyn," Jack said, "go down on deck and throw Bill our docking lines."

"Me?" she exclaimed. "I don't even know what you're talking about."

"The ropes that Les and Arlo untied before we left," he said. "Toss them to that guy down there … one at a time."

"I hope you know what I'm doing, because I certainly don't," she said as she hurried to comply.

Fortunately for Marilyn and the stranger on the dock, Jack brought the boat in close enough so that she had to do little more than hand him the lines. They were secured in minutes. "Permission to come aboard, Commodore?" the man shouted, laughing as he jumped on board.

"Permission granted, Commodore," Jack laughed as he hurried down to meet the man who instantly wrapped him in a bear hug.

"Jack, you old fart!" he exclaimed. "I couldn't believe it when Sam said you bought tickets to this shindig!"

"Leave it to him to keep a secret," Jack laughed. "Does everybody else know?

"Rita's already half in the bag and ready to sink her hooks into you. Hell, the only reason I'm here is to watch the fireworks," the man said. "Now how about introducing me to the reason for all this commotion?"

"Marilyn," Jack said, "this is Judge Bill Bellingham, one of the Past Commodores of the Club, and a very good friend of mine. Bill," he said, turning toward the judge, "this is Marilyn Dupré, a very special lady."

"You must be special to get this old goat to come to the Summer Fling," Bill said, taking her hand. "But now that you're here I must inform you that since I'm the senior Past Commodore, you'll have to spend the rest of the day with me. It's a very old and unbreakable B.K.Y.C. tradition."

Marilyn looked stricken and turned to Jack. "Bill," he said, "she doesn't know you're kidding."

"Who's kidding? Besides, you'll have enough to do fighting off Rita," Bill said, putting his arm around Marilyn's waist. "Oh, all right, I guess you can tag along if you have to," he finally added to Jack, over his shoulder.

The three of them stepped off the boat and walked past the dock area to the wide lawn where the picnic was already in progress. Jack was greeted as something of a celebrity, and deluged with warm wishes and welcomes.

A woman with short red hair and a thickening figure wedged into slacks a few sizes too small approached them from across the lawn. "Well, Jack," she said in a voice already slurred from too much alcohol, "it's nice to see you again. And you brought your . . . is it your niece? . . . with you."

"Hello, Rita," Jack said curtly.

Bill Bellingham hustled Marilyn off to the other guests where he took great delight in introducing her as "Commodore Townsend's Crew." As he told and re-told the story of her part in the docking maneuver, her role became ever larger, until he was telling people that she had heaved the lines at least fifty or a hundred feet and then single-handedly pulled the vessel to the dock.

"But I've never been on a boat before today," she protested when he finished his latest version of the tale.

"Even better!" Bill exclaimed. "It just shows what natural ability you have."

Jack finally came around and rescued her. "William," he said, taking her hand, "I have come to reclaim my lady fair."

"See that, Darlin'?" Bill said as he let her go. "He looks shifty to me. Don't trust him. Remember, I'll be here if you need me."

They walked in silence for a long time. Finally, Marilyn said, "Is everything all right with Rita?"

"Rita went home early," he replied flatly. They walked on for a while before he stopped and added, "Look, nothing ever happened between Rita and me. I guess a couple of years ago she expected me to . . . It just wasn't right . . ."

"You don't have to explain anything to me," Marilyn interrupted. They began walking again; she slipped her hand into his and laughed, "Of course you know your friend Bill is a certified nut."

"He's one of a kind, that's for sure," Jack replied with a smile. "Billy and I have been through some tough times together. Both of his marriages and divorces, a few really scary night crossings, and a dismasting off *Isla Mujeres* down in Mexico when I honestly thought we were going to die. And then there was . . . the accident."

He said nothing more for another few minutes, and they walked along in silence.

"I was married once," Jack finally said. Marilyn winced as she felt a sudden emptiness. This sounded like it was going to be something that Sister Jean-Marie would not like to hear.

"I guess I should have told you before bringing you here today. Kathy and I met when we were students at Cornell. Although she was born here, her parents were from Peru . . . that made Kathy both a "foreigner" and a "person of color" according to New York society. We dated, fell in love and got married . . . over my family's very strong objections . . . the year I started law school. We couldn't afford to start a family, of course, and our son, Alexander . . . Alex . . . wasn't born until eight years later. That's what I meant when I told you that I was old enough to be your father. If we hadn't waited, Alex might have been around twenty now."

Marilyn did not reply, but let Jack tell the story at this own pace as they walked along the beach.

"After I graduated, we moved to Florida, so that I could make it on my own ... without my family's help. I got a job as an Assistant State Attorney, prosecuting cases in Bonita and the surrounding counties. I really, really liked that job," he said longingly. "It was the only time I was truly happy in this business."

"After a few years, two friends of mine and I started our own law firm. Do you know what that's like?" he asked. She shook her head silently and added, "No," almost in a whisper.

"I'll tell you what it's like," he said, not even paying attention to her answer. "You start representing all kinds of jerks because you need their money to pay the rent and put food on the table. You don't believe in their causes; you don't like them, you don't even know them. You just take their money and do the best job you can. I was a good lawyer, Marilyn. I waltzed a lot of guys out of courtrooms when they should have gone to jail." He sighed and added, "But I made a good living, and" ... he nodded back toward the Yacht Club ... "even managed to become Commodore of this place."

"Anyway, my reputation as a trial lawyer got the better of me. About five years ago ... just about the time Casey

Calkins died . . . some guys from Miami recruited me. Kathy didn't want to go, but I wouldn't listen. I told her that it was my chance to make some real money. I had been offered a partnership by people who were putting together a criminal defense firm: big cases, big clients, and, of course, big money." Jack stopped walking and looked out over the ocean. "I had to be a big success so I could rub their noses in it back home in New York." He looked at Marilyn and added, "I think Kathy suspected I would go with or without her." He pointed to a log under a stand of palm trees and said, "Let's sit down; this story gets kind of difficult."

"We had three years in Miami," he continued, "and I made a ton of money. I represented drug dealers, murderers, you name it. I knew how the system worked: I had learned it from the other side, and now I played it like a violin. One day, we were retained to represent the son of one of our bigger drug clients. The kid had been arrested after he almost killed a woman in an automobile accident. He was D.U.I., driving under the influence of alcohol, and he had blown a point two five on the breathalyzer. That was two and a half times the legal limit back then."

Jack looked off in the distance now. He wasn't talking only to her anymore; he was talking to himself as well, remembering something that had changed his life.

"When I say 'kid,' don't get the wrong idea. This guy wasn't a juvenile. He was a big, fat, sloppy, disgusting twenty-five year old momma's boy who had never done a worthwhile thing in his life. This was his fourth D.U.I., and the State was looking for a prison sentence, especially because everybody knew what his father did for a living but couldn't prove it . . . again thanks to me."

Jack took a deep breath. "I tried the case and won it on a technicality. It doesn't matter what it was; the fact is, the bastard was guilty . . . guilty as hell, and I waltzed him out of there."

"About three weeks later, I picked up Kathy and Alex after work to take them out for a surprise. I was going to show them the new boat that I bought for us. The one I'm living on; that was the surprise."

Jack hesitated for a moment, then continued, "We were crossing Powerline Road up in Lauderdale when a car hit us broadside. The police later said he was doing at least sixty. Kathy was killed instantly. Alex was . . . in the back seat . . ."

Jack's voice cracked, and he stopped talking. Tears formed in his eyes and Marilyn put her arm around him. He was quiet for a moment, and then said, "Alex was catapulted out of the window into a concrete pole. I had a bunch of internal injuries, and kept slipping out of consciousness. I remember asking about him every time I came to, but no one would give me an answer."

Jack's voice was steadier now, as if he had detached himself from the memory and was talking about something he had seen in a television show.

"Alex was alive but not by much," he continued. "They

took us to the same hospital. I remember seeing a lot of activity in the emergency room, and nurses talking about 'the boy.' The next thing I knew, they were telling me to sign consent forms for both of us. They said Alex had a serious head injury and needed immediate surgery. I was bleeding internally and would die if they didn't operate on me right away, too."

"That's the last thing I remember until I woke up in Intensive Care. The next day . . . or maybe two days later . . . I still can't figure it out . . . one of the doctors came in to talk to me. He told me that Alex had survived the surgery, but that he would never be normal. There was too much brain damage. At best, he would need total care for the rest of his life. It turned out the rest of his life was six days. He never regained consciousness. I never even got a chance to say 'goodbye' . . ."

Jack's voice cracked again. This time he could not continue. Tears were streaming down his face. "Jack, please," Marilyn whispered, "you don't have to tell me this."

"No, I have to tell you," he said, his voice trembling now. "I have to tell you something I've never told another living soul. The truth is, I was relieved when they told me he died. All I could think about at that moment was the cost of keeping him alive, and the care that I would have to provide."

He turned and looked at her. "Did you hear me?" he said with a mixture of shame and anger in his voice. "My son died in the hospital, and my first reaction was relief."

"You're a normal human being," Marilyn protested. "You have normal human feelings . . . fears . . . needs. You can't blame yourself for that."

"I can't?" he said angrily. "Well, here's something I *can* blame myself for. The drunk who hit us . . . the scumbag who killed my family and walked away without a scratch . . ." His voice faltered again and suddenly she knew what he was about to say even before he spoke the dreaded words. "Please God, please," she prayed silently, "Not that; anything but that. Don't let it be what I'm thinking . . ."

". . . the scumbag who killed my family," he continued, "was the same one I had waltzed out of a Miami courtroom three weeks earlier. Now do you want to tell me you don't believe in Karma, Marilyn?"

His words pierced her like a dagger. How ironic, she thought. Arlo had been right all along. Jack Townsend is a man on the run. But he isn't running from the law. He's running from the only man he can never lose—himself.

They sat together in silence for a long time. Finally, Jack stood up and helped her to her feet. "Come on," he said softly, "they're probably wondering what happened to us. We better get back."

As they walked along the beach Marilyn put her arm around him and he responded by doing the same to her. It was a spontaneous act of intimacy between two friends. And it was something more, too.

I understand him now, Marilyn thought. I may not know where this is going, but at least I understand him.

Chapter 14

Erlene Rodgers squealed with delight when Arlo hauled in the sheet for the mainsail and the boat heeled over.

"Are you sure you know what y're doin', Arlo?" she giggled as she followed his lead and switched her seat to the windward side of the boat.

"'Course I know what I'm doin'," he replied defensively. "Me an' Dennis sailed this boat all the way to Mexico oncet."

"You did not!"

"Did too," he insisted. "Just me an' him."

"Who's Dennis, anyway?"

"Oh he's my . . . he's a kind a friend a' mine, sort a'," Arlo said, answering her without explaining anything.

Erlene might have asked another question, but Arlo tugged at the mainsheet again and the boat heeled a little more. He sure could have sailed to Mexico, she thought. When he was on his boat, free from the bonds of land, Arlo Woodbrace, the stumbling, bumbling, self-proclaimed handyman became a new person. Out here he was confident, almost masterful. He moved around the deck with a cat-like grace that Erlene never saw him use ashore. The sight of this new and different Arlo gave her goose bumps.

Arlo was too busy working the deck to notice. It was no easy task to handle a thirty-five foot sailboat single handedly, but he accomplished it with ease thanks to his years of experience living and sailing mostly alone. Like Jack Townsend, he had lived alone far too long. He had found the courage to ask Erlene out only after he saw Jack and Marilyn cruise away on the trawler earlier in the day. If Jack Townsend could take a girl out on his boat, well, then, by gosh, Arlo thought, he could do it too. All he had to do was get up enough courage to ask her.

Of course that was the problem. First Arlo had to convince himself that Erlene was on the gas dock, just wishing that she could be as lucky as Miss Dupré. He gave himself a pep talk. "She's prob'ly out there right now," he muttered as he walked away from the trawler's empty berth. "She's just hopin' I'll come along and ast her out for a sail." He kept repeating the thought over and over as he walked around the marina to the other side of the cove entrance as Jack and Marilyn pulled out. He had it all planned. He was going to tell her, "Erlene, I'm takin' my boat out for a sail tonight, and I was hopin' you'd come along."

Naturally it didn't turn out that way. When he got to her gas dock, Erlene said, "That Marilyn Dupré is sure lucky to be goin' out on a boat on such a nice day," and

Arlo forgot his line and just froze up. All he could say was, "Yeah, it sure is a nice day." And after an eternity of a few minutes during which he kicked a lot of shell-rock and put his hands in and out of his pockets at least a dozen times, Erlene rescued him by asking, "Why don't ya' ever take y'r boat out, Arlo?"

Something about that question hit Arlo, and he must have jump-started. "As a matter of fact, I'm goin' out ta'night for a sunset sail," he said. "Want ta' go?"

"A sunset cruise? Gol, that sounds so romantic," Erlene had said dreamily. "I'll have ta' call home an' make sure Faith don't have no plans."

Arlo almost passed out. It sounded like the woman of his dreams had just said "yes." "You mean you want ta' go?" he asked.

"Sure, as long as I c'n call home first."

"Why don't I watch the gas dock for ya' while you call from the office?" Arlo said after the blood ran back up to his head.

"That's a great idea, Arlo. Y're so sweet," Erlene told him, and she ran off down the dock almost bouncing out of her bikini.

Faith did have plans, but she wasn't about to tell that to Erlene. "No, Momma," she lied gracefully, "I was just gonna stay home and watch T.V. tonight."

"Are you sure, Honey?" Erlene asked. "'Cause one of the fellas here at the marina ast me to go sailin' and . . . well, I've kind a' been hopin' he'd ast me f'r a long time."

"You have a good time, Momma," Faith answered. "Tommy and I are gonna rent a video and get a pizza tonight."

Erlene bounced her way back to the gas dock and said, "Well, Arlo, it looks like I'm y'rs for the evenin'." At about that same time, Faith was calling up her friends and telling them her Momma had a date.

After he got the sail trimmed to his satisfaction and the last line cleated, Arlo relaxed and thought about how easy it had been. Erlene, the woman of his dreams, had been waiting for him to ask her out after all. Now she was sitting next to him on his sailboat in the late afternoon sun: Erlene, whose luscious breasts fairly spilled out of the top of her bikini as she leaned back against the heel of the boat. Arlo swallowed hard, like a man who had hooked a shark and wished he hadn't because now he really didn't know what to do with it.

"Want a Pepsi, Erlene?" he asked, trying to start a conversation.

"A beer 'd be better," she replied.

A beer? He hadn't counted on beer. He might have one, someplace, long since buried in the back of the galley refrigerator. With Erlene stretched out the way she was, with her back to the wind and her feet on the sole of the cockpit, Arlo would have to almost climb over her to get below. He thought about it for a minute, then lashed the wheel and prepared to make his way past temptation.

"Hey, where are you goin'?" she demanded.

"To get ya' a beer," he said.

"Well, should ya' be doin' that?" she screeched nervously.

"Doin' what?"

"Leavin' the steerin' wheel like that?" she responded. "I mean, who's gonna' be drivin' this thing?"

"Erlene, ya' don't 'drive' a sailboat," he said patiently. "Once the sails 're set, she goes by herself . . . at least for a while."

"Well, hurry back," she said. "I don't like bein' out here alone."

Women, he thought. They don't know nothin' about boats. Never did. I guess I'll have to teach her everything.

Arlo found two lonely cans of beer in the farthest corner of the small refrigerator in the galley. He was about to open both of them and bring them out on deck, but he thought better of it and exchanged one for a Pepsi.

"Don't ya' drink, Arlo?" Erlene asked when he opened the soft drink.

"Beer gives me a headache," he said truthfully. "An' besides, there's only one more an' I'm savin' it for you."

"That's real nice, Arlo," she said as she took a gulp from the can. "Gol, it's so pretty out here." She pointed to a boat that was silhouetted by the setting sun. "Let's go over there an' see what them people are doin'."

"We prob'ly shouldn't," he replied, squinting at the sailboat anchored in the distance with its sails furled.

"Why not?"

"They prob'ly don't want to be bothered."

"Heck, we ain't gonna bother 'em," she said, taking another gulp from the can. "We're just gonna sail past 'em and wave. Come on. *Please?*"

The 'please' did it. Arlo brought the helm around and headed for the anchored boat. The change in direction took the heel out of the boat and Erlene climbed out on the now-level deck and waved at passing motorboats. Arlo watched in amazement as her taut body moved inside the small pieces of fabric that encased it. Her back was to him, and her legs slightly spread for balance as she gripped a wire shroud with one hand and waved with the other. Erlene looked just as good from this side as she did from the front, Arlo thought. And her front looked real, real good.

The breeze moved them ever closer to the anchored sailboat Erlene had chosen as their destination. As they got closer, she went out on the foredeck for a better view.

"Look, Arlo," she called back to him, "they must be expectin' company. They got their flags flyin' and everything."

"Them ain't flags," he guessed with the knowledge of a sailor who had spent a lot of time on the water.

"Well, what are they?" she demanded.

"My binocs are below," he said. "Get 'em if ya' want. I'll bet ya' a hundred dollars them ain't flags."

"A hundred dollars? Y're on, Buddy," Erlene replied as she worked her way aft to the sailboat's cockpit and then down the companionway to find the binoculars. Arlo could have gone below and retrieved the glasses himself, of course, but it was so much more fun watching Erlene climb around the boat. Various parts of her anatomy bounced and jiggled with every step providing him with a continuing source of amazement and delight.

"Where are they?" she called from the cabin.

"Next ta' the chart table," he shouted.

"Where's that?"

"Across fr'm the galley," he replied.

A few minutes later she was back on deck and working her way forward again. "Remember, a hundred bucks!" she shouted, certain now that she was right. "I'm gonna hold ya' to it, Arlo! Ya' better have y'r money ready," she said as she raised the glasses and focused them for a minute. "Well, I'll be . . ." she began. She put binoculars down and then raised them to her eyes again. "Hey, those things don't look like flags!"

"A hundred bucks, Erlene," Arlo reminded her. "I'm gonna hold ya' to it."

"Arlo!" she shouted. "That's a woman's bikini."

❧ ☙

Marilyn had taken off her tennis shoes and was carrying them as she and Jack walked back to the picnic. Jack said nothing more, and she allowed him the privacy of his thoughts. She silently slipped her free hand in his and walked beside him, holding his hand and leaving bare footprints along the edge of the water. By the time they arrived back at the lawn she could feel he was in better spirits. Bill was there, waiting for them.

"Well, Darlin'," he said with a smile, "as long as he didn't get past your shoes, I guess I can forgive you."

"He was a perfect gentleman, and the shoes were my idea, Commodore," she replied as she slipped them on again. A group of people who were setting up tables under umbrellas called to them. Jack went ahead, but Bill took Marilyn's hand and held her back for a moment.

"How's he doing?" Bill asked seriously when Jack was out of earshot.

"Fine," Marilyn answered, a little surprised at the genuine concern in the judge's voice.

"That's good," Bill said. "I love that guy. I wouldn't want to see him hurt again."

"Don't worry, Commodore," Marilyn said, taking Bill's arm as they walked toward the others, "I won't hurt him. I think I love him, too."

"Just make him happy, okay?" Bill said as he patted her hand.

A bubbly blonde came forward and extended her hand. "Hi," she said. "I'm Judy Hennel. My husband's the Commodore this year."

"Hello," Marilyn replied, taking her hand, "My name is Marilyn Dupré. I'm a guest of Jack Townsend."

"Yes, I know," Judy said with a laugh that was almost a giggle. "Word gets around fast here. Has Bill been behaving himself?"

"Young lady," Bill said pompously, "I'll have you know that I am a Past Commodore of this Club."

"Well, then," Judy said, taking his arm, "you can help us set up the tables. Come on, Marilyn," she added, "it's never too soon to learn that the people with the titles do all of the work around here."

The Club's paid staff would not be arriving until late afternoon to prepare for the evening dinner. The afternoon "picnic" as they called it was a strictly volunteer effort, and Marilyn joined the members who were busy spreading checkered tablecloths and arranging place settings of silverware on the round tables.

"This has gotten pretty formal, hasn't it," Jack complained. "I thought the idea was for the boys to run the afternoon cookout and the girls to run the dance."

"Jack," Judy replied, "I got tired of trying to eat a steak with a plastic knife and fork. I swore that this year, come hell or high water, we would have tablecloths and at least metal flatware on the tables. The staff can put out the good silverware tonight. Let's go," she added, throwing him a cloth, "you and Bill are way behind on your quota."

"He really is a judge, right?" Marilyn whispered. "I've seen him on the news, haven't I?"

"He's only a judge during the week," Judy said, handing her a handful of knives and forks. "Besides, we pick on everybody equally around here. Get to work," she added with wide smile.

"It's funny," Marilyn said as she began arranging the place settings, "I always thought this was such an exclusive club."

"It is," Judy insisted. "You wouldn't let just anyone into your family, would you? And the officers and their wives are sort of a family within a family."

"Did you know Jack's wife?" Marilyn asked, not looking up from what she was doing.

"Kathy? Sure, we all did. That was a horrible tragedy. It's so nice to have Jack back home with us."

"I suppose anyone who's here with him has some pretty big shoes to fill," Marilyn observed, still looking down at the table.

"Old hens are bound to cluck, Marilyn," Judy cautioned her.

"Is one of those hens named 'Rita' something?

"Rita Thomas. Her husband Lenny died of a heart attack a few years ago. She let it be known around here that she had staked out Jack as her personal target."

Marilyn finally looked up. "Is there anyone else I should watch out for tonight?"

"Hers won't be the only nose out of joint tomorrow morning, if that's what you mean," Judy laughed.

"Judy, I'm not very good at pushing myself in where I'm not wanted . . ."

"Just be yourself, kiddo," Judy replied, squeezing her arm. "You'll be fine. If any of those 'clucks' sound like they're saying 'young enough to be his daughter,' let me know. I'll set the old hens straight. Now come on, help me put out the table flags."

"The what?"

"The table flags," Judy repeated. "They're miniature officers' flags," she explained as she opened a box. "The current officers and p.c.'s get them at their place settings."

"Hold it," Marilyn said. "Judy, I don't know anything about this sort of thing. I had never even been on a boat before today."

"That's all right. None of us knew anything about it before our husbands got involved. They're just like kids, with their flags and their caps and everything. Don't worry—you'll pick it up. Here, this little blue flag with the white anchor surrounded by stars is for the Commodore. That's my husband Ron this year. We'll put him right here. The other blue flags . . ."

"These are miniatures of the one on Jack's boat," Marilyn interrupted.

"Right," Judy continued. "Those are for the past commodores. Put two at our table; one for you and Jack, and one for Bill . . . he and Jack are inseparable. The red flag is for the Vice Commodore and the white one is for the Rear Commodore. Put them and all the other p.c. flags on that empty table so the boys can put them wherever they want."

"This really *is* pretty formal for a cookout, isn't it?" Marilyn asked, repeating Jack's earlier comment.

"Wait 'till you come to the Commodore's Ball," Judy responded. "They really go nuts for this kind of stuff then."

"Oh, I don't know . . ." Marilyn began. "I mean, Jack only invited me to this picnic. It's nothing that serious . . .

well, I don't know if I'll be coming to any more functions with him."

Judy stood back and looked at her for a moment as a smile crossed her lips. "You really don't see it, do you?"

"See what?"

"See what you've done to Jack?" Judy said.

"No, I'm afraid I don't see it."

"Honey," Judy said, taking Marilyn's arm, "whether he's told you or not, he's ga-ga over you. Look at him!" She nodded toward Jack who at that moment was tugging on one end of a tablecloth with Bill pulling on the other. "He hasn't shown his face around here for two years," Judy continued, "and today he's back horsing around with Bill. Marilyn, whether you know it or not, you've given him back his life."

Chapter 15

The afternoon picnic was delightful. The food prepared on the outdoor grill by "the boys" was excellent, and the entertainment, provided by Bill Bellingham and Jack was even better. Bill was without a date—or a boat for that matter—and Marilyn sat between him and Jack, across from Judy and her husband. Bill kept them amused with stores of wild races aboard his forty-foot sailboat. "Hey, Jackie," he demanded, "tell your lady fair about *Regata al Sol.*"

"You do such a better job," Jack replied.

"That was 'The Terminator Race'," Bill continued. "It terminated my second marriage."

"It almost terminated us, too, as I recall," Jack added.

"Oh, hell, all we did was lose our sail," Bill laughed.

Jack laughed with him. "Unfortunately it was attached to your mast at the time."

"My God!" Marilyn exclaimed. "What did you do?"

"Hey, when the weather cleared and Jack-o stopped puking his guts out . . ."

"Bill!" Judy protested.

"Excuse me, did I say 'puking'? I meant 'barfing'," Bill continued. "Anyway, the Coast Guard found us. Right, Jack?"

"Oh, yes, 'The Terminator Race'," Jack replied. "It also terminated my racing career." He lifted a glass and said, "Here's to 'The Terminator Race'."

Jack and Bill kept up their banter all though dinner. After they finished with each other they started in on the current commodore, telling him he would soon be the junior member of the 'Old Dead Commodores Association'—that is, if he were found worthy of admission.

"How do I do that?" Ron Hennel asked, joining in the game.

"Well," Bill explained, "first you have to be old and dead."

"Sorry, Bill," Judy interjected, "Ron does *not* qualify."

"You see?" Bill continued. "You've got a problem already. Now Jack here shows up with a sweet young thing. We might have to revoke his membership."

"How about you?" Judy protested. "You've been hanging around her all day."

"I was only being polite," Bill explained, "as befits a person of my position and experience."

Talk of the "Old Dead Commodores Association" led to several toasts to individual Old Dead Commodores of happy or unhappy memory and only concluded when Judy asked Marilyn if she would like to visit the clubhouse.

"What do you girls do in there, anyway?" Bill demanded. "And why can't you do it alone?"

"Sorry, Bill," Judy replied, kissing him on the forehead. "That's our secret. Now try not to get into trouble while we're gone."

"This is so nice," Marilyn said as she and Judy walked together across the lawn, "I've never been here before, but you and your husband . . . and Bill, of course . . . you've all made me feel like . . . well, like I'm home."

"It's easy to feel that way around here," Judy replied. "We're pretty ordinary people in spite of our press releases. Of course there are one or two folks who have allowed all of this 'private club' nonsense to go to their heads, and there are bound to be a few sour apples like our friend Rita, but thank goodness most of us are pretty normal."

The first floor of the clubhouse was dominated by a bar in the shape of the front half of a boat. Judy explained that it had actually been built out of the bow section of a cabin cruiser. To one side comfortable leather couches and chairs were grouped around a fireplace and various sized coffee tables made from what might have been old hatch covers were dotted with boating magazines. The mantle above the fireplace held the obligatory model of a sailing yacht, and trophy cases filled the spaces between the windows. On the far wall across from the bar, track lights illuminated pictures of the past commodores of the Club, and here and there a framed navigational chart filled the remaining wall space. On the whole, the room was a very homey place.

"Come here, I want to show you something," Judy said, directing Marilyn's attention to the photographs on the wall. "The Past Commodores of Bonita Key Yacht Club," she said, with a flourish of her arm. "Recognize anyone?"

"My God, that's Jack!" Marilyn squealed. "And he has a mustache! He looks so young!"

"Youngest commodore ever elected," Judy assured her.

Marilyn studied Jack's picture along with the other photographs—including Bill's—on the wall. "This 'commodore' stuff is pretty important around here . . . even in Bonita, I mean . . . isn't it?"

"Are you kidding?" Judy replied. "There are men in that town who would kill for that title and the silly flag on the table that goes with it."

"Judy, what are those other flags on Jack's boat? Something about some kind of 'squadron' or something?"

"Power Squadron," Judy replied. "Jack was commander of the Bonita Bay Power Squadron, too. It's quite an accomplishment. There are only two or three other men on that wall who have done both."

"I guess people around here really like him," Marilyn observed.

"You'd better believe it," Judy confirmed. "Don't worry about a few old hens, Marilyn. Any guest of Commodore Jack Townsend is going to be accepted around here, whether they cluck or not. Come on, let's hit the head."

On their way back outside, they passed Sam DePasquale who was supervising the bartenders as they set up an outdoor bar and directing the band to its location on the patio—which all the members insisted on calling 'the deck'—on the other side of the French doors. "Expecting a crowd tonight, Sam?" Judy asked kiddingly.

"The Summer Fling is always a big event, Mrs. Hennel," he replied seriously, missing Judy's joke. "The dance keeps getting bigger every year."

"Sam is the best club manager we've ever had," Judy told Marilyn. "But he takes everything so seriously. I think he actually believes all that stuff we put out about being exclusive. Really, how formal can you be when you spend most of your time on a boat?"

"Exactly how formal is this dance?" Marilyn asked.

"Summer dress kind of thing," Judy replied. The men will wear their white uniforms, which means short sleeve shirts with no ties. I guess you could call it 'informally formal'."

"Uniforms?" Marilyn asked. "Are you joking?"

Judy gave Marilyn an knowing look and said slowly, "Marilyn, the difference between men and boys . . ."

". . . is the price of their toys," Marilyn joined in with a laugh.

"Now you've got the idea," Judy giggled as they walked back to the table. "Just don't let them know you know it."

They arrived just in time for everyone to begin leaving. "Time to change, I guess," Ron Hennel said as he took his wife's hand. "You fellows are wearing your whites tonight, right?"

"Sir!" Bill declared with his usual mock dignity, "Would I offend the company by doing otherwise? But I doubt if my friend here will be similarly attired."

"I'll find my whites," Jack said in response. "They're probably in the closet where I left them."

"Jack, don't embarrass us. Scrape off the mold before you put them on," Bill said as he swaggered away toward the clubhouse.

"Come on, Marilyn," Jack said, taking her hand. "This may take me a while."

₭ ₮

Somewhere out on the Gulf of Mexico, Arlo Wood-brace dropped his sail and furled it on the boom. With the agility that was natural to him when he was on a boat, he stepped back into the cockpit where Erlene was finishing the last of the second beer.

"Gol," she said, "that sunset goes right through me."

"It's purdy, ain't it?" Arlo agreed. "There's nothin' better 'n bein' on a boat."

"'Course ya' know I can't pay off that bet," Erlene said as she moved closer to him.

"We'll have to think a' somethin'," he replied.

"Like what?" she asked as she cuddled closer.

"Well, when the pirates caught somebody that didn't have no money, they used ta' make 'em walk the plank," Arlo said.

"Oh, that sounds like it might hurt," Erlene cooed as

she ran her hand over his bare chest. "Couldn't we do somethin' else?"

"Sure," he replied. "But you have to surrender before I can show any mercy. Them 're the rules."

"How do I do that?" she whispered with her lips inches away from his ear.

"Hand over your colors so's I can run 'em up that halyard, a' course," Arlo told her. "That'll make it official."

"You better tie these on good, Arlo," she said as she stood up. "They're all I got out here, and I don't want ta' go home buck naked."

With that, she turned around, reached back and slowly untied the top of her bikini. She turned back with her hands cupping the material to her breasts, took a step closer and handed it to him, revealing herself. Arlo took the first prize and waited.

"That's one flag," she said as she stepped away. She turned away from him again and slowly began to roll down the top of the bikini bottom until she revealed the cleft that separated the twin globes of her behind.

"Gol," she said, "I don't know if I can go through with this." She turned her head to look at Arlo who was sitting, watching her with a fixed gaze that said here, in this world, on his boat, he was the master. He expected the second "flag," but he would not take it; she would have to give it to him.

Erlene sat down and gracefully removed the bottom half of her swimsuit. She stood up and once again held the fabric in front of herself, still covering what would very soon be revealed. She stepped forward, handed the thin garment to him and said, "Here's my second flag, Arlo. I guess I'm y'rs now."

Arlo pulled her to him. If this was what being on a sailboat did to him, Erlene would be happy to never again return to shore.

"Oh, Arlo," she gasped as he ran his hands over her body. "Oh, it's been so long."

"Follow me," he said. He stood up to lead her down the companionway to the cabin.

"No," she protested. "Let's stay here. Outside. Let's make love in the sunset."

Arlo spread the seat cushions on the cockpit sole and they took each other with utter abandon in the open air, concealed only by the freeboard on either side of the boat. It was absolutely the best love either of them had ever made.

₭ ₮

Jack stood behind Marilyn and put his arms around her as they stood on the deck of the Hennel's boat and watched a crimson sun sink beneath the horizon. She held her arms tight over his as they stood together. She was just the right height for him to nuzzle her hair and look over the top of her head, he thought. And it felt good to be there, with her, close to her.

"If you're looking for the 'green flash' you'll need at least three more Pina Coladas," Ron said as he came out on deck and handed them two of the drinks.

"Don't listen to him, Marilyn," Judy said as she joined them. "I've seen it, and I was drinking soda water at the time."

"I've seen it too, but the conditions aren't right tonight," Jack added.

"Well, I've seen lots of sunsets, and I've never seen a flash of green light after the sun goes below the horizon," Marilyn protested, certain they were all playing a joke on her.

"Well, maybe you weren't watching them with an expert," Jack said, holding her closer. "Besides, the only good way to see a sunset is from the deck of a boat."

"You're an expert," Marilyn said, turning her head up toward him, "and we're on a boat. So how come I didn't see it?"

"You have to be on the right boat, and ... well ... certain attire helps a lot," Jack teased. "Now, come on. Let's all get to the party before I get into trouble."

℘ ℘

Erlene lay next to Arlo on the sole of the cockpit. "We should get goin', I guess," she said reluctantly.

"Yeah, I guess we should," he agreed.

"Ya' ever do anythin' like this before, on a first date, I mean?" she asked.

"Nope. You?" he replied.

"No. An' I said I never would, neither. Y're a lot different out here, Arlo," she continued.

"What da' ya' mean?" he asked, laying on his back and looking up into the now darkening sky.

"Back on shore you're so, well . . . I mean out here, on your boat, y're kind a' in charge and everythin'. I like that."

"My old man taught me how ta' sail," Arlo said. "It's about the only good thing he taught me. A sailboat's the only placet I feel at home."

"So how come ya' work nights over on the mainland?" Erlene asked.

"Come on," Arlo replied, avoiding her question. "We better get some clothes on an' start back."

℘ ℃

Dusk brought a new world of wonder to the Bonita Key Yacht Club. When the picnic ended late in the afternoon, the staff quickly rearranged the tables around the patio. Now, crisp white linen replaced the checkered tablecloths of the afternoon. The umbrellas were gone and candles shielded by hurricane globes gave the tables the appearance of floating islands of light. The French doors were opened wide; the light from inside illuminated the outdoor dance floor, and the sweet scent of jasmine filled the night air. A full moon hung in the warm tropic sky—Judy had explained that the Summer Fling was always held on the weekend in June closest to the full moon—and as darkness fell, stars winked on to complete the picture. When the dinner ended, the band struck up "Moonlight Serenade," and Marilyn danced with Jack on what she thought might be the most perfect night of her life.

It was over all too soon, as such nights always are. Before she was aware of the hour, the bandleader announced it was time for the last dance. Jack had said they would be back at Cap'n Kelly's tonight. Now, as she danced in his arms, she wanted to think of reasons for staying. If she could have read his mind at that moment, she would have known that he was trying to think of the same thing. The music faced away and left then standing in a silent embrace on the dance floor.

"We better go," Jack said, breaking the silence.

"Do we have to?" she asked, her cheek pressed against his chest.

"It will take some time to get back," he explained.

Ron and Judy met them back at their table. "Well," Judy asked, "are you two coming to breakfast tomorrow?"

"Breakfast?" Jack inquired.

"We're inviting some friends to have breakfast on our boat in the morning. Bill will be there; won't you, Bill?"

"Wouldn't miss it for the world," Bill replied.

"I don't know," Jack hesitated, unsure of how Marilyn felt about spending the night aboard. "We really hadn't planned on staying overnight. I kind of promised Marilyn we'd be home before now."

"Jack," Ron protested, "you really wouldn't want to make that run this late at night. Why take the chance?"

Marilyn's eyes widened. "Is it dangerous?" she asked.

"Of course not," Jack answered. "It's only to the other end of the island."

"There are unmarked shoals . . ." Ron began.

". . . and sharks, of course," Bill interjected.

"Sharks!" Marilyn exclaimed.

"There aren't any sharks," Jack said firmly, looking at Bill.

"Why? Isn't that salt water?" Bill shot back.

"Well they don't attack boats!" Jack said, more firmly than before.

Bill turned to Marilyn and said, "Unless they're hungry."

"All the same," Judy said, "why go back tonight?" Ron and I have planned a fantastic breakfast, and tomorrow when you're well rested you can go back in daylight. What do you say?"

Marilyn had heard enough. "Actually, I'd prefer to stay here tonight," she said.

Jack looked at her and then back at Judy. "Okay. We'll stay," he agreed.

"See you in the morning, Buddy," Bill said as he slapped Jack on the back. "Goodnight, Sweetheart. Be happy," he added, giving Marilyn a hug before he walked off to the clubhouse and one of the guest rooms kept for visiting dignitaries like himself.

Jack and Marilyn walked to the docks with Ron and Judy. Marilyn took Jack's hand and wondered what would happen when they were alone. Little did she know that he was wondering the same thing.

"Well, goodnight guys," Judy said when they arrived at the trawler.

"Yeah, goodnight. See you in the morning," Ron added.

The current Commodore and his wife walked away, leaving Jack and Marilyn standing in a dark and awkward silence.

"I guess we better go aboard," Jack said quietly.

"Yes, I guess we'd better," Marilyn replied as he helped her onto the boat.

"Look, you don't have to . . . we don't have to stay," he explained as he turned on a small lamp in the salon. "I mean, we could go back tonight, you know."

"Do you really think that's safe?" she asked. "I'd be a lot more comfortable doing it in the daylight." She suddenly realized how that sounded and added, ". . . going back, I mean."

"Yes, well, look," Jack fumbled. "Your things are already up in the guest quarters. It's stocked with fresh towels and linen. I'll be back here in the owner's stateroom if you need anything. I guess we better go to bed . . . uh, you know, go to our rooms."

"Yes, I guess we'd better," she said softly.

Jack bent down and kissed her gently on the lips. "Well, goodnight," he said.

Marilyn fought the impulse to grab him and not let go. She knew how she felt, but she wasn't sure if he was ready: something was still holding him back. Something more might happen someday, but not now—not tonight.

"Goodnight, Jack," she whispered.

It took all of her strength to walk away, and although she didn't know it at the time, it took all of his strength to let her do it. Neither of them slept much that night. They tossed and turned and worried about how they felt—and about how the other one felt.

But they tossed and turned and worried in separate rooms.

Chapter 16

"They ain't back yet," Les Leslie said when Arlo walked past him on his way to his boat Sunday morning.

"Huh?" Arlo had other things on his mind.

"Miss Dupré an' y'r lawyer friend; they ain't back yet," Les repeated.

"The weather was good and they had plenty a' fuel," Arlo said. "They couldn't have got inta' any kind a' trouble on such a short cruise."

"That ain't the kind a' trouble I was thinkin' about."

"Huh? Don't be so old fashioned, Les."

"Old fashioned? Listen . . . I . . . an' since when did *you* get to be such a man a' the world? What happened ta' you last night?"

"Me? What d'ya' mean, what happened ta' me? An' since when did *you* become her father?"

"Whose father?" Les shot back.

"Marilyn . . . Miss Dupré. Since when did you become her father?" Arlo repeated.

"I ain't nobody's father," Les said. "I just don't like ta' see people takin' advantage a' . . . a' people, is all."

"Well, nobody says anybody's takin' advantage a' . . . anybody," Arlo retorted as he turned to walk away.

"Yeah, well nobody says they ain't," Les muttered as he returned to his work.

෩ ෬

Jack guided the trawler away from the Yacht Club dock and back into the Gulf of Mexico. It was another beautiful Florida day, the kind you want to make last as long as possible.

"How about a little cruise?" he asked Marilyn, already turning the wheel to head for open water.

"Commodore," she replied, "I'd love to take a little cruise with you."

As the sun reflected off the clear, blue water, Jack talked about the Club's many trips to Key West and places along the Gulf Coast, and Marilyn understood more than ever why Judy referred to the members as a family. These people really enjoy each other's company, she thought. And it was obvious that Jack missed them as much as they seemed to miss him.

"Has this boat ever been on one of those cruises?" she asked.

"No, it hasn't," Jack replied.

She could feel the regret in his voice. "Well, there's always next time," she said, almost comforting him.

"That's true. There always is a next time, isn't there?"

he responded. "The secret is to grab that 'next time' before your own time runs out."

"You don't have to worry about that, Jack," she said as she leaned against him. "I'm sure you have plenty of 'next times' left in you."

It was late in the afternoon before he changed course and headed for home. He teased Marilyn about getting to work on time the next day, telling her that the owners of the marina were both punctual and demanding.

As Jack guided the trawler back into the slip at Cap'n Kelly's, Marilyn thought of a time long ago when her own small family was still complete and had spent the day at the amusement park on the shore of Lake Pontchartrain. She remembered the feeling she had when the last ride ended that day. She didn't want to get out of her seat, believing—as only a child can believe—that if she could stay there, that day, that perfect day, could last forever. Mama scolded her for not being satisfied with the treat and Papa carried her home in tears. She couldn't make them understand how she felt. It wasn't about being satisfied. She didn't want that day to end; not because she wanted more, but because a deep-seated intuition made her fear what would happen to their little family when they left that magical place and returned to the real world.

Now she didn't want this magical weekend to end. She felt safe here, safe and complete again with this man who had opened his heart to her. Here she once again had been safe and warm and loved by people who cared for each other. If only every day could be like the past two, she thought, then she truly would believe in miracles.

"Give ya' a hand with your lines, Commodore?" Marilyn did not give any indication that she heard Arlo's voice. Jack put the engines into neutral and hurried down to help him with the docking lines.

"Marilyn? Marilyn are you awake?" Jack was calling to her from the deck.

"Oh, I'm sorry. I was just . . . savoring the moment."

"We're home."

"Yes, of course. I really should be going," she said as she climbed down from the bridge.

"Would you like to . . . go out to dinner or something?" he asked.

"I'd love to, but I . . . well, I promised Jennifer that I'd call her. And I have to study for my exam next month. How about another time?"

"Jack smiled at her. "I do know some better places than the Beach House," he offered.

"What's wrong with the Beach House?" she demanded with mock indignation. "It's a great place to study humanity."

There was a long pause. "Well, I really have to go," she said as she reached up on her toes and kissed him lightly. "Thanks for a wonderful time."

"We can have more wonderful times," he said.

"We *will* have more wonderful times," she replied as she broke away. She stepped off the boat and waved to him as she got into the car. He waved back and watched until she drove out of sight. It was only later, when she was on the main road, that she realized she had left her overnight bag and her clothes on the boat.

"Leave them," she said out loud to the empty car and fighting the urge to use them as an excuse to return. "Maybe it's a good omen."

֍ ֎

The telephone was ringing as Marilyn opened the door to her apartment. I'll bet it's Jack, she thought. He's going to tell me about my bag, but really he just wants to talk.

"Marilyn?" It was Jennifer's voice. "Where have you been? I've been trying to get you all day!" She sounded frightened.

"What's the matter, Jen? You sound upset."

"It's Grandma, Marilyn. She's in the hospital."

Marilyn suddenly felt sick. Why did life have to be so cruel after it had been so good? She sat down in a trance, still holding the phone to her ear.

"Marilyn? Are you still there?"

"Yes. Yes, I'm here. What happened?"

"She just got real weak this afternoon," Jennifer explained. "All of a sudden she couldn't even get up to her room. I got really scared and called for an ambulance, and they took her to Bonita Gardens Hospital. I'm here with her now."

"I'll come right over," Marilyn said.

"No, there's no need right now," Jennifer replied. "She's asleep and they want me to leave. I was just wondering if you . . . well, if you would mind staying with me at the house for a few days."

"Of course I'll stay, Jen."

"I have to meet the doctor here tomorrow morning, and . . . and, you know, I don't want to talk to him alone."

"I understand."

"It would be nice to have you there in case . . ."

"Please don't say any more, Jen. I'll meet you at the house. I'm leaving my apartment right now."

"Thanks, Marilyn."

The drive back to Calkins Harbor seemed longer than ever, especially because the drawbridge went up when she was halfway across the causeway. Jennifer was waiting on the front porch and looking very much alone when Marilyn arrived.

"I know this sounds silly but I just didn't want to go in until you got here," she said with an embarrassed look.

"It's not silly at all, Jen," Marilyn replied as she put her arms around her young friend. "How is she?"

"I don't know, Marilyn," Jennifer replied. "She was so weak and pale this morning . . . and then when she didn't give me a hard time about calling an ambulance . . . that's not like her. I'm really scared, Marilyn."

"Come one," Marilyn said. "She's in the best of hands. Let's go inside and have a cup of tea. Things will look a lot better in the morning.

෯ ଔ

"Your grandmother is a very sick woman, I'm afraid." Dr. Greenman had completed his morning rounds and was talking to Jennifer and Marilyn in the hallway outside Mrs. Calkins' room. "She's known about this for some time. I'm surprised she hasn't told you."

"Grandma is very private about some things," Jennifer explained.

"Doctor, just . . . exactly what's wrong with her?" Marilyn asked.

"About a year ago, I diagnosed her with having a form of leukemia," he said. "I've been treating her ever since although, to be honest, treatment in these cases is sometimes little more than hand-holding. There's really not much anybody can do."

"How . . . how long does she . . . does she have?" Jennifer asked.

"It's hard to say. At her age, everything slows down, including the progress of disease. She might have as long as another year."

"What can we do right now?" Marilyn sounded almost demanding.

"Well, we're going to give her a blood transfusion and keep her here for a couple of days. She'll be good as new by then, but . . . this is a progressive disease. These bouts will begin to occur more frequently. You two are going to have your hands full, I'm afraid."

The doctor left. "Listen, Jennifer," Marilyn warned before they entered the room, "no matter what happens . .

. no matter how she looks . . . we're going to be bright and cheerful in there. She knows the story and if she doesn't want to tell us, we're not going to let on that we know. Got it?"

"I've got it," Jennifer nodded. "I just hope I can do it."

Grandma Calkins looked small and frail in the hospital bed. An intravenous tube was dispensing a clear liquid from a plastic bag into a vein in her left arm, and a monitor kept track of her vital signs. She opened her eyes when the women entered the room.

"Well, my two girls," she said in a weak voice. "Have you been working on Jennifer's restaurant idea?"

"I've just about finished the preliminary sketches, Grandma," Jennifer dutifully replied.

"I plan to be there for the grand opening," she said with a weak smile. "And you, young lady," she looked at Marilyn. "How was the Summer Fling?"

Marilyn had planned to be the strong one, but her voice faltered. Finally she managed to stammer, "It was wonderful, Grandma Calkins."

"I plan to dance at your wedding," Mrs. Calkins said. "Don't disappoint me by letting him get away."

A nurse came in with a plastic bag containing a thick red liquid. "Doctor said you're down a couple of pints, Mrs. Calkins," she said cheerfully. "I'm getting you started on a fill up and then I'm going to give you a shot to make you sleep. You'll be fit as a fiddle in no time."

"Excuse me," Jennifer said. "My, uh . . . sister, Marilyn

and I planned to stay with her for the day. Can we take turns or something? In case she needs us?"

"There's no reason to, Dear," the nurse replied. "We plan to keep her knocked out for most the day. Rest is the best medicine for her right now. Why don't you two leave and come back in the morning? There's no reason to stay."

"Go take care of business at the boatyard," Mrs. Calkins added weakly. "I expect to have a progress report tomorrow . . . from both of you."

Jennifer kissed her grandmother tenderly on her forehead. "We'll be back. Now don't give these people a hard time while we're gone."

Gloom filled the car as Marilyn drove them back over the bridge to Bonita Key and Calkins Harbor. Halfway across the bridge Jennifer finally spoke.

"Let's stop home first. I want to change into jeans and a long sleeved shirt before going to the boatyard."

"Jeans and a long sleeved shirt? In this heat? What on earth for?" Marilyn said.

"I'm going to poke around that entire building." Jennifer's voice had the same sound of quiet determination Marilyn had come to associate with her grandmother. "I'm going to measure and sketch every square inch of that place. I'll give her a restaurant that will knock her socks off."

"Jennifer, be practical," Marilyn cautioned. "Something like that will cost a fortune."

"I don't care," Jennifer replied. "I'll borrow the money. I'll steal it if I have to. If it takes a crazy idea like this to keep her going one extra day, I'm going to do it. And you're going to help me, Marilyn."

It seemed that now it was time for Marilyn to take orders. "Whatever you say, Jen," she sighed.

ഏ രു

Jennifer's project kept her out of the office all morning, and Marilyn was alone with too much time to think. This was too much like losing her mother. Just when everything appeared to be going so well, life was going to kick her again. The more she thought about it, the more depressed she became. Even Jack's visit to the office didn't cheer her up.

"Grandma Calkins is in the hospital," she said as soon as he walked in.

"I'm sorry to hear that." Jack studiously avoided commenting on her use of the 'grandma' when referring to Margaret Calkins.

"She's very ill."

"Yes, I know," he replied.

"I suppose that's what she came to see you about last week."

Jack looked at her but did not reply.

"You can't discuss it, can you?"

"No. I'm sorry, but when a client asks me to keep something confidential, that's what I have to do."

"You could have at least told *me*," she insisted.

"Marilyn, you know the rules; you probably know them

better than I do. I'm sorry, I really am, but that's the way it is."

Her eyes flashed at him and she slammed books around her desk while he tried to remind her of the ethical considerations that define a lawyer's world. "Come on," he pleaded, "let me take you out to lunch."

"I'm not hungry," she said flatly. "Besides, I don't want to leave Jennifer here alone."

"I'll take you both out to lunch."

"No," she insisted. "I don't want to be away from the telephone."

"Marilyn, Grandma Calkins is going to be fine for now. This is a progressive thing. Nothing is going to happen quickly. If you really want to help Jennifer, you'll see to it that she takes care of herself. Now give me your keys. I'll get us a take-out order from the Beach House, and we can all have lunch right here on your desk if that's what you want."

"You can't drive," Marilyn reminded him.

"Of course I can drive," he replied.

"Then why do you always make me do it?"

"Never confuse the lack of activity with the lack of ability," he said, trying to make a joke that she either missed or ignored. "Now, give me your keys. I'll be back in half an hour with the best cheeseburgers on the island."

While he was gone, Marilyn called the hospital and was told that Mrs. Calkins was "resting comfortably." Jack returned with the take-out order, and Jennifer joined them around Marilyn's desk. Halfway through lunch the telephone rang. It was Doug Calkins. Marilyn reported that she had some unhappy news: his mother was in the hospital.

"Gee, that's too bad," Doug replied. "What's wrong with her?"

Marilyn was about to tell him the whole story, but a look from Jack stopped her.

"She's a little anemic," Marilyn said. "They're giving her a blood transfusion.

"Oh . . . hold on a minute." Marilyn could hear muffled voices in the background. "Junior says she'll be okay," Doug said when he came back on the line. "Anyway, I only called to tell you the fish are biting and we're going to stay out for an extra couple of weeks."

Marilyn was flabbergasted. "Your mother is in the hospital," she repeated. "Aren't the two of you coming right home?"

"Hold on again," Doug replied. Another discussion took place off the line. When he came back on, Doug said, "Junior says she'll be fine. He says if anything happens to her, my niece can take care of it. See you in a week or three. Bye."

The telephone went dead. Marilyn hung up and turned to Jennifer. "Your uncle says if anything happens, you can take care of it."

"I told you he's useless," Jennifer replied. "What made you think he would do anything?"

Marilyn turned to Jack. "I suppose you know all about that, too."

He did not reply.

℘ ☙

The next morning found Jennifer and Marilyn back at the hospital. This time a much chirpier Grandma Calkins greeted them from her hospital bed.

"Grandma, you look great!" Jennifer said in amazement.

Marilyn had to agree that the change was dramatic if not miraculous.

"The doctor said I'm fine," Mrs. Calkins said. "I just needed some blood and a little rest. Now, what do you two have to tell me? Jennifer, how are your plans progressing?"

Jennifer gave Marilyn an I-told-you-so look and proudly opened the large sketchpad she was carrying. For the next quarter of an hour she went over the current floor plan of the building, discussed where she would build a kitchen, and debated whether an indoor or outdoor stairway would provide better access to the second floor.

"And what does our financial consultant have to say?" Mrs. Calkins asked Marilyn.

"Well, I haven't done a cost analysis yet," Marilyn began. "We'll need a very large construction loan, that's for sure. I'll have to see which banks are available and what their requirements are."

Mrs. Calkins put the sketchpad down on her lap. "Jennifer, have Mr. Townsend make an appointment for the two of you to meet with Robert Meacham. He's a young lawyer in the trust department of the Bank of Bonita. Jack will know what to tell him. You and Marilyn discuss this plan with Mr. Meacham. Grandpa always did all of his business with the Bank of Bonita, and I'm certain Mr. Meacham will be able to help us get a loan. Now, Marilyn, you still haven't told us about the Summer Fling."

Marilyn was astonished by the fact that his woman who appeared to be at death's door only yesterday was still taking such an interest in life. She dutifully reported the details of her weekend at the Bonita Yacht Club and told Mrs. Calkins and Jennifer about the tragic accident that ended Jack's career.

Mrs. Calkins did not appear surprised at the story. If anything, she seemed to be more interested in Saturday night's sleeping arrangements aboard Jack's boat.

"Separate rooms!" she harrumphed. "Marilyn, how are you ever going land him if you sleep in separate rooms?"

"Grandma!" Jennifer exclaimed with a giggle, "You're embarrassing me!"

"Hush, Jennifer," her grandmother replied. "You can't appreciate this right now, but physical love is a beautiful and natural part of life. It's one of the very best gifts God gave us and we're meant to enjoy it with His blessing. Someday you'll understand." Then she turned her attention to Marilyn. "Now you listen to me, Marilyn Dupré," she said. "Jack Townsend has been badly hurt. He can't make a decision yet. He's confused by too many conflicting emotions. You'll just have to make the decision for him. Don't worry, it will turn out all right."

Marilyn took the old woman's hand in hers and said with a smile, "What do you think I should do, Grandma Calkins?"

"Invite him to your place," she said sternly. "Show him you know your way around the kitchen. Feed him. And then seduce him. But don't give in too quickly. And then when he gets you into your bedroom . . ."

"Grandma! I'm blushing!" Jennifer laughed.

"You'd better pay attention to this too, Jennifer," Mrs. Calkins continued, "before you end up old and alone like your Uncle Douglas." She turned to Marilyn and continued, "And when he gets you into your bedroom, Marilyn, you let him think it was his idea."

"How do you suggest I do that?" Marilyn asked.

"You're studying for an examination, aren't you?" Mrs. Calkins replied seriously. "Men love to show us poor women how smart they are." Her voice changed and took on a softer quality, as though she was reminiscing about a time in her own life. "Tell him you need help with your homework. You'll need to sit real close, of course, because you'll be looking at the same book. Lean over and brush against him. Let him smell your perfume. He won't be able to resist for long. Tougher men than Jack Townsend have fallen. Believe me, I know."

Chapter 17

Marilyn would not have given Grandma's advice any serious thought except for two unusual incidents. The first one was their meeting with Mr. Meacham the very next day. Although Jennifer saw nothing unusual in the fact, Marilyn was surprised they were able to get an appointment on short notice. Apparently the name "Calkins" opened many doors in this part of Florida.

Robert Meacham turned out to be the youngest member of the bank's Trust Department. He had the chiseled good looks and cleft chin of a male model, complemented by hazel eyes and dark hair. His *de rigueur* blue pinstripe suit hung gracefully on his tall, lean frame. In all, he looked more like a young actor playing the part of a lawyer than a lawyer in real life.

"Miss Calkins?" he asked as he looked back and forth between Jennifer and Marilyn in the waiting room.

"Uh, well, that's me . . . I guess," Jennifer stammered.

"I'm so glad to meet you," he said, extending his hand. "Your grandmother told me so much about you."

"Oh ... thank you, I guess," Jennifer replied. "This is my ... uh, sister, Marilyn Dupré."

"This is a double pleasure," Meacham replied. "Your grandmother didn't tell me she had two beautiful granddaughters."

"I'm more like a step-sister," Marilyn explained, taking his hand.

"Well, why don't both of you come into my office where we can talk?" he said.

He led them to a small and rather Spartan office. The room was furnished with a standard, nondescript desk, a swivel desk chair and two matching guest chairs. A certificate on the wall announced that Robert Joseph Meacham had recently been admitted to the Florida Bar. Next to it hung a black-and-white news photograph of a football player lying flat on his back while older men examined him and other players stood around. The only other personal item in the office was an ornate brass desk lamp with a green glass shade.

"That's me, after I got flattened in a Gators game," Meacham explained when he saw Jennifer examining the photograph. "I keep it there to remind me that no matter how bad things get around here, nobody's ever flattened me like that."

Somehow that picture hurt Jennifer more than it hurt him and she turned away from it. "What a lovely lamp," she said, changing the subject as she took a seat in front of the desk.

"Thanks," he replied. "It was a gift from my parents. They gave it to me when I passed the bar exam. My Dad always says it was all they could afford after putting me through college and law school."

"Are you an only child?" Jennifer asked.

"Yes, as a matter of fact, I am," he replied with a quizzical look.

"Isn't that interesting? So am I," she replied. "But I always wanted to have a big family. Don't you?"

"Yes, I would. I've always thought that kids from big families have an advantage growing up."

"I'll bet your parents call you R.J.," she said a little dreamily.

"My Dad does when my Mom's not around. She prefers 'Robert,'" he said.

"Well I think 'R.J.' is cuter ... and sexier," she added, with a wink. "I'll just have to be careful around your mother."

There was no possible comeback to that, and conversation died while the two looked at each other for a long moment. Marilyn was beginning to feel like an intruder on someone's first date. She cleared her throat and tried to get back to the purpose of their meeting.

"Mr. Meacham we're here because Grandma . . . Mrs. Calkins . . . told us to see you about a loan, although I don't understand why we're talking to you instead of a loan officer."

Marilyn's statement seemed to bring everyone back to reality—at least for the time being.

"Oh, yes," Meacham replied, "Well, Mrs. Calkins asked me to handle all phases of her account personally. Now, what kind of loan are we talking about?"

"Marilyn and I are remodeling my grandfather's boatyard . . . that is, the main building at the boatyard," Jennifer said. Her blue eyes began to flash with the same excitement they showed whenever she talked about her idea. "We're going to put a restaurant on the second floor, and completely re-do the first floor."

"I see," Meacham said with a smile. "And how much money are we talking about?"

"We don't know yet," Marilyn answered, "but I wouldn't be surprised if it's over a hundred thousand dollars."

"I wouldn't be surprised if it's going to be two or three times that amount," Meacham replied. He looked at Jennifer, chuckled and said, "It shouldn't be a problem."

"Wait a minute," Marilyn said incredulously, "Are you telling me this bank would be willing to lend us two or three hundred thousand dollars to build a restaurant in a building you haven't seen, with no financial statements and no income projections?"

Meacham recovered himself and became a bank lawyer again. "Well, naturally, we'd need a mortgage on the building as collateral. Of course we would have to iron out all of the details."

"Well . . . R.J. . . . ." Jennifer said, "why don't you come over to my grandmother's house some evening so we can do a little ironing?"

"I'd like that," he replied, losing his bank lawyer face again. "When?"

"Well, my grandmother's in the hospital right now . . ."

"I'm so sorry to hear that," he interjected with genuine concern in his voice and on his face.

"Thank you," Jennifer said softly. "I'm sure she'll be fine. Why don't I give you a call later this week? She should be home by then."

"I'll be looking forward to it," he said as he stood up to show them to the door.

"Goodbye, R.J.," Jennifer said taking his hand and looking directly into his eyes. "I hope to see you soon."

"I'm counting on it . . . Jennifer," he replied as he slowly let go of her hand and opened his office door.

They were safely in the car and on their way to the marina before Marilyn spoke. "Jennifer, what's gotten into you?" she exclaimed. "You can't tell a complete stranger his initials are 'sexy'."

"Why not? God, what a hunk!"

"Well there's something funny going on here," Marilyn said.

"Who cares?" replied Jennifer.

"Will you be serious for a minute?"

"I *am* being serious. Did you see that chin? Can you imagine sticking your tongue in that dimple? I'll bet that would drive him crazy!"

"Jennifer! Settle down and be serious for a minute." Marilyn exclaimed.

"Come on, Marilyn! Lighten up! What's the big problem?"

"The big problem is that bankers don't go around handing out loans for hundreds of thousands of dollars to people they don't even know."

"Why not? We'll pay them back. Besides, they haven't handed us anything yet. So far it's just a lot of talk."

"Jennifer, bankers don't even talk to most people about things like that," Marilyn replied.

ℰ ℭℬ

The other unusual incident happened on the day Grandma Calkins was scheduled to return home. On their way to the hospital, Marilyn stopped by the office of Walker & Grant to check her mail. Fred Walker, the senior partner, was just arriving and met her in the hall outside Theo Grant's door. "Well, Marilyn," he said, "is Mrs. Calkins giving you back to us? Theo could really use some help around here."

"He could? But it was Mr. Grant's idea for me to . . ."

Just then Theo stepped out of his office. "Fred, may I see you for a moment . . . in private?" he asked his senior partner. He acted as if he had just noticed Marilyn and added, "Oh, hi, Marilyn. You're doing a great job. Keep up the good work!"

"Mr. Grant," she replied, "is there something going on here that I should know about?"

"Know about?" Theo said. "No, of course not. You're doing a great job, just great. Mr. Walker and I need to discuss a private matter, don't we Fred?"

"If you need my help around here, why . . ."

"I'd love to chat, but Mr. Walker and I really need to straighten out a few things," Theo said abruptly. He put his arm around the older man and ushered him into his office. "You're doing a great job, Marilyn," he said over his shoulder. "Just great. Keep up the good work," he added as he closed the door.

Jennifer was waiting in the car.

"You know, Jen," Marilyn began as she started the engine, "something is just too pat around here. Me working at the marina, being paid to do nothing, and now you being told to talk to that young trust officer about a loan. I think I see Grandma's hand in all of this."

"Oh, Marilyn, relax," Jennifer replied. "You have to learn to take life as it comes. Why, just yesterday R.J. was telling me about . . ."

"R.J.? Yesterday?" Marilyn interrupted. "You mean Mr. Meacham? What were you doing with him yesterday?"

"We had lunch together," Jennifer replied with the forthright innocence that marked most of her conversations. "He really is a hunk, isn't he? And he's smart, too. He graduated *magna cum laude* from law school. He's always wanted to be a trial lawyer, but one of his professors convinced him to spend some time doing trust and estate work. He's only working at the bank until something better comes along."

"You learned all that over lunch?"

"Well, sure. We had to talk. I mean, we couldn't just sit at the Yacht Club like dummies."

"He belongs to the Club, too?"

"No, of course not. Not yet, anyway. I took him there. Grandpa was a member, you know, and I'm his grand-daughter after all. Besides, no one seemed to mind. Mr. DePasquale gave us one of the best tables in the Members' Dining Room."

Marilyn marveled at how much her mannerisms reflected those of her grandmother. She had the same direct, forthright approach and the same iron determination. Perhaps Jennifer's only flaw was a certain naïveté when it came to money and social position. Not that she was a snob—she was far from it. She simply did not pay attention to those things. It would never occur to her that the people at the Yacht Club might not welcome every granddaughter of every deceased member. Jennifer just assumed doors would open for her. And in her case, she was right.

Marilyn said no more until they arrived at the hospital. "Jen, why don't you go to the business office and take care of whatever needs to be signed. I'll go upstairs and make sure Grandma is ready to leave."

Mrs. Calkins was dressed and sitting in a chair. She greeted Marilyn warmly and asked about her "other granddaughter."

"Jen is downstairs getting your release papers. She'll be right up." Marilyn realized she would not have much time alone with the older woman, and got right to the point.

"Grandma Calkins, may I ask you a question?"

"Certainly, Love."

"No, I mean, will you give me a real answer?"

Mrs. Calkins studied her face carefully. "What is on your mind, Marilyn?"

"Walker and Grant haven't been paying my salary these past weeks, you have. And you've also been paying them to allow me to stay at the boatyard, right?"

"Yes, Dear, I have. How did you know?"

"I didn't know for sure. It' s an old lawyer's trick Jack taught me. Why have you been doing it?"

"That's another question, Dear. I only agreed to answer one."

"Was it to bring Jack and me together?" Marilyn persisted.

Mrs. Calkins took her hand and looked into her eyes. "Very well, I'll answer your question if you answer mine first. Do you love him?"

"Yes," Marilyn said softly, "more than anything. I guess I've been in love with him since the first time I met him."

"I knew it!" Mrs. Calkins said triumphantly. "That day when we met in Fred Walker's office; it wasn't a coincidence, you know." She looked deep into Marilyn's eyes and said, "Marilyn, there are no coincidences. I had been searching for you, and I found you. As soon as I saw you I said to myself, 'There's the girl for my Jack.' And then that morning in my kitchen, I told you that you had hooked him, but I could see in your eyes that you had hooked yourself as well."

"Why do you care for him so much?" Marilyn asked.

Mrs. Calkins smiled and patted her hand. "My Dear, now you're asking too many questions." It seemed as though she was about to close the privacy curtain she had closed so often and so effectively, but this time she hesitated. "No, perhaps it's time," she said. "Tonight, after supper, when the time is right. I'll answer all your questions then. Hush, now, Jennifer is coming."

୨୦ ଓୣ

Evening found the three women sitting around the dining room table of the Magnolia Avenue home. When the dishes were cleared, Mrs. Calkins asked Jennifer to get her a glass of sherry, and suggested that she and Marilyn have some too.

Marilyn knew this would not be an ordinary conversation, and in a way she wished she had not caused it by asking so many questions. Maybe it *was* better to accept life without questioning it, but she had to know what it meant and where she fit into all of it. Only one person in the room seemed to have at least some of the answers.

"It's time for you to know the truth, Jennifer," Mrs. Calkins began, "and this concerns Marilyn too, in a way." She put down her sherry and leaned back as she told her story.

"Many years ago, I was a beautiful and strong-willed young girl in Biloxi, Mississippi. My father, Travis Scott, was the town physician. There's where your middle name comes from, Jennifer. You mother insisted on it as a courtesy to me. She was a good woman, Jennifer. Don't ever let your father tell you otherwise.

"One day, shortly after my seventeenth birthday," she continued, "a young widower came to town with two little boys. His name was Kelly Calkins. He had served in the Navy during the Great War . . . World War I as you call it . . . and he came to our town to start a new life for himself and his boys after his wife died. It was 1935 . . . the depths of the Depression . . . and jobs were hard to come by, but, because he was a veteran and a widower, the owners of the shipyard took pity on him and hired him. Oh, he was a dashing man, tall and straight as a ramrod. I believe he was what you would call a hunk, Jennifer," she said with a smile at her granddaughter.

"Many of the women in the town had their sights set on him. They didn't consider me any competition, of course, because I was just a child and he was twice my age. But I knew from the minute I laid eyes on him that I would be his and he would be mine someday.

"I told him that I needed something to do after school, and I offered to look after the two boys while he worked at the shipyard and escorted some of the single ladies around town. Oh, it hurt me to see that, but I had a plan and the more he dated others, the more useful I made myself around the house. I even cooked dinner for him once or twice, Marilyn," she said with a knowing look.

"One night, I asked him to help me with my homework. The boys were asleep in their room. I sat next to Casey on the couch and pressed myself against him, so that we could read out of the same book. He was explaining an algebra equation, and I turned to ask him a question. Our lips were only inches apart, and . . . and he kissed me. I had never before been kissed by a man and it felt like a thousand skyrockets going off inside my head all at once.

"He tried to avoid me after that, but I wouldn't let him. I kept after him, and let nature take its course. It wasn't long before we became lovers." Mrs. Calkins took a sip of her sherry while Jennifer and Marilyn sat in rapt attention.

"Soon I discovered I was in a family way, as they used to say in those days," she continued. "My father would have killed him if he found out . . . killed him and sent me to a home, most likely. Well, he didn't find out until it was too late. Casey scraped together all the money he could beg, borrow or steal and bought that old shrimp boat that sits at the boatyard today. We ran away on it with the two boys and were married here in Florida. I'm told it was a pretty scandal we left behind in Biloxi. I wrote to Father after it was all over, but he disowned me. Well, I didn't care because I was so crazy in love with your grandfather.

"Six months later my little Abigail was born, right on that boat. It was a difficult delivery. There was no doctor in town then, and I only had one of the local women to help me. I suffered terribly, but I didn't care about that either, because I had my little girl and your grandfather at my side."

Mrs. Calkins hand shook slightly as she once again raised the glass to her lips. "But the Good Lord took little Abby from us before the end of her first year. I took it hard, and your grandfather took it even harder. The worst part was that I had been told because of problems during the delivery, I could never again bear children.

"They tell me Father was devastated when he got the news. He blamed himself, you see. He said that if he had been here to take care of me, it would not have happened. I was his only child, and now he blamed himself for not being able to have grandchildren of his own. He came down to see us afterwards and we reconciled. Eventually, it was his money that allowed Casey to make many real estate investments in this area. Most of those investments, Jennifer, will be yours someday.

"This is where you come into the story, Jennifer . . . and you, too, in a way, Marilyn," she added. "You remember, of course, Jennifer, how you came to live with us. As far as I was concerned, the Good Lord had given me back my little girl, and I was complete again. Then your father returned and wanted you back. I wouldn't hear of it, and your grandfather wouldn't hear of it either. You were the apple of his eye. He swore that no power on earth would take you away from us.

"Every lawyer in town told him the case was hopeless. Grandparents just didn't get custody away from natural parents. Every lawyer in town, that is, except one . . . John Townsend."

"Jack had recently left the prosecutor's office where he had made quite a name for himself. More importantly, he had a strong sense of right and wrong. He kept saying it wasn't right for your father to treat us like some kind of orphanage where he could leave you and pick you up whenever it happened to suit his fancy. Unfortunately, Jack couldn't get a judge to agree. We lost, appealed and lost again. We were served with papers for contempt of court . . . oh, it was terrible, but we wouldn't let you go. Jack fought and fought and fought, but finally he told Grandpa the only way we could keep you was if we made some kind of deal with your father.

"Grandpa and Jack had a terrible row over that idea. Grandpa said he'd see Junior in Hell first. He said he and his friends would take your father out on the *Margaret*, wrap him in anchor chain and throw him overboard . . . and I believe he would have too. Captain Kelly Calkins feared no one, and he had some rough and ready friends from the old days who would have followed him to the mouth of Hades if he asked them."

Mrs. Calkins took another sip of sherry. "Well, Jack just shouted Grandpa down and told him he would end up in prison and never see you . . . or me . . . again. When they finally calmed down, Jack called your father's lawyer and made a proposal. Grandpa would take your father back at the boatyard and give him exactly what he gave his brother Douglas . . . your father always claimed Grandpa loved Douglas best. The two boys would manage the boatyard. They would share equally in Grandpa's estate and would never have to worry about money. In return, your father would give up all claim to you, and you would stay with us."

"When it was all over, Grandpa told me that Jack Townsend was the only man who ever stood up to him, and he was glad he did. The two of them became very close. I suspect Grandpa saw in Jack the son he wished he had." Mrs. Calkins turned to Marilyn and added, "I often think Jack wouldn't have left Bonita and gotten off his path if Casey had lived. I'm quite sure Casey would have won that argument. Now do you understand, Marilyn?"

"I understand that my father traded me for a lifetime of easy money," Jennifer said bitterly.

Marilyn put her arm around the younger woman to console her. "There's another way of looking at it, Jen," she said.

"I can't imagine how," Jennifer responded.

"Your grandparents loved you so much they wouldn't stop fighting for you, no matter what the cost."

Jennifer looked at her grandmother. "But Grandma, if you met Grandpa after my father and Uncle Doug were born, then you're not . . ."

"Jennifer, I am and always will be your grandmother," Mrs. Calkins replied. "We are who we are in spite of the accidents of birth, not because of them."

Marilyn at last understood why Grandma brought her and Jack Townsend together. "Each of us has a purpose in this life. We all have tasks to perform, don't we?" she asked.

"Yes, Love, we do," Mrs. Calkins replied. "And it all comes together if you simply have faith and wait long enough."

Chapter 18

"Have you been avoiding me?" Jack asked when he finally trapped Marilyn in her office Friday morning.

"Oh, Jack, I'm sorry," she said. "I've been so busy with Grandma and Jennifer. No, of course I'm not avoiding you."

"Prove it. Have dinner with me tonight."

"I'd love to have dinner with you tonight . . ." she began, and then caught herself in mid-sentence, ". . . but I have to study."

"You're kidding," he replied.

"No, I'm not," she said as innocently as she could. "The bar exam is next month, and taking care of Grandma and Jen has put me way behind. I'm having a lot of trouble with some basic concepts: you know, agency, partnership, that sort of thing. I'm really lost."

Jack held her by the shoulders and looked at her. "You *are* kidding, right?"

"No, I'm *not* kidding," she insisted. "You yourself said it's the most important thing in my life right now."

"So you're going to stay home on a Friday night and study."

"I'm going stay home and study. If you really want to help, you can come over and tutor me."

"Now there's an idea," he said with a mischievous grin. "I'll bet there are a few things I could teach you."

"Don't get smart," she replied. "I'll make us a quick dinner and you can start by explaining the difference between a general partnership and a limited partnership."

"When you pass this exam, what's in it for me?"

"*If* I pass the exam, we'll talk. I'm sure we'll be able to work out something," she smiled.

"Miss Dupré," he said, adopting a professorial tone, "that is an 'agreement to agree.' It's completely unenforceable." Then he smiled and added, "But I'll take the chance. You have hired yourself a tutor." He turned and headed for the door. "I'll meet you here at five o'clock," he said as he headed out the door.

Jack was barely out of the office before Marilyn was on the telephone with Jennifer.

"Jen, I won't be coming home tonight," she began.

"What's up, Marilyn?"

"Jack is coming over to my apartment to help me with my homework."

"Are you going to let nature take its course?"

"I'm not going to stop it if it does. But right now I have to go shopping and then run to my place to get dinner ready and freshen up."

"What's on the menu . . . besides you, I mean?"

"Jennifer, stop," Marilyn said, and then added, "I don't know. It has to be something memorable that I can prepare this afternoon and then just pop into the oven when he's there. That way I can look like 'Little Suzy Homemaker' without spending all night in the kitchen."

"Sounds pretty complicated," Jennifer replied. "Well, good luck, Sis." Then she added in a little sing-song voice, "Call me in the morning."

Jennifer's quip about calling in the morning gave Marilyn a momentary queasy feeling. She suddenly realized that she was planning—really planning—to get Jack into her bed. Tonight! It wasn't that she was opposed to the idea, it was just that this was so . . . premeditated. Well, she thought, I don't have time to think about that now. I've got to shop, get home, prepare dinner, shower and then get back here and pretend I've been slaving away in the office all day. Jack Townsend, I hope you're worth the trouble!

                                       ℘ ☙

Jennifer too was busy. As soon as Marilyn hung up, she called the Bank of Bonita and asked for Mr. Meacham in the trust department.

"Hello, R.J.?" she began. "This is Jennifer."

"It could only be you or my Dad," he said with a laugh.

"I was wondering, could you stop by tonight and talk to Grandma and me about ironing out those details? If you don't have any other plans, I mean."

"No, I don't have any other plans . . . at least nothing that can't be changed," he replied. "What time would be convenient?"

"Well, we usually have dinner around six. Why don't you join us? It'll just be Grandma and me; Marilyn is off on a project of her own."

"I wouldn't want to impose," the young man said.

"Oh, it's no bother. I'm just going to throw together some leftovers."

"If you're sure it won't be any trouble . . ."

"No," Jennifer assured him, "no trouble at all."

"Well, then, I guess I'll see you at six o'clock."

Jennifer hung up the phone and thought, now what the heck am I going to "throw together?"

೫ ೪

Jack appeared in Marilyn's office promptly at five with flowers and a bag containing two bottles of cold champagne.

"Going somewhere special?" she asked jokingly.

"My mother told me never to go to a lady's house empty-handed."

"Was that your mother's advice or your father's?"

"Come to think of it, maybe it *was* my father," he replied.

"The flowers are lovely," she said, taking them from him. "What's in the bag?" she asked, peeking inside.

"Just a little something to go with dinner," he said as he tried to prevent her from looking.

"Champagne? Jack! We're going to be studying, remember?"

"Champagne is just wine with bubbles in it. Besides, it's the best way to study."

"Oh, sure. Study what?"

"Now, look," he replied, leading her to the door and turning off the lights, "which one of us is the teacher?"

ऌ ल

Jennifer spent the afternoon surrounded by cookbooks. She intended to have more than "leftovers" waiting for the man Grandma called "young Mr. Meacham." She finally settled on a menu of Cornish game hens, with fresh bread, vegetables, salad and apple pie for dessert, figuring even someone with her limited experience probably could not botch baking three small chickens. Unfortunately, the fresh bread came from the bakery and the vegetables and pie were frozen. She carefully tore up the wrappers and boxes and hid them in the trash before she started on the salad. She knew how to make a salad. She also knew that Grandma might not approve of her shortcuts, but counted on her to keep mum.

For his part, "young Mr. Meacham" was a perfect gentleman. He complimented Jennifer on everything, declaring it to be the best dinner he ever had. He appeared to be immensely interested in her school and encouraged the idea of pursuing a post-graduate degree, suggesting areas of study that might interest her. Finally, after Jennifer served the pie and poured the tea, Grandma brought the conversation around to the purpose of his visit.

"Well, now, R.J.," she said, adopting Jennifer's pet name for him, "Jennifer tells me that we might be able to iron out the details for a loan for her. You'll want a mortgage on the building, of course."

"Certainly," he replied.

"I'd prefer if my sons were kept in the dark about this for the present, so I won't deed the building to Jennifer."

"Whatever you say," he agreed.

"I'll have Jack Townsend set up a corporation, using himself as the incorporator. I'll deed it to the corporation, and after the official papers are filed, Jack can turn the shares over to Jennifer and Marilyn who will own them equally. Is that all right with you, Dear?" she asked Jennifer.

"Of course, Grandma, if that's what you want."

"You two make such a lovely team. I'd like her to be involved in this, and I'm sure she won't mind."

"Now then, R.J.," Mrs. Calkins continued, turning toward the young man, "the Bank can loan the money to the corporation, and the corporation in turn will give a note and mortgage to the Bank. I, of course, will guarantee the note personally."

"With your personal guarantee, I'm sure there will be no problem, Ma'am," R.J. said.

"Do you understand all of this, Jennifer?" her grandmother asked. "Once the papers are signed, if you and Marilyn don't follow through, I shall be personally responsible for this enormous sum of money. We could lose the boatyard, this house, everything."

Jennifer swallowed hard. "I understand, Grandma," she nodded.

"By the same token, Mr. Meacham and I think you have a wonderful idea. Don't we R.J.?"

Meacham nodded his agreement.

"So I don't want you to get cold feet and give it up. I plan to be here for the grand opening," Mrs. Calkins repeated.

"I understand, Grandma," Jennifer said again.

"Good. Now that it's settled, I think you young people should go out to a movie. What's playing at the Rivoli tonight?"

"Another 'oldie' . . . 'Key Largo'," Jennifer said.

"Bogart *and* Bacall," Mrs. Calkins responded. "You can't miss that. Now hurry along, the dishes can wait."

"Is she always that direct?" R.J. asked when they were out on the porch.

"Grandma knows what she wants and she goes after it," Jennifer replied. Then she added, too softly for him to hear, "and I'm a lot like her."

∞ ∞

Back at her apartment, Marilyn and Jack shared a bottle of champagne in her small kitchen while she prepared Trout Meuniere. "You're going to love this," she promised. "It's a real New Orleans recipe."

She had a delightful way of pronouncing "New Orleans." It wasn't the typical "N'awlins" of Southern drawl, but it wasn't "Noo Orleans" either. It was somewhere in between, kind of like, NewOrleans,' two words with barely a pause separating them: the pronunciation of a Creole girl who went off to a convent school to learn proper English and never got it quite right. On her lips, the sound was devastating. He also noticed that halfway through her second glass of champagne, the pause between the "New" and the "Orleans" got perceptibly shorter. He had once heard the true South Louisiana accent described as "honey dripping off a log." He wondered how much more champagne it would take to get Marilyn to that point, and what other charms she might reveal when she got there.

Marilyn transferred the dinner to two plates and Jack carried them to the glass-topped dining table where salad, rolls, and the second bottle of champagne were waiting. They sat across from each other, and her dark eyes sparkled as they dined and she talked about her childhood.

"I was Papa's girl when Mama was alive. I loved living in the French Quarter . . . especially at Mardi Gras when the parades would come by. I'd dress up in my costume and mask that Papa bought for me, and Papa and Mama would take me up to Rampart Street near the Auditorium. Pretty soon we'd see the flames in the distance, and then the riders would come by on their horses, wearing their brocaded costumes and masks like silk hoods over their faces, and they'd throw us coins from their saddlebags."

"After that the flambeaux would come, all smoky and dripping while the boys danced their way down the street. Then, finally, would come a float, all in gold and green and purple. And the people on it would throw us beads and more coins as they passed. Then came a band, always a band,

and more flambeaux and riders and another float." Her dark eyes were alive and flashing as she finished her champagne and added, "It was so exciting, especially for a little girl."

Jack refilled her glass and imagined her in those happy days, filled with the joy and exuberance of youth. He fell more deeply in love with her as the minutes passed. Only this time it was different; this time he did not try to stop himself. Whatever happened here tonight, there would be no running away from it.

She suddenly changed the topic. "Would you like to help me make Bananas Foster for dessert?"

Jack hadn't been thinking about dessert, or bananas or Mr. Foster—whoever he might be—and her offer caught him off guard. "Sure," he said gamely, "just tell me what to do."

He followed her back into the small kitchen. "The secret to Bananas Foster is to have the ingredients at just the right temperature before you add the rum for the flambé. Now you stand behind me with this long handled match, and when I tell you, light it and touch it to the pan, okay?"

He stood behind her, match at the ready, drinking in the intoxicating fragrance of her hair while she worked on her creation. "Now get ready," she said as she lifted the pan from the stove and poured in the rum.

"Do you always burn everything you cook?" he quipped.

"She looked back at him over her shoulder, her eyes dark as an unexplored Louisiana bayou on a moonless night. "I guess I just like settin' things on fahr," she breathed.

The line caught him completely off guard. It should have been his cue to kiss her, even at the cost of burning down the apartment, but before he could react she turned away and he was left holding a lighted match.

"Okay," she said, "just touch the flame to the pan." He did and the caramelized sugar and rum burst into a blue flame. "That's great; that's just perfect," she said as she stirred the ingredients. "This is going to be wonderful."

Jack blew out the match. He wanted to move her hair aside and begin kissing her neck right behind her ear but, once again, she was a step ahead of him.

"Now, just put a scoop of vanilla ice cream in each of those dessert glasses," she instructed, "and I'll add the bananas and the topping."

He wanted to shout, "To hell with the bananas! To hell with the topping! Let's just smear the vanilla ice cream on you and I'll lick it off!" but she appeared so intensely interested in what she was doing that he began to wonder if he had misread her signals. He quietly scooped the ice cream into the glasses.

"Doesn't it look wonderful?" she asked as she ladled the hot, rich mixture over the cold ice cream.

"Fabulous," he replied, not sure any more what his response was supposed to be.

"Come on, we have to eat these before the ice cream melts."

"Wouldn't want anything to melt," he replied, a little dejectedly as he followed her back to their places at the table.

She drank the champagne Jack had poured earlier while she dug into the dessert. "Bananas Foster is a N'awlins specialty," she said with a much more noticeable drawl.

Bingo! 'LaFayette, we are here!' Jack thought. "Would you care for a little more champagne?" he asked, moving to refill her glass.

Her brow furrowed momentarily. "Jack Townsend, ahr you tryin' to get me drunk?" The drawl was definitely a lot thicker. Not honey on a log yet, but clearly getting there.

"No! Certainly not! Of course not," he protested. "How can you say such a thing?"

"Well, ma'be just a touch," she grinned as he filled her glass to the brim. "But, r'member, we have a lot a' work ta' do tonight."

"We certainly do. Some of us more than others," he replied. I hope to be doing most of it, he thought. "So, tell me more about the flame boys."

"The who?" she asked, sipping from the full glass.

"The flame bo's," he said, attempting to mimic her delicious newly-uncovered accent. "The guys walking with the torches."

This time she giggled harder. "That's 'flambeaux,' silly! It's French. It means 'torches'."

"Oh, well, what do you call the guys carrying them?"

"She took another sip of champagne. "Ah don't know. Flambeaux boys, Ah guess." He had never seen this side of her personality and he was completely captivated by her. "Anyway, the torches aren't j'st any old torches. They have a kind of curvy cross-ahrm with four lamps. And they boys carrin' them don't just walk, they *dance* down the street. An' sometahms the fuel spills out an' little patches of fahr hit the street." She finished the dessert and the champagne and stretched, cat-like. Above her waist, Marilyn is what the ladies' magazines politely describe as being "full-figured," and what men impolitely describe as being "stacked." At the moment, that full figure was being thrust across the table at Jack and he found it difficult to think of anything else. She stood up and pushed in her chair. "Well, tahm to get to work, Ah guess. My books are in the livin' room."

Wait a minute, he thought, what's going on here? Why is she talking about her books? Maybe I *have* misread her signals. After all, I've been out of circulation for a long time. Maybe she doesn't realize what she's doing to me. Sure, right, the other half of his brain responded. And Hitler didn't realize what he was doing to Poland, either. It was all just a little misunderstanding.

"Well, let's get started," he said as he carried the remaining champagne and two glasses into the living room.

"Hey, Ah have to have a clear head for this," she said, referring to the homework.

"You do, but I don't. I already passed this exam, remember? Now where shall we begin?"

Marilyn sat next to him on the couch, took off her shoes and tucked up her legs. It was a position that left no room between their bodies. He was forced to put his arm behind her in order to get comfortable.

"Ah find this really confusing," she began as she opened one of the books to a bookmark. "If you and Ah ahr partners in a business, and Ah do somethin' really crazy, like buy an airplane or somethin', why should you be stuck payin' for it?"

Jack had been studying her profile and missed the question. "Excuse me?" he asked.

Marilyn appeared not to notice his distraction. As she leaned forward to point out the example in the book, she pressed herself into his side. "See, right here," she said, pointing to a particular paragraph while her hair bushed his cheek. "It says that each general partner is completely responsible for the actions of the other."

Her perfume was seductive. Jack found that he was having a great deal of difficulty resisting her. At the moment he wanted very much to nibble her ear.

"Ahr you listenin' to me?" she asked, turning toward him and looking directly into his eyes.

"What? Of course," he replied.

"Well?"

"Well, what?"

"You're not payin' attention," she said. At the moment he *was* paying attention. He was paying a whole lot of attention to the soft yet firm body that was pressed against his own. She pulled away from him momentarily and arched her back to stretch again. The movement thrust her breasts forward against the thin restraining fabric of her blouse. Jack found himself wondering if she was wearing a bra.

He needed to unbutton that blouse and kiss those breasts as soon as possible.

"Ah knew this was goin' to be a waste of tahm," she yawned.

"No, look," he said, suddenly afraid she might get up and end the evening. His eyes fell on one particular paragraph, so he pointed to it to draw her back close to him. "Right here, they talk about reliance by the public."

She pressed against his body again. "Why should the public care about what we do?" she asked in a voice that made him think she was no longer talking about legal concepts.

Jack gulped the champagne in his glass. "It's the nature of a partnership," he began, wondering if he should continue to fight the temptation he was feeling. Was she toying with him? It all seemed so clear until she starting talking about her damn books. What was next, snuggling over the Restatement of Contracts? He took a deep breath and tried again. "If we hold ourselves out as partners, then the public has a right to rely on that representation."

She turned and faced him again. "But should each of us be completely responsible for the other?" she asked softly.

"Completely," he said with his lips too close to hers. It was no use. Her mouth was just too tempting.

"That's a lot of responsibility," she whispered.

Their lips finally met. He had kissed them before—"goodnight" on the boat, "goodbye" when she left the next day—but this was not that kind of kiss. This was the kind of kiss that made people like Grandma talk about a thousand skyrockets going off.

Jack finally released her lips. He began to trace his way down her neck, and the book fell to the floor. She sighed his name softly as he worked his way back up her throat and crushed his mouth to hers once more. Part of his brain was surprised to find that she was now lying across his lap in his arms and wondered how she got that way. The rest of his brain didn't care and told him it didn't matter. She offered no resistance when he moved her around and laid her on the couch. He knelt on the floor next to her and continued to kiss her. Before long, he began to unbutton her blouse and caress the breasts that she had kept just out of his reach all evening. "You're beautiful," he murmured as he kissed her body. He carefully nibbled her exposed flesh and began to remove her skirt. Soon she lay nude before him on the couch. "Not here," she said softly, stopping his progress. "Let's go in the other room where we can take our time."

Standing next to him in her bedroom, Marilyn became the aggressor and performed the same ritual on Jack, slowly undressing him—feasting on him with her eyes and tongue.

"I love you, Jack Townsend," she said.

"I love you, Marilyn Dupré," he responded, holding her close.

Jack had not made love to a woman in a very long time, and the loneliness and despair of the last two years melted away in a torrent of desire. Once more he took command, gently pushing her down and pinning her beneath him on the bed. "I'm going to make you very happy," she said to him as their bodies intertwined and they merged into bliss.

☙ ❧

Late that night, Jennifer and R.J. walked up the brick footpath to the front door of the Magnolia Avenue house.

"I had a wonderful time tonight," she said, as she held his hand. "I hope going to the movies on such short notice wasn't any trouble."

"Jennifer," he replied, "I don't think anything you do could be any trouble for me."

"R.J., do you . . . well, do you sort of believe in fate?"

"I don't know," he said. "I guess I never thought much about it."

"Grandma says that when you're on the right path, doors open in front of you. Do you think that's true?"

"Your grandmother seems to know an awful lot, that's for sure," he said as they arrived at the door.

"Would you like to come in for some coffee or tea . . . or anything?" she asked.

"It's pretty late. I'd better be going."

They stood facing each other in the warm night air. R.J. hesitated for a moment, and then gently kissed her.

"Goodnight, Jennifer," he said.

"Goodnight," she replied, as she watched him walk to his car.

Chapter 19

Early the next morning, Marilyn slipped out of bed into a short silk robe. She felt a strong need to make breakfast and, even though it was contrary to everything she ever said about being a professional woman, she decided to do it.

I must be crazy, she thought as she padded around the kitchen in her bare feet. After all those late-night pizza discussions in the dorm, here I am doing exactly what I said I'd never do—cooking a 'morning after' breakfast for a man. And I'm enjoying it. I can't believe this is happening to me. She smiled and whispered, "Well it *is* happening to me, girls. Finally! So stuff it!"

She wondered briefly about Nick, back in Baton Rouge. She had never felt this way about him—not even at the beginning. She also wondered about Jack's wife, about the nights she must have spent in his arms, and what she did the next morning. She wondered, too, about whether she might someday become "the second Mrs. Townsend." She did not like the sound of that—the "second." No, she thought, I'm not going to think about her. That was another lifetime, and it's over. This is a new one. Whatever happens will happen between Jack and me. I won't spend the rest of my life fighting with a ghost.

ഔ ൟ

Jack woke up alone in Marilyn's bed. Her perfume clung to the pillow beside him and the sheets were still warm from the touch of her body. Through the open bedroom door he could hear her as she busied herself in the kitchen. This was as good a time as any to call his old friend Rick Summers and he reached for the bedside telephone.

Marilyn returned to the bedroom carrying a tray laden with scrambled eggs, bacon, toast and coffee just as his conversation was ending. She smiled, blew him a kiss, which he returned, put the tray on her vanity table and sat down next to him on the bed.

"Okay, Rick, thanks a lot," he said into the receiver. "I won't be late. One o'clock. Okay. Thanks. Goodbye."

"Who was that?" she asked nonchalantly as he hung up.

"Just a client. I have to meet with him this afternoon."

"This afternoon? She pouted. "But I thought . . ."

"What did you think?" he asked with a smile as he reached out and grabbed her around her waist.

"Well, I thought we could spend the day right here," she said, inching closer to him on the bed. "Look, I made us breakfast and everything."

"I can see that," he replied, "but this is important."

"I'm important," she said as she began to nuzzle his neck.

"Yes, you're *very* important," he agreed.

She brought her lips to his ear. "I'll bet I can make you stay," she whispered, and began kissing her way down his body.

"Your breakfast will get cold," Jack warned softly as her lips brushed past his chest.

"You taste better," she replied.

Before long they were locked in another torrid embrace, testing, teasing each other, using caresses they had missed the previous night. They explored the interaction of their minds and bodies that was by turns playful and passionate. Jack was right: the breakfast did get cold. But neither of them cared.

ഇ ര

It was almost noon before the telephone rang in the Calkins home. Jennifer hurried to pick it up. As she expected, it was Marilyn.

"Well? What happened?" Jennifer demanded. "Why didn't you call me earlier?"

"He just left," Marilyn replied with a yawn.

"Just left!" Jennifer exclaimed. "Good Lord, Marilyn, what have the two of you been doing all this time?"

"Well, we slept for a while, and . . ." Marilyn caught herself. "Jennifer! What kind of question is that? Do you expect be to give you a minute-by-minute description?"

"No, of course not. You can leave out the parts about sleeping," Jennifer chuckled. "So where is he now? Please don't say, 'In the shower,' because I won't be able to stand it."

"No, he's out of the shower and gone. He had to meet a client on some top-secret business. Then he's coming back here. He wants to have dinner at the Yacht Club tonight."

"Why at the Club?"

"Darned if I know. He says it's a big night and he wants me to look special. I'm going to spend the afternoon taking a hot bath and doing my hair and nails."

"Maybe you should take a nap, too," Jennifer added. "In case he comes back wanting 'Seconds.' Or should I say 'Thirds'?"

"Jennifer, mind your manners," Marilyn replied as she hung up the phone.

℘ ℘

Later that afternoon, Jennifer returned home from shopping and was surprised to see Marilyn's car parked in front of the Magnolia Avenue house. *I knew she couldn't hold out on me; she's here to tell me everything,* Jennifer thought. She hurried up the front steps, only to find Jack on his way out and Marilyn nowhere in sight.

"I'm afraid I won't be able to make it, Love," she overheard her grandmother say.

"If you change your mind, the invitation is open," he said as he kissed Grandma's cheek. "I wanted you to be among the first to know."

"Well, I think it's a lovely idea," Grandma replied. "Now you will remember to file my papers first thing Monday morning," she added as Jennifer bounded through the screen door.

"Don't give it another thought," he replied. Jack greeted Jennifer warmly and then was out the door. As he drove away in Marilyn's car, her grandmother turned to her.

"Jennifer, do you happen to have the home number of that nice young Mr. Meacham?"

"R.J.?" Jennifer confessed. "Yes, I do. Why?"

"It would be lovely if he would escort you to dinner at the Yacht Club tonight. Say around six o'clock?"

"Grandma! I can't just call him up and ask him to take me to the Yacht Club!"

"Why not, Dear?"

"Gee . . . so soon after making dinner and going to the movies? He'll think I'm chasing him or something."

"Do it, Jennifer. For me. It would make me most happy if the two of you were there this evening."

෨ ෬

It was after five o'clock when Jack finally returned to Marilyn's apartment.

"Jack? Is that you?" she called from the bathroom.

"How many other men have keys to this place?" he joked as he followed the sound of her voice.

She was applying makeup in front of the bathroom mirror, with her hair and body wrapped in towels. He leaned against the doorjamb and watched her for a minute.

"Do you always walk around here like that?" he asked.

She turned and took a step toward him. "No," she said, dropping the towel from her body. "I usually walk around here like this. Now aren't you sorry you left?"

Jack wrapped his arms around her, kissed her and let his hands roam over the soft skin of her back.

"Are you sure you want to go out for dinner?" she sighed.

"Yes, I'm sure," he said. "I even stopped by the boat and got all dressed up . . . white pants and everything."

"I can fix that," Marilyn replied, dropping her hands to his belt buckle.

Jack kissed her again. "I'm going to wait in the living room to avoid further temptation." He slapped her playfully on her behind. "Now, step on it. Our reservation is for six-thirty."

Jack made himself comfortable in the living room and tried to keep his thoughts in there with him. He knew that if he allowed himself to think about her, he would find himself thinking about the softness of her skin and the firmness of her body, all of which awaited him at this moment on the other side of a not-completely-closed door.

Marilyn called from the bedroom, "How shall I dress?"

"Dressy," he replied. "Dressy—dressy. Elegant dressy. This is a big night."

She came out in a silky red dress cut low enough to reveal her fabulous figure without being outright scandalous. The irregular "handkerchief hemline" gave the illusion that the dress had somehow fallen into place on her body and might slip off again at any moment. It was a dress that few women could wear well, and Marilyn wore it perfectly.

Her dark hair was piled high on her head while she fastened a final earring in place. "Will you help me with this, please?" she said, handing Jack a necklace and turning her back toward him. He dutifully fastened the clasp at the back of her neck. The temptation was too great, and he began kissing her there and working his way around to her ear.

"Hey, come on!" she said, pulling away. "You made me go through all of this trouble . . . therefore, you're taking me out, Mister!"

They arrived at the Club in short order. A long table was set up along the far wall of the Members' Dining Room, in anticipation of a big party, she supposed. Bill was in the far corner, holding court with some of the regulars at the Sailors' Table. He acknowledged them with a wave of his hand and a wink. Jennifer and R.J. were also there at a cozy table for two. Jack resisted Marilyn's suggestion to interrupt them, insisting that Jennifer and her new friend would probably rather be alone.

Sam DePasquale escorted them to a table for two, dutifully placed the small flag at Jack's place setting and lit the candle in the hurricane lamp. "Old Fashioned, right Commodore?" he asked. "And for you, Miss Dupré?"

"Instead of that, we'll have a bottle of champagne," Jack replied. He turned to Marilyn and added, "If that's all right with you, of course."

Sam hurried away to place their order with one of the wait staff.

"Champagne again?" Marilyn said after he was gone. "What's the occasion this time?"

"This is a big night," was Jack's only explanation.

"You keep saying that, but I don't see any kind of party," she said.

"Things will get going later. Trust me," he replied.

"He even remembered my name," Marilyn said, referring to the manager. "This place is really wonderful. No wonder everyone likes it so much."

"It's not the Beach House," he smiled.

Marilyn's eyes sparkled in the soft light from the candle on the table. She picked up the flag at Jack's place setting and toyed with it. "The Beach House doesn't have these, either," she said. "I suppose you think you think you should get one wherever you go."

"Well, it is the proper protocol," Jack replied.

"Maybe I should buy one and keep in my apartment," she said. "In case you come over for dinner again."

The mention of visiting her apartment would have been the ideal lead-in for what he had to say: something about not wanting to be apart; how they needed to be together always. It could have been the perfect romantic speech, but the waiter spoiled it by bringing the champagne, opening it and pouring it with a flourish. Jack looked away from Marilyn's eyes for a moment and caught Bill and the people at the Sailors' Table watching them intently. By the time the waiter left, the rhythm of the conversation had been lost. Jack tried to pick it up again.

"You know, there's a reason why I didn't want to go over and sit with Jennifer and her friend," he began.

"Oh?"

"I wanted . . . I thought we should be alone," he continued. "I wanted to discuss . . . that is, I wanted to talk to you about something."

"What?"

"Well . . . that is, I've fallen completely, passionately in love with you, Marilyn. I guess I knew it when I first saw you, even though I tried my best . . . I really did try to fight it."

"I love you, too, Jack," she said. "And I wouldn't mind saying that in front of Jennifer . . . or her friend," she added, smiling at his discomfort.

"Well . . . you see, the thing is," he went on, "I suppose it would make a lot of sense for the two of us to take a while and get to know one another. Now . . . I don't know how you feel about that idea, but I don't like it at all. I mean, I know how I feel right now, and I know myself well enough to know that this feeling's not going to change."

"Jack," she said sympathetically, "for a lawyer, you seem to be having a lot of trouble getting to the point. What's bothering you?"

"Nothing. Nothing's bothering me. I know exactly what I'm doing," he said as he reached into his pocket and took out the small box containing the 4-carat pear-shaped diamond ring he had picked up from Rick Summers earlier in the day. He looked at her intently. "Marilyn Dupré, will you marry me?"

Marilyn gasped slightly. "You don't waste any time, do you?" she asked.

"I've already wasted too much time," he answered.

She smiled, eyes sparkling in the candlelight, but she remained silent. In fact she was silent for much too long.

"Marilyn, if you don't say 'Yes,' I'm going to look very foolish right now," Jack whispered.

"I'd never let that happen to you," she whispered in return. She took his hand and said, loud enough for nearby tables to hear, "Of course I'll marry you, John Townsend. I just wanted to savor the moment."

Jack slipped the ring on her finger and leaned across the table to kiss her. Just as their lips met, they were interrupted by the sound of metal clinking against glass from the far corner of the room. Bill was on his feet.

"Ladies and gentlemen," he boomed to the people in the Members' Dining Room, "as a Past Commodore of this Club, I claim the privilege of the floor." Multiple conversations died away while people looked up with a great deal of curiosity. Past commodores might have "the privilege of the floor" at meetings, but this was the dining room; such things simply did not happen. On the other hand, it was Judge Bill Bellingham who was demanding their attention. Bill again called for order. "It is my happy privilege," he continued, "to announce the engagement of one of our Past Commodores and my dear friend, John Townsend, to the lovely Marilyn Dupré of New Orleans. Now, everybody join me in a toast to the happy couple."

Applause broke out in the dining room, attended by clinking of silverware against glass. Jack had always hated it when people did that at wedding receptions as a way of encouraging the bride and groom to kiss. It seemed so . . . gauche. But here, at their Club, among their friends, it seemed to be a perfectly appropriate thing to do. As the noise rose to a crescendo, Jack stood up, made an exaggerated bow to the dining room, walked around the table, swept Marilyn into his arms and really kissed her—to the sound of cheers and more applause.

Moments after Jack released her, Marilyn found herself being hugged by a tearful Jennifer. "I'm so glad we were here for this," she cried. "How did Grandma know?"

"I don't know," Marilyn replied, looking at Jack, "unless you said something to her."

"Of course!" Jennifer exclaimed. "That's what you were doing at the house this afternoon!"

Jack denied any knowledge of what they were talking about and while Bill and the wait staff moved their drinks and the champagne bucket, and people from around the dining room began taking their places at the long table that been set up for a party. "Come on," Jack said to Jennifer, "why don't you and your friend join us?"

Once again, Marilyn found herself seated next to Bill, who began re-introducing her to many of the people she had met at the Summer Fling, and who "just happened" to be present. They all had perfectly reasonable explanations of why they stopped by the Club on this particular night, and Bill announced an impromptu contest in which he would award points for the most imaginative stories and toast the winners with a round of champagne. Commodore Ron and Judy Hennel earned an eight point five score for a complex tale that began with them coming down to their boat to check a balky bilge pump and ended when their car refused to start in the parking lot, which, of course, resulted in their coming in for dinner while they waited for a repair truck that never arrived. Jennifer's story—that she and R.J. were there at her grandmother's insistence—did not score well at all, even though she kept telling everyone it was the absolute truth. R.J. came to her rescue by "admitting" they were secret members of an America's Cup committee and were researching venues for an upcoming series of races. He added that the committee was planning to ask Bill to lead the United States team.

"There's an explanation that makes sense!" Bill shouted amid gales of laughter. "This guy gets a ten! Why isn't he a member?"

"Because we don't need anyone around here telling us how great you are. We already have you for that," Jack replied, to even more laughter.

The party—that Jack and Bill continued to swear was unplanned—lasted far into the night. It was after midnight before Marilyn found herself alone with Jack in her car and facing the problem of going home. They had spent a delicious night together at her apartment and were now officially engaged. Did that mean he would move in with her? Or that she would move in with him? Or should they maintain separate places? Once upon a time Marilyn would have worried about the answers to those questions; now she decided to do what Grandma would do—let nature take its course. She drove to the marina and parked next to the white trawler.

Jack got out and hesitated for a moment after opening her door. "You're coming aboard . . . aren't you?" he asked.

"Well, there are some things we need to talk about," she suggested.

"Oh, right. Of course. Why don't I get us some coffee or brandy or something," he offered as they stepped aboard the boat.

Once inside Jack poured two snifters of brandy, sat down on the settee and pulled her to his lap.

Marilyn took both brandies, put them on a nearby table and told him they had had enough. She wrapped her arms around his neck and said it was time to talk.

"Okay, what would you like to talk about?" he asked.

"Well," she began, "for instance, I guess we're supposed to set a date or something."

"Any date you want," he replied. "How about tomorrow?"

"I need to take my exam first. And I would like to have my father here, at least."

"Good idea. We can get him a hotel room, or he can even stay here on the boat with us . . . with me . . . on the boat, in the guest quarters."

"About living . . ." she hesitated, unsure of how to say what she was thinking and what his reaction might be. "It really doesn't make any sense . . . financially . . . for us to maintain two places. I mean, if we're getting married and everything."

"There's plenty of room here," he offered. "And it's as close as you can get to your office. It would make a lot of sense for you to . . . well, stay right here. At least for now."

"Jack," she said, running a finger down his chest, "for our honeymoon, I'd love to take you home and show you New Orleans."

"Great idea," he replied. "We can stop there on our way to Paris."

"Paris? Jack, are you serious?"

"Why not? You speak French, don't you?"

"*Certainment, Monsieur,*" she replied.

"Yes, but can you say things like, 'In the bedroom,' and 'My husband needs oxygen,'?" he teased as she began kissing his neck.

"It would be so romantic, wouldn't it?" she continued as she nuzzled his neck some more.

Jack's only answer was to press his lips to hers again. "You don't have to go home tonight, do you?" he asked when he finally broke away.

She looked deep into his eyes. "I am home, Darling," she replied. "I'm not going anywhere. And I'm not sleeping in the guest quarters anymore, either."

His lips found hers again, and they remained locked for a very long time.

"Jack," she whispered, when he finally released them, "it's been an exciting day. Can we go to bed now?"

Chapter 20

Jack awoke the next morning to the sound of tapping on the boat's hull. He luxuriated in the feel of Marilyn's warm skin touching his. She was asleep with her head on his shoulder, one arm curled over his chest and her breasts pressed into his side. Whatever that sound was, Jack hoped it wasn't important because he had no intention of moving.

The tapping started again. Three short taps and a pause followed by a few more. Obviously someone was knocking on the side of the boat, even though people didn't do that sort of thing. Boat people are supposed to respect each other's privacy, Jack mused. It must be important, he decided, and he tried to get up quietly.

"Don't go," Marilyn murmured sleepily.

"I'll be right back," he said as he gently kissed her forehead. "Don't move." He removed her arm, slipped out of bed and retrieved his pants from the floor where Marilyn had tossed them. As he started up into the salon he saw Erlene and Arlo standing on the seawall. Erlene was about to knock on the boat again. Jack stopped her by opening the salon door.

"'Morning, Commodore," Arlo said. "C'n we come aboard?"

"Well, it's kind of early . . ." Jack hesitated.

"Please? It's real important," Erlene added.

Erlene was not usually so insistent and surely Arlo knew better than to go around knocking on people's boats. Whatever was bothering the two of them, it must be really important, Jack thought. "Sure, come aboard," he said.

"We need ta' talk ta' you, Commodore," Erlene began as they entered the salon. "We need a lawyer."

The old Jack Townsend might have thrown them off the boat. But now, with Marilyn waiting for him in the stateroom, life was easier to handle. Jack directed them to the settee and pulled up a chair on the other side of the table. "What's the problem?" he asked.

"My kid's in jail," Arlo began abruptly. "He robbed a jewelry store."

"What?" Jack tried to make sense out of Arlo's statement.

"Arlo's got a son," Erlene explained. "Actually, he's got three kids over on the mainland?" Her inflection made it sound like she was asking a question. "That's why he works nights, ta' support 'em. Anyway, his one son works part time at a jewelry store? An' they said he stole somethin' and now they got him in jail."

"He robbed the place," Arlo emphasized.

"Arlo," Jack said impatiently, "I'm sure you have that

wrong. Robbery is forcible stealing. It's a life offense in Florida."

Arlo's eyes widened. Jack thought it was in reaction to his last statement, but he was not entirely correct. A sleepy voice behind Jack asked, "What's going on?"

He turned and saw Marilyn standing at the top of the stairs that led down to the stateroom. She was wearing Jack's white dress shirt and did not appear to be wearing much else. Her dark hair was erotically disheveled. It was obvious that she had just gotten out of bed and she looked ravishing. Jack made a mental note to keep a lot of dress shirts on board.

"Oh, I'm sorry," Erlene said as she tried to push a stunned Arlo off the settee. "We didn't know you-all had company."

Marilyn crossed over and stood next to Jack, and he instinctively put his arm around her. "No, that's all right," he said. "Miss Dupré and I are engaged. We're going to be married soon."

"Well, congratulations," Erlene replied. "C'mon, Arlo," she added, poking her companion, "we'll come back later."

"No, please don't let me interrupt," Marilyn protested. "What's going on?"

"My kid's goin' ta' jail f'r life," Arlo blurted out.

It was the second time since she met him that Arlo had blurted out something that made Marilyn feel sick to her stomach. "I'd better put on some coffee," she said heading for the galley.

"Arlo, stop saying that," Jack said testily. "Your son is probably charged with larceny. It's a completely different crime."

"Well the paper they give 'im says "Robbery while Armed'," Arlo replied. "An' you said that's life, ain't it?"

That sounded ominous. "Yes, that's life, or it can be," Jack said seriously. "Where is your son now?"

"He's in the county jail," Erlene wailed. "We just come from there. He looks so scared, the poor li'l thing. Commodore, ya' just gotta help him."

"I'm not in practice anymore," Jack protested.

"We don't expect ya' ta' do it f'r nothin'," Erlene said. "We know lawyers cost money." She handed Jack an envelope full of bills. "There's five hundred dollars in that envelope, an' me an' Faith got more in the bank, too. "We've been savin' it for her college, but we'll jus' postpone that f'r a while."

Jack looked at the earnest expression on her face, and then down at the envelope. It contained an assortment of bills of every denomination. Gas money and tips, he thought. He wondered how many hours she sat in the sun and let herself be ogled to collect it. He took one very rumpled dollar bill out of the envelope and handed the rest back to her. "Okay, you've retained me, Erlene," he said. "I'm not telling you I'll try the case. I'm telling you I'll look into it and see what I can do. I can't make any promises, understand?" He looked from Erlene to Arlo as they nodded their heads. "I'll go down to the jail today and talk to him. That's all I can do right now. We'll talk about this again tomorrow."

"Can you at least get him out on bail?" Erlene pleaded as she and Arlo got up to leave.

"I don't know right now. I won't know until I talk to him and see a judge. He's going to be stuck there overnight at least."

Marilyn came back with a coffee pot and mugs. "Won't you stay for coffee?" she asked.

"Oh, no, thanks," Erlene replied, pushing Arlo toward the door. "We've taken up enough of y'all's time. I'm sorry we broke in on ya'll and everythin'. We'll let ourselves out."

Marilyn put the pot and mugs down on the table as Jack looked wearily at the dollar bill. She stood next to him and stroked his hair.

"You're not going to be able to support me if you keep taking cases for a dollar," she said softly, picking up the rumpled bill on the table.

"I didn't say I'd take it," he reminded her.

"It seems you're the only one who can help him," she replied.

"No, don't say that!" he said, suddenly raising his voice. He stood and faced her. "Whatever you say, don't ever say that! I'm nobody's Messiah. I can't solve all the world's problems!"

"Jack!" she exclaimed with a crushed look.

"Do you have any idea what it's like? What it's *really* like?" he demanded, with his voice getting louder. "Do you know how it feels to stand next to some poor bastard when a judge sends him away? How do you think it feels when he looks at you while they're putting on the handcuffs? It's not such a glamorous profession then!"

"As a matter of fact, I do know!" she shouted back at him. "I did legal clinic work in my senior year."

"Oh, then you're an expert," he proclaimed. "Fine. You can come to the jail with me today. You can listen to the sound of steel slamming against steel. You can smell the smell of sweat and greasy food and God-knows-what. That's what this business is all about!"

"I know what it's all about," she exploded angrily, repeating the things she had said so often in her past and that—until this moment—seemed to be a lifetime ago. "It doesn't scare me! You can't scare me!"

"And the lies!" he continued. "Let's not forget about the lies. "Do you have any idea what it's like to listen to people lie to you all day long while you try to figure out the truth? Do you know how it feels never to trust anybody?"

"I know all about lying," she assured him, thinking now of Nick and the bitter arguments in the apartment they once had shared, and the lying she did to Sister about the bruises that sometimes covered her skin afterwards.

"You think this is such a great profession?" Jack continued. "Do you see what happened to us this morning? Get used to it! Get used to calls at all hours of the day and night . . . strangers, criminals, God-knows-who in your living room. Try that for a while and then tell me if it's so great being the wife of a lawyer." He thought of the school plays he had missed and the ruined dinners Kathy had patiently tried to re-heat for him when he was too tired to eat them.

"I didn't say I'd marry you because you're a lawyer," she shouted back with her fists clenched. "I said I'd marry you because I love you . . ." The words almost choked her. The difference between those words and the memories that were surging through her along with the anger she felt at the moment was too strong. She suddenly found her eyes filled with tears she did not want and could not explain.

Seeing her like that brought Jack to his senses. He went to her and put his arms around her. "Honey, honey, I'm sorry. I'm so sorry," he said quietly. "It's not you; it could never be you. I just don't want it anymore. I don't want the responsibility."

"You have to do it, Jack," she sobbed in his arms. "Grandma said it's your path in life. It's what you were meant to do."

"That's just a silly superstition of hers," he said, stroking her hair.

"No it isn't. No it isn't," she sniffled. "When she told me . . . I felt . . . I know it's true, that's all."

"All right, all right," he assured her. "I'll try to help him. I just don't ever want to see you cry again, okay?"

"Okay," she sniffed.

He kissed her softly.

"Let's get dressed. We'll go out for breakfast and then we'll see young Mr. Woodbrace. Maybe it's all some kind of mistake," he said, not really believing his own words.

അ ഝ

They had to stop by Marilyn's apartment for a conservative outfit before going to the jail. Last night's dress was out of the question, of course, and Jack assured her that the outfit she had left on board the weekend of the Summer Fling would probably start a riot. This trip definitely called for baggy slacks and a shirt—an oversized sweatshirt if possible. Marilyn took the opportunity to pack some extra clothes and personal items. There was no telling when they would have time to move all of her things to the boat.

The jail was worse than Jack had described. No law school course—no legal aid office—could have prepared her for the reality of the grim, cold walls and the steel bars caked with layers of chipped paint. Her first impression was one of constant noise. Everyone seemed to be shouting: from the Principal Guard's warning of, "On the gate!" when they entered to the desperate plea of an inmate, "You a lawyer?" as he was being "processed" into the system.

The guards all acted happy to see Jack and engaged him in a sort of gallows humor. He introduced Marilyn as his legal assistant, and, other than to compliment him on his choice of help, no one questioned her presence.

They would see Dennis Woodbrace in a small room with a metal desk and three mismatched chairs. Before they brought Dennis in, Jack instructed her to sit in the chair closest to the door. That way, he explained, in case "anything happened," the guards could get her out first.

Dennis had dark skin that was a shade lighter than his

father's, a product of the multi-cultural and multi-racial mix of South Florida. He was wearing a red jumpsuit. A guard told him to sit at the far end of the desk before he left the room, closing and locking the solid steel door with a sickening hollow clang. The entire room consisted of steel, thick glass and concrete, resulting in an echo that made any conversation unpleasant.

"Dennis," Jack began, "my name is John Townsend. I'm your attorney. This is my legal assistant, Marilyn Dupré. Your father retained us to look into your case."

"Arlo said he was goin' ta' get me a lawyer," Dennis replied. Unlike his father, there was no hint of the Caribbean in Dennis' speech.

"You call your father 'Arlo'," Jack asked.

"Sure, why not? Everybody else does," the young man said with a shrug.

Jack shook his head silently and opened a leather portfolio containing a yellow legal pad. "Tell me . . . tell us what happened," he began.

"I didn't rob nobody . . . and I didn't steal nothin'." Dennis had his father's way of telling a story by beginning with the conclusion. Slowly, with a series of probing questions, Jack extracted the facts.

Dennis was nineteen years old. He had a spotless criminal record, a high-school education and only vague plans about the future. About six months ago, he was lucky enough to get a job at Palm Island Jewelers in Bonita. Tom Morelle, the owner, started him out working around the shop and slowly increased his responsibilities. Morelle seemed to take a genuine interest in him. He treated Dennis well and was teaching him the jewelry business. Dennis began to think of making it a career.

Last night, just before closing time, Morelle asked Dennis to deliver a diamond bracelet to a customer. When Dennis protested that he didn't have a car, Morelle offered his own and gave him the keys.

Dennis had made some deliveries for Morelle in the past but they were wristwatches that customers left for cleaning or repair. Dennis used his own bicycle for those trips. He had never before used Morelle's car or had such an expensive piece of jewelry entrusted to him. Before leaving the store, Morelle reminded him that the bracelet was worth over ten thousand dollars and that he must be extremely careful. He even made Dennis write down the name and address of the customer to whom the item was to be delivered, even though Dennis assured him he would not forget. Dennis had the paper with him when he was arrested.

When he got to the part of town where the house should have been, he could not locate the address. He wondered if he had made a mistake, possibly by transposing the digits in the house number. Dennis stopped at a gas station to call the customer, but there was no listing for the name he had been given. As he drove around, looking for a similar address, the police stopped him. He was ordered out of the car at gunpoint and forced to lie on the ground while he was handcuffed. He kept trying to explain that he had not stolen anything; that he was delivering a package, but no one would listen to him. He was taken directly to jail. Tom Morelle would not accept his calls and no one else could confirm Dennis' story.

Jack's next stop was the police department's detective bureau where they were greeted with the same kind of gallows humor they had received at the jail.

"Don't do it, Jack," a detective said as they took seats opposite him at his desk. "This is a bad one. The kid even pistol-whipped the guy before he ran out." He showed Jack several instant photographs in full color of a man who he identified as Tom Morelle. The left side of his face was horribly bruised and lacerated, and his left eye was swollen almost shut. "Take a look at my report. It's all here," the detective said. "The kid grabbed the bracelet, beat the crap out of the guy and stole his car for the getaway. You better pick a better case than this if you're going to make a comeback, my friend." The detective smiled and added, "Of course, Deke Stoner might be willing to cut a deal if the kid tells us what he did with the rest of the stuff."

"What do you mean, 'rest of the stuff'?" Jack asked.

"Didn't the kid tell you? There's at least two trays of rings missing. It's quite a haul. He's got them stashed somewhere. We're getting a search warrant for his mother's place. Anyway, you can probably cop a plea for him if he cooperates."

Jack was silent as they left the building.

"What do we do now?" Marilyn asked when they were back in her car.

"*We* don't do anything," Jack replied grimly. "Tomorrow morning *I* will go talk to the State Attorney and see if *I* can negotiate a reduced plea."

"A plea?" Marilyn protested. "You mean plead guilty?"

"That's exactly what I mean."

"But you haven't even . . ."

"The kid lied to me," Jack said bitterly.

"He didn't lie, exactly," she pleaded. "He just didn't tell you everything right away. Give him a chance . . ."

"Honey," he said, interrupting her, "you heard his story. Do you think it makes any sense? More importantly, is a jury going to believe it?"

"He might be telling the truth," she insisted.

"Sure, and I *might* be an astronaut." He shot her a look that said further conversation on the subject was not welcome. "Marilyn, would you give that kid a ten thousand dollar bracelet to deliver anywhere?"

Marilyn sensed the beginnings of another argument, and decided to drop the matter for the time being. Right now she needed to move some things aboard the boat. They could discuss Dennis Woodbrace later.

℘ ℭ

A steady rain kept them trapped on board all afternoon. Marilyn busied herself by making room for her things in the stateroom while Jack typed away at the word processor on the salon table. When she could stand it no longer, she joined him in the salon.

"I hate days like this," she said, trying to start a conversation.

"Really? I kind of like them," he replied.

"How can you like all this rain? It's so dreary."

"I don't know, it's sort of nice for a change. Days like this are a reason to stay in bed with a good book . . . or somebody," he joked.

"Honestly," she said with a smile, "Is that all you men think about?"

"No, it's not *all* that we think about. But it's way out ahead of whatever is in second place," he teased. "Why don't you go slip into one of my shirts and we'll see what happens."

She did not respond. They had shared two glorious nights. Now she wondered if they could survive the real test of living together during the day. Her silence got his attention and he looked up from the word processor.

"Hey," he said, holding out a hand to her, "you really are depressed. Come here."

"I guess I just don't know what to do with myself," she said, taking his hand.

"What would you be doing of you were at your apartment?"

"I don't know—watch T.V., or read, I guess," she said gloomily.

"What's really bothering you? It's not the rain, is it?" he asked, pulling her down to his lap.

"I guess I just keep thinking about Arlo's son, sitting in jail. I wonder what he's doing?"

"He's probably doing exactly what you're doing right now: feeling miserable."

"You will help him, won't you, Jack? You won't just tell him to plead guilty?"

"Marilyn, I'll do the best I possibly can for him."

"No," she said as she put her arms around his neck. "Don't do it for him. Do it for me."

"You drive a hard bargain, lady," he said. "Now come with me. We're going to your apartment to get the rest of your things, and then we're going to take in a movie and dinner."

Chapter 21

"John DeWitt Townsend, slumming in Bonita! As I live and breathe!"

"Good morning, Lois. Is The Deacon in?" Jack recognized Stoner's secretary as the pain in the ass she had always been. She had been with the office forever—even before Jack was hired. She was a snippy bitch back then, and she had gotten worse with age and seniority.

"The State Attorney is in a conference with this Chief Assistant. And he prefers to be called by his proper name. May I help you with something?"

Jack wanted to ask, "Just who does have my old job this week, Lois? I hear Deke goes through Assistants pretty rapidly," but he bit his tongue. Lois had no sense of humor, and she was a rat besides. Stoner would surely hear about his "Deacon" comment; there was no use making things worse: especially since Jack was there to do some begging.

"I'll just wait here if I may," he said in his politest possible voice.

Lois took a note in through the door and returned to her desk. It was almost an hour before the State Attorney himself came out to the waiting room. "Jack!" he called out with the insincere political smile that had become his trademark among those who knew him. "I'm sorry you had wait, Buddy. I've been real busy this morning."

Jerking off, no doubt, Jack thought, before he said with a smile of his own, "No problem, Deke. I really didn't have anything to do."

"Come on in," Stoner said, putting a hand on his shoulder. "What can I do for you, Buddy?"

Jack wanted to say, "Can we cut the 'Buddy' crap, Deke?" but he kept his mouth shut.

"It's about the Woodbrace kid, Deke," Jack began.

"Bad kid. Bad crime. I was just getting brought up to speed on it this morning. He damn near killed that jewelry store guy," Stoner interrupted.

"Killed is a little strong, Deke," Jack pointed out.

"Strong? Hell, all he had to do was pull the trigger and he'd be looking at felony murder this morning. He'd be on his way to the electric chair."

"He hasn't been found guilty yet," Jack reminded him.

"How long do you think that's going to take?" Stoner shot back. "Anyway, you didn't come here to debate me. Not unless you're representing this jackoff. You're not, are you?"

"I might be."

"Might be? Come on, Jack. Either you are or you aren't."

"I told the family I'd look into the case."

"Are you retained?" Stoner inquired, a little too nonchalantly.

"I'm not sure that's any of your business, Deke. But, yes, I have accepted a small retainer."

Deke Stoner began to chuckle. "The Great Jack Townsend, accepting a small retainer to 'look into' a criminal case. How small, Jack?"

Jack Townsend tried to control himself. Deke was beginning to get to him. Jack knew it, and he suspected Deke knew it, too.

"What kind of plea is available?" he asked, ignoring Stoner's question about the size of the retainer.

"That depends," Stoner said laconically. "Where's the rest of the stuff?"

"There is no 'rest of the stuff.' The kid says he didn't take anything."

"And you believe him?" Stoner laughed.

"I didn't say that," Jack replied. "But he might be telling the truth."

"You really have gone soft," Stoner shot back.

"Look, Deke, can I get the kid a plea or not?" Jack's patience was at the breaking point, and Stoner pressed him further.

"Why are you talking about a plea? I thought you were an ace trial lawyer."

"That was uncalled for, Deke." Jack said, raising his voice.

"Was it?" Stoner fired back. "You were the hotshot who said Bonita wasn't big enough for you. So why don't you try this case, Mister Hotshot?"

"You never could get it out of your craw that I left here and made more money than you, could you?" Jack was visibly angry now.

"You got that wrong, Jack. Yeah, I stayed behind. I missed out on that Miami money. But . . . see . . . now I'm the State Attorney." Stoner smiled like the cat that ate the canary. "And you're the one coming in here with his tail between his legs trying to cop a plea. You're Mister Hotshot, remember? Why *don't* you try this case?"

"Maybe I will," Jack said grimly.

"You will?" Stoner retorted. "Maybe I'll prosecute it. Personally."

"Don't do it, Deke. Don't turn this kid into a grudge match between the two of us," Jack warned.

"Why not, Jack?" Stoner asked. "I've been taking a lot of heat in the press lately. They're saying I'm afraid to try my own cases. They say I always send in a hotshot Assistant . . . you know, like you used to be. This'll really give them something to write about: 'State Attorney Battles Former Chief Assistant'."

"Maybe I better come back when you cool off," Jack said, getting to his feet.

"This is as cool as I'm going to get with you, Jack." Stoner did not move from his chair. "Oh, and Jack," he added when the other man reached the door, "if your client wants to cop a plea, he can plead guilty . . . straight up."

※ ❧

Jack pounded the steering wheel of Marilyn's car. He couldn't believe he had allowed Deke Stoner to get to him like that. He was in a foul mood when he reached Marilyn's office at the marina.

"How did it go?" she inquired.

"It didn't," Jack replied. "Dennis Woodbrace can either plead guilty as charged or go to trial. Deke Stoner is going to prosecute the case himself."

"Good. I'm glad," Marilyn said firmly.

"Glad? How can you be glad?" Jack shouted.

"He said he's innocent!"

"What the hell does that have to do with it?" Jack demanded. "Every man in that jail says he's innocent!"

"Well some of them must be innocent!"

"Sure, sure, didn't you know?" Jack demanded sarcastically. "The Bonita police have a new policy. They don't have enough to do, so they've started to arrest people at random. The deputies at the jail book them just to fill up the place. And the State Attorney's Office prosecutes them because all the Assistants need trial experience."

"I can do without the sarcasm," Marilyn shot back.

"Honey, look," Jack pleaded, "you're beautiful, you're sexy, you're intelligent. But you're a tax lawyer. Your head is full of concepts like 'basis' and 'cost of goods sold.' I'm a trial lawyer. My head is full of concepts like 'evidence' and 'reasonable doubt.' I'll make a deal with you, Marilyn. From now on, I won't practice your specialty, and you stay out of mine. Okay?" He turned and started to leave. "I'll be on the boat if you need me," he said over his shoulder, and almost ran into Jennifer who was coming in the door.

"What was that all about?" Jennifer asked after Jack slammed the door on his way out.

"Men!" Marilyn shouted, throwing a ledger book at the closed door. "I hate them!"

஋ ஼

Jack sat on the boat and fumed. He was back into it with both feet. He had managed to avoid all of it for two years, and now, in one twenty-four hour period he had been lied to by a client, humiliated by Lois and insulted by Deke Stoner. "Damn!" he shouted to the empty salon. "Damn you, Dennis Woodbrace! Damn you, Arlo! Damn you, Erlene! And damn me for letting myself get sucked into this mess." He poured himself a drink even though it was much too early in the day. What the hell happened? he wondered. Friday night he was in ecstasy with a woman he cherished. Saturday night she accepted his proposal of marriage, and Sunday morning the roof fell in. Now, with every passing minute he was becoming increasingly responsible for the life of a man who appeared to have no way out. Thoughts of the weekend led to thoughts of Marilyn. She was the only thing that made all of it worthwhile, and now he was even fighting with her. Maybe she was right. Maybe the point was to find happiness through it—or in spite of it.

It was shortly after noon before Jack returned to Marilyn's office.

"Hi," he said, a little sheepishly, "can I take you to lunch?"

"Yes," she replied quietly.

"I'm sorry I shouted at you earlier," he offered.

"I'm sorry I threw a book at you," she replied.

"I didn't know about that," he said, pulling her close and kissing her softly. "Where's Jennifer?" he asked when their lips parted.

"At the Yacht Club with R.J.," Marilyn replied with her lips inches from his.

"Are those two in love or something?" he asked.

"Maybe. But I'll take this. I know it's the real thing," Marilyn sighed before kissing him back.

"Hey! The real thing," Jack said, breaking the kiss. "That could mean a lot of things besides love. Come on. I've got to run an errand after lunch."

"Is the honeymoon over already?" she sighed. "I was just getting warmed up."

෩ ෨

After a quick lunch they drove to a quiet residential neighborhood in Bonita. Jack parked in front of a large but not particularly ornate house with a well-tended lawn and bicycles in the driveway. About the only things that struck Marilyn as being unusual were the three-car garage and the elaborate security system that included video cameras at the doors.

"Who lives here?" she finally asked while they waited for someone to let them in.

"You may not believe this," Jack replied, "but you are about to enter the premises of the most prominent custom jeweler in Bonita."

"Come on . . ." Marilyn was interrupted by the sound of a deadbolt being unlocked. A very pleasant man with a cherubic smile and thick glasses opened the door. He was impossibly short: standing, Marilyn judged, at no more than five feet, and he had no discernable neck. His bald head was decorated with a fringe of hair, and, with his thick ears punctuated by hearing aids, he looked more like a fairy tale gnome than a real person.

"Jack Townsend," he croaked, taking Jack's hand and slapping his arm. Then he turned to Marilyn. "And this must be Marilyn Dupré," he exclaimed, taking both her hands in his. He looked at her left hand and raised his glasses to his forehead. "It's a beautiful ring, Jack. Please, come inside."

The man re-locked the door after they entered. He escorted them into a private office where Jack began the introductions.

"Marilyn, this is Rick Summers. I hope you'll be getting to know him very well. Richard, you've already guessed . . ."

Summers silenced him with a wave of one pudgy hand. "Allow me to extend my congratulations, Miss Dupré," he said in his peculiar voice as he stood up and took her hand in both of his again. "I'm probably not the first to congratulate you, but I was the first to know about it. A gentleman's jeweler always is." He pushed his glasses up to his forehead and examined her ring again. "It was an excellent choice, Jack. And the fit is perfect."

Jack took an envelope from his pocket and laid it on the desk. "You're waiting for this, Richard," he said.

Summers slid the envelope into a drawer without opening it. "I wasn't worried, Jack. Not after all these years. Besides, I'm one of the 'in crowd': I know where you live. Remember?" he joked.

"Rick, what's the skinny on this guy Tom Morelle?" Jack asked, changing the subject and getting serious.

"Palm Island Jewelers," Rick replied. "I guess he got boinked pretty good over the weekend. The kid who works for him."

"So the paper says," Jack responded.

"Is it your case?"

"I don't know," Jack reluctantly admitted. "I think I may have gotten myself sucked into it."

"Well, if you ask me," Rick said, "it couldn't have happened to a better guy. Morelle, I mean."

"What? That doesn't sound like you, Rick," Jack said quizzically.

"Not for anything," Rick continued, "I've always thought there was something funny about his operation."

"Talk to me, Richard."

"I don't know anything for sure. It's just that ... well, the guy blew into town a couple of years ago, from nowhere, and made a big splash with all of the new people when he opened that place. Very upscale, very trendy, all that sh . . . all that stuff," he said, smiling at Marilyn.

"Are you sure you're not jealous?" Jack teased.

"Jealous?" Summers fumed. "I've got all the work I can handle right here. Besides, my wife wears more goods than he has in that store. If you ask me, he's got nothing but paste in there."

"Paste? What are you talking about?" Jack asked.

"Paste. Garbage," Rick insisted. "All I know is, he was always coming in here, wanting something made at the last minute. Had to have it 'yesterday.' Always very specific about the color and size and cut. If you ask me, he was showing paste and making up the goods after he got a sale. I finally told him to take gas. Who needs that kind of aggravation?"

"When did you blow him off?" Jack inquired.

"I don't know: six, seven months ago."

Jack looked at Marilyn. She was about to say something, but he cut her off.

"Rick, if I could get you a good look at the bracelet the kid is charged with taking, could you tell me if it's paste?"

"I could tell you if it's paste from across the room," Rick Summers bragged.

"Thanks, Rick. If things go well, I might be back real soon to pick up a souvenir for a lady."

"He was always my best customer," Summers said, winking at Marilyn.

80 Q

"Six or seven months ago is about the time Dennis started working at Palm Island Jewelers," Marilyn reminded Jack when they were back in her car.

"I know that."

"We're going to win this case, aren't we?"

"Don't get your hopes up, Honey. We haven't gotten anywhere yet," Jack cautioned.

"But if the bracelet is paste ..."

"We don't know that it is," he said. "And even if it is, remember, 'value' is not an essential element of the crime of robbery. The forcible taking is the problem."

"So how come you're acting so differently?" she asked.

"Because a little while ago we had nothing. Now we have a glimmer of something, and when you're up against a wall like we are, a glimmer of something is a lot better than nothing."

80 Q

After dinner that evening, they met with Arlo and Erlene on the trawler. This time the couple accepted Marilyn's offer of hospitality and they sat around the table in the salon.

"I'll come right to the point," Jack said after Marilyn poured the coffee. "Dennis is not going to be able to get a reduced plea as long as I'm on the case."

"He don't need no plea," Erlene said. "He didn't do nothin.'"

"Sometimes," Jack said patiently, "it's not a matter of whether a person did anything. It's a matter of whether a jury says he did it."

"We don't want no other lawyer, Commodore," Arlo said.

"That's really up to Dennis," Jack responded.

"He don't want nobody else neither," Erlene added. "He has faith in you, Commodore, an' we do too. We know if anybody can do anythin' for Dennis, y'all can."

"This might cost some money," Jack warned. "If we're going to trial we need to take depositions and do a lot of discovery. Subpoenas aren't free, neither are expert witnesses and court reporters."

"How about you?" Arlo asked.

"Erlene paid my fee," Jack reminded him.

"A dollar? That ain't enough," Erlene protested.

"You let me be the judge of that," Jack said as he stood up and escorted them to the door. "Maybe that's all I'll be worth."

Chapter 22

"Don't forget, I have an appointment for tea this afternoon," Marilyn said before she left the boat for the short walk to her office Wednesday morning.

"Yeeessss, Deeaarr," Jack replied in a suitably nasal whine.

"Jack, I'm serious," she said as she kissed him. "Jennifer and I usually leave here around two o'clock. I'd hate to ask her to drive me back here after she's already home. You *do* want me to stay here tonight, don't you?"

"Do I detect a hint of blackmail?" Jack chided.

"Seriously, okay?"

"I'll have your car back before two o'clock," he replied as she hurried out the door.

When she was gone, he looked over his copy of the police report again and called Gabriel Kingsley, the Chief of Police in Bonita. Gabe had been a deputy sheriff back in the days when Jack was an Assistant State Attorney. They had always had a good relationship and now Jack needed a favor.

"Gabe! Jack Townsend here," Jack said when he was finally connected.

"Uh-oh, here comes trouble," Kingsley responded with a laugh. "I hear you're back in business."

"Damn, can't anyone keep a secret in this town?" Jack said with mock disapproval.

"Secret? The word on the street is you're out gunning for The Deacon," Kingsley replied.

"Stoner? I only spoke with him two days ago."

"Good news travels fast."

"Gabe, I need a favor," Jack said, getting down the reason for his call.

"Name it, guy . . . within reason, of course."

"I need to get a close look at the bracelet the Wood-brace kid is charged with robbing."

"Are you going to give us any crap about chain-of-custody at the trial?" Kingsley asked.

"You know me better than that, Gabe."

"You bet I do; that's why I'm going to let you in here without a court order. Stop by before noon. I'll tell the boys in the evidence room you're coming."

"Thanks, Gabe."

"Anytime, guy."

As Jack prepared to leave the trawler he noticed a car parked alongside on the seawall. A young man got out and waited for him as he stepped off the boat.

"Mr. Townsend?"

"That's me."

"Remember me? I'm Rob Meacham," he said, extending his hand.

Jack took it and hesitated for a moment before he smiled in recognition. "Of course! The famous R.J.!" he said. "I'm sorry, I was a little preoccupied."

"That's okay. May I speak with you for a minute . . . in private?" Rob Meacham asked.

"I guess I've got a minute," Jack replied. "Why don't you come aboard and have a cup of coffee?" He directed the younger man to the settee and was about to go down to the galley.

"That's okay, I'll skip the coffee," Meacham said. "I'd like to get right to the point."

"Okay, what's on your mind?" Jack asked as he took a seat across from the young man.

"I understand you're defending Dennis Woodbrace," Meacham began.

"Did somebody put an ad in the newspaper?" Jack asked sarcastically.

"I'd like to assist you, be your second chair during the trial," Meacham continued, ignoring the interruption.

Jack smiled. "Well, that's very flattering, but I'm kind of a solo act."

"I really want this job, Mr. Townsend," the young man said.

"You have a job," Jack reminded him.

"Yes, at the bank. But that's not what I want. I want to be a trial lawyer . . . like you. I want you to mentor me."

"Are you nuts?" Jack responded, getting up to leave and hoping the younger man would get the message. "Are you out of your mind? Criminal law is a sewer. You've got a nice, respectable job with great security. Do yourself a favor; stick with it."

"It's not what I want," Meacham replied, not leaving his seat.

"Look," Jack continued, beginning to let his impatience show, "let's lay it right on the line. You're going out with a girl who's crazy about you, and who . . . we both know . . . will someday inherit money that hasn't even been counted yet. You don't need to slosh around in the sewer with guys like me."

Robert Meacham stood up, his face suddenly flushed with anger. "You leave Jennifer out of this! That's not why I'm going out with her. My parents didn't put me through law school to be a . . . gigolo. I'm going to be a lawyer, a real lawyer, a trial lawyer. Like you. And if you won't mentor me, I'll find someone who will."

The younger man brushed past Jack on his way to the door. "Sit down, Mr. Meacham," Jack said, grabbing his arm. "Take it easy. I haven't said 'no' yet."

Meacham looked at him. "You haven't?"

"I don't think so," Jack said, resuming his place at the table. "Of course, if we were in a courtroom, I could ask for a read-back." Jack studied the young man as he returned to his seat. "I like your style . . . Rob. Sometimes the best way to get attention is to get a little hot. As long as you don't overdo it," he added with a smile.

Meacham stared self-consciously at the floor. "I'm sorry I got so angry. I just wish . . ." he hesitated for a moment. "I just wish that what you said about Jennifer wasn't true. I really care for her and people at the bank are already starting to talk. I hate having them think about her like that, and I hate it when they think I'm going out with her to get at her grandmother's money."

"Lesson Number One, Rob," Jack said quietly. "A famous man once said, 'Never explain anything. Your friends don't need an explanation and your enemies won't believe it.' Now, can you take the rest of the day off?"

"Right now? Sure," Meacham said eagerly.

"You need experience, and I need transportation. Let's stop at the office and give Marilyn back her keys. Then we'll take a little ride over to police headquarters. Oh, and we'll have to stop on the way there and pick up our expert. You might as well meet him; you'll probably be needing his services someday. Then after lunch we'll have a little chat with our client. It seems he left out a few details the last time I spoke with him."

"Don't you want to see the client first?" R.J. inquired.

"Lesson Number Two, my friend," Jack responded, putting his hand on the younger man's shoulder as they stepped off the boat. "'Never go to the jail on an empty stomach.'"

☙ ❧

Marilyn felt somehow different returning to the Magnolia Avenue house for Wednesday afternoon tea. She had been living with Jack on the trawler since their engagement party Saturday night. Today he was busy with the preparation of Dennis Woodbrace's defense, and she was returning to the house where only a few weeks ago she and Jennifer shared what now seemed to be childhood secrets. It was as if a courtship, marriage and honeymoon had been compressed in time, and that had heightened the experience. She imagined this must be how a married woman felt when she returned to her mother's home. Her relationship with Grandma Calkins and Jennifer had changed. Marilyn had grown. A part of her had been put away. Sharing Jack's bed these past few nights had somehow brought her closer to Grandma and, at the same, time distanced her from Jennifer. "I guess I really am the older sister now," she whispered to herself as she walked up to the front door.

"It's so nice to have you home again, Dear, even if it's only for the afternoon," Mrs. Calkins said as they took their places around the table. "How is Jack?" she added as she poured the tea.

"He's fine, Grandma," Marilyn reported. "He's working very hard on defending Dennis Woodbrace." Marilyn knew enough about confidentiality to know the conversation would have to end there, and Mrs. Calkins was, of course, too polite to ask for details.

"I do hope the young man is innocent," she responded.

"Now it's time for you and Jennifer to get on with your own plans."

"I was wondering," Marilyn began, choosing her words carefully as she went, "so much has changed this past week. Shouldn't I be helping Jack?"

Mrs. Calkins had been stirring her tea quietly. Now she returned her spoon to the saucer and looked directly at Marilyn. "You listen to me, Marilyn Dupré," she said, tapping her forefinger on the table. "It's all well and good that Jack has taken up his profession again and you're to be married. But you must live your own life, too, and have your own career. Each of us is required to make something of ourselves on this earth. That's how we learn: it's how we grow." She smiled and added, "Anyway, you let Jack pay the bills . . . he's a man and that's his job. But you're entitled to your own income. Always keep something in your purse that is your own, Marilyn. I know you're in love, but a girl can't be too careful these days."

Marilyn smiled. "Yes, Grandma," she said dutifully. "What do you want us to do?"

"I think Jennifer has an idea with a lot of merit," Mrs. Calkins responded. "We discussed it with young Mr. Meacham from the Bank. Things will be set up so that you and Jennifer will each own fifty percent of the building and, of course, the business itself. The Bank will loan us the money to start construction. I would like to see things underway before the boys return from their fishing expedition."

The mention of the Calkins brothers brought a cold chill to Jennifer. "Grandma," she said, "you don't expect us to go ahead with this while they're at the boatyard, do you?"

"And why not?" Mrs. Calkins demanded.

"Well, Uncle Doug is okay, I guess. But my father . . ."

"Are you afraid of him, Jennifer?" Mrs. Calkins asked.

"Well, no, not exactly. It's just that I'd rather not be around him."

Mrs. Calkins put down her teacup. "Jennifer, each of us has a monster in our life that terrifies and weakens us. It is a thing we must overcome sooner or later. I regret very much that your father happens to be yours. I wish it were otherwise, I truly do, but it isn't. You have the finest people at your side to help you, and if there must be a confrontation, I would prefer that it come now, while I can still be of assistance. Now, ladies, the boys will likely return soon. I suggest that we plan our strategy."

80 Q

When Marilyn returned home she found Jack in the engine room, working on one of two massive diesel engines.

"What are you doing in there?" she called out as she looked down into a world she had never seen.

He was drenched with sweat and his face was streaked with oil. "That's not the kind of question you ask someone who's spent the afternoon changing fuel filters," he said, wiping his hands.

"Are we going somewhere?"

"No, just regular maintenance," he said as he turned off

the lights and returned to the salon.

She watched him in silence as he carefully wiped oil from his hands and arms. "Want to tell me what's wrong?" she finally asked.

"What makes you think anything's wrong?"

"Changing oil when you don't need to is a sign that a person wants to get his mind off something," she said. "I save up sewing for days like the day I'll bet you had."

He did not reply for a few minutes and Marilyn waited. "Ice!" he finally shouted, throwing the rag into the trash. She looked at him quizzically. "Rick said the bracelet was 'real ice . . . nice goods, too.' He was surprised it was only appraised for ten thousand. He said he figured it was worth at least twelve." Jack smiled grimly. "I don't know who was more disappointed, Rick or me."

"But you said value had nothing to do with it," Marilyn reminded him.

"I know . . . it doesn't. It's just that I was hoping for some kind of break. I guess I was hoping that Morelle was operating some sort of scam, and that Dennis got caught in the middle of it."

Neither of them spoke for a minute; then it was Marilyn's turn to break the silence.

"Jack," she said, hesitantly, "I've been thinking." He did not reply and she continued. "You once told me my head was full of concepts like 'cost of goods sold.' Well, I know this: if you want to maximize profits, you have to minimize the cost of those goods."

"So?" he asked.

"So even Rick Summers was impressed by the 'big splash' Morelle made when he opened Palm Island Jewelers. Well, maybe it was only a splash. Maybe Rick was right . . . most of the jewelry was fake."

"So what?" Jack retorted. "So Morelle's a four-flusher. So are most self-proclaimed big shots."

"But suppose Morelle was forced to go out of business," Marilyn continued. "Let's say his supply of real jewelry dried up. Rick said he stopped doing business with him six or seven months ago. That's about the time Dennis started working for him."

"Are you suggesting Morelle staged the robbery?" Jack asked. There was no sarcasm in his voice now.

"That's exactly what I'm suggesting: bankruptcy fraud!" Marilyn replied with all the certainty of a recent law school graduate who needs to put her knowledge to work.

"Go on," Jack urged, assuming the role of professor.

"He has to go out of business. He hides the assets . . . the rings . . . and stages a robbery to explain their loss. Then he puts the business into bankruptcy. Of course! It's so simple."

"If the rings are worthless, why bother to hide them?" Jack probed, still playing the role of law school professor.

"That's right," Marilyn agreed, falling into the trap of changing the direction of her argument—much as a typical student would do. "The rings aren't worthless; they're real after all."

"How about the insurance proceeds?" Jack inquired. "Don't they become an asset of the bankrupt estate? Doesn't the Trustee take them?"

Marilyn put both hands on her hips and raised one eyebrow. "Have you been practicing my specialty?" she demanded.

"I know a little bit about the subject," Jack replied.

"Well, okay, maybe he doesn't have insurance," she waffled.

"Maybe he does," Jack shot back, waiting for an answer.

"I don't know, bankruptcy fraud sounded good, but . . . just . . . forget it. Forget I said anything." She began to walk away.

"Wait a minute, we're not finished," Jack said, holding her back. "Let's explore your idea. So Morelle has to go out of business. Why not just close the place?"

"I don't know," Marilyn admitted. "If it were bankruptcy fraud, why would he have to implicate Dennis? If he wanted to stage a robbery, he could just say he couldn't identify the perpetrator. Those bankruptcy trustees are always too busy to look into things like that." At least that's what she had heard. She looked at Jack and added, "Aren't they?"

"They may not care about the criminal case, but they're not too busy to ask about insurance proceeds, that's for sure," Jack replied. "But you're on to something. Think about it, Honey. The guy comes here 'from nowhere' and opens the store with a 'big splash.' What's the first thing he gets? Insurance! Marilyn, have you talked to anyone about the possibility of that jewelry being fake?"

"No, not really," she replied. "Well, I mean just Jennifer, but she . . ."

"Call her up," he demanded. "Tell her to come over here tonight. And tell her not to talk to anyone about anything before she gets here. And get Rob's home number; she must have it."

"Who?" she asked.

"Rob Meacham . . . R.J. He's going to be my co-counsel. I need him to come over here, too. Tonight. Why don't we call the Chinese Kitchen and order a take-out dinner for the four of us? I need to talk to Rob, and I need to make absolutely sure Jennifer forgets everything the two of you discussed."

He pulled Marilyn close and planted an oily kiss on her lips. "I knew there was more to you than a sexy body."

"Stop!" she squealed. "You're going to get oil all over my clothes!"

"So take them off and join me in the shower," he teased. "But while you do that tell me, when did I say you only knew about things like 'cost of goods sold'?"

"Right before I threw a ledger at you," she said, kissing him back.

"Come on," he said, breaking away momentarily, "please make those phone calls while I get cleaned up. We may have a defense after all."

Chapter 23

L ate that night the two couples sat around a salon table covered with the ubiquitous boxes and remains of a take-out Chinese dinner. "I love this stuff," R.J. proclaimed. "I just wish I could remember what you call it so that I could order it again."

"All I ever remember is Moo Goo Gai Pan," Jennifer added, "and I don't even remember if I like that or not."

"All right, boys and girls," Jack said, finishing the last of his pressed duck, "let's get down to business. I'm going to start with a little story."

"Once upon a time, I was a very young prosecutor . . . this was a long time ago . . . and I was assigned to my very first felony trial. We were 'Ready One,' which meant that we would pick a jury as soon as the current trial in front of our judge ended. Anyway, the day after we were notified of our status, I was on the elevator in the courthouse with two guys who looked like lawyers. All of a sudden, they started talking about my case. By the time we got to the first floor, they had laid out their entire defense strategy right before my very open ears. That night I worked late and I researched the very same points on which they planned to rely. Two days later when the trial started, I pounded them. I don't think they ever figured it out. They probably didn't even remember being on the elevator and talking about the case."

"The point is this . . . what we discuss here must be left here. Don't talk about it to anyone: not Arlo, not Les Leslie, not even Grandma. Don't even talk about it to each other when other people are around. Understand?"

Three heads nodded in agreement and Jack added, "Dennis Woodbrace's freedom may depend on whether or not you remember that. Now let's discuss our theory of the case. Rob and I worked on it today . . ."

Jennifer looked at R.J. who shrugged at her and looked away in reply.

"Didn't he tell you?" Jack asked.

"No," Jennifer replied frostily, "he didn't.

"Good man, Rob. That's the idea," Jack said to him, as he continued. "Our client, who is still in jail, insists he doesn't know 'nuthin' about no rings'. We also found out that the bracelet that was found on him when he was arrested is very real, and worth at least ten thousand dollars. I figured we had run into a brick wall and I'm sure Rob agreed. So I came home and began changing fuel filters." Jack looked at R.J. "And you probably went back to the Bank and said wills and trusts aren't so bad after all, right, Rob?"

"Well, I didn't say it, but I was thinking about it," R.J. confirmed.

"Then my brilliant and not-to-mention sexy bride-to-be came home and started talking about 'cost of goods sold' and bankruptcy fraud. She had this crazy idea about fake jewelry. And that got us talking about insurance."

"Oh, Lord, this is beginning to sound like the plot of an old Grade B movie," Jennifer said.

"Yes, but it you think about it objectively, it's really not that far-fetched," Jack replied.

"Thank you for the credit, Darling," Marilyn interjected, "but I didn't come up with the fake jewelry idea. I was talking about bankruptcy fraud."

"But you mentioned the word 'fraud.' Let's forget about bankruptcy fraud. It only adds another layer of complication. Think about simple insurance fraud," Jack told her. "You put Rick Summers' suspicions into focus for us. Up to the point of the robbery, what difference did it make if the jewelry in the store was fake? It would just be a way of keeping down the cost of inventory. But what if it were insured as if it were real? Morelle might even have had real jewelry in there at one time, and after it was insured he might have slowly replaced it with paste . . . a piece at a time. He would still have to keep one or two real pieces around in case anyone got suspicious. A ten thousand dollar bracelet would go a long way toward diverting attention away from the fake stuff."

"Jack, this really *is* a little far-fetched," R.J. observed.

"Is it?" Jack shot back. "Look at the facts. What other theory fits all of them?"

"That Dennis Woodbrace took the jewelry, whacked Morelle on the head and took off in his car," R.J. offered.

"Then why won't he tell us where the rest of the loot is?" Jack demanded. "You saw him today. He's scared as hell. He thinks he's facing life in prison . . . and he might be. He's certainly facing a long stretch. He knows he can't survive inside the walls; he can barely make it in the county jail. You can't convince me that Dennis Woodbrace is willing to trade years of his life . . . and maybe even his entire life . . . for money, no matter how much money."

"But your theory requires Morelle to hit himself in the face . . ." R.J. protested.

"Is that any less believable than Dennis volunteering to do hard time?" Jack interrupted. "You were there. We told him *you* might be able to get him a plea . . . a couple of years, maybe even less, and a lot of probation. All he had to do was tell us where the rest of the stuff is. And what did he say?" Jack asked rhetorically.

"He said he didn't know 'nuthin' about no rings'," R.J. confirmed.

"Maybe, just maybe, he really doesn't know 'nuthin' about no rings'," Jack continued. "Maybe this so-called robbery is just a way of getting rid of a lot of paste and charging it to an insurance company."

"I don't know, Jack," R. J. said, "This really is starting to sound like a movie script."

"Sometimes life imitates art, my friend," Jack said. "Anyway, it's this or plead guilty. Deke Stoner isn't giving us much of a choice."

"At least Stoner will be concentrating on the bracelet," R.J. said. It looked like he was at last warming to Jack's theory of the case.

"Right. And as far as we're concerned, the bracelet is irrelevant," Jack said. "We're going to concentrate on the other items . . . the so-called 'missing' items. We're going to do a discovery deposition on Mr. Morelle, and when we're finished, we're going to subpoena some records. Lots of records. We're going to track every missing item back to its source."

"Where do Jennifer and I come in?" Marilyn asked. "Why get us involved, even if you insist on giving me credit for your idea?"

"You're involved because one of you is a lawyer . . . almost," Jack said quickly. "And even if you're not directly on the case, you're married to the lawyers." Jennifer smiled and looked at R.J. who looked embarrassed. "Well, one of you is . . . almost married . . . and the other is, well . . . 'involved'," Jack fumbled.

"Don't try to explain, Darling," Marilyn said. "You're only making things worse. We understand: you're afraid we might overhear something."

Jack nodded. "If this is going to be as much work as I think it will be, we'll probably need your help, too. The most important thing is this: whatever we do, whatever you see, whatever you hear, it must be forgotten. Think of my elevator story. Okay?"

Jennifer and Marilyn nodded their agreement.

Jack continued, "All right. Rob, tomorrow find out how much vacation time you have coming from the Bank. We have a lot of work to do and not much time to do it. I don't want to waive our client's right to a speedy trial. If he's innocent, let's get him out. If he's guilty, he might as well start doing his time." He paused, and then added, "Oh, and one more thing . . ." Jack took a half-dollar out of his pocket and slapped it down on the table in front of R.J.

"What's that?" the younger man asked.

"Your half of the retainer," Jack replied. "Now it's official."

"I'll take that," Jennifer announced grandly, as she picked up the coin. "After all, if I'm going to be 'involved' with a lawyer, I might as well get into practice!"

℘ ℭ

Marilyn was at her desk bright and early the next morning making a list of things that needed to be done before her July bar examination. As she worked, Jennifer looked out the window at nothing in particular. "What's it like, being married?" she asked dreamily, finally putting her thoughts into words.

"I don't know," Marilyn replied, not looking up from her work. "I'm not married yet."

"Sure you are. You just haven't gone through a ceremony yet. You'll never be very far away from Jack."

"No, I guess I won't," Marilyn said as she continued to make notes.

"What's it like? I mean, do you guys 'do it' every night?"

"Jennifer!" That question got Marilyn's attention and she put down her pencil.

"What's the matter?" Jennifer asked, turning away from the window.

"That's a rather personal question, don't you think?" Marilyn said with a shocked laugh.

"Well, gosh, who can I ask if not you?" Jennifer said.

Marilyn smiled. Sometimes Jennifer could be so charmingly naïve.

"I guess we 'do it' quite a bit," Marilyn admitted, almost blushing. "But that will wear off after a while."

"How can you be so sure?"

"That's what everyone says, and besides I . . . well, let's just say I know," Marilyn said.

"You've done it before, haven't you?" Jennifer said excitedly. "Come on, tell me everything."

"I lived with a guy in Baton Rouge while I was in law school," Marilyn began. "God, Sister Jean-Marie would have had a fit if she had known about it . . . especially since she arranged for my scholarship. 'Living in sin' wasn't the kind of thing a girl who was raised at Sainte Anne's was supposed to do."

"Did you love him?" Jennifer asked.

"Who?"

"The guy you were living with," Jennifer replied testily.

"Nicholas? He was all right, I guess. I thought I loved him. He was getting his Master's in Business Administration and I was working and going to law school. All my friends were either married or living with people. I suppose I wanted the security of doing the same thing. And I was so tired of living in a dorm."

"So why did you break up?"

"Nick hated the idea of me being a lawyer. I guess he must have felt threatened or something. He treated our relationship like . . . like a business. He used to keep track of which one of us went grocery shopping and how much we each spent. He expected me to pay half the rent and utilities. That was all right in a way, I guess, but he was just so . . . businesslike. It was always 'mine' and 'yours.' Nick never thought in terms of 'us.' Maybe he was just being modern or something . . . you know, all that stuff you're supposed to think about a relationship being a 'partnership.' The problem was, I *wanted* a relationship, not a business deal. I never knew if he cared about me or my checkbook." Marilyn looked down at the desk and began toying with her pencil. "It's just as well," she added after a short pause. "I found out that I didn't care about him. I guess what I was looking for was love; I just didn't know what that word really meant back then."

"So what does it mean?" Jennifer asked.

"Well, it's not just 'doing it' . . . even though that's a lot of fun. And it's not just living together, either. Love is knowing the other person's innermost self . . . and accepting it;

being comfortable with it. I guess it's true . . . what they say about someone being your missing half. I couldn't imagine living without Jack anymore." She paused; there was nothing more to say.

"I think that's the way I feel about R.J.," Jennifer began. "He's so nice to be around. I'm really comfortable with him, but sometimes I just don't know what I want."

"You have plenty of time, Jen."

"But I want to be getting on with my life," she replied.

"Well, it wouldn't be fair to either of you to make a commitment until you know yourself better. You have to know yourself before you can really know anyone else," Marilyn warned. "Come on," she added, pushing a phone book across the desk. "Grandma wants us to get things underway. You can start by calling someone to get rid of all that junk upstairs. Try 'trash removal' or 'hauling.' Then we'll have to get an architect in here and get some bids from general contractors. Ask R.J. who he would recommend. Grandma wants action, and we'll give it to her."

"Now you're talking, Sis," Jennifer agreed as she picked up the telephone.

಄ ಐ

Les Leslie and Arlo Woodbrace watched in silence as a container truck rumbled up to the marina office and workmen punched a hole in the wall of the second floor of the building. Jennifer was dressed in her standard tee shirt and jeans, and now sported a hard hat that the foremen insisted she wear while she walked around the site with her ever-present clipboard. Amid the noise and dust, Marilyn talked to two men who unrolled blueprints on the hood of an automobile and gestured toward the building.

"Changes," Les finally said with a grunt. "They're makin' changes. This don't look good, Arlo."

Chapter 24

The Calkins brothers' station wagon made the turn off the highway and nearly collided with a truck that was barreling up the shell-rock road from the marina.

"What the hell is going on in there?" Junior demanded as Doug guided the car though the dust the truck left hanging in the hot summer air.

The scene that greeted them did not give Junior any reassurance. Workmen swarmed over the building, tearing off siding and pitching debris out of several new openings in the second-floor wall. Worst of all, his daughter appeared to be directing the operation. He was in a rage even before Doug found a place to park.

Jennifer saw the car and retreated into the office with her father close on her heels.

"What the god-damn-hell is going on?" he stormed. "And what the god-damn-hell are you doing here?"

Jennifer appeared to wilt in terror before her father. The brightness in her eyes faded, and her face became a frozen mask.

Marilyn stood up and moved between them. "Your mother has decided to make some changes in the building," she began, using the explanation that she and Jennifer had rehearsed many times.

"Oh she did, did she?" Junior ranted. "And who the god-damn-hell told her she could make any changes?" His face was livid and the veins on his neck and forehead looked as though they might burst at any second.

"Well, it . . . it's her building . . ." Marilyn said as Jennifer cowered behind her.

"Oh it is, is it?" he raged. "Well, you've got a lot to learn, Sweetie, and so does that old bitch!"

"Junior, come on, settle down," Doug said, taking his brother's arm and trying to calm him.

"Let go of me, you god-damn weasel!" Junior shouted. "This is all your god-damn fault! I told you we should have put the old bitch away in a nursing home years ago. Who knows what other screwy ideas she's cooked up?"

"Junior, take it easy," Doug pleaded.

"Shut up, stupid!" A foam of saliva had formed at the corners of Junior's mouth and some of it sprayed on Doug.

"Mr. Calkins," Marilyn began, trying with all her might to remain cool and professional, "your mother . . ."

"Don't call that old bitch my mother!" Junior shouted. His eyes bugged out, and Marilyn thought he might have a stroke. "As for you, Sweetie Pie," he raged as he turned his venom on her, "I knew you were trouble the minute you walked in here. Now you can pack your shit and get out. I'm going to settle things with that old bitch once and for all . . . and I don't want to see you here when I get back! Come on, Doug," he shouted as he turned for the door.

It was then that something snapped in Jennifer. "No!" she shouted as she rushed past Marilyn and blocked the door. "You leave my grandmother alone!"

"Well, well, what do we have here? A little bitch in training," Junior sneered.

Jennifer was too angry to be afraid. Her only thought was to protect her grandmother. "You might as well know Grandma has nothing to do with this," she shouted defiantly. "She gave this building to me . . . me and Marilyn. It's all done, and there's nothing you can do about it! And if you want to stay here, you'll have to deal with us!"

"Oh, I will, will I?" Junior exploded. "Here!" He struck her across her face with the full force of the back of his hand. The blow sent her reeling over a pile of debris and into freestanding metal shelves that wobbled precariously. Only Marilyn's quick response kept the contents from falling on Jennifer who lay sprawled on the greasy floor with a small trickle of blood at the corner of her mouth. "That's how I deal with bitches!" Junior shouted at her. "And I'll give you a few more if that wasn't enough!"

"Junior!" Doug exclaimed, holding his brother back. Junior's temper had always gotten him into trouble, but

Doug had never seen him this violent. He plainly did not like what he saw.

Jennifer pushed away Marilyn's proffered help and got to her feet. Her face was already beginning to discolor and she had a distinct ringing in her ears. But her blue eyes were ice cold as she looked at her tormentor. She wiped the blood from her mouth with the back of her hand. "Thank you very much, Mister Calkins," she said, her trembling voice filled with contempt and rage. "That settles things nicely between us. Now get out of my life and don't come back, because if you do I'll have you arrested."

Junior shook Doug off. "We'll see about that," he said as he bolted for the door.

"I better go with him," Doug said apologetically before he followed his brother out the door. "I've never seen Junior this bad."

ઈ ભ

Mrs. Calkins stirred her tea in the living room as she waited for her two stepsons. Although she appreciated Marilyn's warning call, she scoffed at her suggestion of telephoning anyone for protection. She had lived through Junior's tantrums before and she knew how to handle him. Besides, she had control over the one thing Junior loved more than life itself: Captain Kelly's money. It wasn't long before Junior stormed into the house with Doug close behind trying to calm him.

"All right, just what the hell is going on around here?" Junior demanded.

"Why, Junior, how nice to see you," Mrs. Calkins said, returning her teaspoon to her saucer. "And Douglas, too! What a pleasant surprise. The two of you haven't been here since your father passed on."

"Don't give me any of your polite-society-put-on crap," Junior raged.

"Would you care for some tea?" Mrs. Calkins asked, ignoring his last remark. "Douglas?" Doug shook his head in response.

Junior could see that his temper tantrum would get him nowhere. Trying to bully her had always been useless: that was why he kept Doug around, to cajole her when necessary. But there was no time for Doug now. Junior would have to try persuading her himself. "Now listen here," he said, moderating his voice and sitting down on the love seat across from her. "We had a deal."

Mrs. Calkins smiled at this attempted diplomacy. "Yes, indeed," she said quietly, "We *have* a deal. Your father gave his word and I intend to keep it."

"But you gave away the boatyard!" he said, his voice escalating.

"No, I didn't. Not yet, anyway. I gave them only the building."

"The yard will be next." Junior was about to start shouting again.

"It might be."

"But god-damn it . . ."

Mrs. Calkins looked at him severely and Junior's eyes

dropped. She did not allow profanity in her home. She would not allow Casey to use it, and she would not accept it from a man who did not deserve to speak his name, much less carry it.

"Our 'deal' as you call it was . . . and is . . . that you and Douglas will be treated equally. I should like to remind you that 'equally' might mean one dollar . . . each."

Doug's eyes widened and Junior was on his feet in an instant. "You wouldn't dare . . ." he began.

"Wouldn't I?" she said icily. She turned and looked directly at the younger brother. "Douglas, I suggest you take your brother outside. Anything he says from this point forward might have an injurious effect on your financial future."

"Come on, Junior, let's go," Doug said nervously as he took his older brother's arm.

Junior could see money slipping away, and along with it his indolent lifestyle. One more word out of him might put them both on the unemployment line, or worse, having to work for a living. "Who's going to collect the rents?" he pleaded, trying to reason with her one last time.

"You and Douglas. And you'll divide the money between yourselves and send me the bills, just as you always have."

"But we won't have an office," Junior protested.

"I'm sure the new owners will rent you space if you ask them politely," Mrs. Calkins replied. "Of course, I might allow you to move aboard the *Margaret*."

"That old tub . . ." Junior began before his brother cut him off.

"Come on, Junior, please," Doug said, pulling him toward the door. "Let's get out of here."

୨୦ ଓଡ

"I'm not gonna ask anybody for anything," Junior fumed when they were back inside the car, "especially not that little bitch back at the yard. She thinks she's got me cornered. Well, we'll see about that. I'll put up a storage shed on one of the piers and we'll operate our office out of there."

"Junior, I'm not going to spend my days sitting in a storage shed," Doug protested.

"You'll sit your god-damn fat ass wherever I god-damn tell you to sit it," Junior bellowed. "I'm the boss," he screamed, "and don't you forget it."

It was the same line Junior had used on Doug to bully him since they were kids, and Doug knew better than to answer him. Junior was building himself up for another explosion and any opposition would only make matters worse. By the time they arrived back at the boatyard, Junior was ready to erupt again. The green and white sheriff's cars parked near the building did nothing to cool his anger. Two large uniformed deputies were talking to Jennifer and Marilyn in the office doorway. One of the men turned and blocked Junior's way as he walked toward the building. "Sorry, Mr. Calkins," the deputy said, "you can't go in there."

"Get the god-damn-hell out of my way," Junior demanded, as he pushed the deputy with his forearm. Both

officers immediately responded by grabbing him and pinning his arms behind his back. For a minute it looked
like Junior was about to learn he had made a very serious
mistake, but an unmarked white car entered the parking
lot and drew everyone's attention. A large man unfolded
himself from behind the steering wheel and walked toward
the combatants. His uniform was nothing more than a knit
polo shirt and casual slacks but even the enraged Junior
could not mistake his air of authority. Sheriff Beverly
"Bear" Harper was making a personal appearance.

The Bear's six-foot, two-inch frame was topped by
a patch of hair the color and consistency of steel wool,
and he sported a nose that looked like it had been in too
many barroom brawls. His arms still carried the sinewy
muscles he had developed at his job carrying sides of beef
in the packing house when he was a young man. In all, he
looked like a man who could easily handle Junior along
with two or three of his friends simultaneously—that is, if
Junior had any friends. The Bear sauntered over to where
his deputies held the man who was now their prisoner.
"Relax, boys, Ah'll handle this," he drawled as his men
let Junior go.

"Junior, we haven't had many dealin's, but Ah knew
your Daddy pretty well, and Ah figure Ah owed him this,"
Sheriff Harper explained. "Naow these boys'll tell you Ah
don't make many house calls anymore, so if Ah were you,
Ah'd listen real careful."

"We've had a call of a disturbance and a possible assault

and battery out here, Junior. Out of respect for your Daddy, Ah sure would hate to have these boys take anybody into custody, but Ah will if there's a victim heah who wants ta' press cha'ges." He looked at Jennifer who shook her head from side to side in response.

"That's good," the Bear nodded. "Casey wouldn't a' cared to see this in the papers." Then he turned to Junior. "It seems you're not wanted here, Junior," the Sheriff said softly. "Now whah don't you just go on down the road and be thankful you're not spendin' the night as a guest in mah jail."

"I'll fight this. I'll get a lawyer . . ." Junior said with a vicious snarl.

"That sounds like a fahn eye-deah," Sheriff Harper responded. "You get yourself a lawyah. Whatever problem you think you got here, you settle it in civil court."

"Come on, Doug, " Junior said. "Let's beat it."

"No!"

"What?" Junior whirled and glared at his younger brother. "What did you say to me?"

Doug's knees shook visibly. His mouth moved but he made no sound at first. "I said 'no', Junior," he finally blurted out. "I've had it with you. You've bullied me all my life, but today . . . this was too much. You won't bully me anymore." He threw Junior the car keys. "You can leave. I'm not going with you."

"Just what do you think you'll do without me, you worthless piece of shit?"

"I'll do what I've always done: run the boatyard from right here." Doug looked past his brother at Jennifer and Marilyn and added, "That is, if the ladies will let me."

"You think I'm going to trust you with my money?" Junior screamed.

"You'll get your half, every month, same as always," Doug said disgustedly.

"You listen to me, you weasel," Junior said, shaking a finger at this brother. "If I ever think you're cheating me, this stupid redneck"—he jerked his thumb at Sheriff Harper—"and his whole god-damn department won't be able to keep me outta here."

Doug walked over and stood next to Jennifer. "I won't take your money, Junior. I couldn't be bothered."

Junior Calkins had no response. He was a beaten man. He glared at them in silence but his shoulders sagged noticeably. He turned and walked to the station wagon without another word. In a moment the engine roared to life and he was bouncing his way out of the parking lot, leaving a cloud of dust behind. Jennifer stood between her uncle and Marilyn, holding their hands. As she watched her father drive away she felt . . . nothing.

❧❦

Later that afternoon, Marilyn and Grandma Calkins tended to Jennifer in her bedroom at the Magnolia Avenue house. Jennifer's head was pounding so hard she could not lift it off the pillow and she felt she might get sick to her stomach any minute.

"You'll have quite a shiner for a few days, Love, but you'll survive," Grandma said applying witch hazel to Jennifer's puffy face while Marilyn held an ice bag on her eye, which was now swollen almost completely shut.

"I'm so sorry, Grandma," Jennifer moaned. "I guess I blew it."

"Nonsense, Dear, you did nothing of the kind," her grandmother reassured her.

"But all the trouble you went through with Jack and R.J. to make it so our names wouldn't appear ... and then I went and just blurted it out."

"That secrecy business was a foolish idea of mine, Dearest. I was trying to protect you, while it seems you were trying to protect me. It doesn't matter now. It all had to come out, sooner or later. It's better this way. Now it's out in the open and you can get on with your life."

⁛ ⁚

Down in the kitchen, Jack and R.J. stood together as men do when their only job is to stay out of the way of women.

"Damn it, Jack. We should have been there. I should have been there!" R.J. muttered, trying to contain the anger in his voice.

"We were at a bail hearing ... which we lost ... remember?" Jack said, pouring two glasses of Mrs. Calkins' rum.

"They could have called us," R.J. protested.

"You don't call people in courtrooms, Rob," Jack responded. "Here, drink this. It'll mellow you out a little."

R.J. raised the glass to his lips and coughed slightly. "God, this stuff is strong," he whispered. "What is it?"

"Casey Calkins liked hundred-proof Navy Rum. I can't tell you how many bottles of this stuff I went through with him and his cronies. She still keeps it around after all these years; same brand, and in the same cupboard, too." Jack went to the refrigerator and took out an ice tray. "I never understood why he wouldn't let her buy a new 'frige with an automatic icemaker," he continued.

"Jennifer told me they would never buy anything until the old one wore out completely. They were the last ones in town with a black and white television," R.J. said.

"That sounds like Casey," Jack said as he put a handful of ice into the younger man's glass "Here, this will knock it down a little."

"All right now, what could you have done about it if had been there? Jack asked rhetorically.

"I could have beaten the son-of-a-bitch senseless," R.J. muttered, clenching his fist.

"And then you could have gone to jail . . . and gotten disbarred," Jack added. "Listen, Rob, the relationship between Jennifer and her father has been a boil festering in this family for a long time. It had to be lanced, sooner or later, and Jennifer was the only one who could do it."

"He didn't have to hit her like that," R.J. protested.

"Bruises heal quickly, Rob," Jack replied. "Emotional wounds take a lot longer. You'll have to help her with those."

Chapter 25

W ord of Jennifer's black eye surged though the marina like a rogue wave. The construction workers closed ranks around her. Her unabashed enthusiasm combined with her willingness to jump in and tackle anything made her their darling. Some of the men let it be known around the island that it would be best for Junior Calkins to keep his distance in the future. Construction sites are dangerous places, they reminded people, and strangers who wander around them unbidden have been known to have serious and sometimes fatal accidents.

Jennifer was back on the job a few days later, still bearing the marks of her father's attack. Work came to a complete halt as the men, led by construction foreman Tim Gorman, presented her with a brand-new white hard hat with her name across the back and the words "Boss Lady" emblazoned on the front. From that day on, Jennifer was the undisputed queen of the job site and, for her part, her evening reports to Grandma were filled with expressions of pride in the work "our guys" were doing.

Marilyn, too, was busy juggling her professional and personal lives. She and Jack agreed to put their wedding on hold until after both the bar exam and the Woodbrace trial were over, but that didn't stop her from giving up her apartment and moving aboard the trawler where she spent much of her time studying. Living aboard was the practical thing to do, she insisted when Jennifer questioned her about the arrangement. "Oh, I agree completely," Jennifer told her. "And besides," she added with a knowing smile, "the fringe benefits must be nice."

With the trawler turned into a study hall for Marilyn, Jack spent most of his days in R.J.'s office at the Bank where they poured over reams of documents. The missing rings were never found, and Jack was determined to track each one of them back to its source.

The frenetic pace of their four lives left much of the detail work of the marina to Doug Calkins who settled into his old office. With his brother out of the way, Doug surprised everyone with his eagerness to please. For the first time the residents of the place found themselves treated like valued customers when they entered the office. Doug's only fault continued to be his inability to accept responsibility. He deferred to Marilyn or Jennifer whenever a decision had to be made. It seemed as though all self-confidence had been crushed out of him when he was a child, and now, even though he was no longer under his brother's heavy hand, he could not function on his own.

As construction progressed, it became apparent that the real problem was none of them had any experience in operating a restaurant. Jennifer could meet with architects and inspectors all day long but, when it came down to the nitty gritty of knowing how things should actually work once the place opened, she relied on pure guesswork aided by Marilyn's intuition. It was not a good way to spend money, Marilyn kept reminding her.

The two of them were pondering the situation in the office one morning amid the noise and bustle of construction when Jim Lacey caught up with them.

"Excuse me?" he said, poking his head in the door.

They were studying the blueprints for the thousandth time and did not hear him. The crew needed a final answer on the doors in and out of the kitchen. The architect had provided for two, but their placement bothered Marilyn. Something told her that "in" and "out" needed to be reversed.

"You want the 'in' door on this side," the man said, touching the blueprint with a wrinkled but firm finger.

"I thought so, but why?" The question slipped out before Marilyn realized there was a third person in the room.

"Most servers carry trays on the left," the voice explained. "If you set it up the way he's drawn it, they'll be running into each other. Of course, you could put them at opposite ends and set up a circular traffic pattern. And it doesn't have to take up any more room if you plan the kitchen properly now."

Suddenly it looked a lot clearer. "He's right, Marilyn," Jennifer said. "If we move this counter out of the corner . . ."

"Wait a minute, Jen," Marilyn interrupted. She looked at the man who by then was hunched over the blueprints with them. "Excuse me. Who are you, and how do you know about this?"

"Oh, I'm sorry. I'm Jim Lacey," the man said. "My friend Eddie and I live on the boat behind yours: the one with the flowers."

"Mr. Lacey!" Marilyn exclaimed. "I've spoken with Eddie many times, but I don't think we've ever met."

"We haven't. I keep to myself a lot."

"What can we do for you, Mr. Lacey?" Jennifer asked.

"Well, actually, I was wondering if I could do something for you," he replied.

"What do you mean?" Marilyn said.

"Well, Miss Dupré . . . Miss Calkins . . ." he sat down across from them and folded his hands almost in prayer. His face appeared youthful, but from his white hair and wizened hands, Marilyn guessed he was in his early sixties.

"You see, I've been retired for four years," he explained, "and I hate it. If I don't get to work pretty soon, I'm going to go nuts. What's worse is that Eddie hates boats. He's never said it, but I've come to realize that's how he feels. That's why I keep building flower boxes and trying to make the place look like a cottage . . . trying to make him happy. Of course, he doesn't know that I know he isn't . . . happy."

"I think I understand, Mr. Lacey," Marilyn replied, "but I don't see what this has to do with us."

"Maybe I should start at the beginning," Lacey said, unclasping and re-clasping his hands. "I used to own a restaurant in Detroit. It was a nice place, not too big. Well, I guess I let the pressure of things get to me and four years ago I had a heart attack. A bad one. It scared the hell out of Eddie. We had been together for a long time, and he forced ... well, urged me ... to sell out and take my disability payments. We stayed in Detroit for a year and I was miserable. I was stuck in the house most of the time and always looking at magazines about boats and Florida and the Caribbean." He unclasped and re-clasped his hands again. Obviously he was nervous. "Eddie didn't want to leave the States because of my health and ... we wound up here in Calkins Harbor.

"You have your boat and he has a cottage. That seems like a fair compromise," Marilyn observed.

"Well, that's what we thought, but see ... I had never owned a boat, Mrs. .... Miss Dupré. It was all a fantasy. And like most fantasies, it was better as a fantasy than it is in real life."

"It does take some getting used to," Marilyn agreed.

"Yes, well, I found that out too late. My life was in the food business. I hate fishing. I hate building flower boxes. And if I don't find something to do with myself pretty soon I'll go crazy."

"Does Eddie know about this?" Jennifer sounded like a cross between a pop psychologist and a personal counselor.

"Heck, no. He'd have a fit if he knew I was here asking for a job. He's always following me around, hovering over me, reminding me to take my pills. He makes me feel like I'm going to keel over any minute. I've got to get back to work!"

"Is that what you're doing, asking for a job?" Marilyn inquired.

"Arlo Woodbrace said you folks were building a restaurant up here. Well, that's my line, all right. I figured if you didn't have anybody in mind to manage the place . . . I could tell Eddie that I'm just helping you out by showing you the ropes. He really likes the two of you."

Marilyn smiled when she thought of Eddie Miles, tending his flowers and trying to make a houseboat into a country cottage. She hoped she could be that devoted to Jack if the time ever came.

"Look, I won't die on you or anything," Lacey blurted out.

"What?" Jennifer was startled by the suggestion.

"In spite of what Eddie thinks. I'm not going to keel over. I'm as healthy as an ox."

"We really can't take that kind of responsibility . . ." Marilyn began. She stopped suddenly. Grandma's words about everyone having a purpose in life rushed back to her. She looked at Jennifer.

"You promise you'll tell us right away if you're ever . . . not feeling well?" Jennifer asked.

"I promise."

"You'll only be helping us out," Marilyn reminded him. "There would be no reason to get . . . well, to get upset if things didn't go right. Understand?"

"You got it."

"We'll expect you to go home and take a nap or something every afternoon," Jennifer added.

"Anything!" Lacey agreed.

Marilyn and Jennifer exchanged one more glance before Marilyn turned and extended her hand. "Welcome aboard, Mr. Lacey," she said. "Now tell us what we're supposed to do about our friends 'in' and 'out'."

"Call me Jim . . . and let me at those blueprints."

∞ ⌒

At the Magnolia Avenue house, Les Leslie struggled to hold the china teacup in his thick hands without crushing it.

"Would you prefer a mug, Mr. Leslie?" Mrs. Calkins asked politely.

"No, Ma'am. No, this is fine," he assured her.

They were sitting in the dining room, a place that made him uncomfortable all by itself. He didn't need the added distraction of a china teacup and silver service.

"There are big changes happening at the boatyard," she observed.

"Yes, Ma'am, there sure are."

"You don't care much for change, I know."

"No, Ma'am. No, it ain't one of my favorite things," he admitted.

He couldn't figure out what she was getting at. He had been her caretaker for a number of years. The work was easy. "Money for old rope," his father would have called it. The hardest part of the job was times like these when no one else was available and he was pressed into service, drinking tea with her. Today, with Jennifer at the boatyard and Marilyn in her last week of preparation for her bar examination, his job was once again to make polite conversation over china cups.

"Would you care for more pie?" she asked.

"Yes, Ma'am, thank you. That would be nice," he said as she cut him a large slice.

"I'm afraid it's not homemade," she apologized.

"That's all right, Ma'am. It's fine."

She did make the best Key Lime pie he'd ever eaten, he had to give her that. The one on the table was not up to her standard of perfection but it was good enough to warrant another round.

"Tell me about Elena, Mr. Leslie," she said.

"Well," he began, lifting the fork to his mouth, "I've got her decked over, and her hull is just about finished. She'll be ready for the water any day now."

"That's very nice," Mrs. Calkins said. "Now tell me about the real Elena."

That question caught him off his guard. Most of their teatime discussions involved the boatyard and its residents. She had never before put him on the spot by asking a direct, personal question. He wasn't sure how to handle it.

"What do you mean, Ma'am?" he asked, putting down the fork and stalling for time.

She smiled a little. "You know what I mean, Cecil. Men don't name boats by picking names out of the air. As often as we've spoken, you've never told me about Elena. Now, who is she?"

This was serious. Nobody—*nobody*—ever called Les Leslie by his given name. Most people didn't even know his real name, and for sure Mrs. Calkins had never used it. He fidgeted in his chair, but could not think of a polite way to escape.

"Well?" She was waiting for an answer.

"She's . . . she was . . . a friend of mine," he muttered, looking down at his plate.

"I guessed that. Where is she?"

The conversation brought back thoughts of the young girl he left behind when he was forced to ship out long ago. When he closed his eyes some nights he could picture her there, like his buddies told him later, looking small and alone on the Sicilian quay, clutching flowers he had asked them to take to her.

"She's in Italy, I guess; or Sicily, rather. If she's still alive," he mused, pushing away the plate. He didn't feel much like pie anymore.

"You don't know?"

"I was an eighteen year old swabbie. I got over there with the Navy a year before the War ended. Her father, well, the less said about him the better. Anyways, I promised 'er I'd send for her. I wrote f'r a while. I don't know if my letters ever got through. I guess I kind a' lost track."

"I want you to go back there and find her, Cecil."

"What? Oh, now, Ma'am, that's crazy."

"No it isn't," Mrs. Calkins replied firmly. "I'll pay for your trip and for any expenses. But you must go there and find her."

"It's crazy, I tell you. What would I do with her if I found her? She's prob'ly married . . . or dead."

"She might not be. As for what you do with her when you find her, well, I suppose that's up to you . . . and her, of course."

"Now, look, Ma'am, I appreciate the thought, I really do. But it's a crazy idea. That was over a long time ago."

"People say it's never over until a certain obese woman sings, Cecil."

"That's 'fat lady,' Ma'am. 'It's not over until the fat lady sings'," Les explained.

"Well I've never been quite sure of who she is but I don't believe she's gotten to your song yet." Mrs. Calkins took his callused hands in hers. "Cecil, we've known each other a long time. Your friendship has meant a great deal to me . . . and to many people at the boatyard. Now I want you to do one last thing for me: I want you to promise me that you'll find Elena."

"I promise you that I'll look for her," he replied.

"If you look for her, you'll find her."

℘ ℘

Erlene Rodgers lay next to Arlo in the cabin of his sailboat. With Faith getting ready for college and Tommy home for the summer, she could not spend as much time with Arlo as she would like, and their lives had begun drifting apart. Dennis' upcoming trial did not help the situation. When he was faced with a problem, Arlo closed in upon himself. Erlene had learned that even in the best of times he was not good at showing his feelings, and these were certainly not the best of times. She found herself reaching out more and more to an Arlo who always retreated just a little bit more ahead of her.

"Arlo?" she asked as she ran his hand over his bare chest, "What're ya' thinkin'?"

"Nothin'"

"Wouldn't it be nice ta' just take this boat an' sail away for a couple a' days. Just go somewheres?"

"I guess," he replied without sounding like he meant it.

"Would ya' like that? Just you and me?"

"I guess."

She sat up suddenly and the sheet fell away as she looked at him. "Arlo, do I mean anything to you?" she demanded.

"What? What's that supposed to mean?"

"It's a question. It's supposed ta' mean, 'Do I mean anything to you'?"

"Well, sure, I guess."

"You guess? You guess? Don't ya' know?"

"Well, sure I know, I guess ... I mean, sure," he fumbled.

"Maybe I better just get out a' here until you *are* sure,"

she said as she jumped out of the bed and began searching for her clothes.

"Aw, now look, Erlene," Arlo began.

"Don't you 'Look Erlene' me!" she fumed as she jiggled into her tee shirt. "Maybe I made a mistake ... another mistake. I seem to be makin' mistakes about men all the time."

"Now don't say that, Erlene!" he pleaded.

"I thought you was different, Arlo. That's why I fell .. . that's why I ... did what I did with you. But you're just like the rest of 'em." She stuffed the tee shirt into her jeans and fought to pull up the zipper.

"C'm on, Erlene, don't be like that. It's just that I'm kind a' worried about the trial an' all."

"I know you're worried, Arlo. I'm worried too. Everybody is. But we can't stop livin' because of it. You never talk ta' me, Arlo. I didn't even know about y're kids until this trial business come up. What else didn't ya' tell me? I'll tell ya' one thing ya' never told me ... you never once told me that you love me."

"I guess I'm just not much good at talkin' ..."

"Y're good at talkin', Arlo," she continued. "Y're real good at talkin'. Y're just not good at sayin' anythin'." She stomped out of the cabin and started up the ladder to the deck in her skin-tight jeans.

He wrapped the bedsheet around his waist and stood in the doorway. "Don't go, Erlene," he pleaded.

She turned back and looked at him. "Whah? Whah shouldn't I go?"

"Please?"

"I'd like ta' please you, Arlo; I really would. I just don't know how."

"I . . . I guess I love you, Erlene," he muttered, looking down at the cabin sole.

"Still guessin', Arlo?"

He looked up and faced her. "No, I don't guess, Erlene. I know. I do love you."

She stepped off the ladder. "Well, maybe I better stay for a minute and see what else ya' got ta' say."

"Can Ah at least get dressed first?" he asked.

"Whah?" she smirked. "What a' you got under that sheet that Ah ain't seen?"

"C'mon, Erlene," he pleaded, "Come back to bed."

"There's more ta' life than just bed, Arlo," she replied.

"Suppose we . . . kind a' make it permanent?"

"Are you proposin' to me? 'Cause if ya' are, I'd kind a' like ta' remember this. I ain't never been proposed ta' by a man wearin' a bedsheet before."

"It won't be easy. I still got to pay for them kids."

"Are you proposin'?" she demanded.

"Maybe once Faith starts college, you and Tommy could kind a' live right here on the boat f'r a while."

"Arlo, are you proposin' or ain't you?"

"I'm proposin'," he replied.

"In that case, I'm acceptin'."

"Now will you come back in here?" he pleaded.

"Only if you get rid a' that silly sheet," she said.

80 03

Marilyn's big day finally came. Late afternoon found Jack Townsend waiting for her with an armful of flowers at the bar of the Bonita Sands Hotel, where the bar exam was being administered.

"Hi," she said brightly as she walked out of the ballroom filled with desks, chairs, and the last few candidates. She kissed him lightly. "Are these for me?" she asked, picking up the bouquet.

"Well, you seem pleased with yourself," he observed. "Think you did okay?"

"I'd say so. I know I really killed them on that last essay question."

"Oh?"

She looked at him with eyes that spoke volumes. "General and limited partnerships," she explained. "I had a very good teacher for that. Remember?"

Chapter 26

Judge Regis Horatio MacIntyre drew himself up to his full five-foot-four-inch height, peered over the top of his bench and intoned in a slow drawl, "Ahr the lawyahs ready to proceed? Theah will be no continuances heayh."

"The State is ready, Your Honor," Deke Stoner, dressed in a three-piece suit, was on his feet toying with his half-glasses and already playing to the gallery.

"Verah well." Judge MacIntyre turned aside and spat into a tin cup. "Mistah Bailiff, bring in the venire."

Marilyn was watching from the first row. Despite Jack's warning of the previous night she was surprised by the fact that MacIntyre chewed tobacco on the bench and dribbled the juice into a tin cup decorated with a Santa Claus painted by his granddaughter. "I'm *not* kidding," Jack had insisted in response to her protestations. "If you're going to come down to watch, make sure you've eaten a good breakfast."

The judge greeted the prospective jurors who were brought into the courtroom, and ordered the clerk to draw the names of the first six who would be seated in the jury box for questioning. "Let's keep it shaht, gen'lemen," Judge MacIntyre drawled. "We have a not insubstantial numbah of cases on the calandah. Mistah State Attahney, you may proceed."

Deke Stoner went first, questioning the prospective jurors about their attitudes and attempting to engage them with too-slick sincerity, Marilyn thought. She tried to concentrate on what was happening and read thoughts into each answer, but it was not easy. Stoner kept asking people whether they agreed with this or that principle of law, and most of their answers were confined to very brief yeses and noes. Finally, it was Jack's turn. Marilyn smiled quietly when he turned to the first juror and said, "Tell me a little about yourself, Mrs. Seidell."

"Well, I have three beautiful grandchildren . . ." the woman began, and Marilyn wondered how long it would take Jack to learn as much about this stranger as he had learned about her on their first date that evening at the Beach House.

The questioning ground on. Every now and then the attorneys would meet at the bench and various jurors would be excused for no apparent reason. New ones would take their places, and the questioning would begin again. Judge MacIntyre did not appear to be happy with the amount of time it was taking, and more than once interrupted either Jack or Deke with the comment that a question had been asked before and the juror's mind "likely has not changed in the pahst twenty minutes." Neither attorney seemed particularly rattled by the interruption. When it happened each of them thanked the judge and sidestepped into another question.

As the hands of the courtroom clock crept past eleven, Marilyn began to study Judge MacIntyre in earnest. She noticed, for example, that he had begun to turn away from the jury and spit into his cup with increasing frequency. Jack had told her that the senior criminal court judge was known as "Hangin' Mac," and enjoyed the fact that he was hated and feared throughout the circuit. Judge MacIntyre took great delight in calling strange lawyers, especially the ones he called "the Miamah boys," up to the bench for a personal examination of their bar cards—an identification issued by the Florida Bar to every practicing attorney— to determine if they were indeed licensed to practice law. On days when he felt particularly cantankerous, the ritual examination would end with Mac expressing amazement to his clerk and bailiff that his latest victim had indeed passed the bar examination.

Jack was not happy with the assignment of Dennis' case to Judge MacIntyre, and confided to Marilyn that a guilty verdict would almost certainly result in a long prison sentence. "Still," she heard him tell R.J. in one of their late-night strategy discussions aboard the boat, "Mac's got guts. He won't hesitate to pull the plug if he smells a rat. And I think I have enough credibility with him to get some leeway on cross-examination."

It was nearing noon. Both sides were down to quibbling over the alternate juror, and the judge was down to his last 'chaw' of tobacco. Each attorney began to excuse whomever the other accepted. Marilyn thought it looked like two small boys who had each decided not to be the first one to give in. Judge MacIntyre must have gotten the same idea. "Ah wish to remahd Counsel that as the issahs in this case ahr straight-forwahd and the likelihood of a jurah becoming incapacitated remote, the Coaht is considerin' dispensin' with an alternate."

In other words, Marilyn thought, he's saying "Get on with it, boys. If you keep fooling around, I might get tired of this and take the marbles away from both of you." With that, an alternate juror was quickly accepted by both sides, the jury was sworn and the judge announced a forty-five minute luncheon recess.

"I thought we were supposed to get an hour and a half," R.J. complained in the windowless attorney's conference room as he and Jack ate cold sandwiches from the courthouse coffee shop.

"You've been watching too many movies, Rob," Jack replied. "It's early in the week and he's in a good mood . . . that's why we're getting forty-five minutes. If this thing starts to drag, we'll soon be down to thirty."

"That doesn't give us much time to prepare," R.J. said.

"Prepare what? If we can't anticipate the answer to every question by now, we've lost. That's what we've been doing these past two months, remember?"

"What do you think Stoner will start with?"

"After opening statements, Deke will call somebody from the Crime Scene Unit. Deke prides himself on thinking he's methodical ... even though he isn't, and everyone's afraid to tell him so. He'll call some detective who'll put the jury to sleep by testifying about the sizes of room and the directions things face. The jurors who don't fall asleep will be so confused they'll be lost. Why don't you handle the cross-examination?"

"Me?" R.J. suddenly looked ill. "I've never done this before. What am I supposed to say? Maybe I should just sit and watch you."

"You want to be a trial lawyer, don't you?" Jack responded. "This is it. Just keep it short, and for God's sake don't piss off Judge Mac by going over things that have already been asked."

"Jack, I don't know ..."

"Sure you do. This is it, Rob. This afternoon, you're going to become a real lawyer."

Deke Stoner was the first to feel Judge MacIntyre's afternoon wrath by haranguing the jury with an overly long opening statement. Jack watched the judge twisting his neck and pointed out the signal to R.J. with a nudge. An explosion was imminent, but Stoner was apparently too carried away by the sound of his own voice to notice. Finally, it happened.

"Mistah State Attahney, the Coaht would like to remind you that soonah or latah you will need to call a witness. The jurah cannot convict based on speeches."

Bang, you're dead, Jack thought, as Stoner tried to recover gracefully and at least one juror snickered. After Deke sat down, Jack kept his opening statement very brief.

The afternoon went reasonably well. True to form, Stoner called a crime scene detective who, as expected, confused everyone—including the State Attorney himself in one memorable exchange:

"Does the counter run north and south, or east and west?"

"Both, Mr. Stoner."

"What do you mean?"

"It's a L-shaped counter."

"Well which way does the north-south portion of it run?"

"North and south."

"And the other portion?"

"East and west."

The judge had begun to twist his neck again, and Jack could see another shot coming. "Mistah Stonah, is theah a point heayh, or are we meahly gettin' a geography lesson?"

Stoner moved on to the sizes and distances, and the judge turned away from the jury to take a discrete chaw. Finally, it was R.J.'s turn. Jack was pleasantly surprised that Mac did not subject him to the "bar card" ritual and took it as a good sign. R.J. did a good job, Jack thought, and even managed to score a few points of his own:

"Officer, can you tell us whether the security cameras in the store were in operation?"

Stoner objected on the basis that the question was outside the scope of direct examination, but R.J. argued, "Excuse me, Your Honor, but I believe the witness testified as to the location of two cameras during direct examination."

"The young man's got ya theah, Mistah Stonah," Judge MacIntyre said, looking at his notes. "Ovahruled. The witness is dahrectecd to ansah the question."

"No, they were not operating."

"Why not?"

"The owner told me . . . ."

Stoner was on his feet again, objecting to an answer that had to be hearsay—but which, if he had done is homework—he would have known could help him. Bob Schover, the owner of Guardian Electronics and a fellow member of the Yacht Club, had confided to Jack that the system had been turned off because of non-payment. "Better not let the jury hear that," Jack had warned R.J. "Let them infer that Morelle shut it off himself."

Thankfully, R.J. had enough sense to "withdraw the question," so the judge did not have to sustain the objection. Now Jack hoped that Deke would forget to follow up on the subject. He planned to use the point in his summation if the trial got that far. He would ask the jury, "Why had it been turned off?" and let them reach their own conclusion. Of course, that idea might go down the tubes if Deke thought things out and asked Morelle about the security cameras. The Judge began his neck-twisting routine again. R.J. was a fast learner; he ended his questions and sat down quickly.

The next witness was the police department's fingerprint expert who testified that Dennis' fingerprints had not been found on the gun—and then took half an hour to explain why that was not necessarily unusual. Deke's learning, Jack thought. Without this testimony, Jack would have had another point on summation, asking the jury why the State didn't even bother to check for fingerprints. Jack scribbled a note and pushed it in front of R.J. "Ask him if Morelle's prints were on the gun."

"Detective, were *any* fingerprints found on the gun?" R.J. asked in cross-examination.

"Yes."

"In particular, were Mr. Morelle's fingerprints found on the gun?"

"Yes, but that's not unusual either."

"Counsellah, theah has been testimony that Mistah Mohrelle owned the gun. Ah would be saprahsed if his fingahprints wheah not on it." Judge MacIntyre interjected.

R.J. mumbled that he had no further questions and sat down. "I guess I walked into that one," he whispered to Jack.

"Don't worry about it, you did fine," Jack replied. "We had to get that fact in."

The final witness of the afternoon was the investigating detective. Marilyn recognized him as the man they had met at the Bonita Police Department on the Sunday Arlo and Erlene first came to the boat. He testified that the only jewelry recovered was the bracelet. The rings were never found although he had conducted an extensive search. He also identified the gun that was found at the scene of the crime. He said it was Morelle's gun, and it was normally kept—Morelle told him—him under the counter. Jack did not object to the hearsay statement in spite of R.J.'s insistent poke in the ribs. Finally, the detective identified the picture he took of Tom Morelle the night of the robbery— the one Jack and Marilyn had seen at police headquarters—that showed the left side of Morelle's face swollen and bruised.

Jack handled the cross-examination and was careful to avoid any mention of the rings. He concentrated instead on the fact that the robber had abandoned the gun and the note that the police found in Dennis' pocket.

"That's pretty unusual, isn't it, for a robber to leave a gun behind?"

"Objection, Your Honor. That calls for a conclusion of the witness," Stoner demanded.

"Your Honor, an expert witness can state an opinion. I've known this officer for years, and I'm sure he's an expert in his field. I can't believe the State Attorney would object to him giving us his opinion."

Judge MacIntyre smiled a little. "He's your witness, Mistah Stonah. Do you object to him offerin' an expert opinion?"

Stoner was trapped. If he objected, it would appear that he was not vouching for his detective's credibility.

"Well, he wasn't offered as an expert, Your Honor, but I certainly don't have an objection to him giving an expert opinion."

"The witness is dahrected to ansah the question," Judge MacIntyre intoned.

"Well, it's not necessarily unusual," the detective said. "It could be the sign of an amateur who got scared and dropped it."

Now it was Deke Stoner who smiled. That description fit Jack's client; Jack had walked into that one, all right.

"This address," Jack continued, without missing a beat, "it's in my client's own handwriting, isn't it?"

"I'm not a handwriting expert, Counselor," the detective replied.

"Did he tell you he wrote it?"

"Yes."

"Is there any such address?"

"No."

"In fact, are there any residences on that street in the area of the number he had written?"

"No."

"Wouldn't he have to be pretty stupid to make up an address like that and then try to use it as an alibi?"

Stoner objected instantly, and this time he was sustained as Jack expected he would be. The question was completely improper, of course, but the point had been made. Judge MacIntyre's only comment was, "Mistah Townsend, let's confine ouahselves to facts rathah than speculations."

"Certainly, Your Honor. Thank you, I have no further questions," Jack said. Not bad, he thought as he sat down next to R.J. He had gotten a little slap upside the head, but he deserved it. It was not bad at all for that kind of question.

"Mistah State Attahney, call youah next witness."

Stoner stood up and toyed with his glasses again. Here comes an announcement, Jack thought. He was not disappointed.

"Your Honor, the State's next witness is the victim Thomas Morelle, after which the State will rest. Mr. Morelle will not be available until tomorrow morning. In view of the lateness of the hour the State would beg the Court's indulgence . . ."

Judge MacIntyre couldn't deny the reasonableness of the request. It was getting late, and the trial was going much faster than anyone had planned. Even "Hangin' Mac" was happy. "Ladies and Gen'lmen of the jurah," he said, cutting off Deke Stoner in mid-sentence, "in view of the ouah, we will adjohrn until nahn thirty tomorrah moahnin'. The Coaht has othah business to attend to at nahn. You are dahrected to be heah promptly at nahn-fifteen, and not to discuss this case or allow it to be discussed in youah presence durin' the evenin' recess."

The bailiff knew the speech well, and solemnly intoned "Everyone rise!" as soon as the judge stood up.

"Is that it?" Dennis Woodbrace after the judge left the courtroom. "It's goin' awful fast, ain't it?"

"Hang in there, Dennis," Jack assured him. "We'll be over to see you tonight."

R.J. was bursting with questions as he rode down the elevator with Jack, Marilyn and Jennifer, but he dared not say a word. Finally, in the parking lot, he could stand it no longer.

"How did I do?" he blurted out to Jack.

"Never poke me . . . I know when to object. If I don't do it, I don't do it for a reason. And for God's sake *never* ask a witness to tell you 'Why'."

"I know . . . I know. It just slipped out," R.J. apologized, as Marilyn tried to avoid the hurt look in Jennifer's eyes.

Jack noticed their exchanged glance and relented a little. "Hey, come on. You did great," he said, slapping R.J.'s arm. "You survived MacIntyre your first time out; that alone puts you in a very exclusive club. Just remember, at least one of those jurors is watching your every move."

"Are we getting together tonight?" R.J. asked, suitably humbled.

"Pick me up at the boat after dinner. I guess we owe Dennis a visit . . . to keep his spirits up if nothing else. Other than that, we know what Morelle's going to say, and we know what we have to do. We're as prepared as we're going to get." Jack shook his hand. "You're a good lawyer, Rob. You're a damn good lawyer. I'll see you later."

Jack appeared to have a lot on his mind as Marilyn drove back home to the trawler. Finally, Jack broke the silence.

"He *is* a damn good lawyer. God, he's gutsy. I would have dropped my drawers if someone had given me ten minutes notice and told me I was going to cross-examine a witness in front of Judge Mac my first time out."

"You were a little hard on him, don't you think?" Marilyn asked softly.

"No! Hell, no! A guy that gutsy needs to be sat on a little bit or he'll get himself into trouble. Believe me."

"Are you sure the gutsy guy we're talking about isn't the one with the initials J.D.T.?" she chided.

"Yes, that goes for him, too."

"Well I, for one, am glad *that* guy turned out exactly the way he did," she said, turning toward him momentarily.

"I love you, Marilyn," he said, reaching across and caressing her hair.

"I love you, too," she replied, glancing at him again.

"Good. Now keep your eyes on the road and get us home. We'll have a few hours before R.J. catches up with us."

€ &#x08;

"It's goin' awful fast, ain't it?" Dennis Woodbrace was pacing back and forth in the attorney's conference room at the county jail and he was worried.

"Sometimes trials go fast, and sometimes they don't," Jack assured him.

"Yeah, but Ah mean, this one's goin' *awful* fast. It don't seem rhaht. Ah mean, ain't you guys suppose' ta' be doin' somethin'?"

"What, exactly, do you expect us to do?" Jack asked.

"Ah don't know! Y'all are the lawyers!"

"That's right, we are, Dennis. Now you just hang in there and trust us for one more day. Okay?" Jack said.

"Okay, if you say so," Dennis responded. "But Ah still think it's goin' awful fast."

$$\wp \quad \wp$$

"He's right, you know. It is going awfully fast," Jack said when they were in R.J.'s car.

"What does that mean?" the younger man said.

"I'll let you in on a little secret, but I don't want you to think about it right now. I think it might mean that Deke is so confident about this case that he didn't do any homework."

"You think that's possible?" R.J. asked.

"I've seen him do it before."

"So now what?"

"So now nothing," Jack replied. "I've said it; now we both forget it. Never, never underestimate the opposition . . . not even Deke Stoner. We have a big day ahead of us tomorrow, and if things don't break our way, Dennis Woodbrace won't see the sunshine for a long, long time.

Chapter 27

"Everyone rise. Pursuant to recess, the Circuit Court of the Twenty-first Judicial Circuit of Florida is now in session; the Honorable Regis H. MacIntyre presiding. Be seated."

The bailiff opened court the next morning with well-practiced ease and Jack felt the old knot forming in his stomach. This is it, he thought. Today was the day. No matter how many times he had done it, he had never gotten used to it.

As promised, Deke Stoner called Tom Morelle to the stand and led him through a description of the robbery. True to form, he even dramatized the event by handing Morelle the gun and having him demonstrate how Dennis had pistol-whipped him before fleeing the jewelry store in Morelle's own car. Direct examination lasted no more than thirty minutes. Then it was Jack's turn.

He carefully led Morelle through his version of what happened the night of the crime, nailing down the details as he went. He seems to have thought of everything, Jack thought. But there was still the evidence of the photograph that didn't fit Morelle's version of the facts. It was the key—it had to be the key—that would release Dennis Woodbrace from prison. Jack knew he was going to have to take the chance he had been planning, and he began to change the focus of his questions. It would take some time, but it was now or never.

"Mr. Morelle, you testified that the bracelet is worth over ten thousand dollars, isn't that correct?"

"That's what I paid for it when I bought it from Cartier," Morelle replied smugly.

"Do you often buy jewelry from Cartier?"

"I buy jewelry from all over, Mr. Townsend."

"In fact, the missing rings, they weren't from Cartier, were they?"

"I don't know where they came from. I'd have to check my records."

"I *have* checked your records. They weren't from Cartier, were they?"

"If you know so much about my business, maybe you should tell me."

"I object, Your Honor," Deke Stoner interjected. "The State is trying to be patient, but counsel's questions are completely irrelevant."

"Mistah Townsend, you do intend to connect this up, somewhah, don't you?" Judge MacIntyre demanded.

"Yes, Your Honor. I promise." This was it. If Judge Mac didn't let him pursue this line of questioning, it would all be over before it started. "I just beg the Court's indulgence for a few minutes," Jack added, looking directly at the judge and pleading with his eyes.

"Verah well. The objection is ovahruled for naowh. But see that you don't stray too fahr." A slight smile flickered across the judge's thin lips.

Green light, Jack thought. Now he would nail this bastard.

"Mr. Morelle," he said, turning toward the witness and showing him a paper that R.J. had handed him from the stack on the counsel table, "can you identify this document?"

Morelle shifted slightly in the witness chair. "Yes, that's a copy of one of my purchase receipts."

"It shows you purchased certain rings from Northwest Gemstones in Portland, Oregon, doesn't it?"

"Yes."

"Can you tell the jury what these numbers mean?" Jack asked, pointing to a series of numbers on the paper.

"Those are stock numbers that we use for inventory control purposes."

"And you reported those same six rings as stolen, didn't you, Mr. Morelle?"

"If you say so, Mr. Townsend. You seem to know more about my business than I do."

Jack took another piece of paper from R.J. and turned on Morelle coldly. "Did you report those rings stolen or not?"

"Yes, I suppose those were among the many that your client stole, and that the police never recovered."

"Mr. Morelle, who owns Northwest Gemstones?"

"Objection!" It was Stoner again. "Your Honor, I have really tried to be patient, but this is totally irrelevant."

"Mistah Townsend," the judge said in a chiding tone, "you are trahin' the patience of the Coaht as well."

"Please, Judge," Jack said. "Just one more minute. Please."

Judge MacIntyre hesitated for a moment. "Ovahruled. The witness is dahrected to ansah the question."

"Mr. Morelle," Jack repeated, "I'm holding a certified copy of a certificate of incorporation from the state capital in Salem, Oregon. Who owns Northwest Gemstones?"

"My wife and I own it," Morelle admitted, shifting uncomfortably in the witness chair. A murmur ran through the courtroom and the judge banged his gavel. "There's nothing wrong with that," Morelle added defensively. "People in business do it all the time . . . for tax purposes."

Jack picked up another piece of paper. "Ten of the missing rings came from M&T Jewelry Wholesalers in Dover, Delaware, didn't they, Mr. Morelle?"

"I . . . I'm not sure."

"Would you care to see a copy of your purchase order?"

"They might have. Yes, I suppose they did."

"Do you know who owns M&T Jewelry?"

"I . . . I'm not sure. I'm really not sure."

"In fact, you and your wife own that one too, don't you, Mr. Morelle?"

"It may . . . we may. It was probably set up by our accountant."

Deke Stoner could see his airtight case slipping away into a morass of innuendo, and he was not about to let Jack get away with it. "Objection! Objection, Your Honor. The essential element if this crime is taking by force. Where the rings came from is completely irrelevant."

"The Coaht does not need instruction on the law, Mistah Stonah." Judge MacIntyre turned to Jack. "Well, Mistah Townsend?"

"Just two more questions, please, Your Honor. Please."

"I'm countin' Mistah Townsend."

Jack walked back to the counsel table where R.J. handed him a sheaf of papers. "In fact, every single missing ring came from a company owned by you or you and your wife, isn't that true, Mr. Morelle?"

"I . . . yes, I suppose that might be possible. But that doesn't mean . . ."

Jack cut him off. "There never was a robbery, Mr. Morelle. This is nothing more than a case of plain old insurance fraud, isn't it?"

Morelle turned white, and Deke Stoner was on his fee in an instant. "Objection! Objection! Your Honor, I demand a mistrial!"

"A mistahl? Mistah Stonah do you know what you're requestin'? Jeopahdy has attached in this case. The State may well be precluded from trahin' the defendant again."

Deke was obviously flustered. "I . . . withdraw my request for a mistrial, Your Honor, but my objection stands. This is completely out of order. Mr. Townsend knows better than this. He should be censured by the Court, and the jury should be instructed to disregard that last remark."

"Youah objection is ovahruled," Mistah Stonah." Judge MacIntyre turned and looked directly at Morelle who seemed to have recovered himself during the commotion. He pointed a finger at Morelle. "The witness is dahrected to ansah the question," he said with a piercing look.

"Your client robbed me, Mr. Townsend," he whined.

Please not that old chestnut, Jack thought. Deke Stoner had a bad habit of instructing witnesses to use that line if they got into trouble. Jack could almost hear Stoner prompting him, "Remember if you get into any trouble . . . if you can't answer a question, just turn it around and say, 'Your client robbed me!'" Jack looked at Morelle icily and raised his voice a notch.

"Did he? Did he rob you?"

"Yes, he did! He robbed me. And then he assaulted me. Unless you think I did that to myself!"

Show us, Mr. Morelle," Jack goaded him. "Show us again how he robbed you."

Morelle extended his hand with his fingers in the shape of a gun. "He put the gun in my face like this . . ."

"He robbed you with a finger?" Jack mocked.

"He used a gun!" Morelle shouted. He pointed to the State's exhibit on the Clerk's table. "He used that gun over there!"

Jack picked it up and asked, "This one?"

"Yes, that's the one!" the witness insisted.

"Here," Jack said, handing it to him. "Take the gun. Show us like you did before, with the gun."

They were facing each other across the rail of the witness box. Morelle angrily snatched the gun away from Jack and held it in his right hand. "He pointed the gun at me like this . . ."

"He wasn't sitting down, was he?" Jack interrupted, goading him again.

Morelle stood up in the witness box. Now he was visibly angry. Standing in the box he towered over Jack and looked down at him with an expression of pure hatred. "He put the gun in my face like this," he shouted, his hand shaking from emotion. "And then he hit me with it like this . . ." He swung at Jack who grabbed his hand inches away from the left side of his face.

"You still haven't noticed it, have you?" Jack asked quietly as he took the gun out of Morelle's hand.

"Noticed? Noticed what?"

"My client shares a peculiar characteristic with his father," Jack said coldly. "They're both left-handed."

Morelle looked like he had been shot. The color drained from his face again and he collapsed into the witness chair, gasping for breath.

"You hit yourself on the wrong side, Mr. Morelle," Jack said quietly.

"I . . . I . . ." Morelle began.

Stoner was on his feet again. "Your Honor, the State would request a brief recess . . ."

"Youah goin' to need more than an *brief* recess, Mistah Stonah. The Coaht will recess until nahn thirty tomorrah moahnin'. The jurah is dahrected to be heah promptly at nahn fifteen, and not to discuss this case among youahselves or allow it to be discussed in youah presence durin' the evenin' recess. The jurah is excused."

The jurors filed out, some of them looking over their shoulders at Tom Morelle who was still slumped in the witness box. After the courtroom door closed, Judge MacIntyre turned to Jack.

"Mistah Townsend, at this tahm the Coaht will entahtain a motion to release youah client in youah custahdy."

"I so move, Your Honor."

"Granted. This Coaht is in recess until nahn thirty tomorrah moahnin'."

The spectators rose in response to the bailiff's command when Judge MacIntyre left the bench and Morelle bolted for the door.

"Bailiff! Stop him!" Deke Stoner shouted. "Hold on there, Mr. Morelle. We need to have a little talk in my office." The two walked out with the bailiff close behind.

Jack melted into the counsel chair and looked up at the clock. It was almost noon and he was drenched with sweat. Time flies when you're killing yourself, he thought. In a moment, Marilyn, Jennifer, Arlo and Erlene were crowded around the counsel table. Erlene hugged Dennis and Arlo shook his hand and slapped him on the back in what, for Arlo, was an overwhelming display of affection.

"What happens now, Commodore?" Erlene asked. "C'n he come home with us? . . . Commodore?"

"Jack? . . . Jack?" It was R.J.'s voice.

"Nothing happens," Jack replied wearily. "Nothing. Not a God-damn thing. Tomorrow morning, Deke Stoner will send some poor assistant in here to announce that the case has been nolle prossed, and that'll be the end of it. No comment; no press release; no apology. Nothing." He turned to Dennis Woodbrace. "Go home with your family, Dennis. Just make sure you're here bright and early tomorrow morning for the final act."

℘ ℭ

"Pursuant to recess, the Circuit Court . . ."

The bailiff opened court the next morning with his usual monologue, but this time Melanie Dale was sitting at the prosecutor's table instead of Deke Stoner. The judge recognized her as the senior Assistant State Attorney who was regularly assigned to his courtroom.

"Miss Dale, the State Attahney is not present with us this moahnin'?"

Melanie stood up. One *never* addressed Judge Mac from a seated position. "No, Your Honor," she replied, attempting to suppress the smile that came to her naturally.

"Ah see. Ahr you ready to proceed in the mattah of State versus Woodbrace?" She had worked with Judge Mac long enough to be able to read his features. He knows what's coming, she thought, and he's going to put on a show.

"No, Your Honor. The State Attorney has nolle prossed that case."

"Ah see. And whah is Mistah Stonah this moahnin', if I may inquiah?"

"His secretary informed me that he left for an important prosecutor's conference in Denver, Your Honor," she replied truthfully. In fact, Lois had provided that information when Melanie got to the office that very morning, and she immediately reported to Judge Mac's courtroom. She had no idea of whether or not The Deacon was actually in Denver, and under the circumstances it was better not to ask.

Judge MacIntyre turned toward the jury. "Ladies and Gen'l'men, the State Attahney has tahminated this case by the filin' of an ordah of Nolle Prosequi, which is a fohmal declahration that the State will not phrasecute the mattah. This Coaht is without jurisdiction to inquiah into his reasons but I trust that bah and bah, when he retuahns to ouah State, he will shah those reasons with the votahs. At this tahm, you ahr dischahged with the thanks of the Coaht."

Some of the jurors half stood, unsure if that meant they were supposed to leave. "Of couahs, you may stay and watch the rest of the proceedin's," the judge added. They sat down immediately. No one was walking out early on this show.

"Will the defendant please rahase?" Dennis, Jack and R.J. stood up in unison. "Dennis Woodbrace, an ordah of

Nolle Prosequi havin' been entahed by the State Attahney, you ahr heahbah dischaged. Thah bein' no furthah business befoah the Coaht, we will stand in recess. Ah'd like to see Counsel in mah chambahs."

The bailiff commanded everyone to rise as the judge left the bench. Jack, R.J. and Miss Dale followed the judge into his office.

"That was a naice job, Jack," Judge MacIntyre said as he lit a hand-rolled cigarette and brushed one of the burning embers off his robe. "Ah cut you a little extrah slack, but you didn't disappoint me."

"Thanks, Judge."

MacIntyre turned to R.J. "Well, young man, you've suahvived a trahl befoah Judge MacIntyre. Youah a *real* lawyah naow."

"Yes, sir." R.J. was not sure how to respond. Nobody in law school ever told him that sometimes judges behave just like regular people.

"Ahr you and Mistah Townsend goin' to be settin' up shop togethah?"

"Well, sir, I don't . . . we haven't discussed that, sir."

"Well discuss it with him!" the judge insisted. "It's about tahm he gets back to woahk." He turned to Jack and added softly, "Don't you think it's about tham, Jack?"

"We'll talk about it, Judge."

MacIntyre's wizened face lit up with the hint of a smile and his eyes danced behind his glasses. "See that you do moah th'n just talk," he warned. He turned to the young prosecutor. "Miss Dale, Ah trust youah office has anothah case ready foah me to try this moahin'."

"We're ready to pick a jury in the Paige case, Your Honor," Melanie replied. "It was supposed to go ahead of Woodbrace anyway."

"Well, let's get to it." Judge MacIntyre turned to Jack and R.J. once more and extended his hand. "Naice to see you heah wheah you belong, Jack. And Mistah Meacham," he said, turning to R.J., "Ah'll be seein' you again, Ah hope."

"Yes, sir. Yes sir, you sure will," R.J. said, taking the judge's hand and shaking it after Jack let it go. He was still riding a wave of adrenaline when they met Marilyn and Jennifer outside on the courthouse steps.

"Did you hear that, Jack? 'I'll be seeing you again, I hope.' My very first trial, Jen! It was great! He doesn't say that to everyone, does he, Jack?"

"I know for a fact he doesn't," Jack assured him.

"He said we were supposed to talk," R.J. reminded him when they reached the sidewalk.

"Yes, he did," Jack agreed.

"Well?"

"Well, what?"

"Well aren't we going to?"

"Right now Marilyn and I have a date with a certain jeweler," Jack Townsend replied. "Why don't the four of us get together for dinner at the Club tonight? Somehow I think this is going to be a very long conversation."

"Tonight's a good idea," Jennifer interjected. "I have an errand to run right now."

"Me too," Marilyn added. "I'll go with you, Jen."

R.J. looked stricken and Jack protested, but Marilyn insisted she and Jennifer had important things to do.

"Okay, come on," Jack said to R.J. "You can hang out with me. We'll meet the ladies at the Club at six o'clock."

Marilyn gave Jack a peck on the lips. "Please don't do anything extravagant," she whispered.

"I only got a dollar. Remember?" he replied.

ဪ ၉

"Look, Rob," Jack began as the two men drove away. "It's not that I don't like lawyering . . . it's the clients I can't stand."

R.J. glanced away from the road and looked at him quizzically.

"What we did today was a fine piece of work and we felt good about it," Jack continued. "But we felt good because we knew we were right. How would you feel if we knew that Dennis Woodbrace really did rob Morelle?"

"Not very good, I suppose," the younger man admitted. "But couldn't we just stick with the cases we believe in?"

"That cuts down on your pool of available clients, Rob. Besides, it only happens that way in the movies." Jack was silent for a minute and then added, "On the other hand, I've got a few bucks stashed away; we wouldn't need to practice for a living. We could probably even work out an 'of counsel' arrangement for you with Monty Holcombe at the bank . . . something where you could draw a salary and still have time available for your own cases." Jack was silent again, and then said—almost to himself—"Let's think about this Rob. Let's think about it very carefully."

Neither of the men spoke until they arrived at Rick Summers' house. Suddenly in the driveway Jack turned to R.J. and said, "I don't believe in partnership agreements. If we can't trust each other, there's no use getting into this. It will have to be done on a handshake, okay?"

"Okay. Right. Anything you say," R.J. replied.

"No, it's not anything I say," Jack insisted. "Anything we do, we do fifty-fifty. It's like getting married, Rob."

"Right. Anything you say . . . I mean, I agree completely."

"Okay, put it there, partner," Jack said, extending his hand.

R.J. took it. "You mean that's it?"

"What else is there? If something feels right, you go with it. Haven't you learned that yet?"

℘ ℭ

"So how did we spend our day?" Marilyn asked after Sam DePasquale seated the four of them at a table in the Members Dining Room of the Yacht Club.

"We talked," Jack reported. "And we went to see a friend of ours in Bonita. And . . . Oh, yes, I almost forgot, I got this out of one of those gumball machines where we had lunch. I saved it for you."

He pulled a gold bracelet out of his pocket and reached across the table to fasten it around her wrist.

"Jack, this didn't come out of any gumball machine," Marilyn protested.

"Yes it did. Didn't it, Rob?"

"I wasn't watching, but if my partner says it did, then I'm sure it did," R.J. confirmed.

"Well, I have something for you, too." She handed Jack a package. "It's a little souvenir." He opened it and took out a wooden plaque on which a crumpled and worn one-dollar bill had been mounted. Beneath the bill a brass plate was engraved with the words, "Some of them *are* innocent. M.D."

"Thanks," he said, taking her hand. "In case I ever need to be reminded again."

"I have a little souvenir for you, too, R.J.," Jennifer interjected, handing him a small package of her own.

"Jen, I really didn't expect . . ." R.J. began. His words trailed off when he saw the gold watch chain with a half dollar attached to one end.

"Your first fee," she reminded him. "Now you'll never be broke."

R.J. hesitated for a moment. "Jennifer, I didn't expect to be getting a gift from you . . ."

"That's all right, you didn't have to get me anything," she interrupted.

"That's not the problem," he replied. "I do have something for you. Actually, I was going to save this for later . . ." He handed her a small box. Jennifer opened it and gasped.

"R.J., this is an engagement ring."

"It's only an engagement ring if you want it to be," he replied.

"Do *you* want it to be?" she asked.

"I want it to be if you want it to be."

"I want it to be, R.J."

"I want it to be, too. But we can't do anything about it right away. It'll take me a while just to pay for it."

"I can wait," she promised.

There was a long pause before Jack spoke. "Robert, are you going to kiss her, or are we going to discuss this issue all night?"

R.J. kissed her. And after dinner two young people who were very much in love floated back to Calkins Harbor to report the news to Grandma Calkins: another door on the path of life had just opened.

Chapter 28

The summer plodded along, as Florida summers do. The heat and humidity leveled off at "unbearable" and everyone who could do so spent as much time as possible in air conditioning. Shortly before Labor Day, Jack walked back from the post office with a thick envelope addressed to Marilyn and casually laid it on the salon table of their floating home at Cap'n Kelly's Marina.

"Oh, there's something on the table for you," he said nonchalantly looking up from his word processor when she returned from her office at the opposite end of the cove.

She picked up the envelope and looked at the return address. It was from the Florida Board of Bar Examiners.

"Why didn't you tell me about this?" she demanded.

"Is it important?" he inquired innocently.

She crossed herself and closed her eyes for a moment.

"Marilyn, it's too late for that now," he suggested.

She did not respond.

"Marilyn, are you going to open it?"

She opened her eyes and looked at him. "Will you be quiet for a minute? I'm busy praying."

"Praying about it isn't going to help now."

"I can't help it if you're a heathen."

"Protestant," he corrected her.

"Same thing," she teased, as she tore open the envelope. She looked at the letter for a moment. "I passed!" she shouted. "I passed! Thank God! My life is my own again!"

He pulled her to his lap and kissed her. "Congratulations," he said. "A thick envelope always means you passed. They have to tell you how to go about getting admitted." He took a small package from his nearby briefcase and handed it to her. "Here's a little something to remember the day."

She tore open the gift wrap and excitedly opened the velvet box that contained a diamond-studded wristwatch. "Jack!" she gasped, "This must have cost a fortune!"

"I got a deal from a jeweler friend of mine in Bonita," he explained in between her kisses. "We'll have it engraved with the date when you're sworn in."

"And now we can set our date," she said, kissing him again.

"Honey, *you* don't set the date; the court does. It's all right there in the letter."

"I was talking about our wedding. Or have you forgotten?"

"I'm sorry. I thought we were talking about your admission to the bar."

"We were, but we're finished with that," she said, curling her arms around his neck. "What would you think about Christmas week? The Saturday after Christmas?"

"I think if it makes you happy, it's a great idea."

"It would really solve a lot of problems. I could invite Papa down for the holidays ... if that's all right with you."

"That's fine. Maybe I should even invite my mother," Jack replied with a smile.

"Your mother?" Marilyn said, laughing now. "Jack, you don't have a mother!"

"Of course I have a mother. How do you think I got here?"

"Well, I mean, you don't have a *living* mother. Do you?"

"She was living the last time I checked."

"This is terrible!" Marilyn said, getting to her feet. "You have a mother! Why didn't you tell me this before?" Although she might suppress it, Marilyn's native temperament was French Creole and, like the weather in her adopted South Florida home, it could change quickly— and not always for the better. Jack had lived with her long enough to recognize the signs of an approaching squall. Her voice now carried the unmistakable sound of far-off thunder and the wind appeared to be picking up considerably.

"Why are you so upset?" he asked.

"John Townsend, we've been living together for three months ..."

"Two and a half," he corrected.

" . . . and you never told me that you have a mother!"

"But you're not living with her," he protested.

"I should have called her . . ."

"For what? To get her approval?"

" . . . or at least I should have sent her a card," Marilyn continued.

"That would be nice. Let see, 'Dear Mrs. Townsend, I'm sleeping with your son John. He has lovely manners. Thank you for doing such a nice job. Sincerely, Marilyn Dupré.'"

"Jack, I'm serious. Your mother is going to think I'm some kind of bimbo."

"What about your father?"

"That's *different*. Besides, I called my father."

"You did? When?"

"Right after we got engaged, of course. Don't tell me you didn't call your mother?" Marilyn was at gale force now, and the wind was still freshening. Jack hesitated before he answered.

"Well, no, frankly. I didn't think it was . . ." He broke off when he saw the look in her eyes.

"You didn't think it was important. That's what you were going to say, isn't it?" The gale was now a full-blown storm, the last step before a hurricane. The prudent thing would be to take shelter and wait for it to blow over. But Jack Townsend never backed down from a fight, especially one that touched on the sore subject of his mother.

"No, I was not going to say that," he lied, his voice rising to match hers. "It isn't a question of importance. It's a question of necessity. I don't speak to my mother all that often and telling her about it just didn't seem necessary." Marilyn looked at him coldly, and he added, "Anyway, why should I tell her? What's she going to do, refuse to give me permission?"

"You don't speak to your mother?" Marilyn demanded. She showed no signs of backing down either. "Your own mother, and you don't speak to her? Hers is one of the noses you had to rub in it, isn't it? And don't change the subject!"

"What do you mean, 'change the subject'?"

"She's going to be my mother-in-law, and I don't even know her!"

"And with any luck, you won't have to. Besides, I don't know your father."

"That's *different!*" she shouted, more forcefully than before.

"Why do you keep saying that? Why is it different?" Jack failed to grasp whatever logic it was that Marilyn found so simple.

"We have to take care of this right away," she continued, handing him the telephone. "You call her right now. But don't tell her we got engaged three months ago. Tell her we just did it last night."

"Why can't I call her later? And if I *must* speak to her, why can't I at least tell her the truth?"

"Call her right now!" Marilyn insisted. She looked at him and her tone changed to a plea. "Please. Do it for me.

Tell her you proposed to me last night. It will make her feel so good."

Jack took the telephone from her hand. "She's probably at the racetrack," he groused.

"I'm sure your mother doesn't play the horses," she gently scolded.

"How do you know? She's my mother. Besides, she doesn't *play* the horses . . . she *owns* the horses."

He dialed the familiar number of the family's summer home in Saratoga, New York. "She's probably not home," he repeated while the number rang, hoping he was right.

"Hello, Mother?"

"John," a woman's voice said, "this is a surprise. What's wrong?"

"Nothing's wrong, Mother. Everything's fine. I have some news for you. Are you sitting down?"

"What have you done now?"

"I'm getting married."

"Well . . ." Mrs. Townsend paused as if she need time to think of something to say. Finally she managed to ask, "Who's the lucky girl? Is she anyone I know?"

That did it. Suddenly all the old resentment, the arguments and the bitterness left behind from his first marriage welled up inside him. When would she stop interfering in his life? "She's a seventeen year old stripper from Miami, Mother," Jack replied icily. "I hope you'll approve this time."

Marilyn nearly ripped off his ear as she grabbed the receiver out of his hand. "Give me that!" she shouted, then, into the telephone she added demurely, "Mrs. Townsend? My name is Marilyn Dupré. I am *not* a seventeen year old ..."

"She's really sixteen," Jack shouted in the background.

"Would you hold on for a moment, please?" Marilyn said into the receiver. She turned to Jack with a look that could freeze burning napalm. "Will you *stop it?*"

"And I'm definitely not a ... anything of the sort," she added into the telephone. "In fact, I was educated in a convent school." Suddenly the words began tumbling out of her mouth as if she thought this might be her only chance to get everything in. "My family is from New Orleans, and I'm an attorney ... well, I've passed the bar examination and I'm about to be admitted any day, and I have a Master of Laws degree in taxation—which, I might add," she said looking at Jack, "your son does *not* have. And I'm part owner of a restaurant here in Calkins Harbor." She paused for a moment and added, "And I want to apologize for your son's disgraceful behavior just now."

"Don't pay attention to anything my son says, Marilyn," Mrs. Townsend said with a sigh. "I've spent most of my life apologizing for him. John hasn't been 'right' since he cracked his head after he convinced our gardener to take the training wheels off his bicycle." She paused for a moment and said, "Tell me the truth: did you force him to make this call?"

"Yes, as a matter of fact, I did."

"Well, then, I like you already."The older woman's voice grew warmer and she asked, "When is the big day?"

"I was . . . we were thinking about the Saturday after Christmas."

"That's a splendid idea. I can come down for the holidays. Is John still living on a boat?"

"Yes . . . yes, he is." Oh my God, Marilyn thought, she might be thinking about staying on board with us!

"Then he can make arrangements for me at a hotel. Put him back on the line. Oh, and Marilyn . . ."

"Yes?"

"Congratulations, but I'm afraid you'll have your work cut out for you. John was a very difficult child."

"Thank you for the warning," Marilyn replied as she handed the receiver back to Jack.

"What did she say?" he whispered.

"She said you were a difficult child and that I have my work cut out for me," she repeated as he took back the phone.

"John, I haven't seen you since the . . . since that horrible accident,"Mrs. Townsend said when Jack was back on the line.

Since the funeral, he thought. She was going to say she hadn't seen him since Kathy and Alex's funeral. He was in the hospital at the time and she was the one who had made all of the arrangements. He never properly thanked her for that. Even now she was sparing his feelings by not using that word.

"Perhaps we could be a little more cordial to each other for your bride's sake?" Mrs. Townsend continued.

Maybe he had misread her. The 'anyone I know?' might have just been a polite way of making conversation. It didn't have to be that old, '*But who is she?*' crap from long ago. The seventeen-year-old stripper comment of his was way out of line—even for him. "I'm . . . I'm sorry, Mom," Jack said quietly. "I wasn't thinking . . . it was a bad joke. I'm very sorry."

"She seems like a very nice young lady, John. I'm happy for you. I'm happy for both of you. I truly am."

"She *is* a nice lady, Mom. I'm sure you'll approve."

"Let's not re-live those days, John. If you invite me to your wedding, I'll come as a guest. You don't need my approval.

Jack felt a lump form in his throat as he said, "I would very much like for you to come to my wedding, Mother."

"In that case, I wouldn't miss it for the world," Mrs. Townsend said softly as tears began to well up in her eyes.

ℴ ℙ

Jennifer, too, was concerned about setting a date, but the date she had in mind was for the opening of Sisters' Restaurant. Her problem was a much more critical one. Grandma's health had been failing miserably and Jennifer found herself locked in a race with an unforgiving adversary. Grandma's second trip to the hospital for another transfusion late in September did nothing to lessen Jennifer's fears. She began to pressure Tim Gorman, the construction foreman, when she was on one of her regular inspection visits.

"Tim, we've got to get this project finished."

"Well, Jen, the crews are doing the best they can, but we keep getting held up by the inspectors. We were down for two days last week because the electrical inspector didn't show up and I can't cover the walls until he gives the okay."

"The problem is, Tim, I'm going to open this place with a Halloween costume party, and the customers are going to want food . . . and walls."

"Never happen, Jen. This place'll never be ready to open by the end of next month."

"It's got to happen, Tim. Hire more men. Go sit in the inspector's office. Do whatever it takes but this place has got to open by the end of next month." Jennifer was insistent.

"Okay, Jen. We'll try."

"Don' try, Tim. Just do it!" Jennifer walked away carrying her clipboard. These people didn't understand, she thought. It wasn't about a restaurant. The whole thing was about a job Grandma expected her to do and, by golly, the job was going to get done. It was going to get done—and Grandma was going to be there to see it done. Jennifer didn't want to hear any excuses. From anybody. She was in the same frame of mind when she burst into Marilyn's office a short time later.

"Where's Jim Lacey?" she asked. "I've got to talk to him right away."

Marilyn was looking at a bridal magazine and not thinking about restaurant openings. "Jen, is the Saturday after Christmas okay with you?"

"No way, Marilyn. We're doing it on Halloween."

"Halloween? I can't possibly be ready by then!"

"You'll have to be, Marilyn."

"Jennifer! I should think that I could pick out the date for my own wedding!"

"Wedding?" Jennifer responded. "Who's talking about a wedding?"

"We are. Aren't we?"

"I'm talking about our grand opening," Jennifer replied.

"Jen, I'm sorry. I guess I haven't been thinking about business."

"That's okay, Marilyn. Where's Jim?"

"He's on his boat, I guess," Marilyn replied. She appeared to be piqued about something, but Jennifer didn't have time to chat.

"Okay, I'll catch up with him there," she said as she bolted for the door.

"Jennifer!" This time Marilyn was visibly upset.

"What?"

"How about the Saturday after Christmas? I'd like you to be my maid of honor."

"Sure, Marilyn. That's fine. I've got to talk to Jim Lacey about ordering equipment right away. We'll talk about this later, okay?"

Jennifer was out the door before Marilyn had time to protest. She doesn't understand either, Jennifer thought as she trudged out. Marilyn's life was settled. She didn't care anymore. It was all up to Jennifer now.

Back inside the office, Marilyn picked up the phone and began making wedding arrangements.

₧ ₨

Jim Lacey had just finished his second cup of decaffeinated coffee—the only kind his friend Eddie Miles allowed him to drink following his heart attack—when Jennifer caught up with him aboard their houseboat.

"Mr. Lacey . . . Jim . . . we need to talk," Jennifer began. She had been growing increasingly abrupt in their discussions over the past weeks. Now, as she stood before him with her clipboard in hand and her blue eyes flashing, he secretly regretted having volunteered for this job.

"Sure, Jennifer," he began cautiously, "What can I do for you?

"I need to get that restaurant open, Jim. I want to get it open for Halloween."

"Halloween? That's a little more than a month away!" he protested.

"I know when Halloween is," she replied.

"Jennifer, the construction isn't finished. We don't have a chef or a staff; we don't have kitchen equipment. We don't even have tables and chairs!"

"We can advertise for people. As far as the equipment and tables and chairs, you must know somebody."

"Well, if I was back home, I'd call my buddy Frank Tesla at Nationwide Distributors. But he's in Detroit. I don't know how fast . . ."

"Call him, Jim. Tell him it's a rush. Tell him you'll pay extra. I don't care how much it costs. I just need to have the place open. Got it?"

"Okay, if you say so."

"I do say so." Jennifer turned and began to walk away. She hesitated and turned back to the older man. "Jim . . . Mr. Lacey . . . I don't mean to put you under any pressure, but it's really important that we get this place finished while Grandma is still . . ." she hesitated again, groping for the right words. The she bit her lower lip and added ". . . while Grandma is still in good health. Okay?"

"I understand, Jennifer," he said softly. "We'll get it finished. I give you my word." She began to walk away again, but Lacey touched her elbow and held her back for a moment. "And Jennifer," he added, "thanks for the explanation."

She nodded her head silently and walked away.

Chapter 29

"Jen, do you think you'll have time to go to St. Peter's with Jack and me one day soon?" Marilyn asked the following afternoon when Jennifer seemed a little more relaxed.

"Sure, Marilyn. Why?"

"I guess the Saturday after Christmas wasn't such a good idea. They're pretty busy at that time of the year, and Father Valencia said we'd better get over there right away to make our arrangements."

"Why am I going along?"

"When Father Valencia heard you were going to be my maid of honor, he made me promise to bring you. I guess he really wants to meet you.

"Meet me?" Jennifer responded. "What on earth for?"

"I don't know, but he made me promise, and I don't want to disappoint him. I think I'll have enough problems with the date and this wedding . . . and with Jack not being Catholic and everything. I don't want to give Father Valencia anything to complain about. You will come, won't you?"

"Of course I'll come, Sis." Jennifer said as she hugged her. "And Marilyn," she added, "I'm really sorry I haven't been more involved with planning your wedding."

"Jen, I'm sorry I haven't been more help to you."

"That's okay. I guess we both have special projects going on right now.

ೞ ಖ

St. Peter's was a Spanish style stucco building in the center of Calkins Harbor. It was a rather small church, but it housed some of the most beautiful stained glass windows Marilyn had ever seen. Those windows combined with the open-beamed ceiling gave the whole place an air of homey nostalgia that was so different from the more modern houses of worship on the mainland. This is what a 'church' should look like, Marilyn thought when she first entered it a few months earlier. Now, as she showed Jack and Jennifer around the sanctuary, she marveled to herself that she soon would be married here.

An older man with a shock of unruly white hair and thick, horn-rimmed glasses appeared from somewhere behind the main altar. He was dressed in an ordinary white tee shirt and black pants and, except for the fact that Marilyn recognized him, he might have passed for the janitor.

"Hello, hello. Welcome," Father Valencia said, as he wiped paint from his hands. "Marilyn, it's so good to see you again. And this must be the lucky bridegroom. Excuse the messy hands. Just doing a little touch-up work around the altar."

"Father, this is John Townsend," Marilyn began by way of introduction.

"Well, John, it will all be over soon," the priest said as he grasped Jack's hand and vigorously pumped his arm. "We'll try to make it as painless as possible. And this must be Jennifer Calkins," he said, turning toward the young blonde and gently taking her hand. "My dear, it's so nice to meet you. Your grandfather was a good friend of mine. He did so much for our parish."

"Grandpa Calkins?" Jennifer asked incredulously.

"I didn't call him 'Grandpa,' of course," the priest said patting her hand. "We old timers knew him as 'Casey.'"

"I didn't know Grandpa had anything to do with your church," Jennifer continued.

"There are many people in this community who owe your family a great deal, Jennifer. Have you seen our 'Calkins Window'?"

"Excuse me?"

"Our 'Calkins Window'—the window your grandfather donated, along with the land for this church. His name isn't on it, of course. Casey always believed in doing things quietly."

Father Valencia led them to a side window that depicted a number of straining, sweating fishermen hauling in a net overflowing with fish. To one side a calm, almost aloof figure in a scarlet robe raised a reassuring hand to an older man who knelt in awe, while below them a desperate fish jumped out of the azure water and fought to get a place inside the net. Each of the figures had a unique expression and a distinct personality that shone through the glass. The window was a translucent work of art, and Marilyn spent many Sundays looking at it when Father Valencia's sermon lasted a little too long. Beneath the window a small plaque announced: "Gift of A Friend—Luke 12:48."

"Beautiful isn't it?" Father Valencia said as he admired the window with them.

"Casting their net," Jennifer replied. "Is that from Luke 12:48?"

"Oh no, my dear. The 'casting their net' story is in chapter five. Luke 12:48 was your grandfather's ... well, it's what our Protestant brethren call his 'life verse.' You know about things like that, don't you John?" he asked, playfully squeezing Jack's arm.

"I guess I've heard the expression once or twice," Jack replied with a self-conscious smile.

"Well, what is it? The verse, I mean," Jennifer persisted.

"I have a Bible in the rectory," Father Valencia said with a smile. "Let's go look it up while we make our arrangements, shall we?"

"Father, there's just one thing," Jennifer said, holding him back. "My grandfather ... he wasn't a member of your faith, was he?"

The priest put his hand to his chin and thought for a moment. "Well, now, that's difficult to say," he replied.

"You mean Captain Kelly was Catholic?" Marilyn asked. This time it was her turn to be incredulous.

"Oh no, I don't mean that," Father Valencia chuckled. "Casey was not a member of our religion; there's no doubt about that. But the young lady asked me if he was a member of our 'faith.' Now, faith ... that's another matter." He turned to the younger woman and continued, "Jennifer, I honestly don't know what your grandfather's religious preference was ... or even if he had one at all. But I do believe we shared the same faith ... as does our friend Rabbi Frankel over in Bonita. Your grandfather donated the land for his synagogue, too. If you ever get over there, I'm sure Eli will be happy to show you their 'Calkins Window' ... although it's not from the New Testament and, to be honest"—he gave her a conspiratorial wink—"I like ours better." Father Valencia chuckled at his own joke. "Come on now," he said, "let's go into the rectory. We've held these good people long enough. They have wedding arrangements to make. Now that I've gotten you here, there's no reason for you to be a stranger. You can always come back to hear more stories about your grandfather."

℘ ℀

Grandma's traditional Wednesday afternoon tea party was quiet and subdued. There was no lavish spread on the dining room table this time. Grandma had only returned from the hospital a few days earlier, and it was obvious that she had not bounced back as well as she had in the past. Now she was bundled in a housecoat and slippers, and huddled in a corner in one of the living room loveseats as she apologized for her lack of formality.

"I recall our resolution to have chocolate every Wednesday afternoon," she said in a weak voice. "I was so happy when that young girl came to the door selling cookies yesterday. These chocolate-covered mints are just fine, don't you think?"

Marilyn took one of the mints from the saucer and passed it to Jennifer. This was unbearable, and she hated herself for her inability to cope with it. The woman who had done so much for them, the person who always had the answers, was slipping away from them—and there was nothing they could do about it. She remembered herself as a young girl, being taken to the hospital to visit her mother who was being consumed by a disease she did not understand. The possibility of death was not real then. Mama had always been there, like the house and the flowers on the balcony. Of course Papa was worried, but grownups were always worried about something. So in those days, she worried too. She worried because the grownups worried, even though she could not really be frightened of a terror she did not yet understand. But now she was a grownup herself. She understood life all too well, and she recognized that Grandma's was coming to an end, as all mortal lives must.

And yet, even as the older woman's life force ebbed, Jennifer seemed to grow stronger. It was as if something greater than all of them was preparing the next generation for—for what? That was a question Marilyn could not answer, not yet, anyway. For now, all she could do was witness the drama that was unfolding before her unwilling eyes.

"Now, tell me how our restaurant is coming along," Mrs. Calkins said as she put her teacup down with an unsteady hand that made it rattle against the saucer. Marilyn shivered involuntarily at the sound.

"Fine, Grandma," Jennifer replied, matter-of-factly. "I had Tim Gorman sit in the electrical inspector's office until we got some cooperation. I'll have the walls covered by the end of the week. The floor is next. I have Hap Winkman all lined up and waiting. And I went ahead and ordered all of the equipment with Jim Lacey."

"My, you certainly have been a busy young woman," Grandma said with unmistakable admiration in her eyes. "And you, Marilyn, have you set the date yet?"

"The Saturday after Christmas, Grandma. It's all set with Father Valencia at St. Peter's."

"All set with the groom too, I trust," Grandma added with a weak smile. "Oh, Marilyn . . . I found you for him, and I shall be there to dance at your wedding."

"I'm . . . I'm sure you will, Grandma," Marilyn choked, wishing that she could believe her own words.

"That's a promise," Mrs. Calkins added. "But now I must get my rest. Jennifer, would you help me upstairs?"

"Why not just take a nap right here on the couch, Grandma?" Jennifer asked.

"Well . . . perhaps you're right, Dear. It's such a decadent thing to do, but then, this is a Decadent Wednesday, and we've had our chocolate. A nap on the couch may be just the right finishing touch."

"I'll get a pillow and blanket, and then I really have to get back to the office," Marilyn said, grateful for any excuse to leave. "I promised Uncle Doug I'd be back."

"Well, then, you go ahead, Dear," Mrs. Calkins said feebly. "Jennifer can take care of things here. Heaven knows Douglas never could stand on his own two feet."

℘ ℃

County Judge Bill Bellingham was holding court at the Sailors' Table in the corner of the Bonita Key Yacht Club, and his friend Jack Townsend—one of the few "stinkpotters" ever allowed to sit at the sacred circle—had returned to his old haunt with his new law partner. "So, my colleague Judge MacIntyre tells me you're going to be opening an office soon," Bill said to Jack, and, at the same time, reporting the news to the regulars of the round table.

"Why is everyone so concerned about my future?" Jack complained aloud.

"Your friends are worried about you, Jack," Bill replied. "You're about to get married. You're going to have responsibilities. You have to give up this indolent lifestyle of yours." Bill looked at him and patted his hand. "You need a job, Jack."

"I have a job, Bill. I'm writing a book."

"That's not a job!"

"Tell that to Ernest Hemmingway."

"I will, if I happen to see him. Look, Jack, Ben here is

a pretty good golfer, but you don't see him running off to join Arnold Palmer on the pro tour."

"Maybe he should. How about it, Benny?" Jack asked, deflecting the conversation to the man in question. "Don't the philosophers say we're supposed to follow our bliss?"

"I think my wife might have something to say about that," the man replied glumly.

"Jack, you're marrying a beautiful woman; you're well off financially, and you're living on a boat," Bill reminded him. "That's as much bliss as anyone's allowed to have in one lifetime."

Jack laughed along with everyone else at the round table. "Okay, William, you win. If it makes you any happier, you might as well know that Rob and I have been out looking at office space. Now are you satisfied?"

"No, but it's a step in the right direction. I'll only be satisfied when I see your 'John Hancock' on the lease and 'Townsend & Meacham' in gold leaf on the door."

৯০ ৫৩

Later that day, Rob Meacham was in the living room of the Magnolia Avenue house while Jennifer got her grandmother settled upstairs. She returned looking very tired and sat down heavily beside him.

"Jack and I were out looking at office space today," he told her as he began massaging her neck.

"I'm just so worried about her, R.J. I don't know how much longer this can go on." Jennifer turned away from him and appeared to be enjoying the attention to her neck.

"Jack thinks it might be good to rent a small suite in the Bank of Bonita building, so that I can stay 'of counsel' to their trust department."

"I want so much to get this stupid restaurant open, to show her that I can do it. I'm pushing everybody as hard as I can, I just don't know if it will be enough."

"Jennifer!"

"What?" She turned around and faced him.

"You haven't heard a thing I've said," R.J. complained.

"Yes I have. You and Jack looked at office space. You want to stay in the bank building so that you can still be tied in with the trust department and they'll pay you. We talked all about this, R.J."

He turned away glumly. "You don't care what I do."

"Yes, I do," she said, toying with the hair over his ear. "I just have a life of my own right now, that's all."

"This life of yours doesn't seem to have any room in it for me."

"Don't ever say that, R.J. Come on," she gently teased him. When he didn't respond, she continued, "R.J., I was always the little girl who sat home, read books and played the piano for Grandma. Then when I got out into the world, I learned that I *like* making decisions." She took his chin in her hand and turned his face toward hers. "I really like it, R.J. And I'm good at it. Why can't I do it and have a life with you as well?"

"I don't mean that you should give it up, but you're just so . . . involved all the time. There isn't enough of you left over for me."

"I know I've been pushing, but it's only because I'm try-ing to get things finished while . . . she's still with us. Once the place is open, it will be different. You'll see. Okay?"

"I once said that nothing you did could be any trouble, Jennifer. I hope I don't live to regret saying it."

"You won't. I promise."

℘ ℠

"Jack, she's not the same person I proposed to," R.J. complained as they prepared to meet with the leasing agent at the Bank of Bonita building.

"So what else is new? She won't be the same person after you marry her, either. Neither will you."

"How can you say that? People don't change."

"I don't know about that. Maybe basic attitudes don't change. Good people are always good people, and jerks are always jerks, pretty much. But people *do* mature. When you met Jennifer she was a kid. And even though it wasn't that long ago, she's done a lot of growing up these past months. And she'll do more. So will you. You know what's facing her when Margaret Calkins dies."

"I'd hardly call that a problem," R.J. interrupted.

"Don't be so sure, Rob. Some people think wealth is the ultimate test of character. I'm one of them. It's pretty hard to keep your feet on the ground when you can afford a magic carpet. Anyway, if you're going to bail out on her, you better do it now."

"I could never do that to Jennifer!"

"I didn't think you could."

"Do you think I should tell her?"

"Tell her what?"

"What's facing her, as you put it."

"You don't know anything right now, Rob. Neither do I. Margaret might have changed that Will a dozen times since last summer."

"I doubt it."

"Don't be so sure. Margaret knows her way around. I wouldn't be surprised if your engagement to her granddaughter didn't trigger another visit to Monty Holcombe at the bank . . . on a day when you were conveniently unavailable."

"You know something, don't you?"

"No, I don't. If I did, I'd tell you . . . you're my partner, remember? But even then you wouldn't be able to reveal the confidential communications of a client to anyone else . . . not even your fiancée."

"But Jennifer's her granddaughter!"

"That's right, and if Margaret Calkins wants her granddaughter to know what lies ahead, it's up to Margaret Calkins to tell her. It's not up to you . . . or me . . . regardless of any present or future relationship."

R.J. nodded somberly.

"Come on, limber up your hand," Jack continued, slapping him on the back. "We've got a lease to sign."

Chapter 30

In early October everything began coming apart. The Florida weather, usually so dry and predictable at that time of year, degenerated into a series of violent thunderstorms that local pundits attributed to the power of Hurricane Juan that ran up the Gulf of Mexico and battered the Louisiana coast. Whatever the cause, the rain made it impossible to work on the outside of the building and any thought of paving the parking lot was sheer folly. Things were no better inside. Jim Lacey reported that Frank Tesla, a man who—he assured Jennifer—had always been a bedrock of stability, had retired. His son, Steve, now owned Nationwide Distributors. Steve seemed to know only one phrase: "It's on back-order." Local distributors were no better and even when equipment did manage to arrive on time the always-present, ever-lethargic inspectors found a way of delaying its installation.

Jennifer's dogged determination overcame all of it. She found new sources for equipment; she kept the paving contractor on standby; blacktop was put down whenever the rain stopped. She personally visited county and state offices to win over recalcitrant inspectors. Toward the end of the month, it looked like she might even pull it off. The kitchen was fully operational, tables and chairs were in place, a staff was hired and invitations for a grand opening costume party had been sent out. Then Jennifer found herself up against an adversary that even she could not overcome. Grandma was taken back to the hospital. Halloween afternoon found two depressed couples huddled at the Bonita Gardens Hospital, waiting for Doctor Greenman.

"Tonight was supposed to be the big opening," Jennifer said quietly to no one in particular.

Marilyn moved next to her on the waiting room couch and held her close. "Don't think about that, Jen. We'll do it another time."

"I don't think so, Marilyn," Jennifer responded. "I don't think she's going to make it this time."

R.J. knelt down next to her and took her hand. "Come on, of course she'll make it. You told me the doctor said this could go on for a year."

"I've never seen her look this bad, R.J.," she moaned. "Never."

Jack stood a little apart from them, looking out a window and lost in his own thoughts. "You don't know anything right now, Jennifer. None of us knows anything. We're just going to have to wait for Doctor Greenman."

He had barely finished speaking when a man in a white lab coat entered the waiting room. The fear in Jennifer's

eyes reflected the anxious scowl that clouded Dr. Greenman's youthful features. He went directly to the couch
where she was sitting, and hunched down on the coffee
table across from her.

"Jennifer, I'm afraid this doesn't look good." Jennifer's
hand tightened around R.J.'s, and Marilyn huddled closer.
"It appears that she's developed some internal bleeding, and
I don't know if we're going to be able to stop it. We're giving
her another transfusion right now, but if we don't get this
situation under control pretty soon . . . we may lose her."
Jennifer's knuckles were white on R.J.'s hand. "She's asking to see you and Marilyn right now. Please try to keep it
short." The two women stood up silently and clung to each
other as they left the waiting room. When they were gone,
Jack turned to the doctor and asked, "How bad is it, Jeff?"

"It's very bad, Jack. I'll be surprised if she makes it
through the night," Dr. Greenman replied.

"There must be something you can do," R.J. insisted.
"Money is no object."

"It's not a question of money, it's a question of time. I
wish there were something I could do. I honestly thought
she would last longer than this, but things are breaking
down faster than anyone can fix them. I'm afraid it really
is just a question of time now."

The hospital room was grim and cheerless in spite of
the freshly painted yellow walls. Patterned curtains framed
a pitifully small, sealed window that looked out onto an
adjoining roof that was still being splattered by a persistent,

dreary rain. The air in the room was unbearably close, as though every breath was being counted and tallied by the hospital's head cashier. A single hospital bed backed by a wall of electronic gadgetry dominated the interior, and two chairs took up the little remaining space. Grandma Calkins was almost devoured by the seeming miles of tubes and wires that both sustained and monitored her tenuous hold on life. She smiled weakly when Jennifer and Marilyn entered. "Well, my two girls," she said feebly, "I'm sorry I spoiled your grand opening."

Jennifer went to her bedside and took her free hand. "You didn't spoil anything, Grandma. We really weren't ready anyway. We'll just postpone it for a couple of weeks so you can be there. Things will be fine. You'll see."

"I'm afraid I won't be there, my Darling. Not the way you expect, anyway. But I'll see it all the same."

Marilyn sat next to the bed. "You promised you'd dance at my wedding," she said, choking back tears.

"And I shall, my Dear. I'll be dancing in the arms of the only man I ever loved. He's come for me already, and I expect to be with him soon."

Marilyn buried her head in the sheets and began to cry. "But then I won't be able to see you," she sobbed.

Grandma released Jennifer's hand and began to stoke Marilyn's hair. "You'll be able to see me if you look carefully," she said softly. "And I'll see you; that's what's important."

"I want you there," Marilyn cried. "I won't have my mother there, and now you . . . I want you there!"

Mrs. Calkins caressed her face gently and looked deep into her eyes. "Marilyn, I promise you I will be at your wedding. And I'll find a way to let you know I'm there . . . I promise." Marilyn sniffed and nodded her reply. "Now dry your tears while I tell Jennifer something."

"I'm here, Grandma."

"Jennifer, you will soon be saddled with a great deal of responsibility. I've tried to surround you with the best people to help you, but ultimately the responsibility will be yours."

"Yes, Grandma."

"I want you to rely on Jack and Marilyn. They'll be your family now. And of course, R.J.; I found him too, didn't I?"

"Yes, you did. You did a wonderful job, Grandma."

"And you will have a wonderful life with him," Mrs. Calkins continued. Her eyes brightened for a moment and she chided, "Don't disappoint me by letting him get away."

"I won't, Grandma."

"But the most important thing of all is this: those who receive much are expected to do more. Do you understand?"

"I understand, Grandma," Jennifer said solemnly.

"You don't understand, not yet. I haven't told you everything, Jennifer, and Grandpa isn't very happy about that. He says I sheltered you too much. Perhaps he's right." Mrs. Calkins took her hand and squeezed it with all of her remaining strength as if to force her words into Jennifer's soul. "Promise me you'll remember: those who receive much are expected to do more. Promise me you'll remember that, Jennifer."

"I . . . I promise, Grandma."

Mrs. Calkins released her hand. "As long as you promise me that, I can rest easily."

"Those who receive much are expected to do more; I won't forget, Grandma. I promise."

"I'm very tired, my dears. I would like to sleep now," Mrs. Calkins sighed.

Jennifer bent down and gently kissed her forehead. "Goodnight, Grandma. I love you."

Marilyn pulled her back softly. Although Marilyn was now blinded by her own tears, Jennifer seemed strangely composed. Just as she stood up, the door opened a crack and Doug Calkins peeked into the room. "Mother, may I come in? Can I talk to you for a minute?"

Mrs. Calkins opened her eyes. "Why, Douglas, how nice of you to stop by," she answered with a wan smile. "Please come in."

"Come on, Marilyn," Jennifer said as she put her arm around her. "Let's wait outside."

Jack was standing with R.J. in a corner of the waiting room, and Marilyn hurried to him for comfort. "She's dying," Marilyn sobbed against Jack's chest. "I won't be able to see her anymore."

R.J. looked at Jennifer helplessly. "Your uncle is here," he said lamely. "I thought I should call him."

"Thank you," Jennifer said quietly. "He's in there now." She hesitated for a moment and then said, "R.J., it's all up to me now." She appeared to be too calm for the situation.

"What do you mean?" he asked.

"I don't know for sure. But she said it's all up to me, now. Whatever it is; it's up to me."

A few minutes went by before Doug Jenkins returned. His face wore the expression of a new kid in school looking for a familiar face in the lunchroom, and he gravitated toward Jennifer and R.J. as if by default. "She's resting now," he said, obviously attempting to start a conversation.

Jennifer nodded her understanding.

"Jennifer, I ... well, I called your ... I called Junior. To let him know about ... everything. That was okay, wasn't it?"

"I'm sure my father won't come," she replied flatly.

"Well, I thought he should know," Doug added by way of apology.

Jennifer looked at him and smiled sympathetically. She put her arm around him. "Of course you're right, Uncle Doug. I'm sorry. I just wasn't thinking."

"I told her ... I guess I shouldn't have listened to him all those years, but, you know, he's my older brother. We grew up together. I guess I never thought he could be wrong."

"Don't think about it, Uncle Doug. That's all behind us now."

"I guess it is," he said, quietly shaking his head. "Somehow I never thought things would turn out like this."

It was a few minutes before Jack and Marilyn joined them. "Jen," she began, "why don't the three of you go down to the cafeteria for a while? Jack and I will wait here."

"I'm fine, Marilyn."

"Jennifer," Jack added, "nobody's leaving here until we have some definite word. That could be a long time. It would be best if you and R.J. took a break. Go downstairs for a cup of coffee or something."

Jennifer raised her head proudly, as stiff and dignified as her grandmother would have been in such circumstances, Jack thought. "No, Jack. I'll be fine. You and Marilyn go. We'll wait here."

Jack Townsend had been around the family long enough to recognize the Calkins determination when he saw it and he knew better than to argue against it. "Come on, Honey," he said to Marilyn, gently taking her arm. "Let's take a walk."

"This is awful," Marilyn said as they walked down the deserted hospital corridor to the all-night coffee shop. "Did the doctor say anything?"

Jack put his arm around her tenderly. "Honey, I want you to understand something: Margaret Calkins won't be going home to Magnolia Avenue."

Marilyn hung her head in defeat. "I know. She knows it, too."

The coffee shop was too harshly lit and much too alive with the sound of clattering china to suit their thoughts. They sat in silence until the coffee got cold. There was nothing to say—nothing that could be said. Sitting there seemed so useless, but leaving and attempting to go on with life was impossible. So they sat and waited for the inevitable to happen, and all the while Marilyn prayed the inevitable would not happen.

She finally broke their self-imposed silence. "We'd better get back upstairs. I'd like to be with Jennifer."

Jack nodded. The whole experience was calling up images of long ago—images he thought he had forgotten when he fell in love with Marilyn Dupré. Now the feeling of those horrible days following the accident once again gripped him. There was nothing he could do then, either: no way he could save his own son. At least then he had nurses who would come in every few hours with hypodermic needles and he could drift away from it all. He had blamed the drugs for his inability to cry when Alex finally died. It was all too unreal, he said. But now the sights and sounds and smells of the hospital were very real indeed. They were tearing at him, and part of him wished that Margaret would die quickly so that he could run away into the comfort of the night and the security of his boat.

Jennifer was in her grandmother's room when they got back to the floor. "I'll go in and sit with her," Marilyn said. It confirmed what Jack had always suspected: women are the stronger sex at times like this. He retreated to the relative safety of the waiting room where R.J. and Doug Calkins waited for some word.

Inside the room Jennifer and Marilyn kept watch, the silence broken only by Grandma's labored breathing. Marilyn idly paged through a Gideon Bible someone had left behind and thought about the verse they had seen on the window.

"Jen, look at this: Luke 12:48, the verse on the window. This is what Grandma was telling you, about how those who receive much are required to do more."

"I know," Jennifer replied quietly. "Father Valencia showed it to me at the church that day."

"It's the exact verse," Marilyn repeated, "but what did she mean?"

"I don't know that," Jennifer replied, looking at the frail figure of her grandmother in the hospital bed. "And I don't know what she meant about not telling me everything, either." She turned and faced Marilyn whom she now saw, more than ever, as her older sister, even though she also felt new-found strength building in herself. "Whatever it is, we're going to do it."

"But what's the 'much' and what are we supposed to do?"

Jennifer's response was cut short when R.J. entered the room. "Your Uncle Doug is asleep in front of the television set," he announced. "And Jack is staring out the window and won't talk to me. Can't I do something?"

Jennifer shook her head and then went over to him and took his hand. "I guess it's not the way we expected to spend tonight, is it?" she said with a sad smile.

"Jennifer!" Marilyn's voice called her attention back to Grandma whose breathing had suddenly become more erratic.

"R.J., please get one of the nurses," Jennifer said quietly. "And you'd better call Jack and Uncle Doug, too."

R.J. hurried out of the room and within moments a nurse came through the door.

"You'll have to step outside, Miss Calkins," the nurse said, taking Jennifer by the arm.

"No, there's no need," she replied quietly. "My grandmother is dying. My sister and I would like to be with her when she passes, if you don't mind."

The nurse looked at her. "We don't allow . . ."

"Please," Jennifer insisted with a reserved calm. "It will be all right."

R.J. returned with Jack and Doug Calkins, and the family stood by quietly. It was more than a life passing, Jack thought. An era was ending in Calkins Harbor. The queen was dying and, whether the princess knew it or not, she was about to take her place. "And whether we like it or not," Jack told himself, "we're all going to be a part of the story."

Jennifer and Marilyn held each other and watched while Grandma Calkins peacefully breathed her last.

Chapter 31

A week after the funeral, the same small group of people gathered at the office of Montague Holcombe, general counsel for the Bank of Bonita, only this time Junior and Les Leslie were with them. Junior occupied a red leather chair and chewed on a foul-looking but thankfully unlit cigar while Les tried to be as inconspicuous as possible in the corner of the walnut-paneled conference room. Everyone sat and waited for the proceedings to begin.

"This is most unusual," the balding, portly Monty Holcombe said by way of introduction as he took a seat at the long mahogany table. "I'm sure Mr. Townsend and Mr. Meacham can confirm that a 'Reading of the Will' is a motion picture affectation which has crept into our culture. Ordinarily, we just send out copies of the Will to the heirs." He looked around the room. No one spoke. "However," he continued, "this 'reading' was specifically requested by Margaret Calkins, and I intend to carry out her wish."

"Grandma never did anything in an ordinary way," Jennifer said quietly from her place on the leather couch next to Marilyn.

"There are two documents. One is the Last Will and Testament of Margaret Calkins, and the other is a letter, composed by her and written in her own hand. I have not seen the contents of the letter, but her instructions were to read it concomitantly with the Will itself to the named legatees as soon as practicable after her death." He adjusted his glasses and began with the legal document.

"In the Name of God, Amen. I, Margaret Scott Calkins, being of sound mind and disposing memory, do hereby make, publish and declare this to be my Last Will and Testament, hereby revoking all other Wills and Codicils heretofore made by me."

Mr. Holcombe stopped, opened the envelope and turned his attention to the letter.

"*My Dears, This will be my last message to you. I wanted to write it all in my Will, but Mr. Holcombe told me that doing so might cause some legal difficulty. You lawyers! Always so afraid of your own shadows! If Casey were here, he would simply have told his friends what he wanted done, and they would have done it without question. Well, that's all in the past, and Mr. Holcombe knows best, I suppose. What must be, will be.*"

"I direct that my just debts and funeral expense be paid as soon as practicable after my death."

"*'The undertaker always gets paid first,' Casey used to say, 'he'll be the last one to let you down.' I do hope that I had a nice funeral, and that there wasn't a whole lot of crying and carrying on. So much fuss about an old, worn-out body! Why, people have been dying since time began. It's just an ordinary part of life, my Dears. Don't let it frighten you. There is no real death. The life in each of us lives on. I know mine will. There is still so much for me to do."*

"To my step-son, Kelly Calkins, Jr., I give, devise and bequeath the sum of Five Hundred Thousand Dollars, together with an undivided one-half interest in the buildings known as the Cornwall Apartments, to be his, absolutely and forever."

"You should have gotten nothing, Junior. God knows, you deserved nothing. But your father made an agreement, and he told me what I should leave you, and I would not defy Casey Calkins for all the gold on earth. If you invest this money wisely and treat your tenants (God help them!) with a little respect, you should be able to live your life in comfort doing as little work as you have ever done."

"To my step-son Douglas Calkins, I give, devise and bequeath the sum of Five Hundred Thousand Dollars, together with an undivided one-half interest in the buildings known as the Cornwall Apartments, to be his, absolutely and forever."

"Douglas, I hope that someday you will wake up and see that your brother has done nothing for you but make your life miserable and isolate you from the people who love you. I would have preferred not to put you into another partnership with him, but your father wanted it this way. If you're smart, you'll

take my advice: give him the title to the entire apartment com-
plex and get away from him once and for all."

"To Marilyn Dupré, whom I have loved as a granddaughter, and to John Townsend, my beloved counselor
and friend, I give, devise and bequeath the sum of Five
Hundred Thousand Dollars, together with the empty lot
adjoining my home on Magnolia Avenue in the Town of
Calkins Harbor, to be theirs, as joint owners, absolutely
and forever. It is my hope that they will use the funds
hereby bequeathed to construct a house on the land afore-
said and make it their home."

"Marilyn, I promised you I would dance at your wedding,
and I shall. Whether I am with you in body or not does not
matter. You have brought me great joy by allowing me to help
you go about your task in life. Now I'm counting on you to help
Jennifer with hers. Don't let me down!

"Jack, dear, I know you don't need the money, and you will
probably be upset with me for having left it to you and Marilyn.
But Mr. Holcombe has assured me there is no legal reason to pre-
vent me from doing so, and I want my Marilyn to have a real
home. Boats are all right for you boys, but a proper lady needs a
proper house. Build one for her close to Jennifer and, I trust, R.J.,
and look after them and their children as I would have done."

"To my dear friend Cecil Leslie, I give, devise and
bequeath the sum of Two Hundred Fifty Thousand Dollars, on the condition that he use some part of it to travel
to the country of Italy and find his lost love. If he should
not use some part of this bequest for that purpose, then, in

that event, the entire bequest shall lapse and become part of my residuary estate."

"You promised me that you would look for Elena, Mr. Leslie, and I expect you to keep your world. This money should be more than enough for that purpose. No excuses, now, Mr. Leslie, or you shall lose this gift along with the person you still hold most dear. If you look for her, you will find her. And remember: change is a part of life—don't be frightened by it."

"I give, devise and bequeath all of my right, title and interest in the property known as Cap'n Kelly's Marina to those people who are residents of it at the time of my death, in equal shares, share and share alike."

"The Boatyard. Oh, yes, the Boatyard! It's the place that Casey and I worked so hard to build all those years and the only thing that kept his sons around. Casey put a lot of his life into that place, as did I, but all they wanted to do with it was wait for the two of us to die so they could sell it to some condominium developer. Well, they won't be able to do that! The Boatyard is going to the people who care about it the most: the people who live there. I don't know if they are ready to govern themselves or not, but I suspect they'll take better care of the place than those who wanted it only for the money it would bring."

"I give, devise and bequeath all of the rest, residue and remainder of my estate, of whatever kind and wherever located, to my beloved granddaughter, Jennifer Scott Calkins, to be hers, absolutely and forever."

"My Darling Jennifer: Well the lawyers finally got something right: 'beloved granddaughter.' Those aren't just legal

mumbo-jumbo words. You truly are my 'beloved.' Everything else—all that your grandfather and I worked for—is yours. And I can't think of anyone better to have it. You will have the house and the contents and the rest of the property—R.J. will tell you about it. And you'll have Marilyn and Jack close by and your children will grow up with theirs. You'll have a wonderful life, Jennifer. But remember, you must use what you have been given to do good. Much will be required of you, my Darling, but I know you can handle it. I have surrounded you with the very best people. Trust them as you would me."

"If any beneficiary should challenge any provision of this, my Last Will and Testament, then, in that event, the bequest to that beneficiary shall lapse, and the said bequest shall become part of my residuary estate."

"This is for your benefit, Douglas. I expect that your brother won't like what I have done in my Will, but if he wishes to challenge it, you had better let him do so himself and not inveigle you into doing his dirty work for him. Somehow I don't think Junior will be willing to risk a half million dollars of his own money on a Will contest, and if he tries to get you to do it, don't listen to him! If either of you challenges this Will, you will do nothing but bring shame and grief to yourself and your family name, and you will lose your inheritance as well."

"I nominate my attorneys, John D. Townsend and Robert J. Meacham the Executors of this, my Last Will and Testament, and provide that they shall serve without bond."

"Bond! What nonsense! I've already entrusted you two boys

with the ones I hold most dear. How could mere money ever equate to that? I'm counting on the two of you to see that my wishes are carried out, and more importantly, to bring up my great-grandchildren as I would have done. Don't let them forget their great-grandfather or me. Casey Calkins was a wonderful man. There may be some hope for the Calkins family after all."

"In Witness Whereof, I have hereunto set my hand and seal in the presence of witnesses as by law provided."

"Well, my Darlings, it's time for me to go. I've kept Casey waiting for five years now, and he was never much good at that sort of thing. Please take care of each other as I have tried to take care of each of you. I shall see you all again. Goodbye. Love, Grandma."

Mr. Holcombe cleared his throat. "The Will was properly executed and witnessed by myself and two secretaries. There is no question about its validity in spite of the unusual circumstances of this . . . presentation."

There was a long silence in the room. Suddenly Junior stood up. "It looks like the old bitch boxed me in pretty good," he said. "Send me a check. I'm going over to have a look at those apartments." He slammed the conference room door and was gone.

Jennifer was still in shock, trying to make sense out of the numbers she had been hearing. "Well, that's it, I guess," she sighed, not moving from her place on the couch next to Marilyn. "I hope there's enough left over to do a little remodeling."

Marilyn put her arm around her. "Jennifer, don't be silly. Jack and I don't have any intention of accepting that money. Do we, Jack?"

"What do you mean? Of course we're going to accept it!" he replied with a barely-concealed smile.

"That's all right, I understand," Jennifer said, sniffing back a tear and searching her purse for a tissue.

"Oh, Jennifer, he's just teasing," Marilyn said, giving her a playful squeeze. "Aren't you, *Darling*?" Marilyn's eyes flashed lightning across the room at Jack as she spoke.

"No, I'm not; not at all," he replied. "Margaret wanted us to have that money, and I intend to take it. Every dime." Now R.J. too was smiling at some private joke.

Jennifer dabbed her eyes. "That's all right, Marilyn. I understand. Really," she said.

"*John, this is not funny!*" Marilyn warned through clenched teeth.

Jack turned to Monty Holcombe. "Counselor, perhaps you should tell our client what the residuary estate consists of."

"Well, Mr. Meacham is more familiar with all of the appraisals than I am," he said, as he put the Will and letter back into his file. "We have tried to keep up with things over the years, of course. But I'm afraid it will still take some time to sort it all out."

"What does he mean? What appraisals? What's going on, R.J.?" Jennifer asked.

"Jennifer, your grandmother owned a lot more property

than was mentioned here today. And everything else, whatever wasn't specifically mentioned, goes to you," he explained.

She looked at him. "What? What wasn't mentioned?"

"Well, there's a lot of real estate. Some of it has been developed, but there's a lot more that hasn't been touched. And there are some other investments. We don't have current appraisals on everything, but the holdings are substantial."

"How substantial, R.J.?" Marilyn asked.

"After federal inheritance taxes, and leaving out the specific bequests, I'd say that the net remainder is in the neighborhood of ... I don't know ... probably in the neighborhood of twenty or thirty million dollars."

Jennifer let out a small gasp and grabbed Marilyn's hand.

"That's a very nice neighborhood, Jenny," Marilyn murmured.

"Of course, that doesn't include your interest in this bank, and the Bonita Key Yacht Club," R.J. added.

Jennifer looked stricken. "You mean I own the Bank and the Club too?" she wailed.

"Only a one-third interest in the Bank. Your grandfather was one of our founders," Monty Holcombe explained. "And as for the Club, they are leasing the land from your family on very good terms. Casey Calkins bought a lot of land, but he seldom sold any."

Jennifer stood up. "No!" she protested. "No, I can't do this!"

"What do you mean, you can't do this?" Marilyn said, standing up beside her.

"I can't do it! Marilyn you heard what she said: 'Those who receive much are expected to do more.' I don't want this much responsibility. A few thousand dollars, maybe, or the boatyard, or the restaurant, something like that. But I don't want to be responsible for anything like this."

"I'm afraid you don't have much of a choice, young lady," Mr. Holcombe said. "You'll get used to it."

"I don't want to get used to it!" she cried. "R.J., I don't have to accept it, do I?"

"Well . . . no, but . . . Jennifer, you're not thinking clearly right now. Give yourself a little time," he said.

"Jennifer, are you crazy? Marilyn cut in. "You'll be able to have everything you ever wanted."

"But I don't want anything!" she insisted. "All I want is my life back the way it was!"

Marilyn put her arm around her. "Jennifer, this is a great opportunity. Think of all you'll be able to do. You can set up a trust fund, or a scholarship at the college. Maybe even donate a building. There are all kinds of possibilities."

Suddenly it was as if a light had been switched on. "Marilyn, you'll help me with that, won't you?" Jennifer asked. "And you R.J., and of course Jack. You won't just leave this all up to me, will you? If I accept this, we'll really have to do something. We'll have to do things to make this town better. Marilyn, that's a wonderful idea about a scholarship. How soon can we do that, R.J.?"

"Miss Calkins," Monty Holcombe protested, "first your grandmother's estate has to be probated. That might take a year or more."

"That's fine; that's good. That will give us time to make plans," Jennifer replied. "So I don't have to do anything until next summer?" she asked looking at each of them.

"No, next summer will be soon enough," Jack reassured her.

"Okay. Next summer it is," she said. "R.J. we'd better make our wedding plans right away, too. We're going to have a lot going on next summer."

Chapter 32

I don't know, Jack; I never planned on marrying an heiress," R.J. said as he filled two coffee mugs in the kitchenette of their new office suite in the Bank of Bonita Building.

"We're not back on that again, are we?" Jack complained. "We've been over this a dozen times, Rob. If you're so worried about it, maybe you *should* break up with her."

"Break up with her? That's insane!" the younger man said. "I can't do that; I love her. And she needs me. But she's been acting so ... different lately. I just want her back the way she was."

"Forget it. That's not going to happen," Jack explained for what seemed to be the hundredth time. "All people change. You had better get used it, because brides change even more as their big day approaches. Look at Marilyn: the wedding's a month away and she goes and moves in with Jennifer! Why? Because she doesn't want her father to know we've been living together!" He took a gulp of coffee and asked, "Does that make any sense?"

"Maybe she's embarrassed or something," R.J. suggested.

"About what, for God's sake? We've both been adults for a long time. Besides, he's not even arriving until next week!" Jack exploded. It sounded like he had already fought—and lost—this argument countless times.

Their secretary found them and cut off further conversation by announcing that two clients were in the waiting room.

"Clients? What clients? I thought I was going to do some writing," Jack protested.

"Arlo Woodbrace and Les Leslie," R.J. replied. "I took the call yesterday. They want to talk about the Will. It was either do it here or they'd have wound up on your boat last night."

"And you're complaining about *your* life being screwed up?" Jack said as they took their coffee mugs into his office.

"'Mornin' Commodore; Mr. R.J.," Les said as Ms. Crowley ushered them in.

"Real nice office," Arlo added.

They declined Jack's offer of coffee and shifted around uncomfortably in their chairs while they checked out the oil painting of the sailing ship and Jack's diplomas and certificates on the wood paneled walls before getting down to the point of their visit. Les spoke first. "It's about Miz Calkins' Will," he began.

"'bout them shares," Arlo interrupted.

"Will ya' let me tell it?" Les said over his shoulder. He turned back to Jack. "Ya' see, Commodore, it's like this.

Now, that Will says is everybody who lives at the marina is supposed ta' get a share. Ain't that right?"

Jack confirmed that Les had summed up the situation pretty well.

"Well, what we was wonderin' was, does that mean *everybody*?" Les inquired.

"My recollection is that the language of the Will is pretty straightforward: residents at the time of her death, share and share alike," R.J. replied.

"Yeah, but does that mean *everybody*, Commodore?" Arlo asked, directing his question to Jack and ignoring the younger lawyer. Apparently he did not like R.J.'s answer.

"Who seems to be the problem, Les?" Jack inquired.

"Well, no one, exactly . . ." His answer trailed off.

"Howard Garner," Arlo interjected. "He's gonna make trouble, sure as anythin'."

"Garner? Isn't that the guy who moved in a few months ago on the Connie?" Jack asked, using the familiar nickname for a Chris-Craft Constellation.

"That's the one," Arlo replied. "He's tighter'n a two-dollar watch, and he's gonna make trouble. Ya' c'n count on it."

"He just ain't like us, Commodore," Les complained.

"How can he not be like us, Les? He lives on a boat, for God's sake." Jack protested.

"But he's new," Les shot back. "An' he don't think like the rest a' us."

"There's no law against thinking, Les," Jack replied.

"He's tighter'n a two-dollar watch, an' he's gonna make trouble," Arlo repeated.

Jack looked at R.J. for support. "I don't think there's anything we can do about it. The Will is quite specific. If he was a resident of the marina on the date of Margaret Calkins' death, he gets a share the same as everybody else."

"She didn't make any exceptions," R.J. confirmed. "And she didn't provide for any kind of acceptance procedure."

"Well, we was afraid a' that," Les said, getting up to go. "But he sure ain't like the rest a' us."

"He's gonna make trouble," Arlo added as the two men shook the lawyers' hands and left.

Jack looked at R.J. after they were gone. "And you think you've got problems? I'm *living* there!"

"By the way, Jack," R.J. quipped as he ducked out the door with his coffee mug, "exactly how tight is a two-dollar watch, anyway?"

෨ ෬

Marilyn wasn't thinking about watches, two-dollar ones or otherwise as she washed the breakfast dishes in the gray kitchen of the house on Magnolia Avenue. Papa's visit hadn't been her only reason for moving ashore. Uncle Doug had stayed at the house for a few weeks after Grandma's death, and Jennifer had busied herself with Marilyn, addressing wedding invitations and going for bridal gown fittings. After Uncle Doug returned to his own place, Jennifer had become increasingly moody and depressed. Her visits to the boatyard tapered off and, when they stopped altogether, Marilyn knew she had to move in. Jack didn't like it, of course, but anyway, she really didn't want to be living with him when Papa—and especially—Sister Jean-Marie arrived. She had thought that by moving into the house she could solve the problem of living arrangements and look after Jennifer at the same time, but Jennifer appeared to be no closer to coming out of her shell than she was before.

"Maybe you should think about getting a dishwasher," she said as she handed Jennifer a plate to dry.

"Grandma thinks ... thought ... they were a silly affectation," the younger woman replied quietly.

"Are you going to class today?" Marilyn asked, handing her a glass.

"No, I thought I'd stay home and study. I'm way behind," came the flat reply.

"Well, I thought I'd go over to the marina for a while and check on the place. Wouldn't you like to come out for a ride?"

"No, not really."

"Jen we have to do something about that restaurant," Marilyn brought up the subject for the umpteenth time as gently as she could.

"I hate that place, Marilyn," Jennifer suddenly blurted out. "I'm never going back there."

Jennifer had been keeping her emotions bottled up, and her outburst startled Marilyn. "But we have to open it," she said, trying to reason with the younger woman.

"We don't have to open it!" Jennifer's voice rose a notch.

"Jen, be reasonable," Marilyn said, trying to calm her. "A lot of people are counting on us."

"Well let them count on somebody else," Jennifer shouted. "I don't have to do it and I'm not going to do it!"

"But Jennifer, we borrowed all that money from the bank . . ."

Jennifer suddenly threw the dish she was wiping to the floor where it shattered into a million pieces. "Who cares about the stupid bank?" she screamed. "I own the stupid bank, remember?"

Marilyn looked at her in shock. "I'm sorry. I'm sorry," Jennifer said suddenly, "I'll pick it up. I'll take care of it." As she stooped down to gather up the pieces her hands began to shake violently. Marilyn grabbed them and held her tightly. "It's all right, Jen," she whispered. "Leave it. It's all right," she said quietly.

Jennifer began to weep bitterly as Marilyn hugged her. "I only did it for her," she sobbed. "I built it for her and now she isn't even here to see it. I hate that place, Marilyn. I hate it and I'm never going back there." The pent-up words were tumbling out of her now. "And you can't make me. Nobody can make me go back there. I'm never going to open it. Never."

"It's all right, Jenny. It's all right," Marilyn assured her. "We don't have to do anything you don't want to do. Okay?"

Jennifer shook her head and her body trembled as she went on, her voice punctuated with sobs. "All that work. I did it for her, to prove that I could, to make her live. And it didn't matter. She died anyway. She isn't here, and . . ." She broke down completely and wept bitterly in Marilyn's arms.

"It's all right, Jenny. It'll be all right," Marilyn said softly. "Come on, let's take a ride over to R.J.'s office. You'd like to see him, wouldn't you?"

Jennifer shook her head again. "First I have to clean up this mess," she sniffed.

"No you don't. Leave it; I'll sweep it up later. Come on now. Fix yourself up. We're getting out of here for a while.

80 ca

They were the second visitors of the day at the Law Offices of Townsend & Meacham. Jack was on the telephone with Judge Bill Bellingham, so Marilyn perched on the edge of his desk while R.J. proudly showed Jennifer around and lovingly described how he personally unpacked each of the new law books in the library conference room.

"Bill, I really have to go," Jack protested. "Someone's come in."

"So who's more important than the County Judge?" Bill demanded.

"My fiancée," Jack replied.

"Objection sustained. Call me later."

Jack hung up the receiver. Marilyn moved onto his lap and got comfortable. "Are you ready to come home?" he asked, kissing her neck.

"No."

"You know, this could be considered cruel and unusual punishment." His face was buried in her hair and it smelled wonderful.

"Stop," she protested, without protesting too much. "Jennifer needs my help right now, and besides, waiting will make our honeymoon so much better."

"That's just an old wives' tale," he said, pulling away for a moment. "Besides, I've been cold these last few nights without you to keep me warm."

"I haven't had you to keep me warm either, you know," she reminded him.

"So why don't you come home?"

"I can't right now, and anyway, Papa will be coming soon."

He kissed her: a long, passionate kiss. Her head slid into the crook of his arm and his free hand began creeping up her blouse. It had been a long two weeks. "How is every-thing on the boat?" she asked when she finally pulled her lips away from his.

"Fine. Lonely but fine," he replied.

"No dishes in the sink?"

"I'm perfectly capable of living alone, you know."

"I didn't say you weren't," she sighed as his hand inched farther up her torso. "But maybe I should come over and check."

Now she kissed him. It had been a very long two weeks. Her body began to squirm around on his lap. It was obvi-ous she wasn't tolerating abstinence any better than he was.

Jack hoped that if R.J. wanted to come in for anything, he would have sense enough to knock first.

"It might be a good idea for you to come over . . . to see if you forgot anything," he murmured as his lips left hers and began tracing their way along the side of her face to her ear.

"We could have lunch there," she sighed.

"That's right. We both need to have lunch anyway," he agreed.

"And I'm sure that Jennifer and R.J. can find something to do around here."

"They'll be fine. They don't need a babysitter."

"Let's go," Marilyn said suddenly standing up and grabbing his hand. She straightened out her skirt and opened the door while Jack was still getting himself together.

"Jennifer," Marilyn called out, "Jack and I are going over to the boat . . . for lunch . . . ."

"Isn't it a little early?" Jennifer asked, trying not to sound like she knew perfectly well what was on Marilyn's mind.

"Well, I need to pick up a few things . . . you know, makeup and stuff. I'll catch up with you at home later."

"What do you want me to tell our clients, Jack?" R.J. asked as the almost-newlywed couple was going out the door.

"What clients?"

"Arlo and Les Leslie," R.J. replied.

"Tell them they're all going to have to learn to live with each other."

The drive across the bridge to Bonita Key never seemed longer and to make matters worse the drawbridge went up as they approached the center of the span. Jack impatiently drummed his fingers on the steering wheel of Marilyn's car and tried not to look too impatient. He knew perfectly well what he planned to do when they got aboard the boat, but talking about it seemed somehow crude at the moment.

"So what did Arlo and Les want?" Marilyn asked, obviously doing her best to start a conversation. "Or can't you talk about it?" she added with a coy smile.

"It seems they don't think the 'everybody' in Margaret's Will should include *everybody*," he replied disgustedly. "The fight over shares is beginning already."

"That's too bad," Marilyn signed. "Why can't they just accept life as it comes? It will be a shame if they can't get along after receiving such a windfall."

The temperate winter air blew in through the open car window, and Jack smiled, thinking about how much things had changed in the past months. That was not the kind of thing Marilyn Dupré would have said early last summer.

The bridge came down and they hurried across to Cap'n Kelly's Marina and the private world of their live-aboard yacht. Jack began to undress her as soon as they entered the salon. "Are you sure this is safe?" Marilyn protested while loosening his tie. "Some of them may have seen us come in."

"To hell with them," Jack replied as he covered her mouth with his own. "Let them call Rob. That's why I have a partner," he said, still kissing her.

"At least let's go below," she said as she stripped off his shirt. "Someone may see us up here."

He had her blouse off and her skirt unzipped, and she was tugging at his belt. "Okay, let's go," he agreed.

They hurried down to the dimly lit aft stateroom and the queen-size bed where they had spent so many happy hours in the preceding months. He reached behind her and unfastened her bra while she finished unfastening his belt. It didn't take long for the rest of their clothes to find their way to the floor.

"It's been so long," Marilyn said as she held him close and kissed his bare chest.

"It was your idea to move ashore," he reminded her as he gently pushed her to the bed.

"Shut up and make love to me," she moaned, pulling him down on top of her.

Chapter 33

Jennifer and R.J. sat close together on the leather couch in his office. She toyed with a pencil on the coffee table and avoided his eyes. "Do you think they'll make it all the way home?" she asked. Her voice sounded almost wistful when she broke the silence after Marilyn left with Jack.

"I hope so. I'd hate to have to go bail them out for doing something foolish on the bridge," he replied. "And the Bar Association would not be amused." She didn't respond to the joke, and when she looked at him her sad eyes wilted his grin. "Are you okay?" he asked seriously.

She continued toying with the pencil and avoided his eyes again. "Yeah, I guess. I don't know, I'm just so . . . what should I do, R.J.?" she asked, still staring straight ahead. "I really fell behind at school. Maybe I should just forget about the Master's program." She looked at him, searching for approval, but he remained silent. "And then I ask myself, 'Why bother?'" she continued, looking away again. "I'll never be able to spend all that money. Why should I even bother with another degree?"

He took her hand gently and held it. "You not doing it for the money, Jennifer. You're doing it for yourself."

"Am I? I don't know what I'm doing any more." She looked at him and again and really held his eyes for the first time. "I really don't know, R.J."

"Does that include us?" he asked.

"No, that doesn't include us . . . at least, I don't think it does." He let go of her hand and turned away, stricken. "I'm sorry," she added quickly. "I didn't mean that. I guess I just can't help hurting people today."

"Maybe you need some time," he suggested. "Don't try so hard all the time. Finish out the semester without worrying about being on the Dean's List for a change. Just coast for now; your professors will understand. Then you can start fresh next semester, or even take a year off if you feel like it."

"What about the restaurant? Marilyn thinks we should open it. A lot of people are counting on us."

"Worry about yourself for a while, Jen. If the restaurant is meant to open, it will happen when the time is right for it to happen. Don't push so hard. You'll know when the time is right. Didn't your grandmother always say, 'the doors will open'?"

She stroked the side of his face and toyed with the hair over his ear. "What would I do without you, R.J.?"

"You would do just fine," he replied, "but let's not find out." And he leaned over and kissed her softly.

ℰℒ ⓒ℞

How much d'ya' figure them shares 'r worth?" Arlo asked as he watched Les apply another coat of varnish to *Elena's* new transom. They had just finished covering her foredeck with teak when Les decided they needed to refinish *Elena's* transom to better match the new toerails that would eventually circumscribe her deck.

"How the heck do I know?" Les responded. "Besides, they're only worth somethin' if you c'n sell e'm." He stoked the camel's hair brush only in one direction, taking care to begin each new stroke where the previous one ended. Once upon a time he had tried to teach the technique to Arlo. "Varnish ain't paint," he had warned, "Ya' don't brush back 'n' forth." The younger man just never developed the necessary passion for perfection and he simply would not take the time to do it right.

"Why couldn't we sell 'em?" Arlo demanded as he watched Les and yearned to lend a hand.

"How the heck do I know?" Les said again. "All's I did was tell ya' what I heard's all. An' that's all I know." He continued the careful brushwork. It was the fifth coat of varnish, with at least three more to go: it was tedious, precise work that he could not trust to anyone but himself.

"Well, I think we should go over there an' ast the Commodore," Arlo said, nodding toward Jack's boat.

Les looked up long enough to see Marilyn's car parked beside the trawler. "Will ya' leave them people alone?" he warned. "They prob'ly got a lot ta' talk about right now."

"Yeah, well, so do we," Arlo replied.

"Not as much's they do," Les retorted.

⅚ ⅛

In the stateroom of the trawler, Marilyn snuggled next to Jack under the sheets, their hunger sated at least temporarily. Jack always drifted as times like this, but Marilyn found their lovemaking invigorated her and her mind raced from one subject to the next.

"Jack," she began hesitantly, "Jennifer doesn't want to open the restaurant."

"That's too bad," he murmured heavily. "Margaret dreamed of the two of you making a success of that place. I guess I did too."

"We're going to have to pay back all that money to the bank," Marilyn said, ignoring his comment about Grandma Calkins' plans.

"Yeah," he replied sleepily.

"I don't want her to do it all herself. I mean, we were partners, and it wouldn't be fair."

Jack did not respond.

"I mean," Marilyn continued, "I know she has all that money and everything, but I still think I'm morally responsible for half, don't you?"

"Um-hm," he murmured.

"So what I was wondering was," she went on, running a finger through the hair on his chest, "do you think it would be all right if I used part of the money Grandma left us to pay off my share?"

"Uh-uh. Margaret wanted you to have that money for a proper house. If you really respect her like a grandmother, you should respect her wishes. Don't worry about the loan. I'll take care of it," he replied with a yawn.

She snuggled next to him again and tried to relax, but her mind would not follow her body's lead in the matter. How was he going to 'take care of it' without touching Grandma's bequest? She and Jennifer had borrowed an enormous amount of money—over two hundred thousand dollars. The only possible place to get her half was from the money Grandma had left them. Unless, because of the Calkins family connections with the Bank of Bonita, the whole thing could somehow be swept into a hidden account or something. "You're not going to do anything .. . illegal or anything, are you?" she finally blurted out.

That got his attention and he opened his eyes with a start. "What? What are you talking about?"

"You're not going to do anything like put pressure on the bank to make them forget about it, are you?"

"Honey" Jack laughed, "Monty Holcombe is a good friend but he's also a very ethical lawyer. Not even Casey Calkins would have been able to do that. Now go to sleep."

She put her head on his shoulder and really tried to close her eyes but they would not obey her. "So what are you going to do?" she finally asked.

"I guess I'll write them a check."

She pulled away suddenly and looked at him. "For a hundred thousand dollars?" she exclaimed.

"If that's what it takes," he replied. "Now just stop worrying about it."

She tried to nestle in his arms again but this was too much. She needed an explanation. "Jack," she began softly, "may I ask you a personal question?"

"That's a pretty silly thing to say to a man when you're lying next to him in bed naked," he joked.

"I'm serious."

"So am I," he replied.

"How much . . . I mean, how can you write a check . . . for that much money?"

"For checks that big I usually use a fountain pen," he quipped.

"Will you be serious for a minute?" she protested, pulling away and raising up on one elbow.

"I'm being serious. I like fountain pens. You know that."

"All right, but how much . . . I mean, do we have . . . Well, I mean, do you have . . . any . . ."

"Money in the bank?" he finished the question for her.

"Yes," she said.

"Yes," he replied.

"Well?"

"Well, what?"

"Well how much?"

He looked directly into her eyes. "Would it make a difference?" he asked softly.

"No, of course not," she replied, a little embarrassed. "You know that."

"Then why do you want to know?"

"Just so . . . just so I don't have to worry," she sighed and rolled over unto her back. "I hate worrying about money. I've had to do it my whole life and I just hate it."

"Then don't worry about it."

"But I have to . . ."

"Why?" he insisted.

"Because . . ." her voice trailed off while she tried to think of a good reason.

"Haven't you learned by now that things always work out? Money isn't that important," he reminded her. She could hear Grandma Calkins words in his voice.

"You're not going to tell me, are you?" she said, turning toward him.

"Why are you so upset?" he asked, looking back at her and gently caressing the side of her face.

"I just think that . . . when people care about each other . . . Well, they shouldn't have secrets from each other, that's all. And besides . . ."

"Besides what?" he asked.

"Well, if you must know, I hate being teased," she said. She turned away from him and pulled the sheet around herself. "I always used to get teased at school and I hated that, too."

He turned onto his side, put his arm around her and kissed the back of her bare shoulder. "I'm sorry. I promise I won't tease you."

He kept kissing her warm skin, over her shoulder blade

and around to the back of her neck but she refused to allow herself to respond. It wasn't easy, especially when he got to the area at her hairline. "So how much?" she finally demanded.

Now it was his turn to roll away and stare at the ceiling. "All right, let's see . . . I got two hundred fifty thousand when I left the firm," he said with an exasperated edge to his voice. "I cleared another hundred thousand from the sale of the house . . . real estate was really going crazy and I made a killing. The life insurance . . . we had taken out a million dollar policy on each other. And then there was the settlement. The car was leased, thank God, and there was a million dollar policy on that. We could have gotten the policy limits if we had gone to trial, but I settled it myself for eight hundred fifty thousand because I wanted to get it over with."

She turned and sat up facing him, the sheet falling away from her body. "John Townsend, do you mean to tell me you have two million dollars sitting around in a bank someplace?"

"You have beautiful breasts, you know that?" he said, gently stroking one of them.

"Is that what you're telling me?" she demanded.

"Yes," he assured her. "That is my expert opinion."

"Never mind about my breasts!" She knelt on top of him, grabbed his hands and playfully pinned them over his head on the pillow. "Are you telling me that you have two million dollars sitting in a bank someplace?" she insisted, with the objects of his attention swaying just out of the reach of his lips.

"I'm warning you, I could really get into this kind of kinky foreplay," he said seriously.

"Tell me!" she squealed, grinding her crotch into his chest.

"No," he said finally. "*I* don't have it; *we* have it. And it's not sitting around in a bank someplace, most of it's invested. And it isn't two million dollars, it's closer to four. The insurance provided for double indemnity in case of accident and I've made some very good investments in the past couple of years. Now will you please move forward just a little bit?"

She collapsed on top of him and he nuzzled happily in the delicious fold of her cleavage. "Why didn't you tell me this before?" she sighed as she held him and rolled over so that he was on top of her again.

"You never asked me," he said, kissing her and moving into position between her legs.

She wrapped her arms around his neck. "Jack, let's not tell Papa about this when he gets here."

"About this?" he said, moving forward on top of her.

"About this, and about the money too," she gasped.

"Why not? I thought that people who care about each other aren't supposed to keep secrets," he reminded her.

"They're not," she moaned. "But sometimes it's best if people don't know everything."

ജ ര

"So what'd he say?" How much 're they worth?" Erlene asked Arlo that evening after the dishes were put away and she poured two mugs of coffee in the galley of the sailboat that had become their home.

"He said he don't know." Arlo took one of the mugs and went up the companionway stairs and out into the cockpit that served as both the steering station of the boat and their outdoor patio.

"That's surprisin', him bein' a lawyer an' all," she said following him out on deck.

Arlo took a sip from the steaming mug. Erlene really knew how to make coffee. In fact, Erlene was good at just about everything she did, from sewing to making love. "I was talkin' about Les," he said.

"Well, I wasn't," she shot back. "I figured Les wouldn't know nothin'. I was talkin' about the Commodore."

"Yeah, I figured that out," Arlo replied.

"So?"

"So, I ain't talked ta' him about it yet, exactly."

"So, why not?"

Arlo walked around the cockpit to the other side of the wheel as if a movement of a few feet would give him time to think. He sat down heavily and tried to explain something about what a psychologist might call "male bonding." "Ya' just can't jump inta' things like that, Erlene," he protested. "Ya' gotta sorta' ease up on 'em."

"Well, I sure would like ta' know where we stand," she sighed as she sat down next to him and cupped her mug in her hands. "Easin' up on the subject won't make us find out any quicker, that's for sure."

"Hey, we're doin' all right, ain't we?" Arlo protested. "Livin' here on the boat, we ain't hurtin'. In fact, we're doin' pretty good, ain't we?"

She looked over her shoulder at him and smiled. Faith was living in a dorm at Bonita College, and Tommy was asleep in his room down below. He loved the idea of living on a boat. It was the first time in his life he ever had a room of his very own. Arlo was a good man, a darn good man, and she was lucky, she guessed, even if sometimes he did drive her crazy by not telling her what he was thinking and making her drag it out of him. She was comfortable with him. The cool air of the South Florida winter night made her appreciate the warmth of his body next to hers. Erlene reached down, pulled Arlo's arm around herself and huddled close to him. "Yeah, we're doin' good, Arlo," she assured him. "We're doin' just fine."

Chapter 34

The mid-December sun reflected off the tarmac at the Bonita International Airport. It was a typical tropical small-city setting: a two-story modern terminal building set off with palm trees and an outdoor baggage claim area. The day was just right: not too hot, humidity tolerable: the kind of day tourists pay to have. Papa would have a hard time finding anything to complain about.

"Now don't be nervous," Marilyn said as she straightened Jack's tie while they stood near the fence that separated the public portion of the airport from the landing field beyond.

"Honey, I stopped being nervous after my first jury trial a long time ago."

"I know, but this is different," she said, and she fluffed up the hair on the sides of his head. "You have to make a good impression."

"Or else what?"

"Jack, please. Don't give me a hard time today, all right? Just don't be nervous; there's nothing to be nervous about."

"I promise I won't give you a hard time," he said, kissing her forehead while she brushed dust only she could see off his lapel. "And I won't be nervous, either," he added.

The outdoor speakers announced the arrival of a flight from New Orleans, and Marilyn turned and clutched the chain link fence. "Where? I don't see it," she complained.

"That's because the plane is still a mile up the runway," Jack said soothingly. "Let's go inside."

"No, wait a minute. Maybe we'll be able to see him get off the plane."

It took a few minutes for the big jet to lumber around the corner of the building and, when it did, it's screaming engines made further conversation impossible. The plane continued to inch forward until a member of the ground crew brought two sticks together over his head. The whine of the engines dropped quickly, then stopped altogether and Marilyn stood on her tiptoes at the fence while some men wheeled a stairway into position.

"Remember, don't be nervous," she said to Jack, turning to look at him over her shoulder. "I'm sure Papa will like you."

"I promise I won't be nervous," Jack reassured her.

It seemed to take them forever to get the door open and even after they opened it, nobody came out of the plane.

"What's the matter, why aren't they getting off?" Marilyn protested.

"Give them a chance," Jack replied, stroking her shoulder as she held onto the fence.

They had sent him a first-class ticket. He should have been one of the first people down the stairway but the only faces Marilyn saw were those of strangers, squinting as they stepped out into the bright Florida sunshine. "Oh, God, I hope he didn't miss the plane," she said just before a familiar figure emerged from the dark doorway. "There he is! Papa! Papa, over here!" she yelled, waving a hand in the air.

"He can't hear you, Honey," Jack protested. "At least let him get down the stairway."

"Over here, Papa! Over here!" she continued, waving and shouting, not listening to a thing Jack said.

The man reached the bottom of the stairway and must have heard her because he looked in her direction. He was about sixty, Jack guessed, but his hair was still dark—although it might have been aided by a dye bottle—and he was slightly paunchy, no doubt from too much rich French cooking. He was wearing a gray sport coat over a black turtleneck shirt, and his sagging features lifted into a broad smile when he saw his daughter. He waved a hand in reply and started toward the fence before a member of the ground crew intercepted him.

"Go inside, Papa," Marilyn yelled, pointing toward the doorway where the other passengers were being herded. "We'll meet you inside."

The man dutifully got back into line and followed the directions of the airport personnel.

"Come on," Marilyn said, grabbing Jack's hand, "we've got to get inside."

He held her back for only a moment. "Honey," he said seriously, "I just want you to notice two things: one, he's not wearing a tie . . . and two, I'm not nervous."

The inside of the terminal building was a madhouse of travelers: some families arriving in Florida for the holidays and others going "up North" to be with loved ones and see snow for Christmas. Marilyn pushed her way through the crowd, dragging Jack behind her until she got to the gate area where her father was waiting, looking for her.

"Papa!" she rushed into his arms and kissed him on both cheeks. He hugged her, then pushed her back and held her at arm's length so that he could look at her before he clasped her back to him and kissed her on both cheeks. The Dupré's were a very kissing family, Jack thought.

It took several more hugs and kisses before either of them bothered with Jack. Marilyn broke away from her father's embrace and made what sounded like a very carefully rehearsed introduction: "Papa," she began solemnly, "this is John Townsend. This is the man I'm going to marry."

The elder Dupré raised one eyebrow and looked at Jack with eyes that were the prototype of his daughter's. "So, Jon Tousand," he said, extending his hand and doing nothing to hide his disdain for English diction, "you are the man who will take my last remaining treasure from me, eh?"

Jack took his hand and held it for a moment. "Sometimes a man must give up a treasure to gain greater treasures, Henri Dupré," Jack replied.

The older man looked at him quizzically without releasing his hand. There was a long pause before his face lit up in recognition. "You mean *petit fils*, little ones, eh?" he said. He tossed his head in his daughter's direction. "With this one I had lost hope almost."

"One should never lose hope, Henri," Jack said as the two men finally released each other's hands.

Dupré straightened his jacket and looked at Jack, examining him with carefully pursed lips. "So," he said, "you live on a boat, my daughter tells me. Is this any place for a wife? And a family? A boat?"

"It's a very nice boat, Papa," Marilyn quickly interjected between them.

"Perhaps you would like to come and see it?" Jack suggested.

Dupré nodded. "We shall see. First, I must get my valise," he announced as he started for the exit.

"I knew it," Marilyn muttered as they followed him out to the baggage claim area. "He hates the idea of living on a boat."

"Honey, will you please take it easy?" Jack reassured her. "He's just playing his 'Papa' role. Everything will be fine."

Jack had hired a limousine over Marilyn's objection. "I don't want him thinking we're too well off," she had protested. "But he's your father," Jack argued, "and I hate driving. And with a limo you'll have plenty of time to talk to him on the way back home. Besides, I had to get one for my mother. Anyway, how many times are you going to get married?"

It was the "you only get married once" argument that won out and she had to admit Papa was suitably impressed by the arrangement. "*Tres bon, tres bon,*" he said after the driver loaded his suitcase into the trunk and helped the passengers inside. "They pay you so well at your job? To watch their accounts?"

"The limousine was Jack's idea, Papa," Marilyn told him. "He thought it would give us more time to be together."

"And to impress the bride's papa, eh, Jon?" Dupré said, winking at him.

"To impress the bride's papa doesn't hurt," Jack agreed.

"*Bon,* Papa is impressed," Dupré conceded. "Now tell me everything you have been doing, *ma petite choute.*"

"We've been . . . I've been so busy, Papa," Marilyn began, "I don't know where to begin."

"It is so busy, taking care of accounts?"

"The accounts are nothing, Papa. We were building the restaurant. You know; I told you about it. And . . . well, there was all of that to keep track of. We . . . that is, Jennifer, had everything all set to go when Grandma . . . when Mrs. Calkins died . . ." Marilyn hesitated, unsure of how to finish the story. "And you know I was also studying for the bar exam . . ." she added lamely.

"The restaurant, it is open now?"

"Well . . . no . . . I'm afraid not," she admitted.

"But why?"

"Jennifer is going to need some time to . . . get over her grandmother's death, I guess."

"Janifere . . . she is the one who calls you 'sister,' no? She is not well?"

Marilyn looked at him earnestly. She had not meant to talk about all of this; Papa didn't even know that she was a part owner of Sisters Restaurant. Papa had a way of getting things out of her sometimes. "Jennifer is very depressed, Papa," she finally said quietly, and she looked away.

"I see." Dupré looked out the window of the limo as they crossed the bridge to Bonita Key. "It is a terrible thing to be depressed in such a beautiful place," he said, almost to himself.

They rode the rest of the way in silence, Jack sitting across from them and trying to use his old jury-selection skills to read Henri Dupré. He had been dark and handsome once, that much was certain, but too many nights on Bourbon Street had taken their toll. Up close, he could see streaks of gray in the older man's hair, and although the bags under his eyes made him look tired, they belied his quick wit and a disarming smile. Even Jack found himself susceptible to his French charm. There was something else about Henri Dupré—if his daughter once claimed she always "knew things," she had clearly inherited that gift from her father. Even in this brief encounter, the elder Dupré always seemed to know what questions to ask, as if he had the answers already in his pocket. He would have made a hell of a trial lawyer, Jack thought.

                ❧ ❧

"Well, the famous French chef has arrived," Jim Lacey commented looking out of the window of their houseboat as the limousine ground to a stop next to Jack's trawler.

"Marilyn's father? Let me see," Lacey's partner Eddie Miles elbowed him out of the way.

"I had that place all set to go, Eddie. All set. Kitchen equipment, tables, chairs," Lacey quickly warmed to his usual subject of recent days. "Listen, I had Steve Tesla practically standing on his head getting stuff for me. And the help! They were all lined up, Eddie. They were expecting jobs! And those two women are going to turn it all over to Frenchy because he's her father."

"Don't be silly," Eddie responded without turning from the window. "Marilyn doesn't want him around here anymore than you do." He watched Dupré get out of the car and go aboard the trawler with his daughter and Jack. "Although he's a handsome devil, I must admit," he added.

"Get away from that window!" Lacey insisted. "Do you want them to see you?"

"I'm just cleaning a spot off the glass, Jim," he said, taking a paper towel out of his apron pocket. "There's no law against that, is there?"

"How do you know that she doesn't want him here?" he demanded.

"You'd know things too, if you stopped shouting at people all the time and listened for a change."

"To who? To you?"

"To everybody. This is a small community, Jim. People talk."

"Talk! They're probably talking about being let down! People were counting on those jobs, Eddie. I wouldn't be surprised if some of them quit what they were doing just so they could get themselves ready to come with us. We let them down."

"Yes, Jim," Eddie said patiently. "And all the time you put into it."

"Yes, all the time I put into it," he shouted. "And what did I get out of it? I'll tell you what I got out of it: nothing! That's what I got out of it! Every time I ask anybody about it, they tell me 'everything's on hold until Jennifer decides'."

"She's a young girl, Jim. She needs time."

"She's a young girl with twenty-five million dollars and no need to worry like the rest of us!"

"You've no need to worry," his partner reminded him. "You never did need to worry. You do it because you like to worry. And you like to shout. And one of these days you're going to worry and shout yourself into another heart attack."

80 03

On the Chris-Craft Constellation berthed along the wall opposite Jack's trawler, Howard Garner hunched over a pocket calculator that was too small to hold the numbers he tried to punch into it. It didn't matter. All he had to do was leave off a few zeroes and tack them back on after he got the answer. The real problem was knowing what the numbers were and that depended on how you interpreted Mrs. Calkins' Will: "one share to each resident." How about people like Jim Lacey and Eddie Miles, he wondered. Everybody knew they were a couple, but did they get two shares because there were two of them? And that girl at the gas dock, Erlene what-was-her-name. What about her? Was she entitled to a share just because she was living with that fellow Arlo? And didn't the same question apply to Marilyn Dupré? Was she a "resident"?— not that she needed the money; the Calkins family had taken pretty good care of her.

The numbers were important to Howard because the more shares there were, the less money each one would be worth. Money was very important to Howard. The only thing he was certain of was that he was entitled to one— and only one—share, whatever it might be. So he spent most of his time alone on his boat, congratulating himself on his stroke of luck and figuring and re-figuring what his net worth might now be.

The limousine didn't surprise him. Even in his self-imposed isolation he had heard about Henri Dupré's impending visit. He hoped the future Mrs. Townsend wasn't going to try to pull a fast one by claiming her father was a resident and get a share, too. That would be too much for Howard, and he might have to do something drastic, like hire a lawyer. Lawyers were expensive he though, unless he could call in a favor from his days as a real estate agent. But even cheap lawyers cost money. Howard didn't want to think about spending money, so instead he brooded over his small calculator and wished that it held more zeroes.

Chapter 35

"*Pas mal*; it is not bad here," Dupré reported as he examined the interior of the trawler. "*C'est comfortable.* The kitchen is small but adequate."

"It's called a galley, Papa," Marilyn corrected him, searching Jack's face for his reaction to this invasion of their—his—privacy. "A kitchen on a boat is called a galley."

"It is where they keep the galley slave, eh, Jon?" Dupré said from below with a laugh. "And the wine cellar? Where is that?" he asked opening the cupboards below the countertop.

"Boats don't have cellars, Papa," Marilyn said patiently as she went down to shoo him up to the salon. "We don't have much . . . Jack doesn't have much room for storage. Do you, Dear?" Her husband-to-be did not reply, preferring to remain silent and watch the interplay between his bride and her father.

"Would you like *café au lait*, Papa?" Marilyn asked. "I have . . . Jack has . . . the coffee sent from Café du Monde on Decatur Street."

"New Orleans coffee one does not refuse. With a drop or two of cognac from the cabinet over the sink, it would be even better."

She hadn't even seen him open that damn cupboard. Jack must be having a fit by now, she thought as she busied herself with the coffee maker. Papa had only been in Florida for an hour and already her nerves were on edge. It was going to be a long two weeks. She couldn't understand why Jack was taking it so well. Nothing Papa did seemed to bother him, not even his nosing around in the galley cupboards. He even insisted on taking Papa to the fly bridge to enjoy the view while the "galley slave" toiled down below, setting out a tray of pastries she had bought to go along with the coffee.

"Here we are," she announced, the perfect little hostess as Jack helped her get the tray up to the bridge. "*Café au lait* just the way you like it, Papa, with cognac and a napoleon on the side."

"Just like home," he said, taking a coffee mug and plate from her. "No, it is better than home. At home I do not have *une belle fille* bringing it to me."

"Like old times, Papa," she replied with a trace of bitterness in her voice.

"So, when will I meet this Janifere, this new sister of yours?" he asked as he dug into the pastry.

"Oh, ah … well, I hadn't thought about that," she hesitated.

"There is something wrong? You are ashamed of your Papa?" he teased.

"No, of course not," she replied. "It's nothing like that.

I suppose we could take a ride over there later, couldn't we, Jack?"

"I've already met Jennifer," he said, smiling. "And I have some writing to do. Why don't you and your father go?"

"*Bon*," Dupré agreed. "First we will finish the *café* and then I will meet my new daughter."

Marilyn went below to telephone Jennifer with a quick warning, and after the dishes were put away did her best to keep up a pleasant conversation on the short drive to the Magnolia Avenue house. She couldn't understand why she felt so uneasy with him; it wasn't like he could send her back to Sainte Anne's if she didn't live up to his expectations. But there she was, a lawyer—with a Master of Laws degree—trying to keep up polite chatter and feeling as out of place as if she had found herself at the wrong cocktail party.

Thankfully Jennifer was home and, if she wasn't delighted, at least she wasn't opposed to the idea of meeting Papa. She was waiting for them on the porch and came down the front steps while Marilyn parked in front of the house.

"Jennifer, this is my father, Henri Dupré," Marilyn announced when they had gotten out of the car. "Papa, this is Jennifer Calkins."

Dupré took Jennifer's hand and bowed as he kissed it. "*Enchanté, Mademoiselle*," he said gallantly.

"Oh, well, it's so nice to meet you . . . Mister Dupré," Jennifer blushed.

Dupré's brow furrowed into a serious-looking scowl. "You are not the one who calls my daughter '*soeur*' . . . 'sister'?"

"Yes, I guess I kind of started that . . ." Jennifer admitted.

"Then why you do not call me 'Papa' as she does?" he demanded with one raised eyebrow.

"Oh, well, yes, I guess I could . . . do that . . . Papa," Jennifer replied.

"*Bon. Deux belle filles.* Two beautiful daughters. What more could any man ask?"

"Maybe we should go inside," Marilyn suggested as she gently pushed Henri Dupré ahead of her into the house.

"Can I get you something?" Jennifer asked politely after they were all seated in the living room.

"One as pretty as you is not meant to be a waitress, Janifere," Dupré said, waving a finger as though he were lecturing a student.

"Thanks, but we just had coffee," Marilyn said, secretly wondering if the "waitress" remark was a comment on the way she had worked her way through college.

"It is for me to prepare something for you," Dupré added.

"Oh . . . no, that's all right," Jennifer protested.

"You must eat, *ne pas*? You are too pale. *Oeufs a'la Florentine* will put some color in your cheeks."

"No . . . really," Jennifer protested.

"I see a kitchen through that doorway. You remain here with your *soeur* and speak about whatever it is young girls speak about. Papa will make your luncheon," he said as he headed for the inner sanctum of the house.

"You might as well give up, Jennifer. You're going to get Eggs Florentine whether you want them or not," Marilyn warned.

"He's kind of cute, isn't he?" Jennifer commented.

"Yeah, so's a baby rhino. But try living with one for a while. He hasn't been here for half a day, and already he's driving me crazy."

"Oh relax, Marilyn. Let him have fun. I might even like Eggs Florentine."

"Let him have fun. Relax," Marilyn repeated. "That's what Jack says. Why is it that Papa doesn't bother anybody except me?"

Jennifer looked at her but did not say anything.

"And what's that supposed to mean?" Marilyn demanded.

"What?"

"That . . . that look. You think it's me, don't you?"

"Marilyn, I didn't say anything."

"But you were thinking it!"

"Janifere, *ma bellotte*, you have no spinach?" Dupré called from the kitchen.

"There's some in the freezer . . . Papa," Jennifer replied, raising her voice so that he could hear.

"Frozen," he complained aloud. "Well, *j'ai pas vraiment d'choix*. I have no other choice, eh?"

"What's a *bellotte*?" Jennifer whispered to Marilyn in the living room.

"Pretty. 'My pretty one'," she scowled.

"He is so sweet, isn't he," Jennifer gushed.

"Jennifer, you're just falling for the same old French banana oil charm he uses on everybody. You don't know him like I do."

"Oh, knock it off, Marilyn. Chill out. Take a pill or something. You know what? I feel like playing the piano."

In a moment the strains of "Lebensraum" filled the house and Papa joined in, humming from the kitchen. "This is going to be an awfully long two weeks," Marilyn said glumly.

℘ ℭ

Back at the boatyard, Howard Garner ventured off his boat long enough to watch Arlo watch Les lay on another coat of varnish.

"Whatcha doing fellas?" Garner said.

"Waitin' for a streetcar. What's it look like?" Arlo demanded.

"Just layin' on another coat a' varnish, Howard," Les replied, not missing a stroke.

"Need some help?"

"Not fr'm you," Arlo replied defensively. "This here's real precise work."

"I'm just takin' my time, Howard," Les replied. "No need ta' rush."

"Rushing is the worst thing you can do," Howard Garner agreed. "When I do my brightwork, I always take it nice and slow."

"You do your own brightwork??" Les stopped what he was doing and looked at Garner with an expression that might grow into respect.

"Sure. You got any idea what some of them thieves want for doing stuff like this? Anyway, there's not much to it: you just lay it on in one direction, like you're doing, and take it easy so you don't get any sags."

"Yeah, that's right; that's the idea," Les agreed. "Like to try out this brush?"

"Sure, I'll give it a try," Garner replied, taking the brush from him and stepping up to the work.

"That's pure camel hair," Les warned him. "I paid sixty dollars f'r that brush an' it's worth every penny."

Garner whistled. "Sixty dollars! That's a lot of money for a brush."

"Yeah, but look, ya' don't see a line when y're layin' on that varnish. Not one line. An' ya' won't see one, neither."

"You're right about that," Garner agreed. "Goes on as smooth as silk. But sixty dollars! I don't know. That's a lot of money for a brush."

"Tools make the master, Howard. That's what my Pa used ta' say."

"I got some purty good tools over on my boat," Arlo put in.

"Ya' know," Les continued, "I got a set of chisels from Japan . . . ya' could shave with 'em, Howard."

Garner whistled again. "I'd sure like to take a look at those."

"I got me some chisels from Sears . . . Craftsman, I mean," Arlo reported. "Them babies 're slick. Darn near cut my finger off with one of 'em one time."

"Why don't we finish this up, and ya' c'n come on board," Les said to the newcomer.

"Sure you won't mind?"

" 's no trouble at all," Les assured him. "I'll throw on a pot a' somethin' 'r other and maybe scare up a couple 'a doughnuts."

"Well, I gotta go," Arlo said. "Ya' know, things ta' do an' everythin'."

"Huh? Oh, yeah. Okay, Arlo," Les replied. "Drop over anytime. We're just about ready for the water, wouldn't ya' say?"

"Yeah, sure. One a' these days. Ready f'r the water," Arlo murmured to himself as he slowly walked away.

ℝ ℞

"That was delicious, Papa," Jennifer said as she ran a last piece of toast over her plate. "I don't know when I ever had anything so good."

"No, you are too kind. It is a pity we did not have fresh spinach and the proper cheeses; then I could have created something worthy of your praises . . . and your beauty, *ma chére*."

"Yes, well, we really should be going, Papa," Marilyn said. "I'll help Jennifer with the dishes and then we can leave."

"Leave, but why?" Dupré protested. "I have nowhere to go. *Peut-etre* Janifere and I can make groceries together, and tonight I will make *Crevettes a'la Creole.*"

The combination of French mixed with New Orleans idiom left Jennifer looking blank. "I don't think Jennifer likes Shrimp Creole, Papa. And we don't need to buy more groceries; there's just the two of us here."

"I love Shrimp Creole!" Jennifer insisted. "And I'd love to get out of his house for a while. And tonight we can have R.J. and Jack come over to help us eat it . . . if that's not too much trouble, Papa?" she asked looking at Dupré for his approval.

"Trouble? How could anything be trouble for one as lovely as you *mon fille*? We go, eh? We must find *les crevettes* . . . and they must be fresh no? And for the sauce Creole we must have cayenne pepper . . . Janifere, there is none in the kitchen, *mon Dieu*! Always we must have cayenne pepper!"

"Yes, Papa. I'll make sure of that," she said, nodding her head dramatically.

"We go now, eh? Marilyn, you tell Jon to be here at half past six . . . no, seven o'clock, *tres bien*?

"Yes, Papa," Marilyn replied with a sigh.

"Janifere, we must stop at the wine store. *Vin blanc*, no?"

"Certainly, Papa. White wine with fish," Jennifer agreed seriously.

"And Marilyn, you will bring the *café* from Café du Monde, *mais oui*? And do not forget the cognac."

"Of course; the cognac," she replied.

"*Tres bien*. Let us depart, Janifere. We have much to do now."

Henri Dupré hustled the young blonde out of the house in an instant. Only after they were gone did Marilyn realize that the dishes were still on the table and the pans were in the sink. She turned to the task grimly. And the galley slave gets left behind, she thought.

෨ ෬

Dinner was superb. Dupré had the touch, no doubt about it. The shrimp were tender and succulent, and the Creole sauce was just hot enough to delight the tongue without making their eyes water. Henri fawned over the diners—especially Jennifer—as if he expected a sizable tip after the table was cleared.

"I really have to go," R.J. announced, looking at his watch. "Judge MacIntyre wants to see me first thing in the morning about taking an assigned criminal case."

"You're kidding!" Jack protested.

"No, why? Didn't I mention it to you?"

"No."

"Is there some problem?" R.J. asked.

"No, not at all," Jack responded. "I just didn't think you wanted to swim around in that sewer so soon after our last dip."

"You got me started, partner," R.J. replied, smiling at him.

"Well, I guess I'd better be going too," Jack said. "Someone will have to be at the office in case the phone rings."

"Jon, you will leave me at *un hotel bon-marché*, no? Something modest to suit my means?"

"Papa, we wouldn't think of having you stay at a hotel, would we Jack?" Marilyn said quickly. "Besides, it's much too late to get a room," she added before Jack could offer an opinion on a hotel. "Why don't you stay on the boat with Jack tonight? We can make other arrangements tomorrow."

"If it is no trouble," Dupré answered, hesitating.

"Oh, no, it's no trouble at all, is it, Dear?" Marilyn said, looking at Jack who still did not respond.

"What the hell are you talking about, 'no trouble'?" he hissed at Marilyn while Jennifer escorted Papa to the door. "It certainly is trouble! A hell of a lot of trouble!"

"Jack, it's only for one night," she apologized. "I don't want to just dump him in some strange hotel. After all, he's my father."

"My mother always stays in a hotel," he protested. Marilyn looked at him. "I know, I know, 'that's different'," he added before she could get the words out.

ജ ര

"*Alors*, Jon, my daughter does not . . . live with Janifere, I think," Dupré said as they opened a new bottle of cognac in the salon of the trawler.

"No, she doesn't," Jack confirmed when he had poured two nightcaps.

"So why is she not here tonight? With you? Where she belongs?"

"She didn't want to do anything that might offend you, Henri."

"Offend me?!" Dupré exploded. "I am French! How did my daughter become so . . . American?" He said the word as if he were speaking the name of a contagious disease.

Jack wanted to say that it might have something to do with being sent away from home as a child to be raised by nuns, but he kept his thoughts to himself and instead took a sip from his glass.

"Your daughter needs your approval, Henri" he said finally. "She wants you to think well of her."

Dupré leaned back in his chair and looked at the overhead before speaking. "I have not been a good father, Jon," he mused. "Sometimes because of this"—he held up his glass and looked at the liquor that remained in it—"and sometimes because of . . . other temptations." He brought the glass down, leaned forward and fixed Jack with his eyes. "You will be a better husband to her than I was a father, no?"

"Yes. But just for the record, I don't think you were such a bad father."

"We do what we must do, Jon," Henri Dupré said, finishing his drink in a single swallow and lowering his eyes. "We do what we must do."

Chapter 36

"It just ain't natural, Erlene," Arlo complained as they dawdled over a second cup of coffee in the cockpit of the sailboat after Tommy went off to school. "Les 's been hangin' around with that guy f'r a week solid."

"Aw . . . lost y'er boyfriend, Arl?" she chided.

"It ain't that, it's just that . . . he ain't like us, that's all. Always hangin' around, 'Need some help?' 'C'n I give ya' a hand?' It just ain't natural."

"Y'er always helpin' people too, Arl. Maybe he's just tryin' ta' be friendly, that's all," she suggested. "Seein's how he's gonna be livin' here an' all."

"Yeah, well I still say it ain't natural," Arlo muttered.

80 03

A fine layer of dust settled into the crows' feet at the corners of Les Leslie's eyes as he and Howard Garner carefully sanded off part of the varnish they had laid on the day before. The secret of good brightwork, they agreed, is to sand off half the varnish you lay on, wipe the work with a good tack rag, and lay on another coat.

Then do it again. And again. It takes time, and Arlo didn't have the patience for it. "What's the sense of varnishin' if you're just gonna sand it off?" he would demand whenever Les would try to explain the process. Now, Howie Garner was different. He didn't mind takin' his time. Les liked that. And Howie kept his mouth shut; he wasn't always chatterin' on about things that was either none a' his business or didn't matter anyhow, Les thought. Les liked that, too.

It was early morning of the kind of day that made Les happy to be alive. The weather was still comfortably cool and the humidity low; tee shirt weather and perfect for laying on varnish. Howard was working on one side of *Elena's* transom and Les on the other, hand-sanding the previous day's work. It was a fine way to spend a morning, Les thought. One of these days, Elena would be ready for the water, but for now he was happy enough to just run his hand over her unfinished white hull and the mahogany transom that would soon have the appearance of fine furniture.

"Want a cup a' coffee, Howie?" Les asked. It was time for a break, when they could sit on one of the many piles of lumber and contemplate their handiwork.

"Sound's like a good idea," Garner agreed as Les began climbing the ladder to *Elena's* galley to pour out the last two mugs full of coffee from the pot they had put on earlier that morning. Les carefully handed one of the mugs to Garner and gingerly climbed back down the ladder with his own.

"So when are you going to Italy?" Garner asked when they had taken their usual seats on the lumber piles.

"What are ya' talkin' about?" Les asked, feigning ignorance.

"Well, the old lady left you all that money to go to Italy. I just thought you might like some company, that's all."

"Oh, ya' did, did ya'? An' I suppose ya' thought ya'd be the 'company'," Les demanded, turning to him.

"Hey, you don't have to get defensive about it."

"'Defensive'?" I ain't 'defensive'. I just don't want people talkin' about my business is all."

"Well, when an old lady dies and leaves someone two hundred and fifty grand to go to Italy, people are going to talk about it," Garner observed dryly.

"An' how da' ya' know about the money?" Les demanded.

"Everybody knows about it, Les. It's public record."

"'Public Record'? What in blazes are ya' talkin' about, Howard?"

"Public record: down at the courthouse. Once a person dies anybody can go down there and look up their Will."

"An' I suppose ya'd know all about that, too, wouldn't ya'?"

"Yeah, sure," Garner responded. "Everybody knows about public records. You'd be surprised at the things you can look up down there. What's the big fuss?"

Les stood up and faced him directly. "The 'Big Fuss' is about me not wantin' people knowin' my business; that's what the 'Big Fuss' is about."

"Well, maybe you don't want people knowing it, but that's the way it is," Garner replied, getting to his feet.

"No, that ain't the way it is. Just because records is public 's no reason for people to be goin' down there lookin' at 'em."

"That's pretty stupid," Garner said.

"'Stupid'?" Les boomed. "Listen, just 'cause somebody's got their winda' blinds open don't mean ya' c'n look in their winda', does it?"

"Sure it does."

"It does?! You an' me are gonna part brass rags on this 'un, Howard," Les shouted. "You mean ta' tell me you think just 'cause somethin's public record gives ya' the right ta' go look at it?"

"Hey, I didn't say I went down and looked at it," Garner backpedaled.

"Ya' didn't? Ya' didn't?! Well what in Hades did ya' say?"

"I said that after a person dies, their Will is public record and anybody can go down to the Courthouse and look at it. But I never said I did it."

"Then how did ya' know about the money?"

"Well, I . . . knew about it. What's the big deal? So the old lady left you two hundred and fifty thousand dollars. So what?"

Les took the coffee mug out of Garner's hand and flung the contents to the ground. "I'd appreciate it if ya' didn't refer to Miz Calkins as an 'ol' lady'," he demanded. "And I'd also appreciate it if ya' didn't drink my coffee. An' mostly I'd appreciate it if ya' just minded y'er own gol-darn business. Now scat!"

"You're saying you don't want my help anymore?"

"I'm sayin' I don't want nobody around here stickin' his nose where it ain't wanted!"

"Well, that's fine with me," Garner shouted as he stalked away.

"An' it's fine with me. An' it'll be fine with everybody else aroun' here, too," Les shouted back at the receding figure of Howard Garner.

ⅎ ℂ

"Do you think you'll have a little time to review the facts of this case with me before you go to the airport?" R.J. asked as he leaned against the jamb in the doorway of Jack's office. It was the body language he used whenever he didn't want to intrude, even though he knew he was intruding.

Jack looked up from his word processor. At the rate he was going, he would never reach his goal of finishing his novel before the wedding. "Sure, Rob. What's up?"

"Only if you have the time . . ."

"The limo's picking me up here at eleven-thirty. Mom's plane lands at noon, then we have lunch and run back to the airport to pick up Sister Jean-Marie, whoever she is. You better get me while you can."

"Well, since you insist," R.J. said, stepping into the room and sitting in a chair across the desk from Jack. "This kid's charged with armed robbery, and he says he didn't do it."

Jack was about to speak, but R.J. held up his hand. "I know, 'that's what they all say,' but this kid's wife backs him up. She says he was home in bed with her at the time of the robbery."

"Was she 'in bed' with him, or *asleep* in bed with him?" Jack asked. "There's a difference."

"Oh, come on . . ."

"If she says she was asleep in bed with him, and she was asleep, how does she know he was there? Now if they were in bed for another reason, he might have an alibi."

"Damn, I never thought . . . I didn't want to ask her anything that personal."

"Ask her, Rob. Your client's liberty is at stake . . . nothing's too personal. You have to know everything. If they're going to use the 'he was in bed with me' defense, you want to know whether they used a condom . . . and if they did, you want a receipt from the drugstore. Do you really think this guy's innocent?"

"I think so, Jack. I really do."

"Never happen, Rob. Dennis Woodbrace was the first innocent client I had in twenty years of practice. I'm betting we don't get two in a row."

80 ଔ

The jumbo jet from LaGuardia airport was already beginning its final descent in the clear blue Florida sky when Jack and Marilyn jumped out of the limousine and ran into the terminal building.

"I told you we should have gotten here sooner," Marilyn complained.

"What for?" Jack replied. "My mother knows enough to find a seat somewhere and wait for us."

"Wait for us? You expect *her* to wait for *us*?"

"Why not? She's a grown woman; she won't wander away."

"Oh, God," Marilyn exclaimed putting a hand to her forehead. "Thank the Lord Sister Jean-Marie isn't going to arrive until one-thirty. I suppose you'd expect her to wait for us, too?"

Jack didn't answer. He was about to say, "Of course. Why not?" but that didn't seem to be the thing that Marilyn wanted to hear at the moment, so he hurried her over to the gate area.

"Do I look all right?" She was wearing a sleeveless floral print dress. It was as modest as possible in light of her figure. "This dress isn't too casual, is it?"

"Honey, it's going up to eighty-two degrees," he replied, reminding her of the unusually warm December weather. "You're supposed to be casual."

"But is it too, you know, revealing?" she asked.

"Are you asking for an expert opinion?" he asked as he leaned over and attempted to peer down her cleavage.

"What's the use of asking you?" she complained, pulling away. "You're only interested in seeing me naked!"

"Now, that's not true," he chided. "I could also appreciate you in a thong bikini. You should buy a few."

"Will you behave?" she complained. "Your mother is about to arrive!"

"My mother is a very worldly woman."

"Well Sister Jean-Marie isn't!" she warned. "And she'll be here in an hour and a half. So start practicing. Have you decided where we're going to take your mother for lunch?"

"Sure: the Yacht Club."

"The Club? Jack! We can't go all the way back over to the island and get back here by one-thirty! Besides, I thought we would take them to the Club for dinner tonight. I made reservations for the five of us."

"Five?" Jack inquired. "I have the distinct impression that I missed something."

"Your mother, Sister Jean-Marie, my father and the two of us," she explained in an exasperated tone.

"What happened to Jennifer and Rob?"

"I thought it would be nice to be alone for once," she said, looking away at the still-closed door.

Jack wanted to point out that five people did not exactly constitute being alone, but he was getting Marilyn's vibes that said it, too, was not the right thing to say at the moment.

"Where has your father been running off to every day, anyway?"

"He's teaching 'Janifere' how to cook. Or if it's not that, they're out together 'making groceries'. And when they're not shopping for food, they're out buying cooking gadgets. Honestly, I never knew there were so many gourmet food stores in Bonita." She looked away again as an attendant opened the door. "Do you really think I look all right?" she asked as they watched the first passengers come into the terminal.

"Fine. You look just fine," Jack replied as he looked over her head, scanning the approaching faces until he saw one that he recognized. "Mom! Mom, over here!"

A well-dressed blond woman who appeared much younger than her assessed sixty-plus years looked in their direction and smiled. She was wearing a dignified peach-colored business suit, and unlike the other passengers who were all toting various parcels, she carried only a small handbag and an elegant black fur coat.

"John, it's so nice to see you," she said, reaching up and hugging him around the neck with her free arm. "And you must be Marilyn," she added, turning to the bride-to-be with a polite hug and a press of her cheek. "I've finally gotten to meet you."

"It's a pleasure to meet you, Mrs. Townsend," Marilyn said with her best convent-school manners as the woman released her.

"Well, now, we'll have to forego that 'Mrs. Townsend' business, especially since you'll be one yourself in a few days. Why don't you just call me 'Victoria'?"

"Certainly, if that's what you prefer, Victoria."

Victoria Townsend wrinkled her nose and patted Marilyn's hand conspiratorially. "'Mother Townsend' makes me sound too old, don't you think? You never know when some eligible bachelor might be standing around . . . especially here in Florida."

Marilyn wasn't sure of what it was she had been expecting from Jack's mother, but she knew that a discussion of eligible bachelors wasn't it. She began to have second thoughts about putting her in the same hotel with Sister Jean-Marie.

"Well now, John," Victoria Townsend said, handing him her black sable coat, "where are you taking me for lunch? Airline food hasn't gotten any better, you know."

Jack shot Marilyn an "I-told-you-so" look and said, "I wanted to take you to the Yacht Club, but my bride has made a reservation for tonight. Besides, we have to wait for Sister Jean-Marie, who's coming in at one-thirty."

"One of my teachers," Marilyn explained. "My favorite teacher, really. She's a nun. That's why they call her 'Sister'."

"Yes Dear, I'm familiar with Catholic nuns. Well, I suppose we can spend some time right here, as long as the airport lounge has Blue Label."

"Johnny Walker Blue Label," Jack explained as he escorted them both from the gate. "It's her favorite Scotch. Some Townsend women have favorite nuns, and some have favorite Scotches."

෨ ଓ

Lunch with the society matron from New York was nowhere near as stiff and forbidding as Marilyn had expected it to be. Thankfully, Victoria and Jack confined themselves to one Scotch each while Marilyn sipped ginger ale. It wouldn't do to introduce them to Sister if they were all "half-in-the-bag" as Judge Bill Bellingham would say.

"Now, I just happen to have some pictures of John when he was a child," Victoria said, reaching for her purse after the table was cleared. "Of course the family albums are in one of my suitcases."

"Mother, not now," Jack protested.

"Why not? Afraid I might show her that one of your bare bum? Ha! Don't tell me she hasn't seen it already."

"Mom, please!" Jack protested as Marilyn did her best to suppress a laugh behind her napkin.

"We really should be getting back to the gate," Marilyn said. "I wouldn't want to miss Sister."

"Well, all right. Perhaps later," Victoria said as Jack held his mother's chair.

"You owe me one," Marilyn whispered to him as they walked back to the gate. "And I definitely want to see that picture."

Once more they went through the arrival ritual, searching the faces that came through the door, looking for the nun from Baton Rouge. Only this time there was no light of recognition as the strangers passed by. Finally a woman in a plain dress with short, shaggy hair approached them. "Marilyn!" she cried, embracing her and kissing her twice on each cheek.

"Sister?"

"Don't recognize me without the uniform, huh?"

"Well, I . . . that is, you look so different without your habit."

"And see? I'm not bald after all," the nun laughed, running her hand through her dark hair flecked with gray.

"I . . . I never thought you were," Marilyn protested.

"Oh, sure you did. All the girls did. Well, that's ancient history now. You must be Jack Townsend," she said, extending her hand to Jack.

"Guilty as charged. And this is my mother, Victoria," Jack said by way of introduction.

"So nice to meet you Sister," Mrs. Townsend said, extending her hand. "At last I'll have someone to show my pictures to."

"As a matter fact, I just happen to have some of Marilyn in her school uniform," Sister Jean-Marie said, opening a large black purse.

"Well, I have some of my son wearing somewhat less than that," Victoria Townsend laughed. "But of course, he was a baby at the time. Tell me, do you play cards?"

"I'm afraid that's one skill I never mastered," the nun said.

"I'll teach you," Victoria replied. "We're going to get on famously."

Chapter 37

J ennifer hummed softly while she set out two place settings of her grandmother's best china. Tonight she and R.J. would have a quiet dinner alone. If only Marilyn would stay out late and the weather cool off enough to justify lighting a fire in the living room fireplace, the evening would be perfect.

"You're sure everything will be all right?" Marilyn asked as she came bustling into the dining room.

Jennifer frowned. "I'm a big girl, Marilyn. I can take care of myself."

"I didn't mean you couldn't." Marilyn stopped at a mirror and checked her makeup one last time.

"By the way," Jennifer said absently as she arranged the sterling silver next to the plates, "what does *ma petite choute* mean? Is that like 'my little flower' or something?"

"No, actually it means 'my little cabbage'," Marilyn said, touching up her mascara. "Anyway, where did you hear it?"

"It's what Papa calls me sometimes," Jennifer replied, a little too casually. "I just wanted to know what it meant."

Marilyn turned away from the mirror and looked at her new "sister" who was still playing with the silverware on the table. "You? Really? That was always his pet name for me."

"Is something wrong?" Jennifer asked, looking up at her.

"I'm just surprised, that's all," Marilyn said, abruptly turning back to the mirror.

"Well, I'm sorry. I didn't mean to make you jealous or anything."

"I'm not jealous," Marilyn said, her eyes still on her own reflection in the mirror.

"Yes you are."

"Don't be silly, Jennifer. Why should I be jealous?"

"You certainly are. Look at you! You're jealous!"

"Jennifer, I am not jealous!" Marilyn insisted.

"All right, have it your way," Jennifer replied as she turned around and headed into the kitchen. "I wasn't jealous when my grandmother treated you like her granddaughter, and you aren't jealous just because your father treats me like his daughter."

"This is stupid!" Marilyn shot back. "I am not jealous. I have never been jealous. Go out shopping with him every day. See if I care! Let him slobber all over both of your hands. I'm going out; don't wait up!" She slammed her way out the door.

"I won't!" Jennifer shouted back to the empty house. "And you *are* jealous!"

80 03

Marilyn was still distracted when the manager seated them at their table at the Yacht Club. The whole thing was really stupid. She wasn't jealous. What did she have to be jealous about? She was marrying the most wonderful man in the whole world. So what if Papa paid so much attention to Jennifer? She had Jack, and that was what was important.

"Is something wrong, *ma petite?*"

His voice startled her. "What? No, nothing Papa," she assured him.

"Are you sure, Marilyn?" Jack asked. "You've been awfully quiet."

"Oh, leave her alone," Victoria Townsend insisted. "It's just pre-wedding jitters. Some champagne will make her feel better. John, order us a bottle of Dom Perignon."

Dupré smiled at him. "Your mother has expensive taste, Jon."

"Yes, well, here's hoping Mrs. Townsend the Younger doesn't follow in her footsteps," he replied as he signaled the waiter.

"Nonsense. You pay attention, Marilyn. Make him spend some of that money he's been hoarding. Living on a boat, indeed!" Victoria Townsend made it sound like she could hardly bear the disgrace of her son's unconventional lifestyle. She turned to Sister Jean-Marie, "Now, Sister, you must tell us all about your trip from New Orleans."

"Baton Rouge, actually," the nun replied. "That's where our convent is located. It's where our bride grew up, isn't that right, Marilyn?"

"Here's a toast to Sainte Anne's," Marilyn replied, raising her glass after the waiter finished pouring the champagne.

Marilyn began to brighten up during dinner. Papa lavished his attention on Victoria Townsend, who happened to be the only available woman at the table, Marilyn noted. When Henri wasn't distracting her with something, Victoria and Sister Jean-Marie seemed to enjoy each other's company. It was odd, sitting there, watching Sister's face as she talked about the convent school in Baton Rouge. Marilyn had always felt especially close to her, but back in those days she never really understood the woman who now sat across the table from her. She attributed the change to the lack of a habit. The old garb did more than just hide most of Sister Jean-Marie's features; it also cut her off from other people by making her something more than human. Now, as Marilyn watched Sister's animated face and her intense gray eyes, something stirred within her: an insight, perhaps; a memory that was not a memory. Papa, too, when he wasn't fawning over Victoria Townsend, would sometimes look at the nun with a certain expression—almost of longing—which was silly, of course, because even a ladies' man like Papa would not dare think of a nun in that way.

Dinner was excellent as always and Marilyn took great pride in pointing out to Sister the miniature officer's flag next to Jack's place setting and telling her how Past Commodores of the Club always got this special treatment.

"This is a wonderful place, John," Victoria Townsend agreed. "I'm so glad you decided to have the reception here.

Is this where we'll be doing the rehearsal dinner as well?"

Marilyn had watched Jack at work in the courtroom and up until the moment his mother spoke, she was convinced that nothing could faze him. But at the sound of the words "rehearsal dinner," his face went blank and, just for a second, she thought she saw a look of fear flash across this eyes.

"You *are* having a rehearsal dinner? . . . John?"

"Well, actually . . . to tell you the truth, Mother, I hadn't thought about it. It's a very small wedding party . . ." he explained.

Victoria Townsend rolled her eyes toward heaven. "John! No rehearsal dinner? With out-of-town guests? I shall be a laughingstock!"

"Mother, people don't do that sort of thing anymore."

"We are not 'people'," she reminded him severely. "We have our standards and 'people' have theirs." It sounded like a speech he had heard his whole life.

"Well, I'm afraid there's nothing I can do about it now. Christmas is Wednesday, and the wedding's Saturday. We're in the middle of the tourist season. I'm sure that every place in town is booked."

"You seem to have a lot of 'pull' around here," Victoria protested.

"Mother, I'm sure they're booked, too. And you know how much I hate doing things like that."

"Well, hate it or not, something must be done," she said firmly. "I'll not have out-of-town guests . . . including myself, I might add . . . standing around at sixes and sevens after the church rehearsal. What would the Governor have said?"

"I don't know what your grandfather would have said, Mother," Jack shot back, his voice rising. "I moved to Florida because I got tired of trying to figure out what he would have said."

A few of the other diners had turned and were watching the escalating conversation between mother and son with growing embarrassment. Suddenly, Henri Dupré moved in to Jack's rescue.

"This wedding rehearsal, Jon, it is at the church *Verdredi*, Friday, no?"

Marilyn confirmed that he was right.

"*Tres bien*, something will be done. I shall prepare this *diner*."

"Papa, Jack's boat isn't big enough for that kind of dinner, and Jennifer has plans to be with R.J.'s family for Christmas. A rehearsal party . . . I wouldn't want to ask her to have guests all over her house the very day before the wedding."

"I do not speak of the boat or her house, *ma petite*. Janifere has a perfectly good *restaurant* that is not in use. I shall make your party there."

"I . . . I don't think that's a good idea, Papa," Marilyn protested. "Jennifer has some problems with . . . she doesn't want to open that place. And I don't want to do anything that might hurt her."

"*Mais oui* she will open it if I ask her, *ma petite*." He

turned to Jack's mother. "Madame Tousand, trouble your-self no longer. On *Verdredi*, I shall prepare *un dîner elegant*. Now, Jon, let us celebrate our good fortune with another bottle of this excellent champagne, no?"

☙ ❧

Papa put his plan into operation the next morning. Marilyn had left the Magnolia Avenue house early to pick up Sister Jean-Marie and Victoria Townsend for a day of sightseeing. They were long gone when Papa called Jenni-fer from Jack's boat and asked her for a ride.

"Where are we going today, Papa?" she asked brightly when he got into her car. "What would you like to do?"

"There is one thing I would like to do more than any-thing else, *ma petite choute*," he answered solemnly. "But to grant my wish appears to be beyond even your powers."

"Come on, we have all day," she chided. "Where would you like to go?"

"Where I would like to go, *ma ch*éré, is right here."

"Right here? I don't understand."

He looked in her eyes. "I would very much like to see the *restaurant* you and your *soeur* put there." He nodded in the direction of the building at the other end of the marina.

Jennifer's face fell. "I don't like that place, Papa. I only built it for . . . I don't like it."

Dupré took her hand. "I know why you built it, *ch*éré. I would like to see it one time, with you, *n'est pas?*"

His dark eyes pleaded with her as she studied his face carefully. "Maybe we should go up . . ." she said at last. "Just to see if everything is still there . . . where we left it."

"*Bon*," he agreed. "Let us go. Let us see for ourselves this *restaurant merveilleux*."

Jennifer drove the short distance to the other end of the marina and left the car in the parking lot while the two of them went up the outside stairway. "I have a key here somewhere," she said, looking through her purse. "I hope it works. I've never used it."

The room was eerily quiet when they entered. Tables were set with tablecloths and glass centerpieces held unlit candles. Chairs were ready to seat guests who had never arrived. The only light came through the large windows that overlooked the marina and the bay beyond it. Sunlight sparkled off the water as a sailboat wafted along in the distance. Below them, Erlene silently filled a tank at the gas dock and even Les Leslie appeared surreal as he puttered away on *Elena*. Just as Jennifer had predicted once long ago, the view was spectacular.

"*C'est magnifique*," Dupré murmured before Jennifer left his side to find the light switches. He broke away from the window and followed her, "*Ooh la la*'ing" and "*Aah*'ing" over the *restaurant magnifique*, with the bar and its unused glasses in one corner. When she opened the door to the kitchen, a look of celestial rapture came over his face.

"What I could do here; what I could do here," he kept repeating, almost to himself as he ran his fingers over the gleaming stainless steel. He hefted one of the virgin pots that hung untouched over the new stove. "Never have I seen such a place. Janifere, you have truly created *un restaurant merevilleux*."

"Yes, well, we'd better go," she said quietly from the kitchen doorway.

He returned the utensil to its place and his shoulders appeared to slump as he turned to face her. "You know, Janifere," he said softly, "the greatest sin of all is when we do not use what God has given us."

"I'd really like to go now," she begged.

He went over to her and took her hand. "*Ma bellotte*, I must ask you for one favor more."

"I . . . can't . . ." she protested, anticipating his question.

"We must make *un dîner elegant* for the family. How you call it, *un repetition*, a rehearsal? There is no other place. Please. Let me make it here."

"I can't . . . I can't, Papa. Please don't make me do it," she whispered.

"Your grandmother was a strong woman, Janifere," he reminded her. "She would not be pleased to see you waste all of this."

A single tear rolled down the girl's cheek. Now he took her other hand, and held both of them in his own. "I am a poor man, *ma petite*. I have no money to give my daughter on her wedding day. All I can give her is the work of these hands. Please allow me to do this for her . . . for your *soeur*. Just one time."

It took a long time for Jennifer to nod her head in reply. "All right, we'll do it, Papa," she agreed quietly. "Just one time; no more. One elegant dinner party, and after that we'll close this awful place forever."

He kissed her on each cheek, and once more on her forehead. "*Bon, ma fille*. You have made Papa *tres joyeux*. Now come, we must see Jon about a small matter. You and I shall make groceries today like they have never been made. And the wine, too, we must not forget. We have much to do, Janifere."

ಬಿ ಆ

"Henri! This is a pleasant surprise," Jack said, going out to the waiting room when his secretary announced that Marilyn's father had arrived with Jennifer in tow.

Dupré replied that he hoped the surprise would still be pleasant after Jack heard what he had to say, and asked Jennifer to leave them alone for a moment.

"Is something wrong?" Jack asked when they were safely behind the closed door of his office.

"Janifere has agreed to allow me to use the *restaurant* for *un dîner special*," Dupré began. "We are about to make groceries for it."

It sounded like this might be about money and Jack was not going to put his future father-in-law in the position of having to ask for it. "That's great! Let me give you a check," he volunteered. "How much do you think you'll need?"

"Your home makes me think of the sea, Jon," Dupré said, pacing the office and carefully avoiding the question of cost for the moment. "I would like to begin with *Huit-res a'la Rockefeller*, how you say, Oysters Rockefeller, and perhaps *Caviar sur Canape*. For the main course, perhaps *Langouste avec Sauce Champagne*, lobster with champagne sauce. *Legumes*, vegetables, must be light or they will over-come the *langouste*, no? I have been thinking of *Asperges au Beurre* . . . how is it? . . . asparagus with a simple but-ter sauce, perhaps. For the salad, *naturellement*, Hearts of Palm because we are in Florida. And for dessert, I will create of course my *spécialité, Cerises Jubilee*. It is a conceit of mine to garnish each plate with fresh *cerises*, and I have located a small *épicier* across the bridge in Bonita who can supply them, I think. For the wines, we must have *un vin blanc*, and also the Dom Perignon at your Club was most appealing.

"At their prices it should be," Jack observed dryly, won-dering at the same time who the lucky grocer was who was going to get the assignment of finding fresh cherries in December.

"One does not think of cost at a time like this, *mon fils*," Dupré replied, waving his hand at the subject of money. "And of course we cannot have your guests serve them-selves. We must have someone, perhaps two, to wait on them; *un garcon de comptoir*, one you call a 'barman' for the drinks, and I would be most happy to have one or two others to help me in the kitchen."

It looked like Dupré was never going to get around to predicting how much this *soiree* would cost, but the price seemed to be growing by the minute. At this rate, he would soon be talking about hiring a string quartet.

"The way I see it, Henri," Jack said, taking a checkbook out of his desk, "you're probably going to need at least five hundred dollars just for the wine . . . probably more. I haven't priced caviar lately, but I'll bet it hasn't gotten any cheaper. As for lobsters, well, you'll have to ask my mother how many guests she expects to invite. Knowing her, even for a small party she'll have a hard time keeping the guest list under twenty. As far as help, check with Jim Lacey. He had people all lined up. And tell my mother to make sure to invite Lacey by the way. Jim worked hard on that place. And tell her not to forget Eddie Miles. He's Jim's partner and I wouldn't want to leave him out. Do you think six thousand dollars will be enough to start? Anyone you deal with can bill me for the rest."

Dupré's eyes widened. "Jon, with six thousand dollars I could prepare *un dîner* for the Almighty."

"Take this check downstairs and they'll cash it," Jack instructed, tearing the draft from the book in front of him.

"Jon, I am most grateful. There is no need to tell my daughter about this, eh?"

"You're doing me a big favor by getting me off the hook with my mother, Henri," Jack reminded him. "I'm the one who is grateful to you."

"*Bon.* We are grateful to each other. Let us speak no more of it."

Chapter 38

Les Leslie barely noticed when Arlo greeted him as he stormed past the next morning. Les had other fish to fry and at the moment the fish on his mind was named Howard Garner, a fish Les was planning to skin alive and then broil.

"What's the meanin' a' this?" Les demanded, after he charged, uninvited, onto Garner's boat.

"Maybe I should be asking you that. Aren't you supposed to ask for permission to come aboard?"

"Ask f'r permission? I'll show ya' my permission, ya' low-down, two-timin' thievin' . . . Here! Here's your bill, ya' slimy sea slug! That's my permission!"

"I see you got my invoice," Garner said nonchalantly. "When can I expect payment?"

His question sent Les to even greater heights. "Payment? When c'n ya' expect payment? I'll tell ya' when ya' c'n expect payment! When hell freezes over . . . in fact, the day after hell freezes over! That's when ya' c'n expect payment!"

"So you're not going to pay me?"

"Of course I ain't gonna pay ya'," Les shouted. "Why should I pay ya'?"

"It's all right there in black and white," Garner said matter-of-factly. "Forty hours of my time at twenty-two dollars an hour, comes out to eight hundred and eighty dollars."

"Eight hundred an' eighty dollars!" Les fumed. "Ya' think I'm supposed ta' pay ya' eight hundred an' eighty dollars?"

"That's exactly what I think. That's why I sent you the invoice."

"Well, I'm not payin' ya'!"

"Isn't my work worth it?"

"What in the name a' Saint Elmo is that supposed ta' mean?"

"My work. Wasn't it good enough?"

That question set Les back on his heels for a minute. He had to admit that Howard knew his way around a brush and varnish pot. "Yeah, I guess your work was pretty good," he conceded, lowering his voice.

"Then why don't you want to pay me?"

"Because I never hired ya', ya' low-down thievin' bilge rat!" Les shouted, back up to his full volume.

"You asked for my help."

"Ya' offered ta' help me!"

"You mean you thought I was going it out of charity? Why would I do such a thing?"

Les looked at Garner as if the man had just announced he came from another planet. And in a way, he had. Les lowered his voice again; his father used to say, "When somebody don't speak your language, it's no use shoutin' the words."

"Maybe I thought ya' was bein' a nice guy, Howard," he said with disappointment heavy in his voice. "Maybe I though ya' was bein' normal, just like the rest a' us."

"Normal people don't do things for free, Les," Garner retorted.

"Well around here they do, Howard," Les said disgustedly. "Maybe that's why you'll never really belong here." He turned to go.

"You're not going to pay me, then?"

Les shook his head. "No, I ain't goin' ta' pay ya'," he said without turning back.

"I guess I'll have to sue."

"I guess ya' will, Howard," Les said as he got off Garner's boat. "I guess ya' will."

It was a long walk back to the comfort of Elena. Les felt as if he had gotten stung in an old con game, and even telling himself it was an honest misunderstanding didn't make him feel any better. It was more than just money. Les had begun to think of Howard as a friend. That was what really hurt; he hadn't been keelhauled by some stranger. Howard was someone Les had shared coffee with, and now a guy who he had thought was his friend was going to sue him for eight hundred and eighty dollars.

"Everything all right?" Arlo hadn't moved from the spot he occupied when he greeted Les the first time around.

"Huh? Oh, yeah, Arlo . . . No . . . no it ain't all right."
He thrust the paper at Arlo who studied it for a moment
and let out a low whistle.

"Eight hundred an' eighty dollars, huh? You mean, he
thought you was gonna pay 'im."

"'s what he says he thought."

"You gonna do it? Pay 'im, I mean?"

Les looked at him as if he had lost his mind. "a' course
I ain't gonna pay 'im." His volume increased every time he
thought of such a thing.

"What's he gonna do?"

"Says he's gonna sue me."

"What're you gonna do?"

"I'm gonna go see the Commodore. Want ta' come?"

"Sure." It looked like Arlo was back on the first team.

∽ ∾

"Mr. Townsend isn't in right now. Can Mr. Meacham
help you?" the secretary at Townsend & Meacham asked
in response to Les' request to see the Commodore.

Les and Arlo exchanged an uncertain glance. This was
an important matter, not to be trusted to an inexperienced
hand. Still, Miss Jennifer was going to marry the guy, and
the Commodore had made him his partner. Besides, the
Commodore wasn't available.

"Mr. Leslie? Would you like to see Mr. Meacham
instead?"

The woman was waiting; Les had to make a decision.
"Yeah, okay; R.J.'ll do," he replied.

The secretary did not approve of Les referring to her boss in such a familiar way. She expressed her disapproval with a frown that was lost on the two visitors and she sighed when she picked up the intercom. A few minutes later, they were ushered into R.J.'s office, where he swept aside the papers he was working on and asked them to sit down.

"Are we interruptin' anythin'?" Les asked.

"'Cause we can come back later, when the Commodore's here," Arlo added before Les shot him a "Shut Up" look.

"I'm getting ready for some depositions in a criminal case," R.J. replied. "This other stuff is preliminary appraisals on the estate property so that we can do a federal tax return. What can I do for you?"

"Well, it's like this," Les began. He related the story—with a few minor interruptions from Arlo—of Howard Garner and the unexpected bill for his services.

"No one ever mentioned money before?" R.J. asked when he was finished.

"No one. Never," Les replied.

"I can't see how he thinks you have a contract, Les. Of course, there is a principle of law called *quantum meruit*."

Les' face clouded over, and Arlo's went blank.

"Quanta . . . what?" Les asked.

"'*Quantum meruit*' . . . it means that a worker is entitled to be paid for the value of his work," R.J. explained.

"But that's just it," Les protested. "Ya' see, his work didn't have no value, 'cause I was gonna do it myself. It wasn't that

I couldn't do it; it was just that he offered ta' lend a hand, an' I was kind a' bein' nice, lettin' him do it."

"I understand that," R.J. replied. "But it's still possible . . ." Les tried to say something, but R.J. cut him off with a gesture, ". . . remember, I said 'possible' that he could recover from you on a *quantum meruit* theory. How much does work like that usually cost?"

"Well, I don't know," Les hesitated. "I guess twenty-two an hour might be what some a' them boatyards charge . . . I guess. But . . . look . . . how do I know he spent forty hours doin' it? I mean, I didn't think ta' keep track a' the time."

"He was with you a whole lot, Les," Arlo reminded him before he was cut off with another "Shut Up" look.

"Well, those are the kinds of things that are subject to proof, Les," R.J. explained. "He'd have to prove the reasonable value of his services and the amount of time he spent with you." It sounded like a final answer and the two visitors did not respond. Then, almost to make the day even worse, R.J. added, "Can I see you alone for a minute?"

"I guess I'll go out to the waitin' room," Arlo said, getting up from his chair. "You guys got some real good boatin' magazines out there."

Arlo closed the door behind him, and Les waited to see what would happen next. He had already gotten more information than he needed. All's he wanted to know was whether he had to pay Howard or not. A simple 'yes' or 'no' would've done it. Now R.J. wanted to talk in private and things were gettin' deep. Les knew he should have waited for the Commodore.

Finally, R.J. spoke. "Les, I don't want to pry into your affairs but, you know, you *are* one of the beneficiaries of Mrs. Calkins' Will."

It was the Will again. Les couldn't understand why everybody was so dang interested in the Will.

"She made that bequest to you contingent on you going to Italy. We need to know what your plans are."

"I ain't made any plans just yet, R.J.... Mr. Meacham," Les muttered, looking down at his shoes.

"R.J.'s okay. I'm not that old yet," the lawyer joked. There was a pause that seemed to last half a lifetime before he continued. "Les I don't mean to pressure you, but if you're going to go, we have to know. And if you're not going to go, we have to know that, too. It affects the way we handle the estate."

Les looked up and met his eyes directly. "What you're sayin' is, if I'm gonna go, I gotta get on with it."

"Well, yeah, pretty much," R.J. agreed. "At least let us know for sure one way or the other."

Les nodded. "Okay. Just so long's you tell me I ain't got much ta' worry about from Howard Garner. It's not that I can't pay 'im, ya' know, it's just ..."

"Not right?" R.J. finished the thought for him and Les nodded. "There's a lot of that going around, Les," R.J. said. "But I still need to know if you're going."

Les nodded again. "Gimmie a week; I'll let you know right after Miss Dupré and the Commodore splice their lines."

"Okay, Les, I appreciate that," R.J. said, standing up and extending his hand.

Arlo was waiting for him on the way out. "What'd he want?" he asked, returning the magazine to the cherry coffee table.

"Nuthin' much," the older man replied. "But next time let's wait for th' Commodore."

୨୦ ଓଃ

A few days later Sisters Restaurant was aglow with candles and white poinsettias. The center of the room was dominated by a long table set with freshly unpacked china and glassware as twelve handpicked guests waited for the two couples who made up the wedding party. Three servers circled with trays of *hors d'oeuvres*, while a barman filled champagne glasses. The only thing missing was the string quartet that Jack anticipated his mother would insist on; instead a young lady with a harp accompanied by a single violinist played quietly in a far corner of the room.

"Well, down the hatch, huh, Les?" Arlo was dressed in his best suit with a string tie and cowboy boots that were mostly hidden by his pants and Les tried not to look too uncomfortable rigged out in a sport coat.

"Ya' don't say 'down the hatch' with this stuff," he hissed from the confines of a shirt collar that would not come together and was held in placed by his necktie. "This stuff's French champagne. You're supposed ta' sip it. I wouldn't be surprised if it cost fifteen 'r twenty dollars a bottle."

"G'wan!"

"I kind a' like it, Arl," Erlene observed. "Maybe we could buy some ta' take home."

"Fifteen 'r twenty dollars? You're kiddin', Les. I'm gonna go ast the guy at the bar," Arlo ventured.

"Will ya' try ta' act polite . . . like ya' belong here?" Les warned.

"Hey, I'm only astin' is all," Arlo replied.

"This is a real nice party, Mrs. Townsend," Erlene said as Victoria Townsend came around. "Thanks for invitin' us."

"You're quite welcome, Erlene," Victoria replied. "Marilyn has no one coming from her hometown. She feels very close to all of the people who are here tonight."

"That's real nice a' her," Erlene gushed as Arlo returned to her side and took the champagne glass out of her hand. "Yeah, thanks for the invite," he added.

"What's the idea of takin' my drink?" Erlene demanded after Victoria Townsend moved away.

"Don't get to likin' it, Erlene," Arlo warned. "This stuff goes for a hundred bucks a bottle."

Les nodded sagely. "Told ya'."

"Damn! Got get me another one, Arlo," Erlene said, taking her glass back and emptying it in a single swallow. "I might 's well fill up on this stuff now. I don't guess I'll be gettin' another chancet."

"Mr. Calkins, I'm so glad you could join us this evening," Victoria said to Doug Calkins as she took his arm and escorted him around the room. "Allow me to introduce you to Judge Bill Bellingham, and Commodore Hennel and his wife Judy from the Yacht Club and, of course, you know Jim Lacey and Eddie Miles from the marina. I understand, Mr. Lacey, that you had a great deal to do with the construction of this restaurant."

"It was mostly Jennifer pushing everybody to get things done," Jim added, shaking Doug's hand.

Victoria escorted Doug over to the bar and Jim and Eddie followed. "Well Bill, do you think anything happened on Jack's boat the night of the Summer Fling?" Judy said after they were gone, barely suppressing a giggle with her champagne glass.

"We're standing here tonight, aren't we?" Bill responded with a wink. "I'd say that's pretty good circumstantial evidence."

"Come on you two, behave yourselves," Ron Hennel warned.

"I'd like to think we had something to do with this," Judy said with a sparkling smile.

"Me too," Bill Bellingham agreed, clinking her glass with his.

"Here they are now!" Victoria exclaimed as the final two couples entered the room. "The Bride and Groom, and our next bride and groom, too."

"Well, is it true, Rob? Have you set the date yet?" Bill asked R.J. as he took his hand.

"We've been a little busy . . ." R.J. explained.

"Miss Calkins, I'm Judy Hennel, Ron's wife," the bubbly blonde said, extending her hand to Jennifer. "I just wanted to tell you how beautiful this place is. You must be really proud of what you've done here."

"Oh...well...thank you very much," Jennifer mumbled.

Jim Lacey came up behind Jennifer and put a glass of champagne in her hand. "Come and take a look around," he said quietly. "You really *do* have a lot to be proud of here."

"This is so beautiful, Jennifer," Eddie Miles added. "I didn't believe Jim when he was telling me about it. You've *both* done wonders here."

"What's this little black stuff?" Arlo demanded when one of the servers offered him an *hors d'oeuvre*.

"That's caviar, ya' ninny," Les fumed.

"Well it tastes like crud," Arlo complained after he swallowed it. "What's caviar, anyway?"

"Fish eggs," Erlene answered. "Everybody knows that."

"Fish eggs?! Ya' mean like bait?" Arlo grabbed another glass of champagne from a nearby server and gulped it down. "What the heck 're they doin' feedin' us fish eggs?"

Jack and Marilyn had slipped off by themselves to a quiet corner where one of the servers brought them champagne glasses etched with their monograms. "My mother's touch: I'd recognize it anywhere," Jack observed, handing Marilyn her glass and looking out the window with her at the scattering of lights in the marina below.

Marilyn sipped quietly for a moment. "This is it," she whispered, almost to herself. "I'm really getting married tomorrow: so far from New Orleans and Jackson Square.

It isn't anything like I'd imagined when I was a little girl."
She looked up at Jack. "And it's a million miles away from
Baton Rouge and Sainte Anne's."

"This is your last chance to change your mind," he
warned.

"She looked at him with dark, inviting eyes. "I'm supposed to say that to you," she smiled. "Anyway I can change
my mind right up until noon tomorrow."

"May I intrude for a moment?" The couple turned in
response to Sister Jean-Marie's question.

"Marilyn," the nun said, placing a piece of jewelry in
her hand and covering it with her own, "it's a custom for a
bride to wear something old on her wedding day. This was
my mother's locket. She once told me it had been in our
family for several generations. I want you to have it, and
wear it for me tomorrow."

"Oh, I couldn't . . ." Marilyn protested, looking down at
the treasured item.

"Please," the nun insisted. "It would mean a great deal
to me to know that it's yours now."

"I think we had better be seated," Victoria Townsend
said as she came by. Chef Dupré is ready to begin."

Fifteen diners took their places around the table before
the sixteenth, Henri Dupré—chef and proud father—came
out of the kitchen and took his place between Marilyn and
Jennifer. He was wearing an immaculate white chef's uniform: either he was a very careful cook or he had changed
before coming out. "*Mesdames é Messieurs,*" he announced,

standing at his place, "At the request of Madame Tousand, this evening I have prepared for you *un dîner elegant. Bon appétit!*

Bill Bellingham stood up at his place next to Victoria Townsend. "First, I would like to propose a toast to the Bride," he announced. "Marilyn, God love you, it appears the people in this room are about to become your extended family. Lots of luck with that!"

Everyone applauded and laughed as the servers began the dinner by bringing out Oysters Rockefeller. "This ain't fish eggs, too, is it?" Arlo whispered to Erlene as he poked at the green stuff in the shells that were placed in front of him.

"Hush up and eat it," Erlene hissed.

They worked their way through the hearts of palm salad, asparagus, lobster with champagne sauce, and one or two other treats Henri Dupré decided at the last minute to whip together for his daughter. Then came the crowning moment. As the other guests were finishing up, he excused himself and went into the kitchen. In a few minutes he was back, wearing the traditional tall chef's *toque*—one hundred creases representing one hundred ways to prepare eggs—with the servers and a cart laden with a silver chafing dish and numerous bowls and bottles.

"*Mesdames é Messieurs,*" he announced grandly, "I will now prepare for you my own *spécial Cerises Jubilee.*" He began with preserved cherries and their thick red syrup already in the chafing dish, and added maraschino and kirsch liqueurs. When the mixture was sufficiently reduced he added brandy, stirred a moment longer and touched a long match to the dish that burst into flame. The servers scooped ice cream onto plates and Dupré quickly covered each plate with the flaming mixture and his signature touch—a sprig of fresh cherries—before it was brought to the table and placed before the guest for a spectacular end to the dinner.

At last it was time to go. "I hate to be a party pooper, but I want to check on the boatyard early tomorrow before coming to the church," Doug Calkins said to Marilyn. "I can drive Sister Jean-Marie and Jack's mother back to their hotel. It's on the way to my place."

"I'm afraid the honor of escorting Mrs. Townsend belongs to me, Sir," Judge Bill Bellingham announced.

"Thank you both," Victoria replied, "but I think I'll stay behind for a while and see if Chef Dupré needs my help."

"We'll see you tomorrow, Marilyn," Judy Hennel said, taking the Bride's hand and then hugging her. She turned to Jennifer. "It was so nice meeting you, Jennifer. We had a delightful time. This really is a wonderful place. I just know it'll be a great success."

"Well, Jenny, we did it!" Jim Lacey said, hugging her and giddy from a little too much champagne. "Even if it was only for one night, we showed them all. You did a hell of a job, kid."

"It is beautiful, isn't it, Jim?" she replied, looking around the room filled with soft music, flowers and still-glowing candles. "You know, we could re-cover these walls with some really classy French wallpaper . . ." Lacey looked at her. Even through the haze of the champagne he thought he saw an old spark returning to her eyes. "Not that I would . . . we would . . . I was just thinking . . ." Her voice drifted off.

"Well, goodnight," he said, quietly patting her hand. "We all have a big day tomorrow."

Chapter 39

A white limousine containing the bride and her maid of honor arrived at the church early the next day.

"Jack isn't around, is he?" Marilyn asked fitfully. "He's not supposed to see me until we're inside or it will bring bad luck."

"That's just a superstition," Jennifer protested.

"I'm not taking any chances. Make sure he's not around."

Jennifer got out of the car and scanned the area. Guests were making their way inside, but Jack and R.J. were nowhere in sight. She dutifully reported the coast was clear and the two women made a dash for the door.

"Here, let me help you," Jennifer offered after Marilyn barreled through the door of the small anteroom at the back of the church in a swirl of white satin and lace. "We didn't have to run like that, you know."

"I know . . . I know it's just a silly superstition but I don't want anything to go wrong today. I've waited so long for this."

"Well, here, let's get you fixed up again," Jennifer said, taking Marilyn's bouquet and putting it down next to her own. She began straightening the bridal veil and brushing the pleats of Marilyn's gown. "We can't have you walking down the aisle looking like you just finished running a marathon."

"Jennifer," Marilyn said, taking her hand, "I never had a sister ... I didn't have anybody to share times like this with ... I guess what I'm trying to say is, I'm really glad I have you." She suddenly let go of Jennifer's hand and hugged her close. "I'm sorry if I've been hard to live with these past couple of weeks."

"I'm glad I have you, too, *Sis*," Jennifer said pointedly. "And I'll get my turn in September when you'll have to put up with me."

"Have you and R.J. set the date?" Marilyn squealed excitedly.

"Saturday, September sixth," came the quick reply. "I don't know if it was the church rehearsal or Judge Bellingham's heckling during dinner that did it, but we decided on the way home."

"Jennifer, I'm so happy for you," Marilyn said, hugging her again.

"We'll be doing a replay in nine months, Marilyn. Now let's make sure you're all set."

Jennifer stepped back and again began fussing with her veil. "Marilyn," she finally said, almost too casually, "about last night, I've been thinking. That really is a beautiful place we built, isn't it?"

"It's a place that you built, Jen."

"Grandma would really be upset if she knew it was just sitting there going to waste."

"Yes, I guess she would be," Marilyn said cautiously.

Jennifer's eyes were sparkling again. "Maybe we should go ahead and open it," she suggested.

Marilyn reached out and grabbed both her arms for a moment. "Jennifer, this is the best wedding present you could have given me."

"It's just that . . . while you and Jack are in Paris, would you mind if I made a few small changes . . . just little ones?"

"Anything, Jennifer. Anything that will make you happy."

"Do you really mean that?"

"Absolutely."

"See, I was thinking, I was never really happy with the furniture. I'd like to have something a little more substantial looking, you know, like it had been there for a while."

"Of course," Marilyn agreed. "It would give the place more character.

"Right, exactly." Jennifer clapped her hands excitedly. "And the walls, Marilyn. You know, I really didn't pay much attention to them when we were building the place. It would be so nice to have them covered with wallpaper and maybe a dark wood wainscoting."

"That would really give it an elegant, homey look," Marilyn agreed.

"Like a French chateau," Jennifer added. "And the name, 'Sisters', " Jennifer continued. "That name has got to go."

"Wait a minute, what's wrong with 'Sisters'?"

"Oh, it's nice and everything. That's the problem: it's too nice. It's too cute. It sounds too . . . invented. We need something more European . . . you know, something Continental . . ."

"Like what, for instance?"

"Something like . . ." Jennifer waved her hand through the air in a dramatic arc ". . . something like . . . Dupré's"

Marilyn's dark eyes widened. "Oh no! Don't you dare! Don't get us involved with him, Jennifer. I mean it! Papa's walked out of more restaurants than I can count. That's not all, Jennifer. You don't know him like I do. He's not what you think. He won't be there for us when we need him."

"He's a wonderful chef, Marilyn. And he's so suave."

"He's nothing but trouble!"

"You said I could do anything I wanted; anything that would make me happy!"

"That didn't include getting us into business with my father!"

They were interrupted by the strains of organ music coming from the sanctuary. "Oh my God! They're staring the music. Come on, we have to get out there," Jennifer said as an unsuspecting Henri Dupré walked into the brewing maelstrom.

"It is time, *ma chouchoute* . . ." he began.

"Papa, it's all your fault. This was your idea, wasn't it?" Marilyn demanded.

"I do not . . ."

"Leave him alone, Marilyn! It was my idea. I haven't even talked to him about it. We have to go!"

"I'm not going anywhere until we settle this!"

"We'll have to talk about it later," Jennifer said as she dashed out of the room.

"This was all your idea, wasn't it, Papa?" Marilyn shouted. "It wasn't bad enough that you ruined my life by sending me away. Now that I finally have a life of my own, you want to follow me to Florida and take this one away from me, too!"

"*Ma petite*, I do not know what you are saying."

"You sent me away, Papa. You sent me away when I needed you most. Well don't think you're going to come here now and get anything from me, because you won't!"

Dupré's dark eyes quickly filled with pain. "I did not want to send you away from me, *ma chéré* . . ."

"But you did, Papa. You're the one who sent me to Sainte Anne's after my mother died. You sent me away, and I'll never forgive you for that."

"I sent you away to learn; to become a lady," he pleaded.

"All the way to Baton Rouge? There's an Ursuline Convent on Saint Charles Avenue. I could have stayed home; I could have become a lady there."

"No! Not the Ursulines! It had to be Sainte Anne's. It had to be Baton Rouge."

"Why, Papa? For God's sake, why? So you could get rid of me? So I would be out of your way?"

"It was for you!" he shouted. "I promised Mama. But

she would not come to New *Orléans;* she would not come to us. What more was I to do?"

"What are you talking about? Who wouldn't come to us?"

Dupré looked at her wildly. He had already said too much. "I cannot tell you . . . I promised . . ." Henri Dupré suddenly looked very old and the pain in his eyes threatened to overwhelm her, but Marilyn could not let go. Not now. There was something there, some missing piece of her life, something she needed to know.

"What are you talking about? Please tell me, Papa," his daughter begged.

"I cannot," he replied with tears in his eyes.

Jennifer stuck her head in the door. "Marilyn, they're waiting!" she hissed.

The Bride sat down firmly. "Let them wait! Papa, I'm not going to walk down that aisle with you until you tell me whatever it is you're hiding."

The old man wrung his hands. "I promised Mama I would never tell," he began. "But if I break my promise today, on your wedding day, perhaps on this day of all days, Mama will forgive me, no?"

He went over to her and knelt on one knee next to her chair. "What is it Papa? Please tell me," she whispered.

"One of the Sisters from Sainte Anne's, she was very good to you. She is very close, very *spécial*, no?

"Sister Jean-Marie," Marilyn confirmed. "You know; she's here at my wedding."

Her father looked at her for a moment. "Before she was Sister Jean-Marie, she was Lynette Vereux."

Marilyn recognized the name instantly. It was the maiden name of her mother. "Sister Jean-Marie is my aunt?"

The man looked down and shook his head slowly. "There is more," he said quietly. "When she was young, Lynette Vereux was a high-spirited girl. She fell in love ... terribly in love, with a man ... a married man, and he with her." Dupré looked up at his daughter, his dark eyes mirroring hers. "And she bore him a child ..." His voice faltered. He hung his head. The rest was too painful to tell.

Marilyn's hand went to the locket on her bodice. "So . . . Sister Jean-Marie is my mother," she whispered, almost fearing to speak the words out loud.

"Your grandfather Vereux was a very hard man. He drove Lynette out of his house. She went to the Sisters in Baton Rouge. Mama, because her heart was weak, could not have little ones. She would not let her sister give up . . . the baby girl."

"I knew ... I always knew ..." Marilyn whispered.

Dupré took a deep breath and continued, "*Alors*, we took *la petite criade* from her and Mama raised her as her own. Your grandfather was furious. He never again spoke to either of his daughters."

Marilyn smiled wistfully when she heard herself called a "little screamer." "Was I a lot of trouble Papa?"

"Trouble? You could not be trouble, *chéré*. You were the joy of our life."

"Why didn't you tell me, Papa?" Marilyn demanded softly. "After Mama died, why didn't you tell me?"

"Mama made me promise that I would never tell you. And when she was . . . the last time, in the hospital . . . she made me promise that I would bring Lynette home to care for you. You, too, were high-spirited, *chéré*, and she feared . . ."

"That I would make the same mistake her sister made?"

Dupré nodded. "She loved you very much, *chéré*. Too many times she was afraid to show you that love."

Marilyn gently stroked his hair. "I understand, Papa. I understand a lot of things now."

Dupré's eyes brimmed with tears. His daughter had guessed the words he could not say; but having begun the story, he was compelled to complete it. "Lynette would not give up her vows," he explained. "So I sent you away to her, far away from the temptations of the City, to a place where you would be safe . . . with the one who gave you life, no?"

"But her parents," Marilyn pleaded in a whisper. "They must have known about Mama's death. Surely they didn't hold a grudge after all those years? I never even had a chance to know my grandparents, Papa. Your parents were in France, and Mama said hers were dead."

"To her they were dead, *ma petite*. And to Lynette. And to me." He looked at her. "*Oui,* and also to you. Antoine Vereux paid a terrible price for his rage. His wife died soon of a broken heart. Even then, he would not permit her daughters to pay their final respects to her. And when Mama followed her to the grave, still he would not come."

"It was hard for you, being alone, wasn't it, Papa?" Marilyn said quietly, stroking the side of his face.

"Sometimes life is hard because we make it so, *chéré*," But we do what we must do." His dark eyes pleaded with hers for understanding. "I loved them both very much. They forgave me. Do you find it in your heart to forgive your Papa, *ma petite*?"

"We are who we are in spite of the accidents of birth, Papa, not because of them."

His eyes told her he did not comprehend.

"It's something Grandma Calkins told me. 'We are who we are in spite of the accidents of birth, not because of them.' I believe that, Papa, with all my heart. She took his face in her hands, kissed him on both cheeks and once more on his forehead. The questions that had simmered inside her soul all her life had been answered. She was strangely calm as she took a deep breath. "Come on, Papa," she said, getting to her feet and wiping away a few tears. "It's time for me to get married."

"Marilyn!" Jennifer hissed, poking her head in the door again.

"We're ready. We're all set. Come on, Papa."

To the relief of everyone in the church, especially Jack Townsend, the bride and her father finally appeared at the far end of the aisle. The signal was given, the organist at last broke into the "Wedding March," and Jennifer began walking forward with Marilyn and Henri Dupré the required number of paces behind.

Everything proceeded smoothly until they were halfway to the altar. A small bird suddenly appeared on the ledge under the open lower section of the Calkins Window. It hesitated for a moment, looked directly at the Bride and then flew up into the open rafters of the church. Marilyn gasped when she saw it and stopped for a moment, transfixed.

"Do not be afraid, *ma petite*," her father whispered. "It is only *un oiselet*, a small bird. It means nothing."

Marilyn's face softened into a smile of recognition. "It isn't just a bird, Papa. It's Grandma Calkins. She said she'd find a way to let me know she was here." While she was still speaking, a second bird flew in the same window and took its place next to the first. "And see, Papa, she's brought Mama with her." Marilyn looked at her father and whispered, "They're both here, Papa, and they've come a long way. Let's not keep them waiting."

They finally made it to where Jack waited to take her hand from her father and escort her the last few steps. "What the hell was going on back there?" he demanded in a whisper when they took their places on the altar.

"Sshh! You're in church!" she scolded.

Father Valencia came over to where they stood. "If the two of you are ready, we can start anytime."

Marilyn had chosen the traditional Catholic wedding ceremony, the one she knew by heart, but now it seemed to be happening in a dream. As the priest began speaking her mind was far away, in the French Quarter of New Orleans, re-living her childhood and seeing Mama as she had never before seen her. She remembered, too, the long walks with Sister Jean-Marie in the gardens around Sainte Anne's where they quietly shared their secrets. How could she have guessed that Sister was holding back the greatest secret of all?

"I, John, take you, Marilyn . . ." she heard Jack say.

'Marilyn,' she thought. Mama's name was 'Marie,' and her's was 'Lynette'. Marie and Lynette; they put them together and got 'Marilyn.' I was part of both of them—two sisters helping each other. And Papa, too. He stuck by us all. He did what he had to do.

"Marilyn, repeat after me," Father Valencia's voice broke into her thoughts. "I, Marilyn, take you, John . . ." She repeated the words she had thought about so often, but even as she did her mind drifted away again to a walk along the beach and a secret shared under the palms. You aren't the only one who was given a second chance, John Townsend, she thought as she mouthed the words of the vow she knew so well. You and Jennifer, you knew about your second chances. But mine came a long time ago, long before I ever knew.

"I join you in marriage," Father Valencia said, "in the Name of the Father, and of the Son, and of the Holy Spirit." He turned to the altar boy who held a small platter on which R.J. had placed their rings. "Bless, O Lord, these rings . . ."

My second chance came right at the beginning, Marilyn thought. Marie and Lynette gave it to me. And Papa, too: Papa, who did what was right and never complained, and never told. She felt Jack take her left hand and slip the gold band into place next to the diamond he had given her at the Yacht Club a whole lifetime ago. Then it was her turn. She took Jack's hand in hers and repeated, "In the Name of the Father, and of the Son, and of the Holy Spirit, take and wear this ring as a sign of our marriage vows."

"Look, O Lord, we beseech You . . ." Father Valencia began a final prayer for God's blessing on the newlyweds.

And Mama stuck by him, Marilyn thought. She gave up everything for Papa . . . and for me. She must have loved both of us more than I ever imagined.

She heard Father Valencia inviting Jack to "kiss the Bride," and she felt him chastely kissing her on the lips, so unlike the other kisses they had already shared. Then it was over, and she found herself taking his arm and turning to face the assembled guests in her new life as Mrs. John Townsend. But there was only one face she looked for in that church: Sister Jean-Marie who was standing discretely alone in a pew, close enough for a good view, but not so close that anyone might think she was 'family.' Their eyes met, and Marilyn knew at once that Lynette Vereux knew the secret had been told. And Lynette Vereux approved.

As the newlyweds walked back from the altar and took their first steps together as man and wife, Marilyn broke away from Jack and went to her.

"Papa told me . . ."

The nun put a finger on Marilyn's lips. It was the way she used to silence the girls at Sainte Anne's. "You're a married woman now, Marilyn. Everything is as it should have been. My task is finished, and yours is just beginning."

The Bride's lower lip began to quiver, and the tears she did not shed earlier suddenly filled her eyes. "Will I see you again?" she asked.

"Of course. Sainte Anne's is my home, but it isn't far from here. God willing, we will have many happy times together."

"I love you," Marilyn said softly, her voice choked with emotion.

"And I you," the nun replied. "Now be on your way," she chided. "Your husband is waiting. And may God go with you . . . my child."

Tears streamed down Marilyn's face as she turned away to continue her walk up the aisle with Jack.

"What was *that* all about?" he whispered when she was back at his side.

She stopped again and turned to face him. "Jack, kiss me. Now. Hard. Harder than you ever have before. Please?"

"My pleasure, *Madame*," he replied as he took her in his arms midway up the center aisle of the church and fulfilled her wish.

The two of them barely heard the applause from Father Valencia and the guests as she melted in his arms.

"Want to tell me what's going on here?" he whispered in her ear after his lips left hers.

"Not now," she replied. "Let's go. We have a lot of work to do in this life."

The Bride and Groom were showered with a flurry of confetti and kisses when they got out of the church door. It was several minutes before they and could make their way to the cool shelter of the waiting limo with Jennifer and R.J.

"Boy, I thought we were never going to get out of there," R.J. complained as he opened a bottle of champagne that was waiting in a silver wine cooler. "What was the hold up, anyway?"

"That's what I'd like to know," Jack added.

"Nothing. Just tying up a few loose ends," Marilyn explained without explaining anything as Jennifer helped her touch up her makeup.

"A bride has a sacred right to keep everyone waiting on her wedding day," Jennifer added haughtily. "I, for one, intend to keep everyone waiting for at least an hour."

"Well, here's a toast to Mrs. John Townsend," R.J. said, handing around the glasses as he filled them.

"'Mrs. John Townsend,' that has a nice sound to it," Marilyn smiled, taking a glass from him. "Still, I kind of like the sound of 'Dupré'. It sounds so Continental. Don't you think so, Jennifer?"

"Me? Yes, I like the sound of 'Dupré' very much!"

"Well maybe you should do something about that while Jack and I are gone."

"Do you really mean that?" Jennifer asked.

"I've never meant anything more in my life."

"Hey, what's going on here, you two?" Jack demanded.

"Nothing," Marilyn replied, sipping her champagne. "Besides, sometimes sisters have secrets they never tell."

∽ ∾

It was the second time in two days that Arlo tasted French champagne and he was beginning to like the stuff.

"This is quite a place, ain't it, Les?" he said as the wedding guests mingled at the Bonita Key Yacht Club and waited for the Bride and Groom to appear.

"Yeah," Les Leslie replied absently.

"I mean, I didn't figure guys like us 'd ever get in here unless maybe ta' deliver somethin'."

"Yeah, I guess," Les agreed.

"Ain't you gonna drink that?" Arlo asked, referring to the full glass in Les' hand. "'Cause if ya' ain't, I'll take it off y'er hands."

"Arl, let me ast ya' somethin'," Les said, ignoring the request for the moment. "Da' ya' remember that time I told ya' that ya' only get one chancet in life?"

"Yeah, I sure do. That's what got me off my butt and made me ast Erlene ta' go sailin'. I never really thanked ya'."

"Ya' think that's true?"

"Sure it's true. I'm tellin' ya', aint' I?"

"I don't mean about Erlene, ya' ninny. I'm talkin' about one chancet. D' ya' think we only get one chancet 's what I'm astin'."

"Gosh, I don't know, Les; 's what you told me."

"Just 'cause I said it don't make it true, necessarily." Les paused for a minute, almost to himself. "I think I'm gonna have a little talk with R.J. when they get here. I guess I'd kind a' like ta' see Italy after all." Les hiked up his belt and truly looked at Arlo for the first time. "I need a real drink, Arl, he said handing his friend his glass of champagne: a little a' Nelson's blood. Let's take a walk ta' the bar."

෩ ඥ

"I just love weddin's don't you?" Erlene Rodgers gushed to Victoria Townsend. "'cept I don't think I'm ever gonna be able ta' get Arlo ta' set a date."

"Yes, well, the only way to get some men to the altar is with a good swift kick in the pants," Mrs. Townsend told her.

"Gol, I don't guess I could do anythin' like that," Erlene protested.

"Well, from what I've seen of Mr. Woodbrace, he's one of those men, Erlene. If you can't bring yourself to kick him in the pants you're going to have an awfully long wait. Excuse me. I must have a word with Chef Dupré."

෩ ඥ

The bridal couple and their attendants finally arrived and the reception got underway with R.J. offering the traditional toast, followed by a dinner that Victoria Townsend assured Henri Dupré could not begin to compare to his repast of the previous evening.

"You are too kind, *Madame*," Dupré demurred.

"Nonsense, Henri. You have too much talent to be working for anyone. We must see to it that you are properly recognized—and rewarded—for your ability. Have you ever thought of living in New York?"

"*Madame, la Vieu Carre* . . . how you call it? . . . the old city, the French Quarter . . . it is my home."

"Times change, Henri," she reminded him, "and we must be willing to change with them. Who knows where we'll all be in another year?"

§○ ○§

The afternoon sped by. Jack and Marilyn found, as all bridal couples do, that they barely had time for one dance together before it was time to cut the cake, see to it that Jennifer and R.J. caught the bouquet and garter, and change into traveling outfits before it was time to get into the limousine waiting at the front door of the Yacht Club. They were almost ready to pull away when Victoria Townsend came running out with a fur coat over her arm.

"Mrs. Townsend! Mrs. Townsend!" she shouted. "You forgot your coat." Victoria opened the limo door and thrust the fur onto Marilyn's lap.

"Victoria, this is your coat!" she protested.

"It's Russian sable, Marilyn. It will keep you nice and warm. Paris can be quite unpleasant at this time of year."

"She's been there," Jack assured his Bride.

"I can't take your coat. How will you get home?"

"I've decided to stay in Florida for a while. Besides, I have a cold storage closet full of furs in New York. I'll have another one sent down when I decide to leave."

With a last kiss to her son and new daughter-in-law, Victoria Townsend closed the car door and Jack instructed the driver to take them to the airport.

"The airport? You mean we're not staying here tonight?" Marilyn protested.

"No."

"We're not flying to Paris *tonight*, are we?" she complained as visions of a romantic wedding night began to evaporate.

"Of course not. You should know me better than that. Besides, there aren't any direct flights from Bonita to Paris."

"Then where *are* we going?"

"To a major city that has those kind of flights."

"Miami?"

"I don't need anyone to show me Miami," he said, kissing her lightly. "I've been there."

"Well, where . . .?"

He looked deep into the dark eyes that captivated him the very first time he saw her outside the marina office. "What city in this country would you most like to spend your wedding night in?"

"New Orleans," she said without hesitation. "You're taking me to New Orleans."

"Our flight to Paris leaves from there the day after tomorrow. You'll have forty-eight hours to show me your city."

"No," she replied, caressing his cheek. "New Orleans can wait a little longer. I'll only have forty-eight hours to make love to you before we have to get on that plane."

❧ ☙

Mr. and Mrs. John DeWitt Townsend checked into the Place d'Armes, a boutique hotel off Jackson Square close by the Saint Louis Cathedral later that evening. A cold December wind was blowing in off the Mississippi River, and Marilyn was grateful for Victoria's coat, the crackling fire in the fireplace of their suite, and the hot *café amoretto* Jack had arranged to have delivered.

"Coffee this late?" Marilyn asked as she sat on Jack's lap in front of the fire. "We'll be awake all night."

"That's the idea," he assured her.

"Are you ready for your present?"

"I've been ready for weeks," he said as he began kissing her neck.

Marilyn suddenly got up and went to her suitcase. "Wait a minute, where are you going? Jack protested.

"I'm going to get your wedding present."

"I was just about to unwrap my wedding present," he said.

"Not that present, this one." She returned to her place on his lap and handed him a small, wrapped package.

"What is this?

"It's your wedding present from me. Open it."

Jack unwrapped the box and took out a gold watch. Only it wasn't an ordinary watch: miniature signal flags had replaced the numerals on the face.

"Where did you get this?" Jack asked as he admired the unique piece of jewelry.

"It was custom made by a jeweler friend of mine in Bonita," she replied grandly. "You may even know him. Now, can you read what the flags say?"

"Sorry, I was a commodore, not a flag lieutenant."

"Start here at the twelve o'clock position. You should be able to recognize that blue and white one."

"J?" he guessed.

"Right. And going around the face, the letters spell out, J-T-I-L-O-V-E-Y-O-U-M-D," she explained.

"You're really someone very special, you know that?" he said as he kissed her.

"Now, what do you have for me?" she asked.

"Well, actually, I do have something for you. It's in my briefcase." Excited as a child at Christmas, she got up again, went to where he left it and found the package. "Jack! It's your manuscript! You finished it!" She carried it back to her place on his lap in front of the fire. "May I read it?"

"I think you better . . . but just the first page for now, okay?"

She opened the cover and read the words that told the whole world his story began with her: "Marilyn Dupré stopped her small car at the end of the shell-rock road and sighed . ."

"I remember that day so well," she said quietly. "I can't believe how much my life has changed since then. So much has happened; I've learned so much. I wonder how many more lessons and tasks lie ahead?"

"I have something else for you, too," he added. "But it's a surprise and you won't be able to see it until we get home."

"A surprise? What is it?" she asked excitedly, putting the manuscript down. "Please tell me."

"You'll see it when we get home," he assured her.

"She kissed him deeply and began unbuttoning her dress. "Well I have something else for you, too," she said softly. "And you can see it right now."

ꝏ ꝏ

Two days later a jet bound for Paris streaked across the clear blue Florida sky. Far below, Arlo Woodbrace sat in a dinghy and tried to keep it steady while Les Leslie performed one last job for Commodore Jack Townsend.

"Hold still, will ya', ya' ninny," Les protested. "I don't want ta' be gettin' this on crooked f'r the Commodore an' his Missus."

"I'm tryin', Les," Arlo complained. "But it ain't easy keepin' us this close. C'n we do this some other way?"

"How in Hades are ya' gonna attach a name board ta' a boat? Ya' think ya' c'n stand on top a' the water? Now just hold the dinghy steady."

It was a few more minutes before Les got the hand-carved name board perfectly centered and screwed to the transom of the trawler. "Okay, row us off a little so's we c'n get a good look at it," he instructed.

The morning sun highlighted the gilt letters and reflected their images onto the still water behind the boat.

"Pretty, ain't she?" Les observed.

"Real nice," Arlo agreed.

The two men sat for a minute and admired their handiwork. The white trawler finally had a name.

And the name of the boat, of course, was "MARILYN."

The End—for now.